W9-ANI-644

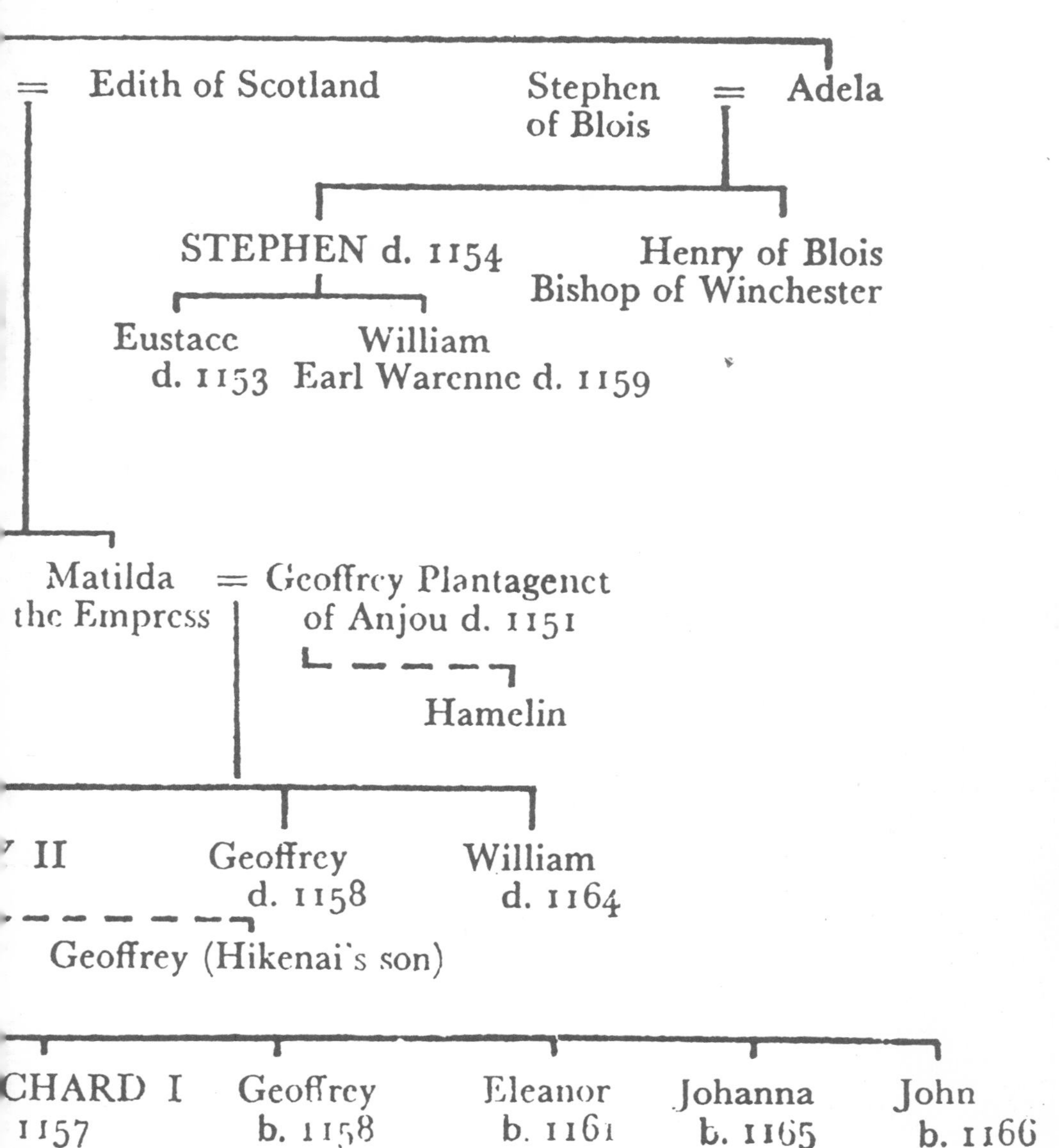
Matilda of Flanders
= Edith of Scotland
Stephen of Blois = Adela
STEPHEN d. 1154
Henry of Blois Bishop of Winchester
Eustace d. 1153
William Earl Warenne d. 1159
Matilda the Empress = Geoffrey Plantagenet of Anjou d. 1151
Hamelin
II
Geoffrey d. 1158
William d. 1164
Geoffrey (Hikenai's son)
CHARD I 1157
Geoffrey b. 1158
Eleanor b. 1161
Johanna b. 1165
John b. 1166

THE LION OF CHRIST

By Margaret Butler

THE LION OF ENGLAND
THE LION OF JUSTICE
THE LION OF CHRIST

THE LION OF CHRIST

Margaret Butler

ASBURY PARK PUBLIC LIBRARY
ASBURY PARK, NEW JERSEY

Coward, McCann & Geoghegan, Inc. New York

First American Edition 1977

First published in Great Britain under the title THIS TURBULENT PRIEST
Copyright © 1977 by Margaret Butler
All rights reserved. This book, or parts thereof, may not
be reproduced in any form without permission in writing from
the publisher.

SBN: 698-10820-5

Library of Congress Cataloging in Publication Data
Butler, Margaret, 1920–
The lion of Christ.
Sequel to The lion of justice.
1. Henry II, King of England, 1133-1189–Fiction.
2. Thomas à Becket, Saint, Abp. of Canterbury,
1118?-1170–Fiction. I. Title.
PZ4.B9865Lh3 [PR6052.U817] 823'.9'14 76-58024

Printed in the United States of America

FOR MY MOTHER

Author's Note

This book, the sequel to *The Lion of England* and *The Lion of Justice*, is a chronicle of the events leading to the death of Archbishop Thomas. I have not distorted any facts known to me though some of my implications are without historical foundation; for instance, there is no record that Queen Eleanor played any part at all in the quarrel between King and Archbishop, nor that she knew anything of the plans of the Poitevin rebels. I believe, though, in the light of her subsequent behaviour, that the thoughts and desires I have imputed to her are in character.

With the exception of Cicely, all of the Fitzurse family are historical figures; their names and relationships are on record, as are those of their le Bret kin, William de Tracy and the de Morville family. But since little else is known of them I have felt free to indulge my imagination here. There is no evidence that de Morville's younger daughter was a mongol child.

An entry in Pipe Roll, 18 Henry II, 75, records that a fine in respect of another murder by Reynold Fitzurse was remitted by royal writ in 1172. It was this and the legendary tales of Hugh de Morville's wickedness (such as the boiling alive of a serf) that led to my assessment of their characters and thus to the invention of the rape and murder at Williton. The reason I appointed Hugh de Morville the evil genius of the four knights was because it always seemed strange to me that he, who did not strike a blow at the Archbishop, should have been considered one of the principals in the murder while Hugh Mauclerk and the de Brocs have been forgotten by all but historians. I apologise to their shades if I have done any of them a fearful injustice.

The references to the old pre-Christian religion are based on the works of Professor Margaret Murray mentioned in the bibliography.

Apart from this the story is authentic history, as is a great deal of the dialogue; even Thomas's dreams have their place in the records. Henry did debauch Eudo de Porhoët's young daughter at the time stated, and I have placed the ending of his association with Annora de Clare and the beginning of his notorious love affair with Rosamund de Clifford where they seem best to accord with legend. I have also taken pains to work into the narrative many trifling but veracious details, such as King Louis' habit of repeating everything twice, Herbert of Bosham's prolixity, Roger of York's unsavoury moral character and the fact that Richard of Ilchester was wall-eyed.

I have, of course, put my own interpretation on Henry's personality and motives, as on the underlying reason for his famous displays of uninhibited Angevin rage. His is a difficult character to assess for he was possessed of many contradictory qualities. He was clever yet obviously blind to the consequences of some of his actions, cold-bloodedly cruel yet given to extravagance in love and grief alike. He hated war but spent half his life in waging it, was careless of royal dignity but swift to punish any flouting of royal authority. It seems in some ways an adolescent temperament and certainly he learned a salutary lesson in the death of Thomas for, while never able completely to control himself if thwarted, his actions thereafter show a guile and caution he rarely exhibited in earlier years.

Thomas himself was nearly as complex; he was forceful, proud and obstinate, no conventional picture of a saint. Gentleness and forbearance were never natural to him and, with all his trying, he could not attain a resigned spirit. That was one battle he lost and it led to his death. The charismatic personality remains. He was beloved by the masses, if not always by his nearest and dearest, and he was an idealist to the end.

Margaret Butler

I
November 1164

Herbert of Bosham, Master in the study of Holy Writ in the diocese of Canterbury, came to the Abbey of Clair-Marais in Flanders only a few days after Richard de Luci, King Henry's Justiciar, having failed to persuade the fugitive Archbishop of Canterbury to return to England, had departed from it in anger. Because the November days were short, Herbert's party had begun the last stage of their journey before dawn and were hammering on the gatehouse door in good time for dinner.

Herbert was at fever pitch in his eagerness to see Archbishop Thomas. A full month had gone by since they had parted at Northampton on that stormy night, neither knowing whether escape or capture by an enraged King would be his lot. Herbert had heard that Thomas was safe across the Channel before he left England but he did not suppose that Thomas could have heard the same of him–indeed, he hoped not because he wished to burst in upon him, unannounced, with the tales of his adventures untarnished by previous telling.

Their reunion was as joyful as even he could wish, and made more so because Herbert had brought with him a number of other clerks and servants, besides a quantity of silver plate and one hundred marks in money which he had filched from the

Canterbury Treasury under the very noses of the King's men. Thomas had to listen to the tale a good many times before Herbert was satisfied that his master finally understood the risks he had undertaken on his behalf. The Archbishop's anxious enquiries after other friends got only the most perfunctory replies and it was not until dinner was over and they were alone that Herbert remembered another interesting titbit of information.

'Oh, I had near forgot–the very day you crossed the Channel a party of the King's men left from Dover. To think they might have sighted you! But you were in God's hands right enough.' He leaned back, smiling and expansive, and prepared to listen now to another voice than his own.

Archbishop Thomas eyed him. He had allowed this valued friend his head, knowing that in the end he would come sooner to the latest news that way. 'Whither bound?' he queried.

'To King Louis in the first instance to ask him to lend you no support, and then to the Pope to present the King's case. But they went first to the Abbey of St Bertin, arriving there at the same time you came here to Clair-Marais.'

'Then they are gone from there, I think, for yesterday I received an invitation from Abbot Godescalc to enjoy his hospitality.'

'St Bertin is continuing its tradition as a place of refuge for English archbishops. Did you not stay there once with Theobald when he fled from King Stephen?'

The Archbishop nodded. That had been sixteen years ago; he was struck by the similarity in the ways of kings–and perhaps of archbishops. He had been plain Thomas of London then–a clerk in Archbishop Theobald's household with no more thought of filling that seat than of gaining the throne of England. Where better to go than St Bertin in the footsteps of Theobald and of Anselm? At least until he knew what Louis of France would do.

He looked at Herbert, who sat silent for once, still savouring his victory over the King's men in the matter of the Canterbury silver; a fair young man, tall and well built, square-featured and with a warrior's eye that belied his cloth. 'Who was in the King's party, Herbert?' he asked.

Herbert numbered the bishops on his fingers. 'York, London, Chichester—'

'Enemies all,' said Thomas.

'Exeter and Worcester are with them. And the Earl of Arundel.' Herbert spoke briskly, hoping to show his master that not all the embassy were against him. He was half prepared for the look Thomas bent on him–resentful but with a flickering sideways glance that betokened a weakening of purpose.

'If they would not support me in England, what hope have I that they will do so now?' Thomas would not voice his real fear: that the Bishops of Exeter and Worcester might have been so shocked at his unchristian behaviour at Northampton when he had rounded on his persecutors that they would withdraw their last halfhearted vestiges of sympathy from him.

Herbert said firmly, 'It is a brave man who will dare the King's wrath to his face. But here, away from him, be sure that Exeter and Worcester will see that the Pope hears both sides of the story. Are they not sons of the Church?'

'So are York, London and Chichester, and you cannot pretend that I shall be quoted honestly by them. In any case, that is not the point. The Pope is in no position to antagonise King Henry while he is threatened by the Emperor and the anti-Pope. You must see as clearly as I do that, if the Pope repudiates me, King Louis will do so too. Am I to be hunted from place to place for the rest of my life?'

'The Pope will not repudiate you. Did he not refuse to ratify unseen the Constitutions that are the cause of all this trouble? And King Louis will grant you asylum in France, I am sure of it. Once they learn of your sufferings in the cause of religion—'

Thomas nodded slowly. He had been struck by an idea.

'There is something I would have you do for me, Herbert,' he said. 'King Louis is at Compiègne, at his castle in the forest. Will you follow those envoys of the King, keeping a day's journey behind them, and watch their moves?'

Herbert's head came up, his eyes eager. 'That's a task to my taste,' he exclaimed. 'I'll be discreet, never fear. I'll take Alexander Llewellyn with me, for the truth is, I'm the only one who can manage him.' He laughed, almost ruefully. 'None of us must bury our talents, eh–but use the gifts God gave us.'

Thomas smiled. Herbert might be full of himself, but he was faithful. He knew then what had been gnawing at him while they spoke. William Fitzstephen was not among the clerks Herbert had brought.

'Fitzstephen?' he brought himself to say.

'William? He did not come.' Herbert's lip curled just a trifle. 'He would try to make his peace with the King, he said.'

Thomas turned his face away. He could see William now, young, flushed and ardent, and hear his voice. 'Let me stay by you always, lord. Beggar or archbishop, it is all one to me. I ask nothing more than to be with you.' It was less than four years since William had spoken those words.

So few of those he had relied upon had remained true to him. One by one they were turning their backs and slipping away. He feared again that the cause was some lack in himself and sought desperately for what it might be. Herbert would say the desertions were from fear of the King, and there was truth in that; but Thomas knew there was something else besides: a gulf between himself and other men he had never known how to span. He was like a traveller lonely on one side of a riverbank who sees across the stream others bound in the same direction, who calls and talks and laughs with them but never can come close.

It had always been so, he realised, until the newly-crowned Henry had entered his life almost exactly ten years ago. They had built a bridge out of love on Henry's part and loneliness on his; they had looked into each other's minds and hearts and had been as one. But at the first breath of storm the ramshackle structure had crashed down. . . . The gift of attracting love was useless without knowledge of the way to keep it. Perhaps it was that he had never truly loved any human being.

The question of women entered his mind; he tried to face it squarely. It was so long since he had considered such things, so long since he had taken his voluntary vow of chastity. Of course he had been moved by mysterious hungers when young but they had seemed to have more to do with the beauty of the world than of women. No, it had not been hard for him. He had often been amazed at the strength of the urge in other men. He wondered, a little fretfully, why God had made it quite so strong. It seemed unnecessary. And certainly it had played its part in separating him from Henry. If he had womanised along with him. . . . The old faint disgust re-asserted itself. There were other sensual pleasures which were equally fulfilling, fine food, sweet scents, the caress of silk on skin–he moved uncomfortably as the hair-shirt pricked him. All were lost to him in any case, sacrificed in favour of the greatest pleasure of all, the service of the Lord. Did God then want everything? Thomas of London, like Job, naked, friendless and alone?

He looked up at the sound of someone at the door and saw it was his personal servant, Roger, carrying wine for the visitor and a cup of fennel-water for the Archbishop.

His thoughts tailed off in shame at the memory of Roger's devoted nursing in his illness and the perils shared in the flight from England. He was not friendless yet, and neither was he helpless. He began to explain to Herbert exactly how to introduce himself to King Louis and how to play upon his well-known piety to gain the place of refuge they so sorely needed.

For most of the week the little party tracked King Henry's

envoys towards Compiègne, questioning wayfarers travelling in the opposite direction, lurking in the misty dusk outside hostelries or monastery gatehouses to be sure the coast was clear before they entered. Herbert was like a boy who has discovered a new game, and was altogether unaware that his fairness, height and accent stamped him as unmistakably English.

It was on a glum, grey morning that they presented themselves at the castle, having first made certain that the delegation they were following had departed on the previous day. It was cold, too, and Herbert had swathed himself in a long, voluminous cloak, sadly mud-spattered, which went ill with his haughty and imperious bearing. They got into the castle easily enough but gaining audience of the French King was another matter.

The hall was full of people chattering away in a French, Herbert thought, as atrocious as any he had ever heard. They all turned to stare at the strangers but only shrugged when asked the whereabouts of the King, brushing aside the enquiries of the bedraggled party as beneath their notice. At last, Alexander Llewellyn spoke loudly in his native Welsh; that took their interest long enough for Herbert to announce himself as ambassador of the Archbishop of Canterbury. A tall man who had been watching them askance came forward then, prepared to listen. Even so, more than an hour passed before they were ushered into the presence of Louis of France.

They found him in a small, unheated chamber in the company of two monks, a Book of Hours on the table before him. His hand rested on the lower corner of the page and he fingered the edge at intervals as though longing to continue his perusal. What they could see of the book was very beautiful, brilliant with colour and burnished gold.

Louis was a small, spare man, yellow of complexion, prim of mouth and distrustful of eye. Nor, unlike his companions', did his expression alter when Herbert, rising from an awkward bow, became entangled in the folds of his long cloak and executed what appeared to be a dance in his efforts to regain his balance. He watched gravely until Herbert subsided, red faced, and then leaned forward.

'You say you are of the Archbishop's household–the Archbishop of Canterbury's household?'

Herbert assured him that this was so and began his carefully rehearsed speech, only to be cut off as Louis turned to Alexander Llewellyn.

'You, too, are of his household and family?'

Alexander drew himself up. 'I am cross-bearer to the Archbishop,' he replied, 'and have served him faithfully since he took office.'

Louis nodded and asked each of the others in turn their standing and length of service with the Archbishop. He repeated nearly every question twice as though he doubted either their hearing or their understanding. Finally he nodded sagely to himself, and, glancing at them very slyly, put to them some innocuous questions requiring answers that proved the extent of their personal involvement with the Archbishop in his time of trouble.

Herbert fidgeted. Did this King of the French suspect them of being spies? But Louis at last professed himself satisfied with their credentials and invited them to sit and tell him the full tale of their woes and privations. This they did, often interrupting one another to amplify or add detail to the account, and, careful as they were not to speak disparagingly of their King in the presence of another monarch, enough came through to show Louis what they thought of royal power misused.

'My brothers,' Louis said. 'My brothers in God, I see that you have suffered for Christ with the Archbishop. But be comforted–here in France we do not persecute our clergy.' He glanced down again, then quickly up at Herbert. 'It may surprise you to know we have but just dismissed the envoys of

King Henry. But I see it does not. No matter. You shall hear what passed between us.' He clapped his hands. 'Bring me the letter from the King of the English,' he said to a clerk who glided from the shadows by the door.

When it was in his hand he motioned Herbert nearer. 'Take and read,' he said.

'To his lord and friend, Louis, King of the French. . . . ' Herbert's eyes hurried over the greeting to the contents. 'Know that Thomas who was Archbishop of Canterbury has been publicly judged in my court by a full council of the barons of the realm as a wicked and perjured traitor to me, and under the manifest name of traitor has wickedly departed, as my envoys will tell you more fully. Wherefore I entreat you not to allow a man infamous for such crimes and treasons, nor his men, to remain in your kingdom. I beg you not to let this great enemy of mine receive any aid or counsel from you or yours, as I would not permit any to be given to your enemies in my kingdom. Rather, I beg you to help me avenge myself for the dishonour inflicted upon me by this great foe as I would do for you if the need arose.'

Who under Heaven, wondered Herbert, had drafted this? He composed his face carefully as he handed it on to Alexander but Louis was not looking at him; he was watching Alexander's expression with a small, detached smile as he in turn perused the letter. Clearly this King of the French was also aware that King Henry's advisers were no statesmen to let him run whining for help to one he had mocked so often in the past.

Louis took back the letter, holding it by the corner between finger and thumb; his smile had broadened now so that they could see the teeth at the side of his mouth, all brown and decayed. 'I asked the envoys'–he said softly–'these English bishops, London and Chichester, why the letter spoke of Thomas who *was* Archbishop of Canterbury. Who deposed him, I asked them, who deposed him? I could get no answer from them on that point. Of a certainty, I said, I am as much a king as the King of the English but *I* do not have the power to depose the meanest clerk in my realm.'

Herbert opened his mouth to speak but Alexander trod hard on his toes; he thought Louis had more to tell.

'Then spoke the Earl of Arundel—' Louis looked at them hard. 'A man without fear of kings, I thought. He spoke to me almost as to an equal—'

As well he might, thought Herbert, seeing he has lain in a king's bed since he married the child-widow of old King Henry.

'He reminded me how as Chancellor the Archbishop had devastated my lands and lopped off a not inconsiderable part of my kingdom and power.' Louis paused, watching them narrowly. No one said anything. Even Herbert could not think of a suitable rejoinder to that mild understatement.

'I informed him that such faithful service to his king seemed to me good and honourable. That appeared to confound him.' Louis' look was bland. 'Yet is it strange that I should defend a vassal's loyalty to his lord?'

Herbert caught Alexander's eye. Perhaps the meeting would go right after all. Deep in him he was amazed that this skinny shrimp of a man, so quiet, so unroyal, had bereft him so easily of words. Therefore he began another oration, only this time feeling free to add the tribulations the Archbishop had endured at the hands of those very men who were King Henry's envoys.

Louis sat nodding to himself throughout. 'In the presence of the envoys,' he told them with satisfaction, 'I instructed the Papal Envoy to tell Pope Alexander that I hoped he would receive the Archbishop with kindness and ignore any unjust accusations against him. Before harrying harshly so great a personage, the lord King of the English should have remembered the verse, "Be ye angry, and sin not".'

'My lord, perhaps he might have remembered if he had

heard it as often in the Canonical Hours as we have,' returned Alexander drily.

Louis laughed as he stood up. 'Piety has other uses than the obvious. Holy Writ may teach us much. Yes, you may rest assured that your Archbishop and lord will have peace and security in France. It is our prerogative to shelter exiles–especially ecclesiastics. You have our permission to let him know this.'

Raising his eyes from Herbert's letter, Thomas gazed thoughtfully through the window of the guest-house of St Bertin. The morning mist was lifting now, revealing the neatly tilled fields outside the walls where not a tree broke that flat expanse. He need not stay here, after all. There in the postscript Herbert urged him to travel with all haste to Soissons, to meet this paragon of piety who would uphold him and righteousness against the persecutions of the wicked. . . .

Well, doubtless Louis was a man of God, though Thomas could not repress the knowledge of Louis' jealousy of his greatest rival quite as well as Herbert had evidently done. Just for an instant he wondered where piety ended and self-interest began. Then, realising that the French king's motives were God's business, not his, he put the thought from him and congratulated himself upon the fact that both were working to his advantage.

He had feared that the Pope, beleaguered by the Emperor Frederick Barbarossa, might sacrifice him on the altar of Henry's support, but if Louis, who was Alexander's host in his exile from Rome, publicly backed him from the outset. . . . That one small factor might tip the scales in his favour. For he was utterly dependent on the Pope's championship of his case–even Henry would not dare face a papal interdict and excommunication. If Alexander would only dismiss his bishops' appeal against him and uphold his own appeal against his condemnation in the King's court, all would yet come right. With rising hope he remembered Theobald's triumphant return to Stephen's England after he had gained the countenance of Pope Eugenius.

According to the letter, Herbert had hurried on to Sens, hoping to arrive before Henry's deputation and witness their discomfiture when the Papal Envoy repeated Louis' message to the Pope. Thomas smiled to himself, his spirits restored. Herbert was quite uncrushable. His loyalty, his frank rejoicing in the defeat of his Archbishop's enemies were unexpectedly endearing.

Thomas called to one of the clerks to give orders for their immediate departure to Soissons.

Gilbert Foliot, Bishop of London, had not missed the tall figure of Herbert of Bosham in the Pope's audience chamber when he scrutinised the assembled company but he ignored both his presence and his inimical glares. Indeed, he had been speaking for a full ten minutes on the incompetence and shortsightedness of the Archbishop of Canterbury before he allowed his saurian eye to stray again to Herbert's indignant face. He continued to harp on his fixed idea that Thomas of London was a fool, as dangerous to others as to himself.

'Father,' he declared with vehemence, 'to you the Catholic Church looks with care and anxiety that the wise may be nurtured by your wisdom for an example of conduct, and that fools may be rebuked and corrected by apostolic authority that they may learn wisdom. But your apostolic wisdom will never account him wise who trusts in his own wisdom and endeavours to disturb the concord of his brethren, the peace of the Church and the devotion of a king. Of late there has arisen in England a dissension between the King and the priesthood on a minor and unimportant matter which might easily have been resolved if a discreet moderation had been shown. But my lord of Canterbury, following his own opinion and not acting on our advice, has pushed the matter to extremes, not considering the evil of the times or what harm might arise from such hostility. Had we given our consent to his proposals, matters would have become worse. But because we would not be led astray by him, as indeed we ought not, he has tried to throw the blame for his own rashness on the lord King, on us and on the whole realm. And to cast infamy on us, his bishops, he has taken to flight, although no violence has been used or even a threat uttered against him—'

Pope Alexander raised his hand. 'Forbear, brother, forbear.'

Gilbert blinked. 'My lord, we shall forbear towards him.'

'Brother, I do not suggest you forbear towards him. Rather, you yourself should forbear.'

Gilbert stood still for a second as the import of the Pope's remark penetrated. Then he sat down abruptly.

Hilary of Chichester, too busy rehearsing his own speech to listen to Gilbert's, had missed the reprimand entirely. He leapt into his display of eloquence with a confidence as misplaced as it was ill-timed, for his latinity lacked the fluency of Gilbert's and several times his listeners winced visibly at his syntactical blunders.

A number of the cardinals smiled or glanced knowingly at a neighbour but the Pope kept his eyes steadfastly lowered. Among the lesser members of the hierarchy some broad grins were evident, and when Hilary solemnly delivered himself of yet another howling error, a few muttered asides began to be heard.

Hilary glanced up doubtfully. '*Oportuit*,' he hastily corrected himself, 'er–*nec aliquando oportuebat*.'

'You're having a hard time getting to port,' yelled a youthful voice derisively, and the whole company burst out laughing. Even the Pope allowed himself a smile.

Hilary would have attempted to continue but the Pope was motioning the Archbishop of York to rise and speak, and he caught Gilbert Foliot's eye; he sat down staring straight ahead in disgruntled silence, trying not to remember the English silver jingling in the pockets of many of the cardinals as they laughed.

Roger of York showed no discomposure. He would retrieve his colleagues' failure. He placed his fat white hand on the crozier that the archiepiscopal ring might show to best advantage, and breathed deeply once or twice.

'Your Holiness, your Eminences, your Graces,' he began unctuously, 'to none are the character and purpose of the Archbishop of Canterbury better known than to me. For I have known the temper of his mind from the first, that he cannot easily be turned from an opinion he has once formed. And there are few he will grant respect enough to listen to. Only Your Holiness, I think'–here Roger made an obsequious inclination in the Pope's direction–'may command that power. Certainly King Henry could not. Wherefore it is easier to believe that this obstinacy proceeds, as of old, from levity.' He paused a moment and, infusing his voice with a studied unwillingness, added, 'I see no way of correcting him, Father, but that your discretion should lay a heavy hand upon him.'

Bartholomew of Exeter said even less. He merely asked for legates to hear the case and decide it.

Earl William of Arundel had waited quietly among his knights until the churchmen had had their say. Being a lettered man, he had missed little of the proceedings but diplomatic cunning enjoined him to hide that fact. So putting on a frank and open countenance he stepped forward and asked in Norman-French if he might be heard.

'My lord,' he addressed the Pope, 'we unlearned men are ignorant of what the bishops have said. It behoves us therefore to explain why we have been sent. It was not that we should be contentious or insult anyone, especially here in the presence of one to whose will and authority all the world rightly bows. But we have come to assure you before the whole Roman court of the love and devotion which our lord King has always borne and still bears towards you. Nowhere is there one more faithful to you or more devoted to God. Nor is there one more anxious to preserve peace. And the lord Archbishop, too, is well versed in his rank and order, discreet and prudent in the things which concern him, although somewhat lacking in clear-sightedness, it appears to some. Were it not for this unfortunate quarrel between them, state and church would enjoy peace and concord under a good prince and the best of shepherds. This, then, is our plea: that Your Holiness do all you can to remove dissension and restore peace and love.'

As murmurs of commendation arose on all sides, Earl William lowered his eyes. The speech was evidently more to Alexander's taste, for he leaned forward and assured the earl that he did indeed remember with gratitude the many favours he had received from the King of the English.

'Then will you declare judgement now on the issue between the lord King and the lord Archbishop?' put in Gilbert Foliot quickly.

The smile on the Pope's lips did not falter as his eyes slid towards Gilbert but William of Arundel gritted his teeth and looked away. Nor was he surprised when he looked back to see Alexander's determined headshake. 'Not in his absence,' he said firmly. 'He must have an opportunity to defend himself. But if you are prepared to await his arrival–it has been reliably reported to me that he is on his way here–I shall be glad to try the suit.'

'We have been strictly commanded to remain only three days,' said Earl William warningly to Gilbert.

Gilbert translated this remark into Latin, adding a question of his own which the earl understood as a request that the Pope order the Archbishop to return to England. Alexander replied shortly–something regarding prisoners and gaols.

The Pope appeared to be agreeing to appoint legates to try the case; then he extended his hand in a gesture of dismissal. They all moved forward to kiss the Fisherman's Ring and as they backed away Earl William fixed Gilbert once more with his eye, but to no avail; no sooner had they reached the door than Gilbert returned to the foot of the dais.

'My lord, what authority will be given to the legates?' came Gilbert's harsh voice.

Alexander looked surprised. 'Due authority, brother.'

'But we ask that they be able to settle the case so that it cannot again be appealed.'

Earl William had a good view of Alexander's face. The Pope closed his eyes for a second. And London believes Canterbury to be a fool! the earl thought. He listened with extra care for the Pope's reply.

'That is my prerogative, which I will not grant to any other,' said Alexander coldly. 'And truly, when he is judged, we and no one else will judge him, for it would be against reason to send him back to England to be judged by his enemies.'

Earl William did not trust his temper sufficiently to wait for the bishops. He rode to his lodgings with his entourage immediately, hoping that by the morrow, when they must depart, he would have cooled enough to be polite to them.

He could manage it only by maintaining an intimidating silence which was made easier by the hard pace he set. Let them sway dangerously in their saddles, these soft clerical lords, or take the chance of being attacked by French knights who, he had heard, were eagerly awaiting a chance to attack his party on their own territory. Old scores could be sweetly avenged on the excuse of championing a persecuted archbishop.

They were well on their way, travelling north up the valley of the Yonne, before one of the outriders yelled a warning and came sliding down the slope in a rattle of stones, his horse almost on its haunches. Earl William's sword was out before the man had stopped, his eyes, narrowed against the low sun's rays, exploring the hillside thickets. The armed men moved in, enclosing the churchmen in a protective square.

'No–no attack, my lord. But see, across the river!'

Earl William looked out across the sloping fields, across the placid river, to the track that wound above the other bank. Dwarfed by distance, indistinct through the milky November air, a great procession rode towards Sens, three or four hundred horsemen at the least.

'The Archbishop,' said the man.

'Aye,' said Arundel bitterly, 'furnished with horsemen by the King of the French. A larger party than our own. Riding in triumph to the Pope as he has done before.' He turned his head as the Bishops of London and Chichester came pushing through the throng. 'There he goes, our fugitive.' His pent-up anger finally flared. 'And how will the Pope, to whom you displayed your spleen and jealousy, receive him, think you? He who, in spite of all you say, has wit enough to dissemble! He'll play the humble penitent before the Holy Father and bring our lord King into disrepute.'

Gilbert swelled, speechless, but Hilary smiled superciliously. 'You grow too hasty, my lord,' he said. 'You do not know what other–ah–commerce–we transacted after the audience.'

'Commerce! Bribery, you mean!'

'Nothing of the kind. It was a free and open offer from the King to collect Peter's Pence from every house in England—'

'You offered that to the Pope in person?'

'Hardly. Protocol must be followed. But you may be sure he knows of it by now.'

Arundel gnawed his lip. 'Every house?'

'Every chimney from which smoke rises.'

Arundel wheeled his horse and waved his arm. The sooner they were out of France and into Normandy the better. But all the way he chewed upon the fact that now, thanks to Becket, everyone must pay that hated Papal tax, and not as it had always been, the villeins only.

From the other bank Thomas's party had sighted the departing envoys, 'running back to King Henry with their tails between their legs' as some of Louis' knights jubilantly put it. Thomas affected not to hear; he did not allow himself to share their confidence.

But as they drew nearer to Sens and the first welcoming trickle of hangers-on at the Papal Court became a flood of highly-placed personages, his heart began to rise. It was like old times, waving and smiling to the crowds, raising his hand in blessing over the bowed heads. He saw now that he had been right to overcome his inner doubts and accept Louis' gift of a retinue befitting his station. The princes of the Church would not have ridden out to greet a beaten and humiliated refugee.

He caught sight of Herbert then, and in his broad grin recognised that the tide was indeed flowing their way. Somehow Herbert's little group fought through to his side but what Herbert had to say was lost in the noise of the excited crowd. But Thomas felt that an army with banners had joined him.

He was confident still when he came to his audience with Pope Alexander. Inside his sleeve he carried the document he had brought away from the Council of Clarendon and now he drew it out and laid it on the pavement where men usually laid gifts.

'Here, my lord and father,' he cried, 'is the reason I am come before you. Give me leave, I pray you, to read it to you and submit it to your decision. For I did not think I had the power to consent to such novelties as are written here.'

The Pope nodded. 'That you shall, my son. And when we have heard what is contained therein we shall order that a cardinal be appointed to defend the document as King Henry's envoys were obliged to leave so precipitately.' He glanced across to where Cardinal William of Pavia had raised his hand. Thomas looked too, and compressed his lips.

Cardinal William was well known to be the dearest friend of King Henry at the Papal Court.

He tried to read the mind behind that benign gaze. Could the issue be decided already? It cannot be so, he told himself. The Pope would never sacrifice righteousness for Henry's friendship. But there was still relief in the memory that they were all in Louis' lands by Louis' favour.

He fixed his eyes on the Pope, feeling the sudden heavy thumping of his heart. Alexander nodded to him to begin reading the Constitutions of Clarendon.

At the sound of his own measured voice repeating the clauses that damned Henry as a would-be tyrant more effectively than any of his own words could do, calm gradually returned to him. He could not resist a brief glance up now and then as he iterated the more telling provisions, but the Pope's face showed nothing. In the hushed hall he could sense no reaction to Henry's insistence on his right to the presentation of benefices, his preservation of royal prerogatives over proprietary churches and abbeys.

With the third clause they came to jurisdiction over criminal behaviour in clerks. Here was the root of his contention with Henry. The cold legal phrases hid the human conflict; he could almost see how some outsider fresh to the issue might see a rough justice in the King's demands. Clerks were to be tried in royal courts if the crime were against common law; only if it were against church law might the ecclesiastical courts have jurisdiction. And even then, if guilty, the miscreant must be handed over to the state for punishment though the church might degrade him from his office first.

As though degradation were not punishment enough. . . . Surely his listeners must see that the state's belief in vengeance and example was against the Christian ethic? Yet he saw no changes in their expressions.

Only when he came to the decree banning the departure of anyone, especially clergy, from the kingdom without licence did he detect a ripple of unrest, and then another at the announcement that no appeal could go beyond the Archbishop's court without the King's permission. The Pope was frowning. Those two were, of course, direct strokes at his authority.

Nor was much notice taken of the King's decision to substitute the custom of assize for wager of battle in suits concerning property. The things which had troubled Thomas most deeply appeared to trouble the Curia least.

While he listened to Cardinal William's long defence of the Constitutions, he was thinking hard. Obviously he must bear most strongly on the points which were troubling them, yet he must also convince them that he had been right to stand firm on those others. And as he took in the import of the cardinal's discourse, he began to see his way. Cardinal William clearly thought of him as a secular man with little or no knowledge of canon law. So, assuming it easy to put down an ignorant layman masquerading as an archbishop, he spoke patronisingly of the dangers of disturbing the Church's peace with trivialities and concentrated on a display of his own erudition rather than on the clauses of the Constitutions which had disturbed the Pope.

When Thomas rose to answer he had himself well under control. He answered the cardinal's interjections with such evident good humour and quick wit that William eventually retired into a scowling silence, leaving the field clear for Thomas to give his own analysis of the Constitutions and of the reasons which underlay King Henry's determination to have them accepted. That the Pope, himself driven out of Rome by Frederick Barbarossa, had seen the obvious parallel was plain.

Herbert was glowing with pride at his master's performance. He saw with satisfaction every gaze fixed on the Archbishop. But at his next words Herbert blinked and stared. 'My lords and fathers,' Thomas was saying, 'every man ought to speak the truth at all times and especially in the presence of

God and yourselves. I freely confess with sighs and groans that these afflictions have befallen the English church through my wretched fault. I climbed into the sheepfold of Christ not through Him who is the door, as one summoned by canonical election, but forcibly intruded by the secular power. And though I accepted this burden unwillingly, nevertheless it was human will, not divine will, which induced me to do so. What wonder then if it has brought me to such straits! Yet had I at the threat of the King renounced the jurisdiction of episcopal authority, as my brother bishops urged me to do, it would have constituted a pernicious precedent, ruinous to the interests of princes and the will of the Catholic Church. I therefore deferred doing so until I appeared before you. But now, recognising that my appointment was far from canonical, dreading lest the consequences should prove the worse for me, realising that my strength is unequal to the burden, and fearing lest I should involve in my own ruin the flock to which, such as I am, I was given as shepherd, I resign into your hands, father, the Archbishopric of Canterbury.'

He took off the archiepiscopal ring and handed it to the Pope. There was a shifting and muttering among the cardinals; some were nodding their evident approval. Herbert saw his own dismay reflected in the face of Alexander Llewellyn at his side.

That the Pope was deeply moved was obvious. He glanced about for a moment so that the murmuring of the cardinals subsided and in the sudden silence his soft voice carried clearly to the farthest reaches of the hall. 'Receive anew at our hands, my son, the cure of archiepiscopal office.' He replaced the ring on Thomas's finger.

Cardinal William of Pavia glanced at his neighbour. 'And they told me this man was a fool!' he whispered. 'I would I had such simpletons in my service. With one speech he has made his position secure. King Henry will never see him deprived now.'

Alexander was speaking again, his voice grave. 'Son Archbishop, we must rebuke you for ever having consented to those customs, old English usage though many of them be. Yet you have risen again after falling and have shown yourself to be a man tried and proved in manifold temptations, far-sighted and prudent, beloved of God and men, and loyal in everything to us and the Holy Roman Church. As you have been made an inseparable partner of our trials, so also, with God's help, we will not fail you–where reason permits.' He raised his head a little and gazed directly at Thomas. 'But in order that you, who have hitherto lived in affluence and luxury, may learn in future what you ought to be, the comforter of the poor–a lesson which can only be learned from poverty herself, the mother of religion–we have decided to commend you to the poor of Christ–I mean to the Abbot of Pontigny and his monks, to be trained by them–not, as I say, to fare sumptuously but in simplicity as befits an exile for Christ. Among them you must for a time abide with but few indispensable companions while the rest are dispersed among friends until the day of consolation comes and peace descends on us from on high. Meanwhile, be strong and of a good courage and manfully resist the disturbers of the peace.'

Herbert stared; the Pope had fixed him with his eye on that last remark. Then he realised that the Pope had meant the agents of the King and, after the first shock at the prospect facing his lord, he looked at Alexander with added respect. He was cleverer than he had thought. He had bought time–so important to him personally–with this gesture, for the King would think Thomas's dismissal to a monastery a punishment and would thus be persuaded to hold his hand.

Herbert's penetrating discernment told him otherwise. 'Indispensable companions . . . ,' he thought with satisfaction. Myself, of course, and Alexander Llewellyn. . . . We shall have peace there to plan our campaign against King Henry. He tried to catch Thomas's eye.

But Thomas would not look his way. He was sitting rather stiffly with a fixed smile that failed to hide the turmoil of his thoughts. That there was to be no place for him in the Pope's court was plain. And try as he might, he could not get beyond the fact that the Pope had not even mentioned the all-important appeals–his own against the judgement of the King's court on himself and his bishops' appeal against his authority.

II
December 1164

Thomas jerked back to consciousness with a start at the sudden jangling of the bell for Prime. He had been kneeling alone for hours in the bitter cold of the unheated chapel and, numbed to the bone, had drifted into a kind of waking dream. He had thought himself back in the old days, warmed by Henry's love and the admiration of his fellows, and the contrast with his present state was almost too much to bear.

He had been at Pontigny nearly three weeks on this St Thomas's Day, the dawn of his forty-sixth birthday, and he had never been so unhappy in his life. If Pope Alexander had intended to humble him, he had done well to send him here. And Thomas had little doubt now that this had been his intention, for when he, not yet a monk, had asked the Holy Father to confer the monastic habit on him, Alexander had sent him a habit of the skimpiest cut and coarsest cloth; and the accompanying message that he himself had blessed it had shown the impossibility of exchanging it for something of more reasonable fit.

After Abbot Guichard had clothed him in a private ceremony he had gone below, hot with embarrassment at the ridiculous figure he cut and ready to be offended at the first sidelong glance. He had met Alexander Llewellyn passing through the cloister garth. Oddly enough, Alexander's whoop of uninhibited mirth at the sight of him had been easier to bear than polite silence. Alexander had turned him round, tugging at the overshort and narrow cowl which barely covered Thomas's crown. 'Well, marry,' he had cried, 'never did I think to see you such a sight! Does the Abbot intend to use you as a scarecrow in his fields?'

Attracted by the laughter, one or two other monks came out and stood by, grinning. Hilarity spread between them until even Thomas was able to enjoy it, ruefully recounting other tales against himself.

'But yesterday it was, when I vested for Mass in an alb too big for me so that it bunched up at the back when I tied the cincture. "Why are your buttocks so inflated, my lord?" he wants to know. Thank Heaven this cowl is too small or he would be saying the same of my head–or accusing me of being hunchbacked!'

That was the only time he could recall laughing in this place. The life of a Cistercian was one long penance. From Advent until Easter–throughout the coldest, darkest months of the year–the monks ate only one scanty meal of gruel each day. Even in his early days with Archbishop Theobald, when he had been the regular butt of Roger de Pont l'Évêque's ridicule, he had not suffered as he was suffering now. Then, at least, his conscience had been clean; he had not been consumed by a remorse as bitter as the gnawing pangs of hunger that were always with him. And the further acts of contrition he was imposing on himself–the refusal to change his vermin-ridden hair-shirt and drawers, the constant immersion of his feet and legs in icy water, the secret flagellations, the long hours spent upon his knees in meditation–eased his soul's burden not at all. He was deserted by God as by man.

He should have remained in England, even if that had meant his death. He should have sat meek under the threats and accusations of the King at Northampton. Instead he had given way to a murderous anger that had enabled him to escape the knights and bring him here to worse misery. He had thwarted God by disobeying the injunction to turn the other cheek. But for that he might now be wearing a martyr's crown in Paradise. . . .

He heard the low chanting of the monks as they filed into the chapel for Prime and tried to rise, wincing as the blood returned to his stiff legs. The chapel was lit only by the red glow of the Sanctuary lamp and the flickering tapers carried by the monks; their breath steamed before them, making a halo round each candle and rising like the smoke of incense. Everything began to grow grey and hazy, the glimmering lights fusing into a far-off glow, the chant dissolving into a fading hum. . . .

Thomas was standing at the Judgement Seat and God wore Gilbert Foliot's face. He spoke in no tongue Thomas could understand but His tones were terrible. His face swelled and receded and Thomas cowered in a dread so fearful that his throat was quite closed up. Helpless, he strained to cry for mercy. . . .

Herbert started back at the cry that burst from Thomas and looked with apprehension at the Infirmarian who shook his head, frowning, and leaning forward, touched Thomas gently on the cheek. 'He has a swelling here,' he said.

'That's a toothache only,' said Herbert promptly. 'He complained of it some days ago. I told him to sit with open mouth over a bowl of steaming water that the worms might be drawn out, but you know how he is—' He stopped, staring in anxiety as Thomas began to mutter low and feverishly. 'He is very hot,' he said.

'He has a fever of some kind,' answered the Infirmarian. 'The problem is to know which.'

'He has laid himself low with his penitential exercises. And this life is too sudden a change for him who has always fed on the finest food. Very little of it, mind, very little, but always of the best—'

'He shall eat meat and lard while he is in my care,' returned the Infirmarian, 'but while the fever is on him he shall eat not at all. That you will agree with, I suppose?'

'Herbert?' said Thomas faintly. 'Herbert?'

'I am here, my lord,' said Herbert. He was aware that the Infirmarian was tired of his presence in his infirmary and he was equally sure that he was not going until he had assured himself that Thomas was on the road to recovery. He settled himself more firmly by the pallet. 'Speak, my lord,' he urged.

But he had to put his head close to Thomas's to make out the Archbishop's words, and even then most of it made no sense whatever.

'Drawers?' he whispered very low and made a face of warning, very slightly shaking his head. Thomas's speech came fast and slurred; he seemed excited, almost angry.

'My hair-drawers. . . . The great rent I could not mend. . . . They were crawling alive but she mended them–she sat beside me. . . . '

Herbert was very conscious of the Infirmarian behind him and also of the fact that drawers of any kind were forbidden to the monks. He had mended those drawers of the Archbishop himself, and washed them too. 'There now,' he said. 'Hush, try to sleep.'

'Our Blessed Lady mended them for me. The Virgin at least has pity—'

The Infirmarian moved closer. 'You are doing no good here,' he said to Herbert. 'You will not make sense of his babbling. Whatever he says now is best ignored.'

Herbert glanced at him quickly and was surprised by the almost conspiratorial quality of his look. Perhaps the Infirmarian was not such a bad fellow after all. And Herbert was very tired. Two nights and a day he had watched over

Thomas, praying and willing him to recover.

'I will confess that I am worried by that swelling on his face,' the Infirmarian continued. 'It seems to me that his sickness stems from that. It may be that we must lance the cheek to find the root of the trouble.' He saw Herbert stiffen and said gently, 'Try not to fret overmuch, Brother Herbert. I can see how weary you are, and we all know the great care you have for the Archbishop. If we must operate I will grant you leave to be present if you wish it.' He laid his large sinewy hand on Herbert's suddenly slumped shoulders. 'Have you ever seen such an operation?'

Herbert shook his head.

'Do not fear the prospect. Sometimes it is the choice between life and death. And you can help both him and me with your prayers.'

Herbert rose stiffly to his feet. 'I shall go directly to the chapel,' he said.

'Better to go and sleep first. Wait, I will give you a draught that will ensure it.'

He returned in a moment with a spoonful or two of liquid in a small cup and stood staring down at the Archbishop while Herbert drank it. Thomas tossed and turned, his anguished cries and fierce, almost inaudible, mutterings reflected in the changing expressions on his gaunt face.

Thomas was standing alone in the Pope's court to argue his case while dozens of cardinals and bishops who took the King's side were ranged against him. Nearer they came and nearer, hands clawed to rend him, until he saw them in their true guise. Imps and devils of Satan they were for all their crimson and violet robes, fanged, horned and tailed. Far away he could hear the Pope crying to them to hold but in the uproar his lonely voice was lost. They drew their swords as they advanced; he could see the light flash on the blades and hear the whistling sounds as the creatures slashed and lunged at him. He felt the silken kiss of the steel on his skin; the blades slid into him like water, like ice, like fire. One of them cut off the crown of his head; it fell forward, blinding him. . . .

Herbert was among the helpers. All his prayers had worked no miracle and a deadly fear was on him. He knew how few men lived to show the scars of operations. He could not look at the sharp knives and little saws lying ready on a scrubbed board but kept his head averted as he bore down relentlessly on Thomas's arm. That was his part in this procedure: to hold the Archbishop's right arm immovable, as others of the largest, strongest monks were holding down his other limbs. For in fever, as in madness, a man's strength increases; and all feared that even the draught of poppy juice and the thick leather straps that bound the patient to the table might not suffice to keep him immobile when the knives cut into living flesh. And this was delicate work, unlike the amputation of a limb.

For the moment, though, Thomas was unconscious. Herbert sucked in a deep breath as the Infirmarian took up a knife. He saw the Infirmarian's hands, large and pale, sorting among the instruments beside him, and then Thomas's face laid open across the cheekbone; there was no sound or movement from the patient. The bone looked dirty, like a decaying tooth. Herbert looked hastily away but not before he had seen the Infirmarian pick up what looked like a small hammer and chisel.

He heard tapping noises and felt Thomas's arm jerk beneath his hands. Sweat broke out on his face. The sounds seemed to go on and on.

'There!' said the Infirmarian. 'We have done well, I think. That piece of bone was like cheese–mortified. Wipe away the blood, brother, that I may see whether there is more. Pull the cut wider–gently, though, gently!'

Herbert dared to take another peep. Thomas's mouth hung open; his face, with blood running down over the ear, was very white.

'Lift his eyelid, brother,' said the Infirmarian sharply to his chief helper. What he saw seemed to satisfy him for the tapping sounds continued, but Herbert did not look again.

He forced back nausea and, hearing again the Devil's congratulations on his strength and fortitude whisper in his mind, took refuge in the silent recitation of the *De Profundis*. But long use had robbed it of meaning for Herbert and he broke off half-way with an anguished cry. Save him, O God! He must not die like this from weakness brought on by his own foolish austerities, the Church's need of him is too great. He must recover!

'Well,' said the Infirmarian at last, 'with God's help we have done all we can. I will sew the cut quickly for I think the drug will not keep him sleeping much longer. Pass me the paste for dressing the wound.'

When he finally rinsed the blood off his hands in a bowl of water he wore a decidedly self-congratulatory air. 'We shall know the result by tomorrow,' he informed them. 'I must go at once to Abbot Guichard to inform him of the success of my work.' He saw the wild joy and relief flood Herbert's face and added warningly, 'By success I mean that he still lives. We shall not know how he fares for a few days. But if the fever abates it is likely he will mend. Pray for that, brother.'

Herbert only nodded so that the Infirmarian wondered for a moment if he fully realised how desperate was the Archbishop's case.

Herbert went quickly, not looking back at the still figure on the trestle, but unlatching the door with haste as though eager to get away. Once outside, though, he paused, then stood surprised. It was snowing hard. He watched a moment, raising his face to the drifting flakes. On the ground the snow was as white as a shroud. He shivered as if an icy splinter had touched his heart, then, pulling up his hood and muffling his hands in his sleeves, he marched quickly through the blizzard to the chapel.

The child, who had been kept awake a long time by the raised voices in the hall, pulled at the wolfskin until she had drawn enough slack inside the woollen blanket that covered her to make a little nest for her cold hands. The harsh feel of the fur brought back the comfort and security of earlier days. The baron had given her the wolfskin for a coverlet when first she came with her mother to live in his household and, matted and moulting as it now was, it symbolised to her the special position she had with him.

Of course she had not known then that she was his daughter, although he had been a familiar figure since her babyhood on his visits to the mill. That knowledge had come only gradually during the four years since Miller's death, picked up from whispers and asides from serfs in the village and servants in the hall. The first hint she had had from Robin–dear Robin, Weaver's son, and her best friend. She felt foolish now, remembering how she had misunderstood, but she had been no more than six or seven. He had tried to warn her then that the baron would separate her from the village people–her mother's people–but she had not taken that in either.

Her hands were warm now in the fur and she wriggled her toes in the coarse blanket. The voices outside rose louder. She had stood listening for a while in the folds of the curtain that separated her sleeping place from the hall; that was why she had been so cold. They were discussing the King and the Archbishop of Canterbury.

He was a kind of king of the church as King Henry was king of the realm, and they had quarrelled so terribly that the Archbishop had fled in fear to a strange country oversea. That had made King Henry angrier because he had wanted to cut off the Archbishop's hands and feet and nose, and cast him into prison. She shuddered again when she thought of it. She had seen a beggar once with a horrible hole where his nose should have been, and stumps instead of hands, and all he had done, according to the baron, was to make false money. Pushing her head down to shut out the voices, she began to whisper a prayer that the Archbishop might escape such a fate.

Half-way through, though, she stopped because she remembered what her mother said about the prayers the priest taught her. Perhaps that was the reason why her father wished to part her from her mother's folk. Because although they went to Mass and observed all the outward forms, they did not really believe the things the baron believed–or if they did, they believed other things too; secret things they took care the baron should not know about. Certainly Robin did. He had told her something about them and she had gone with him sometimes when he left gifts under the elder and the thorn for the Old Gods.

But the powers of the Old Gods had not prevented her father removing her from the servants' quarters and her mother's care to the custody of Dame Ysabel, the baron's daughter-in-law. She had known how the other servants had resented that by the way they turned their faces when she passed and seemed not to hear her requests unless the baron or Sir Robert, his son, or Dame Ysabel was by. Her mother had told her not to complain of it or even to notice and was as she had always been, a broad, heavy, silent woman with a face that seemed too young for her body. Cicely knew she was not young at all though; she was more than thirty years old. It was her magic that kept her looking young.

She had not always known that either; she had only learned of it during the last year. It was after the baron had insisted that she have lessons from his chaplain, Master Lawrence, that Beta had taken her aside one day and questioned her about his teachings. It was in the spring and the air had throbbed with the cooing of the doves as they sunned themselves on the ledges of the cote. A sharp scent of sage rose from the bushes that spread across the path where one of them had bruised the leaves in passing, and there was a steady humming of bees working the foxglove spires by the wall.

Beta had laughed at her answer, her eyes crinkling at the corners. 'Pay no heed to his tales,' she had said. 'I shall teach you truth, not fables.'

'You, mother?' She had had a feeling of what was meant not only from Robin's stories but also from half-remembered hints of hidden knowledge. '*You?*'

Beta looked up at a sky in which a few fat white clouds swam. The black circles in the centres of her eyes shrank to pinpoints and the brilliant light made them the same blinding, heavenly blue.

'Yes, I, my child. Did you not know I work the earth magic here? There's none so many of us now, and less as their religion grows stronger, but some still hold to the old ways. And you are my child and shall learn them from me.'

'When?'

Her mother's face had darkened. 'Not while Dame Ysabel watches you.'

Something cold brushed the child at the memory. For within the month Dame Ysabel was dead and the household at sixes and sevens until the baron gave the household keys into her mother's keeping. Then things had gradually come back to normal except that Sir Robert who had used to pat her head and smile at her did so no longer. She knew well enough that it was not that he had taken any dislike to her but that he simply did not see her, his eyes being inward turned with his great grief. She decided that he must have loved Dame Ysabel dearly, which was strange indeed as he had been her husband.

In her experience, most husbands and wives seemed not to like each other very much, from Godric's wife down in the village who was continually being brought before the Manor Court for beating and abusing her husband to the baron himself who had locked away his Lady in the tower. The baron had good reason, for the Lady was possessed of devils and feared by everyone, including Cicely herself; but it made the blood run cold to hear her howl and fling things about in the night.

She stuck her head out from the covers a moment to be sure that all was quiet up there. It was not far away for the tower was built on the end of the house, and the same end as her little closet. It was quiet–altogether quiet–and she realised the men had done talking in the hall and retired to their beds. She snuggled down again, content. Soon her mother would come, unless she had gone to the baron, and lay herself beside her.

She was nearly asleep when she heard the curtain whisper across the strawing on the floor and saw brightness through her closed eyelids. When no further movement came she rolled her head from side to side like a blind mole shying away from the light of day. 'Are you awake, then?' said her mother's voice. She made an inarticulate mumble.

'Wake up,' said Beta, 'wake up, child. Do you not know this is Midwinter Day? Tonight we celebrate the rebirth of the sun!' She put down the rushlight and sat on the bed, touching the child's cheek with her hand. 'They are all asleep. It is safe to go now.'

Cicely sat up with a jerk and Beta laid a finger on her lips. 'Quiet, now. Come, dress yourself. Tonight is festival.'

It was quite dark outside but not really cold. She hesitated at the plank bridge, thinking of the lookout, but her mother urged her on with whispered words: 'Those who do not join us will not see us. Better for them that they do not. Come away, come lightly.' And they had gone on, her mother, herself and at least a dozen of the house servants, away from the village to where the tree-crowned summits of the little hills thrust towards the sky.

It was the dark of the moon but a faint, diffuse starshine lit the way and a damp breeze, smelling of the sea, blew in their faces. Excitement filled Cicely. She had no idea what she expected to see but it was not what finally met her eyes when they had ascended the hill and come through the trees to a small clearing on the summit. It seemed no more than a harvest-ale, the leaping bonfire in a hollowed stone in the centre, the food and drink set out, the very faces that turned to watch them come all familiar to her. Only they looked at her differently.

And when her mother pushed her forward so that she stood alone they came up one by one and each laid a hand upon her shoulder as they kissed her cheek, and then led her to the feast. Her mother had gone and she sat between Goda and Walburga, replete with ale and mutton pie and sheltered by their bulk from the breeze that shivered the branches of the trees and eddied down among the drifts of last year's leaves at their feet.

She was nearly asleep again when they began to sing so she did not see the coming of the god who, as she learned on later occasions, merely walked from the shadows of the trees. But that first time she thought he had been called from the Other World by the singing and she shrank down between the two women lest the pits of darkness in the blank animal mask light on her and suck her soul away. Then she saw that her mother stood beside him, her hair unbound and flowing on her shoulders, and behind her were others, beast-headed but lacking the great curving horns of the god. He had the head of a stag; they were oxen, horses, goats. . . . There was a smell that reminded her of the stable and the byre, and something else that made her think of mystery and darkness. The fire crackled as they threw handfuls of herbs or seeds on it.

All the people were swaying and singing; they beat the heels of their hands together in a very gradually accelerating témpo, a rhythmic pulse. Faster it went and faster.

Her mother had something in her hands that mewed and struggled; the thin, shrill cries rose above the throbbing chant. There was a small flurry of movement and it was still. Dark splashes stained the front of her mother's robe.

Goda felt the child stiffen and drew her into the circle of her arm. 'See?' she said. 'There's the blood of sacrifice, real blood, not the wine the priest pretends is blood when he drinks it. You don't think the gods don't know the difference?' She cuddled the child closer. 'You don't want to be part of their lies, do you, my pretty? This is the true worship that the grandfathers of our grandfathers knew.'

Cicely looked up into the broad Saxon face and saw the subtle change in it as the woman recalled who were her grandfather and her father, and knew that she said those same words to every child new to the rites, only this child was different in half her blood. . . . She remembered, too, the cold and empty faces of these people as they performed unwilling services for the baron's bastard daughter. And she thought of Robin, whom she loved more dearly than a brother and who belonged wholeheartedly to his folk and their beliefs.

'No,' she said. 'No, I do not believe their lies.'

Goda gave her an approving pat. 'I'll dip a rag in the blood for you. Do it every year and when you marry you'll be fruitful. It's really for the animals–when they breed we pour it on the ground and say the spells and they beget more young—'

Her voice was carried away on a sudden great cry that went up and Cicely saw that the horned god had come forward and seated himself to one side of the fire. Goda pulled her to her feet. 'Go to your mother–there, see, be quick!' She was jostled forward, pushed from hand to hand until she stood by Beta. She did not look like the mother Cicely knew in the blood-spattered robe with a crown of ivy on her long, loose hair; her face was vacant and her eyes looked different. Her hands were dark and sticky and the stickiness was transferred to Cicely's own hands.

Up there the rank beast smell was so strong that it nauseated her. Her mother's hands were on her, pulling off her clothes, pushing her forward to the god. Someone tied her own hands behind her.

She dared not raise her eyes but she saw the long, shining blade slide out and felt it prick her chest. A voice rumbled a question; fear blanked out everything until it pricked deeper. Then she nodded wildly, it must be assent he wanted. The sword withdrew. More questions, more assenting. Arms reached out and took her, strangely gentle. She drank from a proffered cup; the taste made her tongue curl. Then everything swam away in noise and haze.

The next thing she knew she was lying on a deerskin cloak and Robin sat beside her. He leaned down, smiling. 'Are you awake?'

'What happened?' she said in wonder. 'Have I been asleep?'

'It's the drink they give you. Did you dream? Dreams mean something and the first dream is important.'

'I can't remember.' She raised herself. 'What are they doing now?'

'Dancing for the god. They will dance till nearly dawn.' He put his hand on hers. 'I shall be glad when you are old enough to join in. I had rather dance with you.'

'Then you—?'

He could not repress his pride, though he tried in the face of her disappointment. 'This is my first time. Before I was always sent to wait with the old women as you were.'

'Stay here with me.'

He shook his head. 'You will go to sleep again.' And indeed her lids were drooping. 'I will see you again at the monthly meeting.' He squeezed her arm fiercely. 'I am so glad you are one of us.'

He saw that she had gone from him in sleep and gazed at her, torn by a feeling he could not put a name to. Then he looked towards the ring of naked dancers where couples were already clinging to each other and staggering away into the undergrowth, and he ran to join them and discover, if he might, whether he was yet a man.

Behind the shutters of her eyelids Cicely was remembering

the dream she had denied. In it she had been the sacrificial victim–and willing, nay, eager for immolation. The horror of it still lay in her mind. She strained to stay awake, to break the spell that had seduced her into acceptance, into surrender to something that would not be satisfied with less than all of her. But it was hard, too hard. . . . She twitched and sighed and sank to sleep.

The baron, whose name was Sir Richard Fitzurse, did not rest undisturbed that night either, though it was not the great quarrel between King and Archbishop which had dominated the conversation at his table that troubled him. He had long ago lost interest in what did not touch him personally. He was far from the centres of power, and invulnerable on his own lands by virtue of his status as a tenant-in-chief. The heathen revels of his serfs might have concerned him more deeply had he ever taken the trouble to verify his half-formed suspicions. It was as well for him he had not, since the turmoil in his mind was occasioned by the very child who at that time was being led to her initiation.

He loved her more than anything in the world, and throughout that sleepless night his mind returned again and again to the insoluble problem of how he might marry her, child of his villein mistress, as high as the two legitimate daughters for whom he had cared hardly at all. For give her to the Church, as most men did with the offspring bred of servile blood, he would not.

Every feeler towards marriage he had sent out had been met with blank indifference; it seemed that no amount of silver could bridge the chasm that separated noble and villein, and he could think of nowhere else to try. Robert, the only other of his children remaining with him, was a bastard but the attitudes towards him whose mother had been a high-born Norman lady were entirely different. Some of his spleen had spilled over on to Robert on that account.

Aside from that, his son had been forgetful and uncaring of his stewardship since the loss of his wife. Sometimes the baron wondered whether there were more to it than natural grief. He knew that Robert blamed him in some degree for Ysabel's death, and it was true that he could not remain quiet on the subject until Ysabel showed some prospect of producing an heir; but how was he to know that the attempt would kill her? He too missed her quiet presence but it was useless to try and speak of her to Robert; his face would close up and he would make some excuse to be about an urgent task elsewhere, though there were signs of his neglect everywhere. Should he not feel some gratitude that this manor would one day be his? As the law stood, he was entitled to nothing.

Though it was the poorest of his lands, Williton was dearest to Richard Fitzurse's heart; he spent most of his time here apart from the regular autumn journeys to eat up the produce of other nearby manors. Robert's apparent indifference rankled. Even if it had entered his mind the baron would have given no consideration to the fact that Robert's promised inheritance was due more to his determination to deprive his elder son of it than any other reason.

He had never liked Reynold, his heir and only true-born son. Even in childhood the boy had put his teeth on edge; his slow wits, his lack of any finer feelings, his strong likeness to the mother who shared those disabilities. Robert, less than a year younger, had shone by comparison, and when both lads had returned from their education in de Tracy's household he had been thankful to find it was Reynold who was the natural fighter, fired with ambitions to live in camps, and courts, too, if he got the chance. He had been able (though not without trouble, for other people had raised eyebrows at Reynold's bluster) to get him placed in the Chancellor's, Becket's, household and thus put a good many miles between them. And Robert, apparently lacking any sort of ambition, had stayed on and, as his father's health declined, eventually assumed the position of steward.

All this had happened some ten years ago, about a year after Cicely was born. Young Henry FitzEmpress, who had then just gained the throne, had healed the breach caused by the wars between his mother and her cousin, King Stephen, and now here he was splitting England in two once more, but this time the breach was between church and state. Or perhaps the fault lay with his erstwhile Chancellor whom he had made Archbishop of Canterbury. Richard Fitzurse remembered him vaguely, a tall man and handsome in spite of a big nose, with pale, fanatical eyes. The blame might indeed be his but he thought King Henry was not far behind in inflexibility.

Seeking to escape the scurrying thoughts he turned too abruptly in the tumbled bed and was brought up short by pain which made him lie quite still and hold his breath for an interminable moment. It passed, his breath huffed out in a tremulous sigh, and very gingerly he shifted his swaddled leg to a new position. It seemed to weigh a long hundredweight, that leg. He knew now it would never heal.

He had got the wound which had left him with those purulent, gaping sores in the fighting between King Stephen and the Empress. In the rout of Lincoln, to be precise, when he and Baldwin of Clare had fought shoulder to shoulder with Stephen himself in the last, desperate, blood-spattered stand against superior numbers. He remembered the aching of his sword arm and the way the nasal of his helmet had pressed upon his nose; it had been dented by a blow that had almost seen the last of him.

Then Stephen had been felled by a stone and they had been captured and dragged ignominiously before the Empress. He had lain in prison nine months and, though he had been released with Stephen when the tide of war had swung the other way, the neglected wound in his leg had never healed and he had been lame ever since.

Well, a quarrel with the Church was not likely to lead to

battles of that kind. He was not even very sure what it was all about, though it appeared that the chief bone of contention was the Archbishop's refusal to allow clergy to be tried in any but ecclesiastical courts. He had a fellow-feeling with Henry there. If any priest or clerk had committed murder on his lands he could not see himself meekly delivering the malefactor to the bishop, who would do no more than fine or unfrock him. Yet, judging by the furious arguments that had raged that evening, Robert would.

Robert. . . . What he needed was a new wife. The baron began to drift into sleep and then came broad awake as the idea that would solve all his problems came to him. He would marry Cicely to Robert.

It did not strike him as distasteful thus to unite his own children. The Church's ban on consanguinity was so far-reaching, stretching back through four generations to great-great-grandparents in common, that it had become a dead letter; when a marriage between third and fourth cousins was reckoned incestuous the word ceased to have meaning. The divergent blood-lines through their mothers satisfied any qualms about interbreeding; nonetheless, he would have to approach the matter delicately.

The next day, being the Feast of All Saints, was a high day when only absolutely indispensable work was done and everyone might then spend his time as he would. In summer this would mean a general exodus from the house but today a miserable, drizzling rain had set in which kept everyone within doors, and after dinner the baron found that Robert had settled himself nearby on the corner of the great hearthstone where he was attempting to mend a hawking glove which had split open along one finger. He sewed intently; every time he thrust the needle through the two thicknesses of leather his lower lip came forward with the pressure of his tongue between his teeth.

Away down the hall a group of men was engaged in like

tasks; the servants, having taken down the trestles except the one where the men sat, had gone off about their own pleasures. The hall was quieter than usual and rather dim; what little light came through the high, narrow windows of waxed linen served only to illuminate the hazy veil of smoke which hung eternally among the rafters. The lime-washed walls were yellowed by it, the painted scenes upon the arch half-way down were almost invisible; only memory informed the baron that this very house was represented in one of them; others depicted the annual work on the manor, ploughing, sowing, cutting the corn. The largest painting was above the keystone of the arch, a fair picture of knights on horseback riding down on footmen armed with battleaxes who stood with interlocked shields. Richard Fitzurse had always thought this a portrayal of the Saxon shield wall in the battle which won England for William of Normandy. But it, too, was almost lost now in a creeping stain of damp from a leak in the roof. Another of Robert's omissions. . . . He looked across at him.

Robert was finding that as the needle blunted it was becoming more and more difficult to penetrate the tough hide. He swore under his breath and, laying down the offending glove unfinished, caught the dark look his father bent on him.

Some emotion perturbed Robert's face; Richard was not sure what, only that it seemed imperative to say something and thus paper over what he might have glimpsed. So, out of his sudden confusion, he plunged headlong into the subject uppermost in his mind.

'I have it in my mind to find a husband for young Cicely. A man I might trust is difficult to find.'

Robert nodded gravely. If his father was about to ask his advice he must be desperate. 'That is always so,' he said and, after a pause, 'What had you in mind to grant as her dower?'

'Silver. And land.' Robert kept his eyes on the fire. That, perhaps, made it easier to say, 'I would have you marry her when she is old enough.'

Robert turned his head very slowly and stared at his father. 'That is not possible.'

'Not possible? You are wrong. Here my word is law.'

'Under church and king.'

The baron continued to meet his son's gaze unflinchingly.

Robert sat rigid. He means this, he thought, and a whirl of old memories rose in his mind: Lady Maud's accusations about the paternity of her tiring-woman's child, his father's angry denials followed by Beta's immediate wedding to the miller. Why had he denied it? Of course he had not known then that the likeness between them would make denial absurd. Or had he feared what had in fact happened later when he had reinstated his bawd and the child in his house after Miller's death: Lady Maud's attack upon the child? Had she always been possessed of devils or was it her sin in giving way to hatred that had given them entrance? And if so, whose was the fault, hers or his father's?

He said, 'Can you believe I do not know she is my sister?'

'You are not children of the same belly.'

'You think that makes it different? Well, I do not. I'll break no law of God for you or any other man.' And if you had done the same, he thought, none of this would have happened. . . . Yet I am as bad as he, or worse, in that I loved my wife and still consorted with a trull. But had she borne a child to me I'd not have brought it into my own house. . . . His self-examination was quenched by the baron's short bark of laughter.

'You are over-nice, my son. I know of half a dozen cases—'

Robert stood up. 'I care not what you know of others' sins. You'll never marry me to mine own sister. Sooner will I leave here and take service with some lord. I should have done that years ago–but that I thought you needed me. I see now I have been a fool. Well, I'll go—' He stopped because his heart was thudding as if he had run a race but still stood there, paralysed by the uncontrollable jumping of his knees.

In contrast, the baron's voice was flat and unemotional.

'You are making more of it than the matter warrants. Or do you perchance feel that you would be disparaged by such a marriage?'

Robert saw in the glitter of his eyes the danger he faced. His father's hand had tightened on the head of his walking-staff until the knuckles were white. Somehow he must make him see the truth without angering him beyond control.

'Can a bastard be disparaged?' he said. 'You know it is not that. Nor that I do not care for her. It is because I do I will not wed her.'

The baron's hand relaxed; perplexity had replaced the anger in his face. 'What, then? You think it sin?–the blood tie too near? See now, my son, every couple who marry in the vill are more nearly related than are you two. Cousins, all of them–first cousins, generation after generation—'

'Look at them,' said Robert, and then into the quiet, 'I am sorry, truly. It is best that I go from here.'

The baron's eyes searched his face; then, as if recognising defeat, his shoulders slumped. 'Nay, nay,' he said. 'No more. I do need you. I did not know you–felt so strongly.' The side of his mouth twitched suddenly, giving him an oddly defenceless look. His voice sounded different when he said, 'Can we speak of it? I shall not try to coerce you, I swear.'

'What more is there to say?'

'I am afraid for her. If I should die, what will become of her? Had Ysabel lived. . . . Well, no use to dwell on that.'

Robert looked hard at him, suddenly seeing the changes that time had wrought. He was in his mid-fifties, but he looked old, older than de Mohun, their near neighbour, who must be at least ten years his senior. What, indeed, if he should die? That would mean Reynold would be master here, for as far as Robert knew his father had done nothing to implement the promise that Williton should be his. He sat down again on the hearthstone.

'You could send her to Reynold and Beatrice,' he said

carefully. 'Where her background is not known, a marriage might be arranged.'

His father's head came up. 'No,' he said curtly.

'Or to one of your other daughters?'

He did not bother to answer that. There was a short, uneasy silence. When Robert spoke again his voice seemed to him unnaturally loud. 'I had no mind to marry again but if you can find me a wife with lands I shall undertake to promise that my house will be hers until I can secure her future.'

The baron nodded. Robert picked up the glove again and laid it on his knee. His sense of outrage had died but shock remained. He knew himself to be a sinful man, weak against the temptations of the flesh, but he, at least, had never questioned the rulings of the Church, let alone set them aside as of no account as his father had done. Without the guidance of the Church, how could a man hope to be numbered amongst the elect after the great Day of Judgement? If he followed not the teachings, safeguarded himself not with the sacraments, what then? And remembering the talk of the men at table last night he gritted his teeth, angry again at their foolishness in jeopardising that security for such a trifle as earthly justice. He disliked those religious who lived easy, waxed fat and indulged in the grossest sins but he was not prepared to risk what might follow King Henry's defiance of canon law. The dread that lay at the back of his mind was out in the open now: interdict, the excommunication of a whole realm. He saw it all in imagination–the muffled bells, the unattended altars, the churches locked and desolate. Babes unbaptised, young lovers unwed, the dying unshriven. . . .

He drove the needle savagely into the leather. It passed through an unseen hole he had made earlier and straight into his hand.

Although the King had been four days at Marlborough by Christmas Day, Queen Eleanor as yet had had no private conversation with him. She knew, though, that his embassy to the Pope had returned with the tale of their failure; her Chamberlain, Henry Fitzgerold, had been one of the party and he had reported to her as fully on that as on Henry's fury at the news.

Now, as her women prepared her for bed, she was wondering why Henry had decided to spend the Christmas Feast here with her. It might be that he was planning to take Richard from her care; he was now seven years old, the age of young Henry when he had been removed to the Archbishop's household for training. But young Henry had grown too fond of his foster-father. Henry loved his children jealously; it might make him think twice about placing Richard elsewhere.

She did not think it would occur to Henry that he could lose his children as effectively by leaving them with their mother. But she was seeing to it that none of them loved or respected the man who had dragged her pride in the dust. She was his equal at least in breeding and intelligence and the domains she had brought him had helped to make him one of the most powerful men in Europe; yet he had bestowed the love and affection he owed her on a low-born clerk and a villein mistress. That dead whore's bastard lived among her children as a constant reminder.

He was here now with them, though at eight years old Geoffrey had learned enough to efface himself, withdrawing silently with the baby and her nurse when she had visited the children's quarters a day or two ago to see her eldest son. Since he had been accepted by the magnates and granted the title 'The Young King', Henry had been given his own household and their meetings had been few.

He had flung himself upon her, laughing with delight, while she had held him off to exclaim with pride and pleasure on his increased stature and handsome face. He bore a strong likeness to Henry's father, Geoffrey of Anjou, the handsomest man of his day. There was a curious rightness in that; she had known him better than Henry ever guessed–or Louis, who had been her husband at the time. She had quite forgotten that this old memory had ever discomfited her.

She listened enchanted to young Henry's tales of exploits of swordplay and horsemanship, with hound and hawk. (Nothing of books, she noted; he was a warrior born.) He had wanted to hear all she had been doing and when she recounted those stories from the courts of love suitable to his years he capped them with a few which were not. She laughed then, and sighed, seeing how few years were left to him before manhood.

He was sitting at her feet and, hearing the sigh, looked up at her.

'Mother?' he said in quite a different voice.

'My son?'

'You heard what happened at Northampton?'

'Yes,' she said cautiously.

'I heard too. I was not there to see but I was at Clarendon last January. I–I thought then that the King, my father, treated the Archbishop very ill. I was afraid, mother–for the Archbishop, I mean–no, for myself too. My father shouted at me before all his lords—'

'At you?'

'I was crying–I could not help it, truly. I was afraid of what my father might do to the Archbishop.'

'You love him as much as that?'

He was silent, considering his loyalties. 'Not as much as you. But more than him.'

She was silent then. She did not like Thomas Becket, but young Henry did not know that. And he knew nothing of the deeper issues; he saw only a king raging against one he loved. She began to see how that love could further her own ends. If Henry did violence upon the Archbishop the boy would never forgive him. This might be the weapon she had waited for; but with the Archbishop safe in France, and she and Henry scarce on speaking terms. . . .

She ran her hand caressingly over the child's thick, red-gold hair. 'You must know my influence with your father is small.'

'Yes,' he said. She guessed he had been talking to Richard, who missed nothing.

'It will but make him angrier if I speak of it,' she said.

'I know,' he answered. She saw on his face a look of most unchildlike hatred.

She was remembering this while her ladies divested her of the fur-edged night-rail, and helped her into bed. The markings on the wax of the night candle showed an hour before midnight.

Their busy hands stilled suddenly at the deep tones of a man in the ante-chamber and the answering voice of a page; propped against the pillows Eleanor sensed rather than saw their covert looks. The rattle of the latch was loud in the silence. Henry stood in the doorway, alone and unannounced, as he used to come long ago.

She was, for an instant, at a loss, feeling her ladies' suddenly awakened interest; then she stretched out a hand towards him.

'Welcome, my lord.' She forced a smile, seeing with shock that he wore only a bedgown under the cloak that protected him from the chill of the outer passages. Did he think to resume the marital duties he had for so long ignored? And if he did, what of her intentions? Must she soften yet again towards him or could her will withstand the betraying body?

But when a chair was brought for him and the ladies dismissed, his conversation concerned their children and principally Matilda whom he was proposing to betroth to a German princeling. She frowned slightly.

'Is that prince not a cousin and great friend of the Emperor?'

He nodded and began to toy with her fingers. She allowed him to keep her hand but sat up a little straighter. 'And is not the Emperor an enemy of true Christianity in that he has raised up his own Pope?'

He smiled a faint amused smile. 'Oh, come now, Eleanor. That does not sound like you.'

She primmed her mouth a little, eyeing him. 'I will not have my daughter in an enemy camp.'

He dropped her hand and half turned to face her directly. 'Nor I. But will you tell me one good reason why I should continue to support Alexander? He does not support me.'

'Oh, I see. It is true then? That Thomas of London has been received with honour and confirmed Archbishop of Canterbury?' She spoke with sudden passion. 'I tried to warn you of him. Why could you never see until it was too late?'

Henry moved impatiently but bit back the sharp retort about feminine jealousy. He would not get what he wanted by antagonising his wife. Even if he was unwilling to allow that her initial distrust of his dearest friend had proved well-founded, he was at least prepared to admit his mistake in making him Archbishop. But only with reservations. He said, 'He has changed out of recognition. I think he has become a religious fanatic.'

'He has not changed at all. It was there always, only that you could not see it.'

'Oh, and you could, I suppose?' he said sharply, forgetting his good intentions.

'Yes, that I could–and much besides.'

He raised his eyebrows.

'That he was dangerous,' she said, 'as such rigid men are always. He would see all destroyed for his beliefs. Beware of men with conscience, Henry. Pray that the Pope is not another such.'

'Louis . . .,' he said reflectively, 'Louis sides with him against me.'

'But not for the sake of conscience only, I think. He has many an old score to settle.'

In the dim light, with her beautiful mouth curved in a

reminiscent smile, she looked much younger than her years. A faint, sweet scent from her warm flesh assailed his nostrils. He leaned a little nearer, remembering that she had been the greatest prize he had won from Louis.

'Tell me,' he urged, 'how I may separate them. You were married to him, you knew him well enough.' He gave her a look she thought was sly. 'You shall not again have cause to complain that I do not listen.'

Let that be so, she thought. Oh, let that be so, and he may have good cause to complain that he listened! She veiled her eyes.

'Not by threats against Louis,' she said, 'but yes, in the way you are thinking of. Louis will sacrifice him to the Pope's interests. Frighten them both enough and Louis will be persuaded to hand over the Archbishop to you. If you can make him believe you will desert Pope Alexander. . . . For you do not truly mean to recognise the anti-Pope?'

Henry eyed her in silence.

'You must not!' she exclaimed. 'Think–if you do that you will have shot your last bolt and so lost all chance of recovering the person of that traitor. For Louis and the Pope will see you as an enemy and protect him at all costs. Threat is more powerful than action here.'

Her horror at the thought of his failure to apprehend Thomas was too genuine to mistake and it took Henry off guard. She saw the triumph in his eyes as he took her face between his hands and kissed her full on the mouth. It told her why he had come.

All her reservations died before that knowledge. She would truly do all the things she had considered, no matter who suffered. Not for young Henry or Matilda would she hold back–her own heart's treachery was now her only fear. But that was open to proof.

Henry was not the only one who could use bedchamber tricks to gain his ends. She moved the sheet a little. It was up to him whether he chose to read an invitation in it.

'It grows chilly,' he said with an exaggerated shiver. She shifted over an inch or two, making more space on his side of the bed. He began to remove his bedgown, watching her. She closed her eyes as if in modesty, then raised the lids a trifle to study him through her lashes. His belly looked soft, he was growing a paunch. She looked after him coldly as he padded to the privy and back. His nakedness left her unmoved. If it were true that she no longer cared!

He appeared to notice no difference in her attitude towards him. When he rolled away from her afterwards and lay with his arm crooked behind his head, she knew why; he had not been thinking of her at all. For as though there had been no interruption in their conversation he said, 'Who may I entrust with so delicate a task? Who can convey veiled threats as he could? And his serpent's tongue works against me now while I am surrounded by fools.'

Fixed and irrevocable now her decision. She had to wait a moment to find her voice.

'It will be threat enough to send a deputation to the Emperor.'

'To treat of betrothal, then?'

Eleanor recognised the choice between the loss of Matilda to the Germans and recognition of the anti-Pope. She abandoned Matilda with little more compunction than she had felt at leaving her two eldest daughters with Louis. But she lay awake a long time after he slept not knowing whether to sorrow or rejoice that magic dwelt no more in his touch, and that she had used him as he used all women, for pleasure only.

When the King had left, the Privy Council began to break up with much loud, excited talk, the earls and barons gathering into groups while the officials scurried here and there with the rolls which recorded the proceedings and which must be safely stowed away when sealed and witnessed by the Justiciars.

One of the two Justiciars, the Earl of Leicester, moved closer to his colleague, Richard de Luci, until he was looking down over his shoulder. Richard half turned in his seat and, seeing who stood behind him, flattened the roll in front of him with his long, narrow hands that Leicester might read.

'If any clerk or layman in your bailiwick has appealed to the Roman Curia, I command you to seize him and keep him closely in custody until you learn my will. Seize also all the revenues and possessions of the Archbishop's clerks for the Exchequer as Ranulf de Broc and my other officers shall inform you. And the fathers and mothers, brothers and sisters, nephews and nieces of all the clerks who are with the Archbishop you shall put under safe pledges, as well as their chattels, until you learn my will concerning them.' After the King's signature at the bottom was a great spatter of ink, showing the vehemence with which the quill had been driven.

'Ranulf de Broc,' said Leicester softly. 'The greatest ruffian in England.'

'Well, what would you?' de Luci said wearily. 'We shall not like to see the Church despoiled, either of us, but whose is the fault? The King is angry at the Archbishop's desertion of his see and his people.'

Leicester's eyebrows rose. 'Desertion?'

'Disobedience, defiance and desertion,' returned de Luci with a hard look. 'As you know, I was out of England on pilgrimage for more than six months, but even before I went the facts were plain. The Archbishop is the King's vassal.'

Leicester remembered de Luci was Canterbury's man. 'And from vassals there must be unquestioning obedience,' he remarked, not without malice.

De Luci remembered too, and the Archbishop's retort when he had tried to withdraw his homage. He said coldly, 'I saw the Archbishop on my journey home. He was stiff-necked beyond bearing. He would do well to remember a man's first duty is to his prince.'

'Ranulf de Broc would agree with you,' said Leicester sourly. 'He will do the King's will with a right good heart, especially on the Archbishop's close kin who are to be cast penniless adrift. One of his sisters is a nun, the others married with young children.'

De Luci stood up. 'The suffering of innocents must lie at the Archbishop's door. He has the means to discharge his conscience of it.'

'Oh, Richard!' Leicester pulled a face that made de Luci eye him haughtily. Then he said, 'I could better have borne it had the administration of Canterbury been given to an honest man.'

'Yes,' said de Luci. 'Yes—' He looked at Leicester with more sympathy. In this one thing, a detestation of the de Broc family, they were in accord. 'You were there,' he said, 'at the trial. As I have heard it, it was you passed sentence on him. Did it seem to you he was in peril of his life?'

'As any man who stands unarmed on a battlefield,' returned Leicester equably. He saw de Luci's eyes go down again to the parchment. 'Does that read as though the King had mercy in mind?'

De Luci muttered something about the Archbishop merely having to affix his seal to the Constitutions and stopped abruptly at Leicester's hard, angry laugh.

'You, Richard, who are so much a man of God that you have braved the dangers of a pilgrimage oversea at your age, would have an archbishop sign away his hope of Heaven for the sake of peace? Come, you wrote them out, you know what's in them. Will the Pope swallow them? He has seen them now in black and white since Henry so obligingly set them on parchment and forced a copy on Archbishop Thomas. Do you think he will forgo a tittle of his power for the sake of the Archbishop's skin?'

He talked on, keeping his voice low, and what he had to say left de Luci with no doubt at all where his sympathies lay. 'You go too deep for me, my lord,' he said wearily. 'I am a simple man and no theologian. Nor do I care which cardinal calls himself Pope so I see my duty clear and follow it. And neither should you. Henry is King by God's good grace and He will guide him.'

Because he respected Leicester in spite of his faulty judgement and wished him to know that he would mention nothing of what had passed between them, he added, 'Do not let partiality for the Archbishop blind you to his faults. But yet I know it's easy done, though oftener for a woman than a man.'

Leicester, who had always known de Luci silent as the grave, took the olive branch offered.

III
January 1165

In all the manors that belonged to Canterbury there had been troops of armed men for days past; the thin snow had been trodden into a brown slush by their horses and the cattle they had driven off. The great tithe barns stood already empty, their contents transferred to the wains that bumped over the rutted road to Saltwood Castle, and little groups of refugees trudged empty-handed in the freezing wind under the guard of pikemen who prodded the laggards along.

In most of these places only the villeins were left to contemplate the ruin, huddled inside fireless huts lest a curl of smoke betray their presence to the men-at-arms; but some, where the more courageous or less wary had dwelt, were deserted; nothing remained there but a blackened mess, still thinly smouldering, sharp against the whiteness of the winter landscape.

Reynold Fitzurse, coming down the hill with his muster, saw one of them. He had smelt it on the wind a mile off and now he reined in, peering about for any movement in the desolation. But there was only the harsh caw of a solitary crow as it rose, ungainly flapping, from one of the huddled heaps on the ground, proof enough that nothing still lived here. Reynold waved his arm to his men to hurry on. If he did not come up with that gang of cut-throats Ranulf had enlisted they would leave nothing standing between here and Barham.

He wore the King's badge now on his breast and thankful indeed he was to shelter behind it while Canterbury's people were being harried. As an earnest of good faith he and a few others, erstwhile Archbishop's men, had been sent to aid Ranulf de Broc in his work. But thankfulness did nothing to mitigate the vehement ill-humour he felt at having to be abroad in such weather, to prosecute de Broc's tasks for him while he was holed up for the winter in Saltwood Castle. Reynold brooded continually on the misfortunes that had befallen him through no fault of his own.

Here he was, a knight, heir to Sir Richard Fitzurse, a tenant-in-chief of the King, at twenty-eight years old reduced to scouring the countryside because of bad advice from a man he would have trusted with his life. Yet that same man, Hugh de Morville, who had clung so long to the Archbishop and persuaded him to the same, had gained a place at the King's side with no more pledge of loyalty than his given word. He had been made Justice for Cumberland. Why should he be rewarded while Reynold was penalised? But ill luck caused by the jealousy of others had always dogged his footsteps.

For ten years he had been Hugh's faithful satellite and ally, ever since both had joined the household of Thomas the Chancellor in the first year of the King's reign. His father had arranged that and it had always been a source of heartburning to him that he had not been placed with the King. Hugh's pride, too, had been chastened by the obligation of serving something less than the highest; they had each fed the other's resentments until the ostentation of the Chancellor and his even greater vainglory and arrogance when he became Archbishop of Canterbury had made them itch to see him toppled. But when at last it seemed that that might happen Hugh, without a prior word to him, had joined a mismanaged plot hatched by Richard le Bret, a King's man and Reynold's own kinsman by marriage.

Reynold considered le Bret, who was a landless man, with contempt and suspicion. He would have liked to view Hugh with contempt, too, but found himself unable to do so. He did not know why this should be but he was bound to him; where Hugh went, he must follow.

And now he could not. The glowering discontent that filled him turned towards his wife. She was glad he was separated from Hugh; she had always been jealous of their friendship. For months she had been urging him to desert Hugh, to renounce his fealty to the Archbishop and join the King's party. It did not strike him that he would not be in his present position if he had followed her advice. Reynold had never found difficulty in holding two irreconcilable opinions.

He could have borne with all her other faults–the sharpness of her tongue, her barely hidden contempt of him; most of all, the ease with which she won their every argument–had she given him an heir. But one daughter in ten years! He could not see that he owed her anything. He blamed her for their string of stillborn sons.

All at once, as the sun sent a long finger of light through the breaking cloud, he saw the bright wink of steel against the shoulder of the hill. The group they were pursuing was in sight, toiling like ants up the long slope ahead.

Reynold raised himself in the stirrups and sent out a long halloo. It seemed to him they paused a moment, looking back, but they did not stop. He swore and settled himself more securely in the saddle before putting his horse to a hard, pounding gallop. That sergeant would suffer for this when he came up with them.

They had disappeared over the hill by the time Reynold's men began the ascent and the sun was close to setting before they breasted the rise. The land fell away in undulations before them. There was no sign of their quarry.

Furious, Reynold dragged at the horse's mouth and stared

about. Down to their left a thread of smoke was rising. Humbert, Reynold's squire, pointed. 'Down there, my lord.'

'Is it a vill?'

'No. . . . Some shepherd's hut, I fancy.'

'By God,' said Reynold with passion, 'if they're at their games of looting and murder on their own account they shall pay for it. These lands run close by mine. Come on!'

The hut was off the road behind a small copse of trees, but it seemed that de Broc's men, far from wishing to destroy it, were eager to take shelter for the night. They stood, ten or a dozen of them (less than half the number of Reynold's muster), in a wary half-circle around the door where an old crone faced them like a crouching toad.

Reynold drove his horse straight into their midst. The laughter of his own men when they went crashing to the frozen ground dissipated some of his anger over the long chase they had given him.

They sat there rubbing their bruises and staring while the old woman cackled her appreciation.

'Which of you's the sergeant?' demanded Reynold.

A dark-faced fellow picked himself up and approached the stirrup. Reynold hit him across the face with the handle of his whip. 'That's for the run you gave us,' he said. 'Why did you not stop for us to come up with you? I know you saw us.'

The fellow had already taken in the quality of Reynold's horse and accoutrements. Through the hand across his bleeding mouth he set up a loud defensive crying. 'We could not see who you were at that distance, lord. You might have been anyone—'

'Who else rides here in armed bands but King's men?' Reynold grabbed him by the hair; his battered leather helmet still lay on the ground where it had fallen. 'Who gave you leave to burn and destroy round here?'

He muttered something about de Broc and Saltwood Castle, but Reynold's attention was suddenly distracted from him by the old woman who had come hobbling over and stood now by the horse's head. She was withered, toothless and bent nearly double but the small black eyes fixed on his glittered with a vital and ferocious glee.

She cried a question at him. He stared blankly, more astonished by her complete lack of fear than the almost incomprehensible syllables. She made a face of impatience and spoke again. It was a command; there was no mistaking the inflection. She drew her hand across her throat in a universal gesture.

Reynold gave a short bark of laughter, shaking the fellow's head hard enough to rattle his teeth. 'The old mother wants to see your blood, churl. A pity you're de Broc's man or I'd oblige her. What, a' God's name, were you interfering with her for? She's none of Canterbury's people!' He turned to the beldame, startled afresh at the vigour in her bird-like eyes. 'It can't be done this time, mother.'

She pointed at him, then at the ground before her, sharp and peremptory. Staggered, he took a quick glance back at his men. They had all fallen back several paces and were watching in a fixed silence. He saw suddenly that they were scared and ready to run.

Having discarded most of his conventional religious beliefs at Hugh de Morville's prompting, Reynold believed himself to be cynical and sophisticated. But his scepticism did not extend to the lore he had imbibed with his English nurse's milk: the orthology of tree and water spirits and the sacred woods, and of the occult powers of the faery people who still lurked there.

He looked back quickly at the old woman. To his surprise her lips, pleated with age into a drawstring bag, stretched in an ingratiating grin. 'No need for you to fear me, lord,' she said in the dialect of the people. 'Tell your men to wait, and come with me.' Her harsh old voice dropped lower so that he had difficulty in hearing her. 'Come–come away. I will read your future in the smoke.'

He knew now what she was and felt his left hand clench convulsively. Out of the corner of his eye he was aware of the sergeant he had struck crawling away on hands and knees. Then he nerved himself. She had said he had nothing to fear. And they had the Power, these old ones.

The sun had just set. He was suddenly afraid that the instant he entered her hut the silently watching men would take to their heels. He turned and glared at them. 'Wait for me,' he ordered. The sound of his own voice renewed his courage. Perhaps his luck had turned. He had arrived in time to help the old witch; she might help him.

He stooped to go through the low doorway. There was a step down inside; the hut was half underground. The only light came from the flickering fire and the smoke made his eyes water so that he could see nothing but shapes.

She pushed him down on to something soft. Feeling about his hands discovered fur: fox pelts on a bed of fern. There was a bad smell; the pelts poorly cured, or the witch herself; he could not tell.

'What will you have, lord, truth foretold or heart's desire?' She said. 'Philtres for love or vengeance?' At least that was what he thought she said but some of the words she used were unfamiliar.

'Darkness and power?' she said. 'Love and light? Or truth, which comes alone, linked only to itself? Answer, lord, that I may cast the spell.'

Doubt was beginning to rise in Reynold. Why should she give him anything? With her powers she had been in no danger. The gang he had pursued had been ready to flee when he arrived.

'You're cold,' she said, 'and weary from riding. Here, drink this.'

He shook his head but she would take no denial, forcing the horn mug between his hands. He took a sip gingerly and decided it was ale, but there was a curious aftertaste. When he had drunk half of it he put it on the floor by his foot. 'Who are you, mother?' he asked.

He could see better now the iron trivet across the fire on which a couple of pots steamed (he noticed the iron with relief; if she could handle that she was human enough), the bunches of herbs strung up to dry, a yellowed tangle of dead grass on the inverted turves laid across the latticework of poles overhead. She squatted opposite him, hands on her knees.

'Well do you call me "mother",' she said, 'though I be her maiden only. Tell me your choice, future foretold or heart's desire.'

Something about that frightened Reynold. How could a man live knowing the day he would die? His heart began to knock so loudly he could hear it.

She saw it in his face. 'A wish, then?'

'Aye,' he said. It sounded safe.

'Think well on it. It will be granted for good or ill.'

She picked up a knife and went away into the corner. He heard a sudden startled clucking and a whirr of wings. When she turned a fowl struggled frenziedly under one arm. She stretched its neck and cut through it; its wings still beat feebly as the blood spurted into a wooden bowl.

Muttering to herself she moved about in the confined space, adding odds and ends from various containers to the bowl. Reynold wondered how he might phrase a wish to cover all his wants. To have a son that his name might live on; to be at Court; to requite all the indignities continually put on him. . . . Thoughts of his father, his wife, Hugh de Morville moved vaguely in his mind. For the chance to show them all what he could do, were luck not always against him. . . . Yes, he had come at it at last: an imperishable name. For, if not himself, his son. . . . He must be careful how he put it so that he could not be defrauded.

'It is ready. Have you made your wish?'

He nodded firmly. 'Aye.'

'Bare your breast.'

Reynold nervously laid off his jerkin and pulled up the linen shirt underneath. She had drawn blood before he saw the knife in her hand but the immediate realisation that it went no deeper than a scratch held him still while she completed the curious design over his heart.

'Rub the paste into the'–an unknown word–'while speaking the wish.' Her mouth was turned up at the corners but her eyes were blank, unseeing, unsmiling. She looked like a gargoyle on one of the great churches. So must the devil smile, thought Reynold, with an unwonted flash of imagery; but he did not heed the warning.

He worked the mess well into the small wound. 'That my name may live,' he muttered very fast, 'a thousand years.'

'It shall be,' she said, smiling still, and pulled back his shirt into place. 'The wish is granted.'

'How long?' he whispered.

The eyes came back to his from a great distance. 'A summer and a summer and a summer. . . .' She held up five fingers.

'A long time,' he said, disappointed.

'Not long for heart's desire. Some never gain it. You do not want to know the future?'

He shook his head.

'You are wise.' She turned, seeming to hear something. 'Go now. Your men will not wait much longer.'

At the threshold he turned back to look at her. 'Should you not ask my name?'

She smiled, more than ever like a gargoyle, he thought. 'I know it, Fitzurse,' she said.

He left in a hurry, glad to straighten to his full height outside. Only Eudo, his captain, and two bowmen lingered; the rest were waiting a furlong down the road.

Under the open sky, where the first stars shone through broken cloud, Reynold's confidence returned. 'What is that place?' he asked Eudo.

The captain glanced back at the trees spread along the slope. 'They call it the Women's Wood. It is said that few men will go there even in daylight. Those fellows did not know what they were risking.'

'She knew of me,' said Reynold. He began to whistle jauntily to show his assurance. The hush behind him was eloquent of his men's unspoken awe.

Beatrice Fitzurse was dining in her bower with only Ilaria for company when she heard Reynold ride in. Seeing that Beatrice's mind was wandering, Ilaria brought her tale of the wickednesses of one of the serving girls to a hurried conclusion.

Beatrice was discomfited by his early home-coming because little Maud, their daughter, had been soundly whipped today and sent early to bed, and he would undoubtedly demand to see her. The whipping had been well merited for Beatrice had caught her concealed in a closet where she might overhear her mother's private conversation with Ilaria; they had been talking about Reynold.

Ilaria stood up suddenly and bundled the cups and plates into the hutch; then she stood back and tried to make herself invisible. That was difficult because the room was small and Ilaria was a large woman.

But Reynold did not seem to notice her and his first words were not, as they usually were, about his child. Beatrice turned away her head when she heard his tone, which had that hushed, confidential note she knew so well, the note which meant he was about to announce an event of world-shattering importance. He had announced too many inconsequential trifles with just that intonation.

'You will not guess what I have learned,' he said. Ilaria slid quietly through the door.

'No,' she said flatly, 'I dare say not.'

'We *shall* have a son.' He was glowing with repressed excitement.

A sudden rage of fury and disgust shook her. So it was all to start again, the painful and undignified antics in bed, the miserable, useless pregnancies. He had not been near her for months and she had thought. . . . No, she had been sure that he would go away about the King's business, leaving her and Ilaria together, happy and at peace. She remembered the tiny, coffined corpses buried outside the churchyard wall because they had never breathed and therefore had no souls–every one a boy. She could better have borne it had some been girls.

'Who says so?' she said in a voice that plainly bespoke her opinion of him.

He overlooked it. 'Listen—' His tone was urgent. 'There is a wise woman out towards Aylesham. Well, no–a witch. She took me in—'

She pulled back from him. 'A witch! Sweet Christ, what are you at now?'

'I did not seek her out. We were chasing some of de Broc's men and they were harrying her. She–can you not see?–she was grateful to me. I gave her nothing but she scried for me. In five summers, she said.'

Beatrice sat down hard and winced. Her back had ached all day and there it was again, the sensation that she was sitting on a hard lump. Something had happened to her after the last pregnancy, something worse than yet another stillbirth.

'You will never get another living child from me,' she said.

He stared at her. 'How can you know?'

'There is something wrong with me.'

Anger at her reception of his news had been growing in him. 'Yes,' he said through his teeth. 'Yes, there is something wrong with you. But you are my wife. Are you trying to refuse me my rights?'

'Go away,' she said wearily. 'Go away and find some other woman. You have others, that I know.'

'Can I get Fitzurse sons from them?' he shouted.

She knew just how far she could go with him and had no

fancy to be dragged around the chamber by her hair. 'Five years, you said?' she asked as if she were considering the tale. 'Perhaps that is time for me to get my strength again. But there is something not as it should be, Reynold. Why should all our boys die?' She knew, of course, though he did not. But it struck her suddenly that even curses may be lifted by a witch.

He moved away from her and stared into the fire. She did not see the look he bent on her when he turned round and that was just as well for her peace of mind; for he had been coldly thinking that, if all were not well with her, better to know it soon rather than late. If she could not breed now was she like to in five years' time? He doubted it; she would be all of thirty by then.

The thought of a new wife, young and amenable, cheered him so that he answered her almost pleasantly when she asked abruptly if she could see the witch. 'No,' he said. 'No, that I would not risk. It is too dangerous. Besides, it is unnecessary; I have her word on it.'

He began to pull out his shirt from his braies then, preparatory to showing her on his own flesh the visible proof of that promise.

February 1165

When the monks had gone into the church for Vespers, Thomas, Herbert and John of Salisbury, Thomas's oldest friend, went out into the cloister garth. The air was sharp and frosty, clean after the close damp chill of the monastery. John, who had been banished from England more than a year ago, had come for a short visit from Rheims.

Their talk was of King Henry and those actions of his which had resulted in such an increase in the size of Thomas's retinue at Pontigny. For Henry had not merely exiled all those with some connection with the Archbishop; he had extracted a vow from every one of them to present themselves to the author of their misfortunes that he might see the miseries his intransigence had inflicted upon others. For weeks past they had been arriving, underfed, underclothed and despairing, in such numbers that Thomas was finding it increasingly difficult to gain refuge for them. He was having to appeal to friends as far away as Sicily for help.

He had recovered from his operation more quickly than anyone had dared hope and, with returning health, his determination to vindicate himself in the eyes of the world was daily growing stronger. To that end he had been delving in the works of the Fathers in the monastery library, seeking justification for his stand against Henry. This quite uncalled-for harshness of the King could, he thought, only help his case. He had just said as much when Herbert broke in.

'As I have heard, they have a complete collection of the sermons and letters of Yves of Chartres at Auxerre. You would do well to send for them, and also for the works of Anselm wherein you cannot fail to find much that is relevant to your position. It will give you worthwhile occupation during your convalescence and I, of course, out of my knowledge of the Scriptures, will be able to find you many apt quotations with which you may refute the arguments the seculars will bring against you.' He stopped, struck by a sudden thought. 'There must be copies of the old Canterbury privileges in the Papal archives. Why should you not send for them also? In fact, once I turn my mind to it, I can think of any number of works which will be of use to us in our struggle—' He and Thomas looked at each other over the diminutive John's head, both seeing a shining ray of hope in a darkness that so short a time ago had seemed absolute.

Herbert and Thomas talked eagerly, but John had gone quiet, staring upwards, not joining in as they cudgelled their memories for the names of the books on canon law, on English history and other allied subjects. He had to trot to keep up with their long-legged strides. So they turned south in their circuit of the garden, with the mass of the buildings behind them and before them only the roof of the long, low infirmary silhouetted against a sky resplendent with stars. John stopped. The other two broke off and waited enquiringly.

'See,' said John, and waved his arm to encompass the heavens. 'The handiwork of God.' They all stood staring up, silenced by the spectacle. Thomas let out a long, slow, marvelling breath.

Over the refectory hung the evening star; no true star, as John knew, but one of those mysterious wanderers of the heavenly spheres; and close by it another of its kind, much less bright, and reddish. Eastward, caught in the topmost, leafless branches of the trees of the orchard, the Dogstar sparkled, diamond-like after the glowing lamp of Venus, trailing tall Orion who bestrode the southern sky. Strewn across the zenith in garlands and luminescent clusters the great stars glittered; between them, trembling to the limit of sight, myriad scintillating pinpricks dusted the face of Heaven.

To Herbert it came as a shock that so common a sight could be unnerving. God? He could make no connection between this vast and terrible sky and the Lord he served. Cold, indifferent, noumenal, it menaced the cosy edifice of faith in which he dwelt. He felt his soul shrink within him and with a wrench brought his eyes to earth again, to the work of the hands of men. Then his mind steadied, settled back into its comfortable groove. He did not raise his eyes again but contemplated the lighted windows of the refectory instead. Could he perhaps detect a whiff of onion gruel on the air?

Thomas still stood, bereft of words, slowly turning as he scanned each quarter of the sky. When he had come full circle he stumbled a little, then bowed his head and chafed at the back of his neck. 'The heavens shall tell forth His glory,' he murmured very softly.

'Amen,' said John and, seeing Herbert's back turned, caught at his arm. 'I pray you, Thomas,' he said quickly, 'to turn your mind to God and the refuge of prayer. The laws and canons are useful but there is no need of them here. Who rises with conscience stirred from reading the laws?'

They resumed their pacing but this time John had placed himself on Thomas's other side so that Herbert was excluded from his discourse. Thomas laid his arm familiarly across John's shoulders. 'Surely, dear friend, you do not think me so remiss as not to pray? And Herbert and I spend many a happy hour discussing his fresh translation of the Psalms from the Hebrew.'

John shook his head doubtfully. 'I fear such scholastic exercise merely swells the pride of knowledge; it rarely or never kindles devoutness. I would rather have you ruminate on their sentiments and peruse the blessed Gregory's moral books than philosophise as learned men.' When Thomas did not reply he looked up at him but, seeing no more than his cheek with the dark, ruckled scar showing plain through the scanty regrowth of beard, went on more heavily, 'God knows in what spirit and with what devotion I make this suggestion. You must take it as you please.' He felt the weight of Herbert's silent criticism and wondered if he were making any impression at all. 'If you do as I say, God will be your aid so that you need not fear men's intrigues. He knows that in our present troubles we cannot hope for mortal aid, so I think.' Herbert was telling himself he was not prepared to stand by with folded hands and allow King Henry to have his way with none to gainsay him, and nor was his master, or so he thought. The sentiments John had expressed ill became an author whose books must have influenced the Archbishop towards the High Gregorian position he had adopted.

And so, now that they had completed the round of the cloister garth and were in front of the entrance to the warming-house, he went straight in and held open the door for the other two, ready to inform John that the Archbishop had been long enough in the dangerous night air should he show any disposition to linger and go on with his lecturing.

But he did not; they entered and made straight for the fire (the only one in the monastery) where Alan of Tewkesbury and Lombard of Piacenza already sat with a scattering of others of Thomas's train. By the time Herbert had settled the Archbishop's chair in the best position and the rest had rearranged themselves, John had been pushed several places beyond Thomas.

Those who had remained indoors had been discussing the rumour of King Henry's arrival in Normandy which had just reached Pontigny and now fell quiet, not knowing how much Herbert had kept from Thomas. But it was Herbert himself who turned immediately to the bringer of the story, Hugh of Nunant, asking what more he had managed to discover of the King's reasons for leaving England at a time when the Welsh were threatening the border again.

'Well'–Hugh shot a glance at the Archbishop–'I told you that the talk was of his meeting with the Emperor's ambassadors in Rouen. And we can expect a conference with King Louis, to what end we may guess. . . . The only other thing I heard–and there is no certainty about this–is that the King will beg an audience of the Pope.'

Several alarmed looks were exchanged. Thomas looked questioningly at John who had said nothing.

John spoke at last with a hesitation unusual in him. 'In trying to judge what we may hope for, I cannot anticipate any advantage from such an interview. The King will state much against you, much in his own favour and, as is his custom, will alternate promises and bargainings with threats and will thus influence vacillating minds.' Whose vacillating mind he was thinking of hung in the air unstated.

Thomas put up his hand to the scar on his face. 'I shall write,' he said. 'I shall write to Alexander. He has a great feeling for justice; he will not condemn me unheard. I shall beg him not to grant an interview unless I may be present. He will allow me to speak in my own defence. Surely he will allow that?'

Herbert stood up. 'I shall go to see the King,' he said.

They stared at him. 'The King? Why?'

'I am penniless,' said Herbert, 'deprived of my rightful revenues. Is it right that the King should rob me by diverting what is mine to his treasury?'

A great babble decrying him broke out. He ignored it. 'I shall ride to see the King,' he said with the utmost firmness, and sat down.

John looked across at Thomas who nodded slowly. 'I should be heartily glad,' he said, 'that any one of you might make his peace with the King. And particularly,' he smiled wryly, 'if that might lead to an increase in your revenues.'

John's eye caught Herbert's. 'I might even go along with you,' he said.

Herbert was staggered. Making peace of any sort had been far from his mind. Nor did he think John stood any chance of doing so. But if they went together he could keep an eye on him and that might be as well. So he accepted John's offer, though somewhat loftily.

Easter 1165

John and Herbert waited three days in the anteroom of the King's audience chamber while petitioner after petitioner bypassed them. They knew that Henry was aware of their presence and was using this means to shake their confidence. Nonetheless, when John of Salisbury's name was called at last they both jumped a little and looked at each other with more fellow-feeling than they normally felt.

John was not gone very long. Herbert had heard the King's voice indignantly upraised once or twice so he was not surprised at John's rueful expression and the faint headshake he gave when he came out. For himself he had hoped a little. If only he had been called first. . . . For Henry liked a bold man and Herbert had thought that, by delivering himself thus into the lion's den, he might have surprised him into generosity. He had not expected this long wait.

Herbert had calculated rightly in one thing; Henry was diverted by his presumption. After he had sent John off with a flea in his ear he ordered Herbert into his presence and turned to the Norman barons who sat with him. 'Look sharp, now,' he said, grinning. 'You will see a proud man here! We'll have some fun with this one.'

All their eyes were on Herbert as he entered. He was nearly as fond as Thomas had been of fine clothes and, having no intention of being put to shame before a lot of Norman lords by undeserved poverty, he had dressed himself to befit the occasion in a tunic of green cloth of Auxerre with a richly embroidered cloak of the same material carelessly draped over his broad shoulders. It swung in graceful folds almost to his heels in the German fashion.

Henry's eyebrows rose faintly. Here was a different sight from the small, shabbily-clad John. Herbert's expression was different, too; he was inclined always to look down his long, handsome nose but now his head was so erect that his square chin jutted and his eyelids drooped disdainfully. His salutation was decidedly perfunctory.

'My lord King,' he declaimed, 'you see before you no petitioner for favours but an honest man come to claim his own.'

A faint ripple of amusement ran through the group of barons.

Henry leaned forward. 'What do you mean by that?'

'My lord King, I am come to remind you that my revenues are long overdue. No man can exist long without money—'

'Why should you, who have deserted your duties, expect to receive the revenues?' demanded Henry.

'By your leave, my lord, I have not deserted them. I am in

attendance upon my lord the Archbishop as my duty is.' Here Herbert proceeded to review the duties of a master in the study of Holy Writ, raising his voice over the King's interjections in a manner calculated to inflame the mildest monarch.

By the time he had finished Henry's face was black as thunder. He had not missed the delighted expressions on the faces of a number of the barons. They had heard much of the English archbishop who had fled from his wrath but it was plain that few of them had imagined his adherents to be men of such cool nerve. He must appeal to their ferocious, consuming pride of lineage, tell them what this fellow–this nothing–really was.

'For shame!' he ground out. 'Is this son of a priest to trouble my kingdom and disturb my peace?'

Herbert's voice rang through the chamber. 'I do not do so, and neither am I the son of a priest for I was born before, not after, my father was priested. And nor is a man the heir of kings unless his father was a king when he begot him!'

That insult–for Henry's father had never been a king–resulted in pandemonium followed by Herbert's immediate and ignominious ejection; but not before the whole company had heard Jourdain Taisson's admiring cry, 'I don't care whose son he is! I would give half my land to have him my son!'

Herbert relived that moment so many times on their hurried homeward journey that even John's patience finally frayed.

'You were no more successful than I in recovering your revenues,' he commented drily.

'Oh, that,' returned Herbert in an equable tone. 'I did not expect to. My real reasons for going were quite other. I wished to give the Archbishop something more to think on than the King's projected visit to the Pope. And I wanted to show him that we need not cower in fear of anything he may do— Make peace, indeed!' He bent a stern look on John. 'I, too, have read your books,' he said.

'So another lady of the English goes to a German bed?' Ralph de Faye's tone was light but the eyes that followed Matilda's straight, retreating back were alive with interest.

Eleanor relaxed with Matilda's departure. What was it about the child that she could never feel easy with her? There had been something decidedly disconcerting about the way her cool, grey eyes had measured her mother's kinsman and then returned to dwell impassively upon her mother. Yes, it would be well when she had a husband who would know how to deal with her dumb insolence.

Ralph turned the alert gaze on her. 'She seems not to mind the prospect?'

'She is enjoying being the centre of attention.'

'She is a very–composed child. Not at all like you.'

The crease that was almost a dimple appeared at the side of Eleanor's mouth. She knew very well what he meant–it was unfortunately true that Matilda's virtues lay in character rather than looks–but, in parrying, she affected to misunderstand.

'Yes, she comports herself well. She carried off the interview with the Emperor's ambassadors as to the manner born.'

'The Archbishop of Cologne, was it not? The pope-maker?'

The swift question surprised her. 'The great schismatic himself,' she agreed.

Ralph moved from his chair to sit at her feet. 'Stroke my hair,' he said with the amiable assurance of a man who knows his own attractions. She saw that it was shining clean and thanked the saints for a man bred in the warm south with none of the northerner's innate distrust of water.

Gently she ruffled the thick, black locks. It was pleasant to be again with a man of her own degree whom she genuinely liked, with whom she could talk intimately without condescension. She had come to look forward to an hour or so of quiet conversation with him at the end of the day.

'How was he received in England?' he asked lazily, resting his head against her knee.

She laughed. 'Not quite as Henry expected, I think. Earl Robert of Leicester refused him the kiss of peace and ordered all the altars at which he had officiated to be purified. And the bishops were in a flutter. They have never been able to make up their minds whether to be more frightened of Henry or of Pope Alexander. Most of them hid rather than make a direct choice.'

'I understand the Empress refused him an audience in Rouen while Henry was there. Does little Matilda know her grandmother disapproves of her intended match?'

He felt the faint movement as she shrugged and turned his head to look up at her. 'The Emperor's envoys were pleased with her, I take it? But will the match really come to pass?'

'Who can tell? Henry plays a waiting game at the moment. But John of Oxford and Richard of Ilchester have accompanied the envoys back to Germany so the game goes on.'

'A devious game,' he murmured.

'Henry is outclassed here. He is ever apt to underrate the intelligence of his opponents.'

His eyes, long-lashed, dark and deceptively drowsy, met hers. They were close in blood, these two, alike in habit of mind, naturally endowed with a guile and subtlety beyond anything Henry would ever learn. A smile of deepest understanding passed between them.

'Will he recognise Pope Pascal?'

'No,' she said, 'I do not think so. Pope Alexander left Sens last month for Rome so he has judged the imperial cause is weakening. But as long as there are two popes Henry will play one against the other.'

'Pascal might create a subservient Archbishop of Canterbury for him.'

'The English bishops would not accept a remission of sins

from Pascal, let alone an archbishop.'

'Ah,' he said. 'That makes it difficult.'

They both fell silent then, he luxuriating in the probing fingers on his scalp, she conscious of the wide strength of his shoulders against her legs. When they began to talk again it was of light matters from Ralph's great fund of gossip. One of the stories dealt with the reason for the great increase of girth of one of her ladies, and when they had stopped laughing he got up and sat beside her, laying an arm across her shoulders.

'I don't like skinny women,' he said, sliding his hand round and cupping her breast.

'Don't be silly, Ralph,' she said but allowed him to lean closer.

His face was very close to hers. 'I always loved you, you know, even when I was a boy in Poitou and we knew you would be Queen of France.'

'Oh, Ralph . . .' she said and giggled softly. 'Why should you love me?'

'You are the loveliest woman I have ever seen.' There was a note in his voice that made her heart beat.

'Your husband didn't know what he was doing, going off to England and leaving us together.'

Her mouth twisted suddenly. 'It was safe enough. He has left me pregnant.'

'That's a husband's prerogative,' he said lightly, but she did not hear him because the question that had plagued her for weeks echoed too loudly in her mind. What of the heritage of a child conceived in loathing? 'Does it matter?' he was murmuring. She thought he had answered her unspoken question and turned a suddenly softened face towards his. He misunderstood the look and the arm about her tightened.

She felt the tickle of his beard as his mouth came down on hers and in that first startled instant wondered whether displeasure or humour was the best way of saving the situation. Then she knew she should have pushed him off immediately.

But it was pleasant to let go, to relax against the hard strength of his arms, to drift on the warm, familiar, weakening tide.

She was never sure later where that weakness might have led her but for the interruption, or which of them first realised they were not alone. But she remembered the half-shocked, half-delighted face of Mabille de St Valery, her chief lady, for a long time afterwards.

IV
August 1165

Henry sat alone in the great hall of Chester Castle, brooding on his defeat by the accursed Welsh–for defeat it was however his lords and barons might try to gloss over it. They were like quicksilver, those little dark horsemen. They appeared from nowhere, bands of them materialising on the hillsides discharging a shower of arrows while he was bogged down helpless in the mud. Like quicksilver they slid through his grasp time and again, leaving his English screaming and bubbling blood or drowning face-downward in a puddle with an arrow protruding between the shoulder blades. A coward's way of fighting, that, to skulk amongst trees and behind rocks, to lie in ambush, to feint and double back and come upon him in the rear. Why would they not fight like men with sword and lance? That would have made it so much easier to subdue them.

He scowled and poured himself more wine. It was raining still as it had rained all summer, and the damp had got into his bones. He had been warned when the long-haired comet winged across the sky that this would be a disastrous year for England, and he had argued then as he argued now that the comet blazed its evil message as bright in Welsh skies as in English. But the fact remained, he had failed again in Wales.

Sick fury rose in his throat. To be forced to retire to England like a beaten hound! He who could defeat the flower of French chivalry, whom Louis of France regarded with wary respect. To have those black-bearded petty chieftains, Owen Gwynedd and Rhys ap Gruffyd, mock at him behind his back!

Suddenly he remembered the hostages. Their children–that would cut them deep.

'De Mandeville!' he shouted. 'De Balliol!'

The little knot of men far down the hall turned swiftly at the sound of his voice, eyeing one another askance lest any had heard the nervous intake of breath or seen the sudden convulsive movement that betrayed fear. They were all jealous of their reputations, yet not one of them could latterly approach the King without a mental squaring of the shoulders.

He sat there with lowering glance, watching the two barons he had summoned walk towards him–Jocelyn de Balliol, tall and broad, wooden faced, and Geoffrey de Mandeville whom he had raised up to be Earl of Essex; he who had taken the English girl Hikenai to Dame Hermengild so long ago. His little lost love–since her death nothing had been the same.

He looked at the barons with narrowed eyes. 'The hostages must die,' he said. 'I will spoil these Welsh of something they hold dear.'

Neither of them moved and Henry motioned impatiently to the bench. De Balliol went stiffly. 'They are but children—' he began.

The King bellowed with rage. De Balliol felt de Mandeville's hand on his arm. He had scarcely been prepared to argue; only Christian pity had prompted the remark but he saw none was to be found here. He waited for the storm to abate.

'What is it to me that they are children?' screamed the King. 'They were given as hostages with all that entails. I have been attacked and harassed by tribes who owe allegiance to those who gave them. I am within my rights. They shall never see their homes again.'

He began to choke and gibber, beating his hands upon the table, upsetting the wine which ran in a dark stream to drip like blood into the rushes and on de Balliol's knees. De Mandeville sprang to mop it up, busying himself around the King, calming him by his assured movements and easy demeanour.

At last Henry leaned back, breathing in long slow gasps, and by degrees colour returned to his cheeks and the livid line around his mouth dispersed. 'I am resolved on it,' he said harshly, 'for if I do not those Welsh will think they have leave to encroach on my domains; they will imagine themselves invincible.'

At that moment the Earl of Cornwall came in, shaking himself like a dog to rid his cloak of raindrops and, passing the group of onlookers, made to join the King and his counsellors. Cheerful as ever and completely insensitive to atmosphere, he announced, 'I have a riddle for you, and I will wager a fine new pair of gloves that none amongst you will guess the answer! Hearken closely now, 'its a rhyme—'

De Balliol moved uneasily, felt Henry's eyes on him and sat still.

'Not now, good uncle,' said the King, 'we are at more important business than riddles. Tell me, have the Welsh broken the treaty I had with them or have they not?'

Cornwall took a quick glance at the others for guidance and, finding none, took the safest course. 'They be very pestilent villains,' he answered sturdily.

De Balliol's voice was sour. 'That we all know.'

'Well, I will tell you that they have,' said Henry. 'Therefore you will agree that I am within my rights to execute my will on the hostages.'

Cornwall looked blank, then said doubtfully, 'Those babes—'

Henry's tone remained even but savagery underlay it.

'They think to disarm me by offering children as hostages. They shall learn of their mistake.'

De Mandeville took a deep breath and spoke. 'Yet I cannot conceive it a wise course to kill them. We shall have some thin-skinned prelate thundering of latter-day Herods. Can you not hear them, sire, making play on the Massacre of the Holy Innocents?'

Henry raised his chin and stared at him. 'Another weapon in his hand?' he muttered. 'Oh God, that ever I raised such a viper to be archbishop!'

It was not until Cornwall lay down to sleep that night that the King's words started to trouble him. Thirty years had passed since the day when old King Henry died and Cornwall was not given to considering the past, but something in his nephew's look when he spoke of the hostages had brought his royal father back to him. He trembled at the memory of that day when the old King had ordered the blinding of two of his grand-daughters. They were the children of his natural daughter, Juliana, and had been hostages for their father's good behaviour. . . . And there had been that other story of how old Henry as a young man had hurled the leader of a revolt at Rouen from the battlements of the castle with his own hands. God grant that the present Henry had not inherited that appalling lust for personal vengeance.

The involuntary thought surprised him for he had always admired his father's ruthlessness, perhaps in compensation for what he thought of as weakness in himself; now he was not so sure. He had not known his half-sister's children but he had seen the Welsh hostages running and laughing, playing together as children will in any circumstances. He wondered if Henry remembered how he had been treated when King Stephen had captured him in boyhood–how he had carved little wooden puppets for him and played toy soldiers with him in the meadows, using plantain stalks for lances. Of course, Stephen had been a man uncommon soft with children. Even so. . . .

He began to avoid his nephew, busying himself checking what remained of their weapons and stores, and scouring the countryside for provender with a small band of followers. The hostages were not mentioned again in his hearing and he spoke of his fears to no one as though he hoped that silence might avert the issue.

Although de Mandeville's warning had taken root in Henry's mind the cold desire for revenge demanded an outlet. Old Cornwall had been right; Henry's likeness to his grandfather was becoming more pronounced with the years, the boyish good humour diminishing as that streak of cruelty that was the hallmark of the Norman kings showed ever more clearly.

And the Welsh were not the only reason for his anger; it was their misfortune that they were the only ones he might vent it on. When he had been encamped at Oswestry Gilbert Foliot and Robert of Hereford had come bearing a letter from Pope Alexander ostensibly addressed to Gilbert but in reality a sharp rebuke for Henry himself, for it took him to task in no uncertain terms for communicating with schismatics (this was a thrust at Henry's dallyings with Frederick Barbarossa and his creature, the anti-Pope Pascal), for oppressing the clergy of his kingdom and exiling its archbishop.

'Unless the King repents his evil deeds,' the letter ended, 'God will surely visit harsh vengeance on him and his, and we ourselves will no longer be able to endure them with patience.'

It was only a month or two since Alexander had pronounced Thomas's condemnation at Northampton null and void; this had seemed the last straw. Yet there was worse to come when John of Oxford came back from Germany with his report on events at the Diet of Wurzburg. Emperor Frederick, fired by what he considered his ambassadors' success with Henry, had managed to persuade the German bishops to follow his magnates and himself in taking the unparalleled oath devised by the Archbishop of Cologne: never to recognise Alexander as the successor of St Peter and ever to hold the universal Catholic Father, Pascal, in honour, obedience and reverence.

And before Frederick's entire court, John of Oxford and Richard of Ilchester had sworn the same oath on a chestful of relics. But one dissenting voice had been raised there, that of Archbishop Conrad of Mainz who, like Thomas before him, had fled away at dead of night to Pope Alexander.

Henry, perhaps recognising that John and Richard had been caught in a cleft stick, passed little comment on their action but he foresaw well enough the trouble it would cause him. The feeling that events were moving too fast for him was growing, and with it a burning rancour that demanded satisfaction. He laid all his difficulties with the Church at Thomas's door and restrained rage continued to fester in him.

Continued to, that is, until he hit upon a way to punish the Welsh without actually killing their children–and of keeping his oath that they should never see their homes again.

All his chief advisers were present when he gave the order but it was to Ranulf de Broc that he addressed himself. Ranulf did not turn a hair and his little, colourless eyes glinted as at an anticipated pleasure. 'Blind them?' he said. 'Boys and girls alike?'

'Nay,' said Henry with a deliberation that chilled his listeners, 'not the girls. I will have their ears and noses off. Leave them their eyes that they may see my handiwork.'

There was a breathless silence and Cornwall felt his hands begin to shake. He dared not look at his neighbour and, seeing the way the King's head was drawn down between his hunched shoulders and the ominous stillness and watchfulness of his posture, neither dared he say a word.

'So may all traitors' children suffer,' said Ranulf with an atrocious cheerfulness, and went off to see the order executed.

The ill luck the comet brought had not done with Henry. Towards the end of the month, in the midst of preparations to retire to England, news came that after five years of marriage the third wife of Louis of France was delivered of a son– 'a fair boy and like to live' the message ran. It was the end of his hopes of uniting France and England under young Henry.

He threw himself into an orgy of hard, physical work and saw to it that his men, noble and common alike, did the same; anything to stop himself thinking of the ruin of all his plans. One of the great wains got stuck in the mire and he was there yelling at the men to get it out. Another overturned, the load slewed sideways under its covering, and he was among them, tearing at the knotted ropes which rain had tightened, tugging the stiff, cracking hide until his hands were smeared with blood. Included in the rough camaraderie of simple folk he could almost wish to be one of them himself, living like an ox from day to day, ignorant of the care power brings.

It was raining again the day he visited the Welsh Gate. He had jested with the men, as filthy and exhausted as they, knowing that afterwards they would talk amongst themselves, calling him 'Harry' and marvelling at how different he was from those lords of his who stood by looking down their noses; a proper man, not afraid to turn his hand to anything. The comradeship in the guardroom warmed him. He leaned against the wall, seeing their eyes on him, admiring, dog-like, as they hung on his least remark.

From outside came the sound of horses. A big, black-bearded fellow peered out of the slit window and withdrew his head abruptly. They heard the cry of the sentries and a rumble and a crash as the great gate opened. Henry became aware that the men's eyes had fallen away from him; they moved uncertainly, shuffled, and fumbled unnecessarily with belts and weapons.

Henry's head went up. He ignored one of the men who suddenly began urging him to take another sup of ale with them and, putting aside the big man who still blocked the window, put forth his head. He remained there quite a long time, though after the first glance he only stared blindly into space. He did not need to look again. In a split second the picture of that pitiful procession had burned itself into his brain. The hostages were going home to Wales, and the Welsh of Chester with them, on foot, on mules, on pack carts, protectively grouped about the children who raised hideous caricatures of faces to the weeping sky.

When the great gate thudded shut he knew he must turn and face the men who had known they would be passing. It was among the hardest things he had ever had to do. He got away as quickly as he could, wondering at the cheerfulness with which they cursed the weather as they bade him Godspeed–all but Blackbeard, who stood heavy and inexpressive to one side. Perhaps he too thought it meet for Heaven to weep.

He was half-way into England before he remembered Annora. He marvelled that he had not thought of her before; but, after all, he had been too busy to think of women. . . . No, love, not women, he told himself in a sudden access of honesty; no man was ever too tired or too much occupied for women.

But Annora was not just another woman; she would bring him the consolation he so badly needed. He sent messengers ahead to her brother, the Earl of Clare, to wait on him at Clarendon with her.

All the long journey his anticipation grew. In imagination he pictured her quietly listening while he talked until that picture in his mind was blotted out and quite forgotten. But when they rode in she was not there to greet him, though in answer to his anxious queries he was assured she was within the walls. 'The lady is not yet tired fit to greet you,' they said. 'The lady will come in a little while, her woman says.'

'Aye,' he said, 'aye . . . ,' reassuring himself that it was not want of eagerness to see him but only a natural desire to pleasure him with her toilette. Women set great store by such things, never realising that lovers would not notice if they wore sackcloth. In the end he shouted for the barber and went off to attend to his own appearance.

When, after the man had shaved him, he saw his reflection in the polished shield held up for him–he had refused a bath in his impatience–he made an effort to smooth his face into pleasanter lines, shrugging to settle the crimson tunic more comfortably on his shoulders. What had they done to the thing? Surely he could not have put on more flesh? What could she be doing that was more important than greeting him?

It was nearly supper-time and the candles lit before she came to his chamber, but when he saw her his irritability dissolved. She was wearing something green but he was more conscious of the luscious curves and the beautiful, glowing face above them than of the stuff and style of the gown she so proudly displayed.

She gave a shriek and a giggle as he grabbed at her, suddenly cut off as she looked at him for the first time. 'Why, Harry'–the deep, rather too loud voice took him by surprise as always–'what *have* you done with your hair?' A look of sweet and girlish forgiveness spread over her face. 'Oh, you men! Where would you be without us women!'

He held her stiffly a moment before he kissed her. Was external appearance her only care? All at once he could not think of anything to say. His silence passed unremarked since she talked at length, and when she finally asked for his news he could not recall one of the things it had seemed so important to discuss with her. So he listened to her chatter feeling vague discontent, aware of disappointment but unwilling to admit to it, and knowing now that he had run to her for comfort as a hurt child runs to its mother.

But that night he found himself able to tell her what he had been driven to, not excusing himself or pleading for understanding, but flatly, baldly, in words that scourged and, oddly, seemed to cleanse him. While he spoke he scratched, unawares, at the old fleabites that covered him.

He felt her shy away. 'Oh no, love,' he whispered, 'I did not know—'

She had not heard. She sat up straight, her face a mask of disgust. 'Jesu,' she said, 'you are lousy. Mother of God, to come to me thus! I should have known when I saw your hair. You have not even bathed!'

He lay quite still. After a while he said stonily, 'I have no lice about my person now. You know everyone in camp has them. The old bites itch still.'

She stared at him in the dim light. 'Are you sure?'

'Quite sure,' he said. 'You will get nothing from me.'

'Well,' she said, 'I hope you are not going to scratch all night. And do have them wash your hair tomorrow.'

By God, he thought, this is what I raced to meet, this shrewish, chiding scold that speaks to me as if I were her wedded husband–and, sick and raging, remembered what he had forgotten, that she had once dared aspire so high.

'Madam,' he said chokingly, 'I shall spend the morrow with my friends who care not to lay such emphasis on the outward man. And my advice to you is to remember well your position—' He flung back the covers and got out of the bed. In the half light he loomed above her, naked, menacing, so that she gave a little cry and drew back, hand to mouth.

'As for what is between us,' he said, 'I see now what it means to you. And I will leave you now to consider what might have been had you been possessed of a soul instead of the dried and shrivelled walnut I have discovered.'

He left her on that thrust which he had aimed in the sudden certainty that it would reach her brother's ears. For he had seen it all–de Clare's plans to gain the crown matrimonial for his sister and bring himself closer to the throne. Or if not the crown matrimonial, a royal bastard. . . . He no longer expected any kind of comprehension from her, knowing now that those ingenuous and child-like eyes mirrored most truly the emptiness behind them.

By the time he reached his own quarters the small satisfaction he had derived from his spurt of malice had evaporated. Nothing was left but the heavy burden he alone must shoulder.

He rose next morning before cock-crow so that when he went out of a side door and round to the mews the world was dark and still and the last stars still glimmered overhead; even the servants were still sleeping. His heels rang on the cobbles.

It annoyed him, this dim loneliness, making him think of things he did not wish to think about: like being blind, or deaf, or condemned to wander forever in some limbo where time had stopped. 'Where are you?' he yelled, and then heard voices from the stable-yard and the familiar, comforting sounds of horse and hawk. So he had not caught them out in spite of the scant notice they had received of his intention to spend the day in hawking. As well for them!

They brought out the horses by the light of torches; he barked an abrupt order to douse them. Did they not know that one spark in the stables could cause havoc? Under a sky just beginning to pale with the false dawn he paced about, watching, criticising and surreptitiously marking the order in which his invited companions put in an appearance. De Clare came last.

'Come on, come *on*!' said Henry when he arrived. 'I said before the birds began to sing—' The sharpness of his tone brought de Clare's sleep-heavy eyes wide open.

They streamed out of the gate behind him, across the great open fields where the hurdles were down now that the harvest was at last carted. Henry rode with his head up, not looking about, the longing for escape strong in him. But when he had put a couple of miles between himself and Clarendon he eased the pace of his horse and glanced back at his followers, seeing in the strengthening light how the horses' legs were lost in the mist that lay low on the fields like floodwater.

The men behind him checked their headlong pace and murmured soothingly to their mounts, patted steaming necks. They looked furtively one at another, each reluctant to be the first to draw abreast the King. Had Cornwall been with them there would have been no question about who would brave the lion; he never held back, out of a blind faith in his royal nephew's regard for him or (as some thought) an obtuseness that was impregnable. But even he had not seemed so ready to approach Henry of late and had taken off for his Cornish lands, where Henry's writ did not run, as soon as the Welsh campaign had come to its humiliating conclusion.

De Balliol pulled a little harder on the reins to fall back beside Geoffrey de Mandeville and leave the Earl of Clare at the head of the procession. 'The King's temper's none too sweet this morning,' he said out of the side of his mouth, 'considering where he spent last night. If something's gone wrong there, let the lady's brother take the brunt.'

De Mandeville nodded silently and both watched as Roger de Clare closed up alongside the King. Things seemed to go well enough between them, though, or so they thought when they heard de Clare's laugh ring out. But he did not laugh again although the King did, several times; so did the gentlemen behind who could hear what he was saying. There was a forced note in that laughter.

De Mandeville and de Balliol knew every one of Henry's moods and of them all they most dreaded this new one of publicly-conducted, spiteful raillery. He had practised it last year on Becket and seemed to have developed a taste for it. So they fell gradually ever further back until they were practically amongst the falconers and game-retrievers who brought up the rear. Here they could converse as freely as if they were alone.

'So there is a rift in the lute,' said de Balliol.

De Mandeville nodded. 'She has been pushing too hard, perhaps. You know she has her eye on the Queen's seat?'

De Balliol snorted expressively. 'Her–to oust the Queen? That would be a dangerous play indeed. There was a tale—' He edged his horse nearer. He spoke quietly; the name Hikenai, the King's mistress who had died, recurred frequently.

De Mandeville heard him out, though shaking his head with increasing vehemence as the story proceeded. 'That's a tale makes the rounds at intervals,' he declared, 'and not a word of truth in it. I knew that minion of the King's well enough–'twas I played messenger between them at the King's order. She died in Normandy and Queen Eleanor was in England. Poison indeed! Not that I'd put it past her,' he added thoughtfully, 'but there was none near the wench she could have sent. Nay, if she was poisoned it was none of the Queen's doing.'

Beneath de Balliol's solid exterior a surprisingly lurid imagination lay concealed. Allowing it free rein for once he began to suggest various methods whereby the Queen might have accomplished her purpose. Put in plain words it was too much even for him to swallow, yet he was loth to relinquish his picture of the Queen. Beautiful, determined, dangerous. . . . Being tenacious of his opinion he began to speculate on what might happen should Annora de Clare's ambitions reach her ears. At last de Mandeville's cry, 'Look now, they're putting up the hawks!' cut him short and returned his mind to the business in hand.

But he was reminded some hours later when he sighted de Mandeville again, looking tired and hot, riding at the tail-end of a line of bearers whose panniers bulged with small game. 'Ho, Geoffrey! Had enough?' he shouted.

De Mandeville checked his horse to allow two mounted men bearing between them a long pole strung with fifteen or twenty herons to pass. De Balliol fell in beside him and they went at a walk behind the limp, dangling corpses that twirled and swung at the end of long, stick-like legs. From their sharp, pointed beaks an occasional spot of blood dripped and lay round and red like a ruby in the grass.

The afternoon was warm and golden under a hazy blue sky, perfect harvest weather, and they were pleasantly tired after a long day in the open, riding relaxed as the King's loud grating voice and louder laugh drifted back to them on the sweet air.

'His Grace laughs a little too much, I fancy,' offered de Balliol.

De Mandeville looked at him without answering.

'Where's de Clare?'

The other shrugged. 'As far from the King as he can get. As am I.'

De Balliol stroked his horse's neck. 'I cannot say I shall be sorry to see him lie low for a bit. I have thought, among other things, he helped to stir up trouble unnecessarily with the Archbishop in his early days in office. All his advice to the King tends one way–to the benefit of the de Clares.' He glanced at his companion. 'You do not think the King was seriously considering marriage with his sister?'

'I am quite sure he was not. What could she offer to compare with Aquitaine? She doesn't know much about Henry if she thinks that her pretty little paps could make up for that.'

'Well, she's apparently managed to upset him.'

'She–or something else.'

De Balliol looked gloomy. 'Aye–there's enough. After the Welsh, the Scots. King Malcolm has been taken in treasonable correspondence with Louis of France, as I have heard. But at least Becket and the Pope are quiet.' He rode in silence for a few minutes, then turned again to de Mandeville. 'I don't like the way Henry's courting the Emperor any more than Leicester does. We are beginning to feel that we must put it plainly to him that we cannot countenance an abandonment of Pope Alexander.'

De Mandeville nodded to his left where thick coverts of hazel clothed a gentle slope. 'It will be quicker that way.' He had raised his voice so that the bearers could hear him. 'If we get in last we'll be lucky to get our mounts stabled before dinner.'

Under the low-growing trees it was hot and airless, and clouds of small black flies danced ceaselessly in the confined space. De Balliol was sweating after a few minutes but he made no complaint when de Mandeville stopped in the most dim and stifling place and leaned towards him. 'There are stories out of Angers,' he said softly, 'concerning the Queen's behaviour.' De Balliol waited, not even brushing off the flies that settled on his face. 'And of her kinsman, Ralph de Faye.'

'What kind of stories?'

De Mandeville smiled. 'He is a man much beloved of women.'

The other blew through his lips like a horse. 'Who told you?'

'Never mind.'

'Not the King?'

De Mandeville gave a sharp snort of laughter. 'No, not the King. But I got my information from the same source as he did.' He peered at de Balliol. 'Had you not heard a whisper?'

'No. . . . But it's not the first time such tales have been told of her.'

'Not since she rid herself of Louis and married Henry FitzEmpress.'

'No,' said de Balliol. But he was thinking it was the second husband who had taught her the rules of the game.

De Mandeville said, 'I tell you that you may see women have other weapons than poison. She is making him a laughing-stock. It's for you to judge whether this is a good time to argue with him on matters of policy.' He clucked to his horse to urge it onward.

De Balliol followed. He was not particularly surprised. The

Queen was beautiful, and de Faye was a man who was as high born as, from all accounts, he was comely. But he did not believe she would deem anything so petty as revenge. She was a daughter of treacherous and intriguing Aquitaine; her vengeance, he thought, when she took it would be as bloody, as pitiless and as calculated as a man's.

There was a minstrel called in that night after dinner because ladies were present; he sang sweetly of love's pangs but the loud laughter which the King's jeering comments provoked drowned most of it. Still, it all seemed very jocose and only a few of the older members of the company leaned back a little out of the candlelight so that it was less easy for the King's eye to catch theirs.

Henry was looking rather finer than usual for he had changed his clothes and made some effort to order his hair which, sadly thinning on top, had grown overlong and thick at the sides while he was on campaign. But it still had a rough, staring look as if he had combed only the topmost layer and left knots and tangles undisturbed beneath.

He was also rather drunk; not so that anyone who did not know him well would notice, but sufficiently for intimates to recognise. His glittering eyes roved swiftly from face to face, weighing and assessing reactions to his remarks; only in one direction he did not look and that was towards Annora de Clare who had left her seat at his side and taken a place among the circle of young maidens around the minstrel.

A great deal of giggling and shouting was going on down there as the young people cried upon the minstrel for their favourite airs but the King, who had continued to drain his cup long after the others had placed hands over theirs in token of refusal, slumped lower in his chair and lapsed into a heavy, threatening silence. Those near him braced themselves for the storm which they had been expecting to break ever since his venomous baiting of de Clare that morning. De Clare himself was seated at a greater distance from the King than was usual of late, his eyes on his sister who, finding herself ignored, was growing ever noisier in her endeavours to attract the royal interest.

A bitter rage and contempt consumed him as he watched her. What in God's name had she done, thus to wreck everything? Did she not know–or care–that her sins would be visited upon him? He had warned her when she had spoken of her pretensions to marriage that the King would suspect him of complicity. And he did suspect him, so much he had gathered from Henry's barbed remarks earlier in the day. He had had to play the injured innocent, swallowing his rage at the insult to his intelligence as best he might. Henry had not believed him, though; he knew it.

He took a sideways look at him now and, seeing his eyes on Annora, closed his own and began to feel very sorry for himself. Had it been his idea to bargain his sister's body for Tonbridge Castle? No, it had not; but what man, seeing what the King wanted, would not have tried to gain something for himself out of such a situation? It was not as though he could by any means have prevented it, knowing what he knew of his sister.

Henry, having expended most of his malice, was also indulging in self-pity. The combination of minstrelsy and too much wine had made him maudlin. He had been rudely wrenched back from a dream of the happy past by Annora laughing and crying out above the noise of the rest. Why was it that she and the other women were forever gabbling like so many geese, giving a man no peace? Why could she not be like–his mind hesitated a second–like Hikenai?

He raised his head and looked at her hanging on some gallant's arm, tossing her head in that well known gesture, exclaiming over some triviality in the dark, husky voice that he had once found fascinating and which now irritated him beyond bearing.

She saw him watching her and called his name, pert and saucy, holding out her hand. Hikenai would have come to him and knelt before him. Hikenai had called him lord and given him a son, and obeyed him in all things for five long years.

'Come, Harry,' cried the throaty, commanding voice.

Rising, he eyed her, his mouth pulled down at the corners, and very slowly, very definitely shook his head. 'No, madam,' he said. 'Nor shall you come to me since I ride for Winchester at dawn to meet my son, having wasted too much time already.' His eyes went round the table, singling out the few he would choose to accompany him. 'You–and you–and you— See to it.' De Clare was careful to avoid his glance.

In a hushed silence he went down from the dais and stood in front of her. 'Since I know not when we may meet again,' he said in a voice that was rather more clipped than usual, 'I will take this opportunity to bid you adieu, and to tell you it is my most earnest prayer that your kinsfolk may ere long discover you the husband you deserve. For somewhere, hard though it is to believe, I am assured there may be found a man'–he hesitated pointedly–'worthy of you.'

He smiled unpleasantly at her and held out his hand, palm down, as though expecting her to kiss it; when she did no more than stand and gape at him he let it fall and smiled again; but this time with the air of one who has scored his point and is satisfied. And he walked, a little more slowly and carefully than was his habit, to the door, opened it, and passed through without a backward look.

He did not sleep well that night. When he closed his eyes images of Annora and memories of Hikenai jostled in his mind and became confused; he went into a wild dream in which Hikenai spoke to him in Annora's voice and he had his hands about her throat because for him that was the ultimate horror. Awakening in a sudden great sweat he felt his stomach heave; he flung himself off the bed and across the room as far as the corner where he was violently and vilely sick.

He felt not only weak but despairing. What was the purpose of it all? One day when he was dead young Henry would sit in his seat and take decisions that might be very different from the ones he would have taken and he, lying cold in his tomb, would neither know nor care. Surely there should be more in life than fighting to lay up possessions for one's heirs?

Years ago, speaking to Tom of Hikenai, he had said he must have something for himself, something to satisfy his inner needs, and Tom had understood and accepted it. So, for a while, he had had them both, Hikenai, his heart's darling, and Tom, his soul-mate, and he had been complete. Now both were lost to him, and Tom's loss was the more cruel for he still lived.

Was it possible that a man could change as much as he had, or had Eleanor been right when she said he had not changed at all, but that he, Henry, had never seen him as he truly was? Could it be true that he was no judge of character and had lived in a fool's paradise for years? A shiver ran over him. This was something he would not think about; it made him feel unloved–unlovable. Self-blame was preferable. He had given Tom too much so that he had become puffed up with pride and thought himself the equal of a king.

It was because of that, he told himself–because I saw how he was changing towards me–that I deluded myself into believing Annora could fill not only his place in my heart but Hikenai's too. And then, because she refused to conform to his mental picture, he had insulted her, publicly and with a deliberate malice. But it was he who had decked lust in love's fair colours; she had done no more than remain obstinately herself, a pretty, silly, scheming tit.

He had shamed no one but himself, he thought. But he had learned a lesson. He knew now that love is a wilding that blooms when it chooses; forcing produces only counterfeits. So he would fill his emptiness with other things. . . .

The nausea was passing and his unquenchable determination to win every battle, no matter how minor, began to rise again. Tomorrow he would see his son, young Henry. Tomorrow a new chapter would begin.

Word of his coming had run ahead. When he reached Winchester swarms of litigants were already descending upon the town. No matter that his justices now progressed regularly through every quarter of the kingdom, everyone wanted the King himself to hear his case. He could not put a foot outside his private quarters without being pestered by quarrelling groups who demanded his decision on the most unimportant matters.

Nor could he find the time to talk with his son. Not that that would be an easy thing to do had he all the time in the world. He had surprised the boy more than once watching him with an oddly inscrutable expression for a ten-year-old as he gave his judgements; whatever that look meant, it did not bespeak filial respect and admiration. It bothered him; he loved the boy dearly. He was his father; should not the boy love him? He must make the time to befriend him, draw him out.

He tried without much success. Young Henry sat stiffly with straight back, hands on his knees, replying politely to his questions and volunteering nothing. Was there no subject on which they could meet? He had tried swordsmanship, learning, the boy's friends, and he was growing impatient. There was one last thing to try.

'You have heard there is a new heir to France?' he said abruptly.

The child's eyes met his for a split second, then returned to an indeterminate spot mid-way between them. 'Yes,' he said.

'France will have a king now when Louis goes to his reward. Do you see how this has put your nose out of joint? If he had had another girl your wife would still be heiress.' He began to talk quickly, detailing the plans he had made, the reason for the boy's early marriage, trying to show the silent child all he had done for him. 'France, Normandy and England would have been one. Your writ would have run from Scotland to the Middle Sea, a greater empire than that of the Germans.'

'What of my brothers?' said the boy.

'What? Your brothers? They would have ruled in certain of your lands, naturally, but remember they would have held them of you and done homage for them—'

'My wife's little brother is my brother also,' said the childish voice.

Was the boy a fool? Henry felt his temper begin to rise. 'He will be King of *France*,' he said sharply. 'You will hold your French lands of him, remember. He will not hold of *you*.'

'His name is to be Philip Augustus.'

'Yes,' said Henry with difficulty, 'King Philip of France in time to come.' His mouth went down at one corner. 'A noble name, one to live up to. Take care he does not eat you up, my son.'

He wondered why he had said that. He did not believe at all in the possibility of any son of Louis out-manœuvring his own.

He saw the boredom in the boy's face then. He was wasting his time. 'Get along then,' he said, forcing geniality into his voice. 'Get back to the things that interest you.'

As the boy went with more alacrity than was mannerly he called after him, 'Remember–remember you may bring me any of your troubles—' But the door had closed before the last word left his lips.

When it opened again almost immediately he turned swiftly but his expression altered as de Mandeville entered with a murmured apology. 'I saw the young King leave—'

Henry braced his square shoulders as if settling more comfortably an invisible load. 'What is it?' he enquired crisply.

'Sire, Richard de Luci asks me to inform you of the arrival of a number of plaintiffs, all requesting your hearing of their cases—'

'Am I to have no peace? No rest? Do none of them believe they may get justice elsewhere?' He stood up suddenly and glared at de Mandeville as though he were at fault. 'God's Passion, can I be everywhere at once?'

'My lord King, the justness of your judgements is spoken of with awe. And these are simple folk for the most part—'

'Simple folk! Can they not be heard in the honorial or the shire courts? Why must they trouble me over a few bovates of land?'

'If the judge be also the defendant—' De Mandeville left the sentence hanging.

'Are they all pleas of inheritance?'

'The greater part of them.'

'And when they have my writ, justice is done?'

De Mandeville hesitated. Should he, as was his inclination, take the easy course and assure the King that justice was done according to his word, or should he tell the truth and say, 'Not always, for the rich and powerful still have means of procrastinating'? If he drew Henry's attention thus to the power of his own class to thwart him in minor matters, he might risk seeing it curtailed as the power of the Church had been. Yet he still chose the latter remark for he feared the personal grudge against him if he attempted deception more than any loss of baronial authority.

Henry stared at him with narrowed eyes. 'Something must be done,' he said shortly. He walked to the deep window embrasure and stared up at the patch of sky which was the only view the high, narrow slit afforded.

'There is, perhaps, overmuch law in England,' murmured de Mandeville.

Henry whirled round. 'Overmuch law? No! Too much overlapping of jurisdiction, certainly. Too many courts, yes—manorial courts, hundred courts, shire and honorial courts, ecclesiastical courts—' He fixed de Mandeville with a hard look. 'Sit down. Tell me how it comes about that justice is not always done after my writ of right has been issued. Does not the writ order one of my magnates to see that the order is complied with, by force if necessary?'

De Mandeville sat down. Henry on points of law was a different man from the arrogant monarch they had lately seen, but scratch the skin, de Mandeville thought, and the unprincipled despot would show once more. Justice? No, it is not that he wants. The poor and oppressed are no more than a nuisance to him. His real purpose is to take all power to himself. De Mandeville was surprised at his own perception, then he became conscious of Henry's eyes on him and coughed to cover his confusion.

'The defendant will not always accept the authority of an intermediary,' he said hastily, 'but will appeal, sometimes to another court. So that the plaintiff must then try to seek an interview with you, and that may be both costly and difficult if you are oversea. You remember the case of Robert de Valognes and Abbot Roger which dragged on for years?'

'I remember. And I recall that it was Robert who first applied for my writ, saying that he had been unjustly deprived, though in the end it was proved that the woods in question were rightfully the Abbot's.'

De Mandeville agreed that that was so.

Henry nodded thoughtfully. 'Tell the Justiciar that I will hear the cases tomorrow.'

When de Mandeville had gone he recalled the case he had mentioned–the accusations and counter-accusations, the appeals to the Queen, to Leicester, to the Pope. If Robert de Valognes had been trying to defraud anyone less powerful and determined than the Abbot of St Albans he would doubtless have succeeded.

Henry had long sensed some anomaly in the practice of using oath-helpers to back up a man's sworn word–few feared God's vengeance for perjury while they were in good health–but he had never been able to devise a system that satisfied him. Now de Mandeville's words about the judge being also the defendant had given him an idea. Impartiality–there was the nub.

The truth of the plantiff's assertion must be proved before the writ was granted by empanelling impartial witnesses instead of, as heretofore, allowing each party to select his own jurors. Twelve law-worthy men of the shire, he thought, older men of good memory, with no axe to grind. The writ itself should name both plaintiff and defendant and specify the claim exactly. And there should be no appeal.

He got up quickly, filled with sudden excitement. He must find de Luci and have him set down in writing this seed of an idea. Good law, he thought, is justice for all and, moreover, it will relieve me of these constant interruptions. . . .

He went down the steep spiral stair from the little chamber, through the hall and into the covered passage that led to the rooms where official business was transacted. It was dusky in there and he was hurrying, intent only on what was in his mind, so that when he felt a sudden bump and, putting out his hands, touched softness, he was quite taken aback. Then he realised it was a woman–or a lady, judging by the feel of the stuff she was dressed in–and a young one.

'Madam—' he said. 'Forgive me. I was not looking where I was going.' He ran his hand lingeringly down the arm he had grasped to regain his balance and escorted her back the way he had come, ignoring the faint, fluttering protests. Determined to get a look at her, he gripped the arm more firmly to lead her to the light, talking cheerfully all the time of his own clumsiness.

Tantalisingly, she kept her head lowered when they reached the entrance to the hall; he could see no more than the tip of her nose against the curve of the hood that covered her hair. 'Is it your wish to remain incognito, mistress?' he said, suddenly struck by the thought that she might have been returning from a secret assignation. 'I would not embarrass you but'–there was a laugh in his voice–'you may trust my discretion.'

She raised her head then, her eyes earnest and her lower lip caught in as if she had indeed been surprised in some girlish foolishness, and he knew he had seen that face before, though for an instant he could not think where or put a name to it. Then he remembered–and Sir Walter de Clifford's guarded, courtly phrases as he passed on his daughter Rosamund's decisive rejection of the King's advances.

She had known him immediately even in the dimness of the passage. But she must have been alert to avoid him while he was in the castle.

He dropped her arm as though it were hotter than the warmth he could feel in his cheeks and bowed stiffly. 'Mistress de Clifford, is it not?' Inwardly he cursed the urge that drove him always to assess the potentialities of every woman he met. Under the steady gaze that told him she knew what he had been about, he moved restively.

'I had thought—' he said. 'I understood–from your father–that you were to enter Religion, mistress.' I'm floundering here like a green boy, he thought and, angered by it, fixed her with his eyes.

Hers were a pure grey, very wide and clear; he saw them move slightly as she searched his face. If she had been loth to meet him again, she now seemed in no hurry to be gone. Nor could he see that his question had confounded her at all.

'There was a time when I thought that such would be,' she said. 'But since my father's death—'

'Sir Walter is dead!' In his surprise he reached for her hand; he felt it tremble slightly but she let it lie there, small and cold in his.

'This day month,' she said. 'He fell like a tree falling. And after–after, he could not speak but lay three days with his left side unmoving as it were already dead. And then he died.' She tried to smile. 'My mother–oh, sir, my mother is like to die of grief. She–it is she who will enter Religion if she may. But she

is afraid–that is why my brother is here to see the Justiciar—'
Her eyes filled up with tears and she pulled away the hand he was holding to cover them.

'There now,' he said. 'Gently, mistress. Come, you shall tell me all.' He led her to a settle by the screens at the end of the hall, speaking very kindly of his high opinion of Sir Walter to give her time to recover herself. When she was seated and her shoulders had stopped shaking, he leaned forward to look at her and, having quite forgotten his own feelings in concern for hers, took her hand again and sat warming it between his own. 'Tell me, then,' he said, 'and if I may help you, be sure I shall.'

She gave him a watery smile. 'I think,' she said, 'that it is only you who can help. Oh!–I am so glad I met you. I knew, despite all they said, that you were kind—'

Despite all they said, he thought indignantly, but brushed away the thought to listen closely.

'You were so kind to me before and I nobody of importance—'

'Kind?' he said, puzzled.

He saw her pale cheeks grow pink. 'Of course you have forgotten. You spoke once to me of my roses at Corfham. In the garden–but that's of no consequence—'

'I remember.'

She raised her head and looked at him. 'Do you? Truly?'

'Yes,' he said, 'I do. It was growing dusk.'

Her eyes wandered over his face again. Hikenai long ago had gazed at him like that–as though she would learn by heart every feature.

'You never came again,' she said, and looked down at the hand he was holding.

He sat in silence. Did she mean. . . ? And then, because he dared not question further in case he should find he had made a fool of himself a second time, he said more coolly than he had believed himself capable, 'Tell me how I may help you.'

'My mother–as I told you, she wishes to enter Religion,

being now, as she says, dead to the world in her body. But she is afraid that–that she will be forced to remarry. And my brother is even now with the Justiciar pleading that she may not be given again in marriage without her consent. He will offer £50 that she may be left free to choose—'

Henry stared. His control over the marriage of heiresses and widows of tenants-in-chief was a necessary safeguard against the conveyance of property into the hands of his enemies; he had never considered the thoughts and feelings of the women. It had seemed only sensible to remarry them quickly to a loyal vassal ready to pay for the privilege, just as he had remarried Earl Warenne's widow to his bastard half-brother Hamelin when that damned traitor Archbishop had refused to allow her to wed his full-brother William because of some nonsense about consanguinity. He had always blamed Thomas for William's death–poor, weak William who had loved Earl Warenne's widow to distraction and died of sorrow and despair–but he had not once considered the woman's feelings.

'Your mother shall be free to choose,' he said, and almost added 'without payment' until he recalled the state of his finances. She would be glad enough to pay so small a sum. He considered it small indeed for the widow of a tenant-in-chief; he would have got much more by selling her hand to the highest bidder.

'And yourself? he asked. 'What of yourself, mistress? Shall you join your mother in her convent?'

'No,' she said and, lifting the hand that clasped her own, kissed the back of it. 'I go with my brother. His wife is with child and I shall stay there until her time comes. After that–who knows?'

'Who knows?' he echoed and sat staring at her in a sombre way that disturbed her, she thinking that this most masterful yet palpably kind-hearted man was already regretting for his own good reasons what he had promised.

But Henry was regretting nothing unless it were his hurried departure from Corfham a year ago. For it was beginning to seem that Walter de Clifford had exaggerated his daughter's longing for the life of a religious, and perhaps there had been misunderstanding on his side too. He had certainly believed that Sir Walter's warning was at this girl's instigation, yet now she asked him why he had never come again. He could not recall exactly what had been said; his conviction that he had been snubbed had effectively smothered the memory.

Suddenly she sprang up. 'Oh, sir, my brother—' She ran across, leaving Henry seated, and he watched her talking eagerly, now and then turning her head in his direction. Her brother came back with her and went down on one knee.

'My lord King, my sister has told me of your gracious clemency.' He looked up and Henry saw his eyes puzzled, faintly suspicious.

Well, let him wonder, let him suspect. It was true he had wanted this girl last year and he still did. But with a difference. He had been ready to give away his heart that first time; not now. Annora had taught him the folly of that.

He smiled at Walter de Clifford the younger. 'I am glad to be able to grant a favour to any house I value as highly as that of de Clifford. But you must grant one in return.' He tipped up the girl's chin so that he could look again into those candid eyes. 'You must leave this fair rose of your line with us that my court may benefit from her sweet presence.' He saw the grey eyes come wide and nodded at her. 'Is that a fair exchange, mistress?'

She turned to her brother who was looking like a man bidden to choose between hanging and decapitation.

'Oh, sir, may I stay? May I?'

Still down on his knee he mumbled something about gratitude and honour and the King's will.

'Honour?' said Henry. 'The honour will be ours if she be content to bide among us.'

It was not until after they had left and he was closeted with de Luci that it occurred to him that it might have been another kind of honour de Clifford was thinking of.

V
February 1166

When the King had gone the group of officials and barons seated on the dais at the end of the hall in Clarendon Palace relaxed visibly. Between them they had thrashed out the new laws for improving the administration of Justice; most of the ideas had been the King's but they had all played their parts and the last week had been heavy work. Now it was done and, while the King returned to the arms of his latest love at Woodstock, they were left to see that his orders were put into effect.

Leicester yawned and rubbed his eyes. The hair that had been so thick and black was growing grey now; it clung in strands to his broad skull. But his beard and eyebrows, liberally sprinkled with stiff, white whiskers, grew bushier and coarser yet as though its strength had gone to them. De Luci, who was ten years younger, thought that he was showing his age and was glad that it was de Mandeville who was to accompany him on progress as itinerant justice.

Leicester was evidently thinking the same thing for he said, 'There was a time when I would have envied you your travels. Not now. I have too many of the infirmities of age for journeying to be a pleasure any longer.'

De Luci politely decried the idea that he was growing old.

'Na, na.' Leicester waved his hand. 'I cannot see without I hold everything a yard away and I'm getting deaf. But age is the great leveller; it comes to all. I've watched the young pages trying who can piss farthest across the moat and thought–ah, lads, the day will come when you, like me, must stand at the lip of the privy hole and strain to dribble a few drops. It comes to all.' He sighed. 'Except for those who are cut down before the fullness of their years, God rest them,' and he signed himself on the breast and gazed vaguely before him. Speaking like this enabled him to keep the ever-strengthening clawing in his belly in perspective.

De Luci frowned a little, watching. He had not noticed before this preoccupation with mortality in Leicester. Doubtless it was caused by the news that his twin brother was dying. Still, it brought to mind how swiftly his own span, too, was slipping away, each passing year making it less likely that he would ever fulfil his private vow to worship at the Holy Places. He and Leicester had both given their lives to Henry. Would God accept that for service? The making of laws that criminals might more easily be apprehended, that just men might keep the rewards of their own or their kin's industry?

The laws they had just made might count in their favour. Fewer murderers and robbers would escape justice because of them. Twelve law-worthy men of each hundred were to be sworn to tell the truth, and he and de Mandeville would demand of them the names of those commonly reputed to be guilty. And the powers of the justices had been strengthened by the declaration that they were the king's representatives; their courts would now be equivalent to the king's own sessions.

'Certainly these are good laws we have made,' he said, to himself as he thought but Leicester looked round sharply; he was not so hard of hearing that he had not heard the questioning undertone in de Luci's voice.

Now he nodded down the board to where Arundel's voice

could be heard raised in contention. 'There's some cause for argument,' he said, 'and for my part, Richard, I will tell you I'm not sorry I shall not live to see the new world Henry will make. There's a strong new wind blowing and others may come to shipwreck on it besides the Archbishop.'

De Luci ignored the reference. He had enough to think about without Thomas Becket. He said, 'I see no changes. There's nothing in our new assize that was not done in the time of the king's grandfather; only the means have altered.'

'No? What of Novel Disseisin? Do you not see it transfers suits concerning the possession of land from the barons' private courts to the king's? Cast back your mind ten years, Richard. What was the first thing Henry did after he gained the throne?'

'What? Destroyed the barons' castles, you mean? That was understandable at the time.'

'But it was not only the castles of the barons who had upheld Stephen. Did he not also command the faithful followers of his mother, the Empress, to relinquish to him the custody of their castles?'

'Well?' said de Luci.

Leicester heard the challenge in his voice. Little use to talk to him, a man who had inherited no autonomy, whose only power derived directly from his office. He would not care how much the noble houses lost to the king.

'Oh . . . nothing,' he said. 'But there's this investigation into the enfeoffment of knights.' That might cut closer with de Luci; he owned land now. 'They have taken their oaths of fealty to their lords; now the King will have them swear fealty to him also as lord paramount.'

'That should not trouble a loyal lord.'

'No, of course not. But Henry is taking more and more into his own hand.'

'Well,' said de Luci, 'we must needs suffer it. It is the best way in these times—' He turned as de Mandeville touched his arm. 'I'm coming.' He turned back to Leicester. 'I must away. We've arrangements to make for our journey.' He put out his hand and gripped the other man's shoulder in an unaccustomed gesture of friendliness. 'Take care, now. It will not serve the King if you overwork and become ill.'

De Mandeville had overheard the latter part of the conversation and the troubled line between his brows grew a little deeper. So he was not the only one who had noticed how Henry was arrogating more and more power to the Crown. When he and de Luci went out into the February afternoon a small, chill rain was falling and they stopped a moment under the overhanging eaves. The gates stood open and they could see the muddy track, its ruts brimming water, winding away between the leafless trees. It was a dreary prospect and it matched his mood.

March 1166

When he finished reading Eleanor's letter Henry knew that his time of dalliance with Rosamund was at an end. He flung the letter to the floor and put his heel on it, let out several colourful oaths, then picked it up, smoothed it out and reread it. So the bitch sent her duty, did she? He had heard tales enough of what was going on in Angers. It had begun when she was still carrying the daughter she had borne him five months ago and, for all he knew, she was still behaving like a draggle-tail with that uncle, cousin, or whatever he was. Not that he believed for a moment that she had dared to cuckold him; but she had ignored her duties as regent so that rebellion had brewed and broken out in both Maine and Brittany before she noticed anything amiss.

There was no time to be lost, with the Count of Séez on the rampage and only Eleanor there with her mind on other things and burdened with a tribe of children.

He flung open the door and yelled for attendance in a voice

that the servants had almost forgotten, so long had it been since they had heard it raised in anger.

Henry embarked at Southampton a fortnight later with Leicester and the new King of Scots in his train. He was glad to have Leicester with him; he had a wise and subtle head on his shoulders. William of Scotland was an unwelcome companion; Henry distrusted him nearly as much as his brother Malcolm who had died just before Christmas and he was perfectly aware of William's reasons for attaching himself to the party. Earl Cospatric of Northumberland had recently died and William wanted the earldom to push his holdings further south; not only that but his sister was wife to Duke Conan of Brittany, Henry's vassal, and William meant to see that Henry made no treaty with the rebels that might unseat the Duke and thus disinherit his infant daughter.

He need not have worried on that score. Henry was in no mood to treat with rebels. His wife was the first he dealt with.

When he came into the hall at Angers she was calmly waiting to greet him surrounded by their children, all except Henry, the young King, whom he had left in England. For protection, he thought furiously; she must have known that had she been alone he would have struck her to the ground.

She made a low, sweeping curtsey and, when he eyed her coldly, rose with dignity and laid her long, delicate hand upon his arm. 'Welcome, my lord my husband.' She leaned towards him.

'Ha!' he said and stopped short when she motioned forward a nursemaid with a babe-in-arms.

'Your daughter, my lord, who is baptised Johanna as you instructed.'

He stared at her, amazed at her coolness. She looked as smug as a cat cleaning its whiskers after stealing cream. He took a perfunctory glance at the new child, round and pink like any other babe; it looked healthy enough. Now they were bringing the other children to his notice but his eyes caught and held hers; he paid them no attention.

'Madam,' he said, 'I will see you alone. And then I will see your kinsman, Ralph de Faye.'

'Ralph is not here, my lord. He is in arms at Roche-Mabile.'

He swung on her. 'On whose side?' He saw her start and nodded, satisfied. She was not so calm as she appeared. He felt the children's eyes, wide and unsure, on him and the men at his back and suddenly saw the elder Geoffrey on the fringe of the small group. His boy and Hikenai's. He held out his hand to the child, smiling for the first time. He did not see Richard turn his face away.

But after a few stilted words–Henry always had difficulty in communicating with the young–he left him and looked again at Eleanor. 'Alone, madam,' he said.

Eleanor ordered that the little ones be taken back to the nurseries, then turned again to him. 'Surely Richard—'

'Richard may be off about his own concerns,' said Henry briefly. 'Come with me.'

Once in the private chamber his thunderous face left her in no doubt that talebearers had been at work. Let him dare accuse her! Go carefully, she told herself, injured innocence is best; and, after all, was it not the truth? Nothing more than a few fondlings and kissings had passed between her and Ralph.

'Well?' he said. 'And what have you been about that things have come to this pass before you pay heed? By God, you shall never act as regent in my lands again!'

'And that uncle of yours!' he cried. 'If he's not behind it, he's had a hand in it. I know him, I tell you, a treacherous knave and deceiving womaniser that leaves his own wife to go crawling into other men's beds—' He stopped short, staring, as amidst laughter she shook her head at him in marvelling disbelief.

'Henry, Henry!' she said. 'Pots should not draw attention to the soot on kettles. He has not been in my bed, I promise you.

And for the rest, I'm sorry. But you are here and you will quell them. They are cowering already, having barricaded themselves in their castles the instant they had word of your coming.'

In that moment–the first for longer than either of them could remember–something between them met and touched, a sudden mutual acceptance, an unwilling respect for a quality each possessed and saw suddenly in the other.

A wry, reluctant smile played round Henry's mouth. It did not occur to him to wonder at the change in her that she could laugh where once she would have raged; he only thought that had she been a man he might even have liked her.

'Well, no more of that then,' he said, 'but'–he looked into her eyes–'let it be understood that Ralph de Faye had best avoid me.' His glance, calculating, ran over her face, then lingered on the lovely mouth and slid down to her opulent bosom. 'You're looking well.'

Passion of Christ, she thought, if his face was anything to go by he rode in here with thoughts of a weighted sack in the moat at dead of night, and already his mind's on the usual thing! O God, I thank you for denying me the gift of manhood; a woman is tempted by no such siren songs.

But it was with the greatest demureness that she informed him that she was indeed very well and the happier for his coming. 'See you, my lord,' she said, 'I have been lonely here out of my accustomed places. And whatever evil tongues have said of me, let me assure you that all my friendliness with Ralph was on our own behalf.' She began to impart several minor items of information gleaned from her kinsman that might help Henry's interests. How carefully she had sifted them to sow doubt or mistaken confidence to the advantage of her designs was apparent to no one but herself.

Henry stayed no more than twenty-four hours in Angers; next day he was off at breakneck speed to meet up with his army before it reached Alençon. Eleanor watched him go with relief. Their meeting, culminating as it had in a physical reconciliation, had gone off better than she dared hope but she was afraid that deeper probing on his part might have uncovered more than she wished him to know. Besides, with Ralph gone too, she would have more time for Richard.

She was with him that afternoon when her lady Eustachia came breathlessly into the room. 'Here's news!' she cried. 'The de Clare minx is betrothed and the nuptials follow shortly. Well, we all know what *that* means!'

Eleanor made a gesture to stop her; she had seen Richard's eyes slide sideways towards the lady although he did not raise his head from the book on his knee. But Eustachia with a juicy item of gossip was impossible to check.

'Oh, but there's a successor–installed at Woodstock if you please! The daughter of some marcher lord—' Out it all came with an appalling frankness–Eustachia's informant had had it written down and she flourished the scrap of parchment as if it were a battle flag. Seeing that the damage was done Eleanor made no further attempt to stop her but sat stony and unmoving, hearing the tale to the end. Then she dismissed Eustachia.

She looked at Richard. 'We are not interested in gossip about people we hardly know, are we?' she said conversationally.

She saw him go red; he shook his head. His eyes avoided hers, and he stood up. 'I have just remembered. I am promised at the quintain at the ninth hour should the weather be fine.' He turned back in the doorway. 'Shall I tell the lady Eustachia you need her?'

'No,' she said because she was sick at what she had heard. Then, sharply–'Yes!' because at least Eustachia should pay for her thoughtlessness which had somehow tarnished the shining image she wished to present to her favourite son. The slimy track of Henry's adulteries had besmeared her, too; she had seen it in Richard's face.

Easter 1166

Thomas sat in his cell in the Abbey of Pontigny reading *On Grace and Freewill* by Bernard of Clairvaux but he was finding it hard to concentrate. All through Lent he had put aside the books on canon law and restricted himself to a diet of devotional works; he could not be sure whether they had improved his soul's health; it seemed to him that his mind raged with a hunger fiercer even than that of his body. Spring had come, the sap was rising, and Thomas of London longed to be up and doing, fighting the Lord's battle once more after this long winter of inaction.

It was too dim to see the writing any longer; he could with a clear conscience raise his eyes from the page and give himself up to meditation–not on grace and freewill, to be sure, but on the next step in his battle for vindication. Holy Week was here at last, and with the passing of the Easter Feast the spiritual weapons of which he had been deprived would be his to wield once more. For last summer Pope Alexander, playing his usual two-handed game, had added a rider to the letter which announced that Henry's sentence on him had been quashed by apostolic authority, ordering him to take no measures against the King and his land until the following Easter–'for by then God will grant better times and both you and we may safely proceed further in this matter.'

Whether or not God would grant better times he, Thomas, would no longer be forced to confine himself to mild reprimands in writing; he would be empowered to unsheathe the Sword of the Spirit, sharper than any two-edged sword, against the enemies of the Church. And the first he would strike would be the Bishop of Salisbury for daring to disobey his ban on the institution of John of Oxford as Dean. No matter that Henry had ordered it! Jocelin of Salisbury had doubly sinned, both by disobedience to his metropolitan and by the betrayal of his old friend Pope Alexander whom John at Wurzburg had vowed never to recognise as the successor of St Peter.

Henry was in France again and on Sunday–Easter Day– he was to hold a conference at Angers with King Louis. No invitation to himself had arrived so far but there was yet time. It was obvious that he was to be the subject of their discussions. Involuntarily he pressed his hands together. O God, if he saw Henry truly penitent, how swift he would be to forgive–yes, even that atrocity he had committed in Wales last year.

At the time he had thought he never could forgive. It had been weeks before the seething pit of grief and fury in his mind had died, much longer before he could bring himself to refer to Henry as anything but 'that animal'. It had given him the last proof (if proof were needed) that he stood for the right and must hold fast to the end.

Perhaps, then, it had been wise of Alexander to restrain him, to compel him to wait upon the changes time might bring. If he could now consider forgiving Henry, it might not be too much to hope that Henry, too, had had a change of heart. The thought of what he had been reading came to him and with it a silent prayer that God's grace might work its miracle on Henry's all too free will.

May 1166

De Mandeville turned from the usher and muttered, 'Abbot Urban is without, bearing a letter. Do we let him in?'

'Why not?' said Leicester, but then his eyes narrowed and he looked sharply at de Mandeville. 'Abbot Urban? A letter from the Archbishop, you mean?' At the other's nod he frowned unhappily. 'No–wait–let me think.'

He did not want a recurrence of yesterday's scene when the King read the letter sent by the Archbishop to the Empress, full of oblique threats under the guise of imploring a mother's intercession with her son, and bringing the frightening news that the Pope had appointed the writer Legate of the Holy See for all England except the diocese of York.

Henry had read the hidden message clearly enough: the reason why his mother had sent it on to him. He had burst into tears of frustration, crying that 'This Archbishop will deprive me of body and soul alike!' Then the muscles of his jaw had stood out, he had begun to breathe in short, heavy gasps and then to scream, letting fly with anything to hand– parchments, quills, ink-pots, sanding-boxes–all had crashed or fluttered to the floor while his ministers and officials had backed away and the men on the benches further off had stood up, craning to watch with interest. He had howled at them, 'Dogs! Traitors! Traitors all that you take no care to deliver me from the trouble caused by one man! Not a one of you but will sit by and allow him to beard me as he pleases.'

Gilbert Foliot had sat stiff-backed with a red stain of colour creeping up his gaunt cheeks as the King had cursed and sworn at him and York–aye, and at his present favourite, John of Oxford, too–for leading him into the mazes of canon law and there deserting him.

And now Urban, who came direct from Thomas, waited outside. The King's chief minister was only too well aware that if the true business of this Council (which was to prepare for the invasion of Brittany) were thwarted, all their success in Maine would go for naught. The continental dominions would rise as one to throw off the yoke of an excommunicate king.

Leicester got up suddenly. 'I will see him before the King arrives—' But the King was entering with the Abbot on his heels.

Henry had scarcely reached the dais before he rounded on the Abbot and the two clerks with him. They went down speedily on one knee; the Abbot with more care and circumspection for he was not a young man. Henry stood glaring at them without a word.

Leicester could not hear what the Abbot said but he saw the King throw up his head and walk away, leaving them kneeling there. The clerks hoisted the Abbot to his feet but they remained where they were, keeping a safe distance between themselves and Henry.

Once he was seated, Henry turned to Leicester and his other officers, asking sharply about the lists of provisions and weapons, shuffling busily through parchments; all, thought Leicester, to disconcert the Abbot and show him he was of no account. But Urban waited with no sign of discomposure.

'Ha!' said Henry at last, as if he had only now noticed his continued presence. 'I know you. You are he who brought me a letter before from that perjured renegade who still masquerades as archbishop. I wonder that you make so bold as to come before me again after your last reception.'

The Abbot held out his hand and one of the clerks placed a letter in it. He smiled gently upon the King and advanced to the foot of the dais.

'It is no boldness in me but concern for your soul's health that brings me here as messenger, my lord King. As to my last reception, I have long since forgiven your harsh words, knowing, as we all do, that the cares of earthly kingship bear hard on any mortal man and but make more difficult the entry to that Kingdom—'

'Give me the letter,' snarled the King, 'without a sermon.'

There was silence while he broke the seals and spread it out to read, and of all the watchers the Abbot and his clerks breathed easiest. Beside Henry Leicester could not keep his eyes from straying to the parchment; he even leaned away a little to bring the writing into focus and the last sentence sprang out at him: 'Otherwise you may know for certain that you will experience divine severity and vengeance.' So it was not the worst! His eyes flew to the top. '*Desiderio desidaravi*' it began–'With great longing have I desired to see your face again and speak with you; greatly for my sake but even more for yours', and half way down, 'in that you are my son, I am bound by reason of my office to chasten and correct you'. That was as much as he could make out before Henry let the roll run up again and sat with both hands spread on the table before him.

Leicester did not listen to what he was saying to the Abbot; the tone was enough to tell him that this second reception was no kinder than the first. He considered instead what he had just read in Thomas's own hand. 'With great longing have I desired to see your face again. . . .' Of course Becket was disappointed not to have been invited to those discussions of which he was the chief subject. But where was the point? With every passing month it was becoming clearer that the differences between Henry and himself were irreconcilable. God alone knew what the end would be. 'With great longing. . . .' Did he love Henry still?

The Abbot was leaving now, imperturbable as ever. Henry was not shouting this time; he sat sunk in gloom while the letter was passed round among his ministers. 'What have I done to deserve this?' Leicester heard him mutter. 'God knows the fault is none of mine. Have I not always been a dutiful son of the Church? Obeyed the laws? All I have wanted is to keep that which my forefathers had.' He raised his voice. 'You see that he intends to excommunicate me. Come, advise me; tell me how I may avert it.'

Arnulf of Lisieux had sat mumbling with his eyes down; now he lifted his head. 'My lord King, while an excommunicate cannot appeal, being already outside the fold, it is possible to appeal against an impending excommunication. An appeal may procure postponement for as long as a year.' He turned to Foliot. 'Is that not so?'

'It would be necessary to deliver formal notification of the appeal to the Archbishop.'

The King glared from one to the other. 'No, by God's

Passion!' His face had gone darkly red. Then he looked down at his hands and groaned. 'You are sure?'

The bishops conferred together for a few moments and finally announced that they were agreed about the validity of such a procedure but speed was essential since none could know when the Archbishop's patience might run out. Henry eyed them morosely. It was plain that an appeal to Rome, galling as it was, was the only way.

'You will deliver notification of the appeal to Pontigny,' he said to Arnulf, and to Bishop Froger of Séez, 'You, also.' Those two disliked each other heartily and their eagerness to report adversely on the other would safeguard his interests. 'And one other,' he added, 'I care not who.' Rotrou of Rouen volunteered, the King agreed, and so it was decided. They left to put the matter in motion and the real business of the Council could finally begin.

While they listed the stores needed Leicester was deep in thought. Rotrou, like himself, had shown a good deal of sympathy for the Archbishop. Please God that he could see Thomas alone, though how he could find a way to unravel the coil was more than Leicester could see.

Henry was too preoccupied himself to notice his Justiciar's inattention. He was beginning almost to dread the arrival of letters, even from Rosamund. He had heard last month from her that she was pregnant and, torn between his heart and the cold common sense that had made him leave her with no promises of a later reunion, his exasperation against the rebels grew daily more bitter. But for them he could have remained with her until his feelings had run their natural course and he had tired of her, then he could have married her off with no heart-burnings. He had not wanted to love again–did not love her, he assured himself. But how he missed her.

That she loved him he no longer doubted. And now she was with child. . . . Despite himself he felt that well-remembered softening, that glow that warned him that the heart is not bounded by the cold restraint of reason. Perhaps, after the child was born–October, she had said–he could send for her.

It would be better to forget her though, to send money, to pay her off. Why did he feel this shrinking, shame almost, at such a thought? And, absurd as it was, he doubted that she would suffer it. There was a steeliness in her that had been absent in Hikenai, a look in the eye that probed straight to the soul, that said, 'No man has his will of me but by my consent.' That came of her breeding.

Yes, he had had her consent indeed; to a certain degree, he thought with a faint smile, she had seduced him. He had been in no great hurry, being busy with law-making and still savouring the new-found knowledge that she had not found him unattractive after all.

He had met her unexpectedly again in a dim place, she descending, he ascending the steep, stone stair from the hall. She had stood in front of him, one step above, so that their faces were on a level, and had not stepped aside as he expected but remained stock still. He had smiled and put his hands on her waist to help her past on the broader side of the spiral tread and had felt her tremble at his touch. As always, youth and timidity had roused something in him; his hands had slid a little higher and, hearing her fluttering breath, he had leaned closer and drawn her into the angle of the stair-well. And he had felt her arms go round him, felt the pressure of her hands at the back of his neck guiding his head towards her, his mouth to hers.

Taken aback, he had half disengaged himself and then, being so close, had seen her face. 'What is it?' he said.

'I love you,' she said simply.

He gazed at her, the hunter in him for a second affronted, then he saw her eyes. She meant it. He stood there staring, like a prisoner who sees, faint with distance but unmistakable, the first banners of a relieving army; and then, so fast the mind draws parallels, he remembered how he had gazed into

Annora's eyes and heard those same triumphant bugle calls.

That recollection sent his mouth down. He had not known how he looked but he had seen her eyes flinch from his face and recognised in her the same stiff misery he had felt at Corfham. And he had not known how to mend it. 'Love's a large word,' he had ventured.

She had lifted her head. 'It is a large feeling,' she had said. 'I–I thought it could only be for God till I saw you. But I have felt it ever since–a whole year now.'

When she speaks of love she does not mean what I mean, he thought.

'If I have mistaken you—' she began and seemed not to know how to continue. Then she said in a small voice, 'I thought that was why you asked for me at court. My brother thought so too; he would have taken me away but that I gave him the slip.' Colour ran up her cheeks. 'Sir, I am not practised in these things. But I knew the Queen was away oversea—'

He had never heard a woman gently reared speak so plain. He answered as plainly. 'You are offering yourself to me?'

'Yes,' she said.

He was astonished to find himself arguing. 'You will regret it.

'Not I,' she said, and very low, 'You have had others.'

'Not like you,' he came back quickly, knowing it for truth.

'Then I shall go from here.'

To that he could only shake his head with determination.

'Why not? What reason for me to stay?'

He put on a show of sternness. 'Because I so order it.'

It was wrong that a young girl should speak so, he thought, such directness was unwomanly. And he did not welcome the stirrings of interest it roused in him. What he wanted was much simpler. Desire warred with the urge to flee. 'We cannot talk here,' he had said lamely. 'Dine with me tonight in my chamber.'

That was how it had all begun. It had been quite absurd. And now there would be a child who partook of her qualities and his. What sons might they not breed between them!

Eleanor too was pregnant again; he had received confirmation of the news a week ago. It had taken him by surprise in view of her age. God knows she was fertile; he could not complain of her on that score.

Why then should he feel that she had in some way stolen a march on him? He knew the reason for that, too, hide from it as he might. It would now be plain to Rosamund that he had gone straight from her arms to the Queen's. She would not rebuke him by word or look but what was between them would never be quite the same because of it.

Scowling, he tried to force his attention back to the work in hand. If her image were to come between himself and the cares of state to this extent, he must end the thing. He could see the child provided for by intermediaries. A king could not afford to put himself completely in a woman's power, he told himself, and he was, after all, no longer the simple lad who had looked on Hikenai and thought the world well lost for love.

That mythical youth assumed other qualities as time went on, many of which would have caused considerable astonishment to those who could remember the young Henry FitzEmpress.

It was not long before the contents of the Archbishop's letter were common knowledge among the King's entourage and most of them drew from it the same conclusion as the King. A sense of impending disaster settled over Chinon. What little discussion there was was conducted in whispers, suddenly broken off at the approach of one not intimately known. Everyone waited for the return of the bishops.

Ten days later Hugh de Morville and Richard le Bret went down to see the great destriers exercised–a useful euphemism, for Henry would allow no jousts or tourneys in his lands such as the French had. But now, in time of war, a large, sanded space outside the castle walls had been roped off so that the young knights might try their horses one against the other, and the horse-masters were not the only ones to turn a blind eye to the levelled lances and the excited yelling of the onlookers.

It had rained heavily during the night so that the sodden sand was thrown up from the horses' hoofs in heavy clods which broke and sprayed stingingly over the first row of spectators. White clouds raced across a sky too brilliantly blue at this early hour to promise more settled weather. The clarity of the light picked out each grain of sand clinging to le Bret's cheeks and beard as he brought his face closer to Hugh de Morville's ear to be heard above the shouting.

In one thing only these two agreed, it was what brought them together at intervals: hatred of the Archbishop. Le Bret could talk for hours of his thirst for vengeance on behalf of his old master, the Lord William, brother of the King, whom the Archbishop had driven untimely to his grave. This letter had rekindled him. But Hugh thought he seemed singularly unready to make the first move to help the King to his avowed desire to be rid of that turbulent cleric forever.

'Surely the man who succeeded in such a feat would be well rewarded?' he murmured now in his silkiest voice.

'He is under the protection of the King of the French,' le Bret replied gloomily, 'and in his territory.'

'In an undefended monastery. . . .'

Le Bret shook his head. 'Such an act would bring Louis up in arms. The lord King has enough to think about with these rebels. He would not thank us for bringing a hornet's nest about his ears.'

Hugh smiled. Something in that smile riled le Bret. 'What think you of this new King of Scots?' he asked unpleasantly.

Hugh's eyes slid sideways at him under their long, womanish lashes but the patronising smile did not falter. 'As unchancy as the last one, I would say,' he returned. 'My birthplace lies in border country close to the Scots. I think you will agree that I am entitled to be interested in any claims they may be putting forward.'

'In Northumberland?'

'No, in Cumbria hard by Carlisle.'

'Then you need not worry. It's the earldom of Northumberland William's after.'

'And if he gets it my manor will be the last northerly outpost of England.'

'He'll not get it anyway; it's harder to separate land from Henry than gold from a Jew.'

'All the same I think that I shall ride north when I return to England. The rents from Burgh have been declining ever since my mother died.'

Le Bret thought how typical de Morville was, with honours scattered the length and breadth of the land, to worry about the poor returns of some barren northern manor! And to sneer at others, more sensible of their prince's interest, for refusing risks he would not undertake himself. If those others had less to lose, it was all they had. He began to reckon up in his head what he could expect to receive this year from the one manor he had acquired and ended the calculation in a fouler temper than he began it. If this Archbishop had been domiciled in Henry's own lands nothing would have prevented him from carrying out the King's expressed wish, though for the moment he was not sure whether vengeance or the hope of reward would have been the overriding reason.

He suddenly became aware that Hugh was looking past him. He turned, but being shorter than Hugh could see nothing for the press of bodies. 'What is it?' he said.

'Arundel–and Leicester–and in an almighty hurry. The King must have sent for them. I'm going in.' He began to elbow his way through the throng. Le Bret followed. 'Is it the bishops, think you? Have they returned?'

When Hugh and le Bret got there the hall was already half-full and the news was that the bishops had returned and were now closeted with the King.

For all the numbers in the hall there was little noise; all could hear the loud, harsh voice of the King overmastering the voices of the others; it rose finally to what sounded like a screech, then suddenly cut off.

The door flew open with a crash; it was Arundel who stood there wild-eyed, yelling for a physician, and quick about it–he would have a rope about the neck of any who hindered his passage to the King.

'Passion of Christ!' said le Bret. 'Has he done it? Is the King excommunicate?'

No one answered him. 'What good's a physician for that?' he muttered. He heard the silence around him like a ringing in his ears.

Arundel half closed the door and came further into the hall. 'Nothing has happened,' he said, 'except that the bishops were unable to deliver the notice of appeal because the Archbishop had left Pontigny.' His face twisted. 'To go on pilgrimage to Soissons, so it was said.' He looked around. 'The King has fallen ill.' Clearly in his own relief he had forgotten for a moment to be worried about the King. And truly it seemed a small thing to the rest of them compared with what they had feared.

Le Bret sucked in a long breath and looked at Hugh. If he had been a religious man he would have thought he was praying. But since he was not. . . . Not for the first time it occurred to le Bret to wonder why he so often sought out a man he did not like and would never understand.

On that same day Archbishop Thomas arrived at Vézelay from Soissons. It had been no accident that he had left Pontigny before the bishops arrived. In the constant traffic of the King's court strangers passed unnoticed, tongues were loose, and Thomas's spies and secret admirers active. Little happened there which was not reported at Pontigny within a few days.

Herbert had instantly urged him to circumvent Henry by making a pilgrimage to the shrine of St Drausius, that saint who was commonly reputed to make invincible any combatant who would watch all night there in his memory. In the charged atmosphere of piety in that place Herbert had been fired by all the talk of the miraculous finds at Vézelay two years previously. He had pointed out to Thomas that it could be no coincidence that among them were fragments of the clothing of Meshach, Shadrach and Abednego, who with Daniel had defied the mighty Nebuchadnezzar and yet had emerged unharmed from the fiery furnace. It was surely God's way of telling the Archbishop that he too would eventually come unscathed through his ordeal.

Thomas had made no comment, but even before Herbert finished speaking he saw that here was the sign he had been waiting for. A dozen times since Easter he had taken the fateful decision to excommunicate Henry and his chief ministers, and as many times he had changed his mind again. Not to embarrass Louis who was his host, not to risk Henry's swift retribution upon the English monks of the Order which harboured him–were they reasons or mere evasions of responsibility? Where would the Church be now if the saints of old had put the safety of other men before duty to God?

But the Abbey of Vézelay was subject only to the Pope. Through Herbert, God was showing him the one place where he might sentence Henry with impunity. He had bowed his head, thankful that the momentous decision had been taken out of his hands. But still he had said nothing of his intentions to Herbert.

They had ridden to Vézelay in the midst of a great host that, drunk with spiritual excitement (or, in some cases, a more earthly brew), streamed in to keep the Pentecostal Feast. The crowds choked the dusty roads and more than once the rear of the long procession had to stop and wait while the vanguard thinned to a trickle to cross a narrow bridge. It was a long and tiring journey but at last they crossed the Cure, in its valley between precipitous rocks, and came to the fortified gate which marked the entrance to the domains of the Abbot. Slowly then they toiled up the long hill dominating all the countryside to the Abbey church on the summit. There most of them sank down breathless, staring at the stupendous view over the valleys of the Cure and the Yonne to the forested mountains beyond, and the awesome depiction of the Day of Judgement which loomed before them above the great west door.

It was at this scene that Thomas looked, though not for long. He feared it might weaken his resolve. He and his followers pressed on to the Abbey itself.

That night at dinner the Abbot invited his guest to celebrate High Mass on Whit Sunday. Thomas dropped his eyes to his hands neatly folded in his lap. He had been sure enough of the invitation, yet he knew that had God not wished it, it would not have been forthcoming. So He will show us the road, he thought, do we but bide the time.

He thanked the Abbot and then rose, having eaten two courses of the meal. 'If I might visit the church—?'

Coming out from the Frater with the young monk the Abbot had deputed to guide him, the sun was in his eyes for it still stood above the gatehouse; the dovecote too was sunlit with the doves wheeling lazily above. But all the court before him was in shadow, and cool when they passed into it on their way to the cloister. So am I, he thought with sudden wretchedness, pushed out of life's sunlight into shadow. . . . Fearful of these sudden swingings of mood, which came upon him of late with increasing frequency, he started to talk lightly to the young monk, hoping by cheerful conversation to escape the dreadful sense of desolation which always lurked now at the edges of his mind. But the monk went on with measured tread, answering only in monosyllables, awed or perhaps merely shy.

They had reached the cloister door when a hammering on the great gate made them both start and look back; after a quick glance at Thomas the young monk took his hand off the iron ring of the latch and contemplated his feet again. Men with big voices and loud laughs were coming in; they were wearing the livery of the King of France.

Thomas was off with his long, flying stride in an instant. He knew the Constable; Louis had sent messages by him before. There was no mistaking that quick turn of the head and neat black beard, nor the merry eye when he drew closer. 'Welcome,' he called, 'to you who wear the badge of King Louis.'

'My lord.' The Constable came close. 'A message from the King, sent in great haste. The King of the English lies ill at Chinon–so ill that he is unable to attend the conference arranged with King Louis.'

Thomas's face did not alter but his heart gave a great jump. 'Ill?' he heard himself say. 'How ill? Of a fever?'

'None knoweth.' Thomas thought the Constable was looking at him with considerable interest and he turned away to find the young monk had followed him, soft-footed, and now stood behind him listening intently.

'Tell my lord Abbot that the men of King Louis are here,' Thomas said to him. 'No–stay–I will take the Constable to him. You see the men to the guest house.'

Later that evening Thomas sat talking with the Abbot, or more truly, talking to himself in the Abbot's presence, of the news he had received.

'You fear that he may die,' said the old man gently and laid his hand on Thomas's arm. 'It may be that God has sent him this sickness as a reminder of his mortality. And it may work a true repentance in him.'

'I have prayed for that–and yet–I do not know.' He smiled wryly. 'It stretches the imagination to think of King Henry humble and penitent. I think–I fear–that he has always thought of God as an equal.'

The Abbot displayed none of the horror Thomas had expected. 'That is one of the dangers of kingship,' he agreed placidly, 'but remember every man is ultimately responsible for his own soul. You, his spiritual father, have been driven away by him; no blame will attach to you if he dies unrepentant.'

Thomas looked towards the candle where a moth whirred, spiralling closer, ever closer to the flame until a sudden sizzle and the plop of its body to the table marked its end. Dared he excommunicate Henry now?

'Come,' the Abbot was saying. 'Come, and I will show you that which will bring you comfort. The relics are locked away until the Feast but you shall see them now.'

They took a candle apiece to go below to the Treasury. There in the dim, bare, vaulted crypt their doubled shadows loomed enormous, sliding in uncanny silence along the lime-washed walls. When they had closed the low door of the Treasury behind them and placed the candles on one of the great chests, and the Abbot had sorted once more through his keys, Thomas sat himself on another chest and gazed about. He had thought that Vézelay must be rich but the numbers of the great coffers and presses staggered him. Canterbury had nothing to compare with this.

It was a very small box the Abbot finally brought out, bound with iron and with yet another lock on it.

'The reliquaries are not yet made and so we keep them here.' He nodded towards the press whose door stood open. 'It was in that statue they were found.' Thomas saw a small, wooden statue of the Virgin, primitively carved and dark with age. 'She had been placed down here with others of old time since now we have much finer images, painted and gilded. But we keep them all, yes, however old, even those which appear ugly to the sight of modern men.'

He laid back the lid of the box. Within, on silver tissue, lay the precious objects, a little knotted tangle of dark hair, an anonymous piece of bone, brownish with age, and some scraps of cloth, rotting and dun-coloured.

The Abbot breathed heavily, poring over them. 'The Virgin's hairs,' he pronounced. 'A bone of St John the Baptist. . . . Fragments of the robe of Christ.'

Thomas stared at them. The hair looked like nothing so much as the cleanings of a comb. A faint unease touched him.

'As I heard it the stuff was part of the clothing of Daniel's companions—'

The Abbot separated the scraps. 'Those pieces,' he said.

'Ah. . . . ' said Thomas.

'We intend to have them set each in a golden reliquary. Jewelled–yes–many gems have been donated already. St John the Baptist's finger. . . .' The Abbot's voice dreamed on.

Thomas looked at him covertly without moving his head. He was very old. The candlelight cast a soft halo through the scant white hairs that pricked through the tonsure and glittered on the easy, joyful tears coursing down the wrinkled cheek.

Perhaps the eye of faith saw most truly. Gently he touched the ancient, decaying fragments designated as the remains of Abednego's garment. They were brittle and stiff. 'God is good,' he said.

The Abbot squeezed his nose between the knuckle of his forefinger and his thumb and then sniffed noisily. 'If one soul may be saved from damnation because of them. . . .' His voice broke.

'Yes,' said Thomas, 'one soul would be enough.'

Henry's name was absent from the list of those he excommunicated on Whit Sunday. After the Mass was over and he had delivered his sermon to the people he stood a moment in silence, listening to the small scufflings that always preceded the congregation's rush for the open air, and gazing down the long nave to the great doors that gave on the narthex beyond. Just now the doors stood open for even that vast space could not accommodate all the multitude that wished to hear one whose fame had spread to the borders of the world.

He was struck again by the solemn power and severity instinct in the very stones of the great monastic church. The vault of the nave soared loftily, spanned by arcs of stones alternately white and olive green; above the much lower arches on either side was a plain, unbroken surface surmounted by one small narrow window to each bay. It was as stern and unyielding in its rejection of the world as Pontigny. There high, pointed arches rose sharply over narrow aisles from undecorated columns in a long, numinous vista and here the capitals were ornamented with an extraordinary minuteness, yet the strength and dignity of the structure was undiminished by it. Starkly impressive, it was a fitting place to deliver judgement.

He began to speak again and the first half-resentful surprise of the assembly quickly died away as it became plain that they were to be treated to a public exposition of the causes of the quarrel between the King of the English and the man who stood before them. As he drew to a conclusion the Abbot, who had been fidgeting for some while, rose from his throne at the side of the altar and turned eagerly towards the monastery door; he retired again in some confusion to take his place in the procession which Thomas was leading to the narthex.

In that paved and pillared space, overlooked by the great sculpture of Christ in glory above the portal, Thomas lit the candles symbolising the souls of John of Oxford and Richard of Ilchester and dashed them out upon the ground. In the terrifying words of the Liturgy he cast them from the fold of Christendom into outer darkness; and along with them he excommunicated Richard de Luci and Jocelin de Balliol for their part in formulating the Constitutions of Clarendon, and Ranulf de Broc, Hugh de St Clare and Thomas Fitzbernard for laying hands on Canterbury's possessions. He denounced the Constitutions and all who obeyed them, and he absolved the English bishops from their oath to observe them. Then, his voice thick with tears, he warned King Henry to repent lest he, too, should incur the fell sentence.

Not a listener present but quailed before the surge and thunder of that dread anathema, who felt no cold finger touch him at the measured tolling of the knell. When it was over and the last deep reverberations were only a faint shuddering deep in the skull, a stunned silence ensued.

In the Laver before dinner Hugh of Nunant whispered in Herbert's ear though only the two of them were there. 'How is this possible? Surely our lord King appealed on others' behalf as well as his own?'

Herbert had had time to recover from his own shock. 'The notification of appeal to the Archbishop was invalid. The bishops read it publicly but omitted to post it on the monastery gates.'

Hugh breathed a sigh of relief. In common with the others his spirits were rising at this evidence of direct action. 'He was right to do it then?' he said.

Herbert bristled slightly. 'Right? What do you mean–right?'

Hugh was not sure what he had meant himself. But he still found that iron and uncompromising judge hard to reconcile with the master who talked so often of the tender, everlasting love of God.

Thomas followed action by words. The next day he wrote a long letter to his lord and king, expressing at once his longing for the end of their painful conflict and his inflexible determination to carry it through to the bitter end if Henry would not yield.

Day and night, he informed him, he had prayed for him and waited expectantly for him to change his ways, repent and depart from the path of iniquity. He urged him once again to break with the so-called friends whose instigation and advice had caused him to fall into the abyss. And he repeated, as so many times before, the assertion that the authority of priests was greater than the royal power–'for God will demand an accounting of them even in regard to kings.'

It was very quiet in the little closet where Thomas sat. He leaned his head on his hand as he read what he had written. How else could he make Henry understand how he feared for him? He returned to supplication, urging his most beloved son, most serene Highness, most revered lord to follow the example of King David who returned to God with a contrite and humble heart after he had sinned.

'If you do not listen to me,' he wrote, and then carefully examined the end of the quill. He smoothed it against his thumb nail and tried again—'I, who am wont to pray for you before the majesty of Christ's body—' It was beginning to scratch. He discarded it and picked up a fresh one. '—with overflowing tears and sighs,' he continued. But then he stopped again and sat staring before him.

Finally he drew a deep breath and, dipping the quill in the ink-pot, wrote firmly, '—then I shall cry out against you and say, "Arise, O God, judge Your cause. Remember the outrages and the injuries that are being done to You and Yours by the King of the English and his followers. Forget not the ignominies inflicted on Your church which You established with Your blood. Avenge, Lord, the blood of Your servants which has been spilled. Avenge, Lord, the afflictions of Your servants which are infinite in number. The pride of those who hate and persecute You and Yours has grown so great that we can no longer endure it."'

And then, half-aghast himself at seeing the words in black and white, he returned to his theme of wicked advisers and assured Henry that he did not say these things to provoke him to greater anger as would no doubt be suggested by malignant persons, but rather because he wished to persuade his lord to take care for his soul's sake and avoid the ultimate peril.

After deep thought he concluded, 'Consider, where are the emperors, where the kings and other princes, where the archbishops and bishops who preceded us? In truth they toiled and suffered and now others have entered upon their labours. What more is there to say? The glory of this world passes away. Therefore remember your last hour.'

VI
June 1166

Robert Fitzurse rode in cold and wet from Taunton; for after a warm and settled spring the weather had changed at the solstice to a succession of gales and pouring rain. Overhead, torn and shredded by the wind, low scuds of black cloud raced along beneath an impenetrable layer of overcast. Coming over the plank bridge to the house, Robert raised his head to the rain; foolish as he knew it to be in such conditions he was searching for the figure of his wife.

Six months ago he had married for the second time. His bride was Amicia Engaine, the widow of a landed knight. He and her two young sons had drowned in the same shipwreck. But the tragedy of losing her children had meant that his wealth devolved on her.

The merest chance had brought her to Richard Fitzurse's notice. She was cousin to a daughter-in-law of de Mohun of Dunster who had mentioned the disaster; the baron had pricked up his ears and made it his business to discover more. That her marriage was in Leicester's gift had been a stroke of fortune; that she was willing to take Robert had seemed closer to a miracle.

Robert himself had not thought very highly of her at first sight but he could think of no valid excuse for refusing so handsome an endowment. To say that buxom ladies with sorrel-coloured hair made no appeal to him would only have aroused his father's anger after his promise to wed again as soon as a suitable match could be arranged. And as suitability in the baron's eyes meant previous proof of fertility and his own condition of a fat dower had been met, he said nothing and gave little thought to the reason why a rich widow (even one five years his senior) should have settled so easily for the younger son of no very great house, and one with a bend sinister in his escutcheon at that.

In her Robert had found a content he had never before experienced. She was everything to him now though it was to be a little longer before he realised it.

So he faced into the driving rain to look for her, feeling an absurd pang of disappointment that she was not standing there to welcome him. Then he saw the door at the head of the stair open and, hastily dismounting, thrust the bridle into the hand of the nearest fellow and crossed the intervening space in a few long strides. By that time she was at the foot of the steps. He tried to swing her off her feet to kiss her but fourteen stone defeated him; he bent down to her instead.

'You're well?' she said. 'But wet as a drowned rat! So much for sunny June. Did you get the spices?'

'Hold, hold!' he said. 'Let's get inside; you've not put on your mantle. I got most of what you asked for but there's no ginger to be had–or not in Taunton, at any rate. Is all well here?' He tipped his head at the tower.

He made for the fire, dropping his drenched cloak on the floor. The old baron sat there beside it in his chair with Cicely in her usual seat on the hearthstone at his feet. 'Pick up my cloak, child,' Robert addressed her, 'and hang it to dry for me if you will. And tell them to bring wine.' He put his arm about Amicia's ample waist. She leaned against him, her warm hand sliding over his cold one, while the baron drove at the fire with his staff, scattering the smouldering logs and sending a tattered burst of flame leaping up the chimney.

Robert put his wife aside and bent to salute his father. 'I met de Reigny in Taunton with Osbert, de Mohun's steward. They had been talking to the bishop's bailiff,' he said in a low voice. The baron's face did not move but his eyes slid to the man who had appeared with the wine. Robert took the jug from him, saw Cicely behind and frowned.

Amicia looked round. 'Come, Cicely,' she said. 'Come and help me unpack the stuff Sir Robert has brought. There'll be something there for you, I fancy.'

When they had gone Robert sat down opposite his father. 'De Luci is excommunicate,' he said in a taut voice, 'and Jocelin de Balliol, the authors of the Constitutions of Clarendon. It was done at Whitsuntide, they said.'

'Leicester—?'

'No, not Leicester.'

'No. . . . He liked him–helped him, some say. At Whitsuntide? That's not three weeks ago. Ill news travels fast but, by the Rood, that's more than fast; it's near to a miracle with all the ports closed.'

'There be many, both in this land and out of it, who hold by the Archbishop and work his interests,' Robert said.

The baron looked at him keenly. 'This news came from the bishop's bailiff?'

Robert nodded.

'Only those two? Not the King himself?'

'Not the King. But John of Oxford and Richard of Ilchester, Ranulf de Broc–I cannot remember all the names. A goodly number. All those who have despoiled Canterbury's property.'

The baron's mouth tightened a little. Reynold had had a hand in that despoliation.

'And he has suspended the Bishop of Salisbury for disobedience.' Something that was almost a smile lifted Robert's lip. 'Bath has taken to his bed again in terror. The bailiff is putting it about that he is sick unto death.'

'He's an old man.'

'He's a coward.'

The baron shook his head impatiently. 'He has been ill for years.'

Robert shrugged and let it go. 'The King himself was ill when the news came, they said. But he has sent orders to the bishops to convene and appeal to the Pope. That, after swearing that very thing was forbidden under the old English customs!'

'You will learn, my son, that kings frequently find it expedient to ignore the laws which bind their subjects.'

'Well, Bath did not go, of course. The council was some days ago but they had no news of that.'

'Hmm,' said the baron. He did not seem very interested, Robert thought. His father changed the subject to speak of the great rains that had fallen and bade fair to ruin the harvest. But then he asked after a while if Exeter and Worcester had joined in the appeal the King had ordered, so Robert knew the thing was still working in his mind. Robert could not tell him that.

Cicely helped Amicia unpack the goods in the long, dark pantry that adjoined the kitchens. Most of them were foodstuffs they were unable to produce themselves; dried figs, great raisins, spices and the like which came from foreign climes. When they had finished she sat back on her heels and asked what gift there was for her.

Amicia looked at her consideringly. She saw now it had been foolish to say such a thing to a child who was her father's pet. 'I said that to make you come away–to teach you manners–for it was plain to me, as it should have been to you, that the men would speak alone. You are too bold, Cicely, sitting ever at the baron's side, even when men are present. I am surprised that he allows it.'

'He would have told me himself if he had wanted me to go.'

Sheer surprise that an unwed girl should answer back robbed Amicia of words. But not for long. She stepped smartly forward and fetched Cicely a blow on the ear that sent her sprawling. 'Hold your tongue, you saucy wench! I am mistress here and the baron has given you, as well as the servants, into my keeping. Truly it seems to me that the sooner we are gone from here the better, or the baron's hopes for you will never be realised. No man of station will marry with a maid who is not meek and gentle of spirit. Oh, I can see I shall have much trouble with you—' She bent forward to stare into the girl's face. 'But in my own house things will be different, I promise!' She straightened up and dusted her hands down the sides of her skirts as one who has finally accomplished an unpleasant task. 'I shall speak with the baron and Sir Robert to discover how soon we may take you with us into Dorset. In the meantime you may stay here alone until you repent of your impudence.'

Cicely heard her lock the door behind her and go away through the kitchens. She was breathing quickly and nervously but she was not frightened by the darkness and the silence. She rubbed her tingling ear but she scarcely felt that either. A dismay too deep to allow of any other feeling filled her. She was to be sent away from everything she knew and loved–away from Robin. She might never see him again. Then a worse thought struck her. Amicia had spoken of marriage.

She waited until the normal cheerful hubbub from the kitchen told her Amicia had gone and then felt her way to the back of the shed-like structure. Her eyes had grown accustomed to the dark; looking up she could see the long, slanting rafters that were embedded in the kitchen wall. Up there, in the angle where the pantry roof met the wall, and hidden by cobwebs from ignorant eyes, was a small slot window with but one iron bar down the length. After listening a moment, she climbed on the lowest shelf which was of stone and stretched up her arms to the bar. Rotten and flaking with rust, it was only propped in position. Satisfied, she got down and felt around for the pile of sacks she remembered. One would serve for a hood if it still rained. She had not been through that little opening for a long time, and never from this direction, but she was sure she could do it.

When she had climbed the shelves again and removed the bar, she poked out her head. The rain had almost ceased. She struggled through, with an effort, and finally dropped to the soft earth below. There was not a soul about. She swathed herself in the sack, stopping an instant to examine the knee she had skinned on the rough stone. It was bleeding freely but she could still run, if somewhat stiffly.

It was her hobbling gait and the dirty old sack over her head that saved her from detection by the look-out in the hut by the bridge. The two men there gave her only the most perfunctory of glances as she passed out.

Weaver's toft was not far and she was hardly wet, apart from her feet, when she beat on the door. Weaver's wife opened to her and gave a cry of surprise when she saw who it was. But she let her in, hiding her personal misgivings because Weaver, a difficult husband and hard to please in most things, was not at all averse to the continuance of the friendship between his son and the baron's wild young natural. He was an ambitious man and thought there might be gain in it for him if a closer tie should grow from it; his wife had early learned to keep her opinions to herself.

They were all working inside today; even the small girls each held a spindle and the busy twirling never stopped as their heads came round to stare at her. Weaver's own hands continued their deft movements almost independently as he nodded and smiled at Cicely, but the quick flicker of his eyes and jerk of his head towards his wife seemed to mean something to her for she begged in a low, anxious undertone that the visitor would take a cup of ale.

'No–I will not, if you please. It was Robin I came to see.' She saw his parents look at each other, and began to feel uncomfortable. Suddenly conscious of her grimy hands, she hid them behind her.

Weaver was affable. 'Go through into the lanary,' he said, 'if you would speak alone. But be quick.' He gave his son a warning look. 'We must finish this bolt of cloth before nightfall.'

Robin followed her into the dark lanary where the wool was stored, then pulled her on and into the beast-house. It was all under the one roof, houseplace, stable and shippon, but it was warmer where the beasts dwelt.

'Don't go near Black Jake,' said Robin. 'He kicks.' Black Jake was the mule in his stall at the other end. Cicely stopped where she was, close by the place where a cock and his hens were penned behind a lattice of withes.

'Why have you come?' asked Robin when she did not speak.

She felt foolish. Here she was, a grown maid, and because she had been locked up as a punishment she had flown the coop and run to him like a small child. She said all in a rush, 'The Lady says I am to be sent from here. I am to be married.'

Robin turned away. He had grown tall this last year so that he seemed thinner than ever, and there was dark down on his upper lip.

'She locked me in the pantry,' said Cicely.

'How did you get out?'

'Through the hole by the roof. You remember–we got in once and stole some pies.'

'Who are you to marry?'

She was glad then he was not looking at her. 'She did not tell me his name.'

'Well, why do you tell me?' He faced her scowling and, getting no reply, peered closer. 'All maids must marry, I suppose.' He threw out the remark in a gruff, manly tone but his voice played him false as it was still disconcertingly apt to do and rose to an undignified treble on the last syllable.

Her face began to work and she was child enough not to care if he saw it. 'I thought you would care—' Her voice broke on a great sob.

He put his hands on her shoulders hastily. 'I do care. Do not–nay, do not cry. It is that–that I am not surprised. Had you been truly Miller's daughter—'

'Yes? 'She hung on his words.

'Even then,' he said, 'I should have had to marry where my father chose.'

'He would choose me! I know he would. He lets us be alone together.'

He stared about. 'We cannot talk of this now. If the Lady should come back and find you gone. . . . You must return.'

She said, 'I will not! I will run away. Unless— We could run away, Robin–to Taunton–to London even, and be married. They would never find us there. We could find a little house and I would cook for you and you could weave cloth to sell.'

'Yes. Well. . . .' The doubt in his voice was plain. 'Has the baron spoken of this marriage?'

'No, only the Lady. She said–I think she said he hoped for it. But I do not believe her. She thought of it because she does not like me and would be rid of me.'

'Then nothing is sealed. There is no need to worry yet.'

But she was not listening. Her eyes had wandered away and become fixed unseeingly on the chickens that pecked industriously at unseen trifles on the bare earth of their pen. She muttered, 'It may be that my mother will work a magic and she will die as the Lady Ysabel died.'

'Hush!' he said violently. 'Don't speak of death in the same breath as marriage; it is an ill omen. Besides, your mother laid nothing on the Lady Ysabel. She liked her.'

'Yes. Perhaps.' She smudged a hand across her dirty, tear-stained face. 'Let us swear an oath that we will never marry anyone but each other.'

'Where?' he said. 'Not here?'

'Under the sacred tree where the god can hear us.'

'Yes,' he said. 'Yes, we will do that.' He would have promised almost anything just then to get her away. She put her hand out to him but he heard the familiar creak of the door and sprang round just as his father's voice, jovially impatient, boomed at them—'Have done now–have done. That's long enough together!'

Back in the houseplace the young ones were eating bread and lard. That was all they got for dinner on Friday for Weaver was very willing to be a Christian on fast days if he might thereby save a penny. It was this frugality which made his invitation to Cicely to join them less than pressing so that she was able to escape quickly and avoid the necessity of thinking up a lie to account for her visit.

As she ran homeward along the darkening path she thought of the array of dishes on the baron's table even on a fast day and vowed to herself that Robin should never have only bread and lard for his dinner when she had the providing of it; but since her imagination could not take her further than what she knew, it was at a lord's table that she saw them sitting, ordering forth food from a kitchen backed by well-stuffed pantries.

Robin's thoughts moved vaguely round the idea of taking Cicely to wife, but without much hope. Young as he was, he knew the dangers of permitting the gods to overhear the secret longings of the heart.

July–August 1166

Gilbert Foliot ascended the altar steps to say the first Mass of the day. These last nights he had lain awake for hours thinking of the Archbishop's contumelious reply to his protest in the name of all the English bishops, and his eyes still pricked and burned from lack of sleep. That reply had appeared–as did all the exiles' letters–in a manner mysterious and unaccountable, being discovered in his chancery on top of a pile of documents which were to be dealt with that day. Even now, at the foot of the very altar of sacrifice, it was difficult to shut out the memory of those stinging phrases, and the venomous retorts that the evil one had urged upon him.

Not that Gilbert had succumbed to the wiles of Satan. He had not answered the letter at all yet, nor would he, he told himself, until the temptation to respond in kind had left him. But because of it he found himself fidgety and inattentive so that several times he hesitated and lost his way in the familiar prayers. He rattled through the *Munda cor meum* and then, crossing to the Gospel side of the altar, turned his eyes to the Mass Book.

A roll of parchment, sealed with Canterbury's seal, lay between the open pages. Gilbert jerked away as though an adder lurked there, but after a moment he picked it up between finger and thumb and dropped it at the top of the chancel steps. He finished his Mass but his mind was not on it, burning with indignation as he was at the underhand way the letter had come to him. As he genuflected before the altar for the last time he felt about for it and thrust it into his sleeve; he knew the acolyte had seen and that now the news of it would be all round his household before he had sat down to breakfast. The traitor within the gates who had placed it there would think his work well done.

He opened the letter when he was alone. It reiterated all the Archbishop had said before but in even more bitter terms. He sat with it spread out on the table a long time until a clerk came in to inform him that my lord of York was downstairs.

Gilbert sat up quickly. This letter had driven their appointment from his mind. But it was well York was here. He had meant to show him the first one. 'Send him up,' he said.

Roger of York was himself full of the terrible missive Thomas had addressed to the King and those that others of the bishops, including himself, had received from members of the Archbishop's party.

'He lays the blame for this quarrel squarely upon me,' said Gilbert in one of York's infrequent pauses for breath.

'Upon *you*? How so?'

Gilbert's lip turned down. 'He says that I openly oppose truth, stand against justice and confound right and wrong. He also says that I seek to overthrow the establishment of the Holy Church.'

'Surely he is mad?' York picked up the first letter and began to read. Gilbert's eyes followed his down the page; when he came to the words, 'your joint letter which we cannot believe proceeded from your joint wisdom', he looked quickly at York to see if he could detect any change of expression, but York did no more than purse his pink, petulant little mouth and distend his nostrils; it made him look more porcine than ever.

When York read, 'it turned out well for those who were eager for my death and thirsting for my blood', he slapped his hand down on the parchment and cried, 'Always that old story!' but he continued reading and went straight on to the second letter without further comment. Since Gilbert had that practically by heart the words echoed in his brain too. 'If anyone was troubled by my election to the archbishopric, let him not say that his own injury was suffered by the whole kingdom and by the Church. It may possibly be that some ecclesiastics did sigh about that promotion as aspirants generally do when they find themselves disappointed in the hopes they have entertained. And possibly those same persons are now the authors and advisers of the present dissensions, by way of revenge for their misfortune.'

'Well!' said York when he had finally come to an end. 'He certainly sees himself as a lamb of sacrifice.' He began to giggle. '*Do* you blush to stand with the persecutors who in him persecute God? Truly, he is crazed!'

'It is no laughing matter if an archbishop has gone insane.'

The cold rebuke silenced York. 'Yet I do not believe that. His mind is clear enough. But he is a dreadful danger to the Church in that the greater part of the people believe his delusions. Simple folk cannot see through to the overweening pride that lies beneath. You see how incensed he becomes at my truthful observation about his lowly and poor beginnings. He tells me that his family and ancestors were by no means of the lowest station and lists the many benefices he held. Does that show a humble heart?' Gilbert sighed heavily. 'I, of course, mentioned it only to point out how much he owed the King.' He seemed to wait for York to say something, then frowned a little and went on, 'Now that worldliness and pride drive him to ascribe his own ambitions to me!' He regarded York closely. 'When did I ever desire preferment to high office?–I who always knew myself unworthy even to be Bishop of Hereford. Is it known and spoken of me that I am an ambitious man?'

York assured him that it was not, but rather that it was known to all that the Bishop of London was one who followed the scriptural injunction to hide his light under a bushel. But he did not look at Gilbert when he said it, turning his attention instead to the belt about his corpulent middle and easing it out a notch.

The belt was of soft, tooled Spanish leather and the buckle was of gold studded with garnets. The collar of his fine linen shirt was embroidered with gold thread in a design of leaves and flowers, and the stuff of his gown had a sheen that bespoke foreign workmanship.

'Worldliness and pride,' repeated Gilbert as though savouring the words. 'Yea, and love of luxury.'

York clasped his hands over his gold buckle. 'The Pope must act,' he declared. 'When he receives our letter explaining the position here in England he will surely absolve those whom the Archbishop has excommunicated.'

Gilbert moved his eyes slowly up to York's face. 'We must

pray for that,' he intoned. 'We must press him by every means in our power. For indeed'–his voice lost its pulpit timbre–'it is as much for his sake as for ours that he should uphold us against Canterbury. His Holiness cannot realise the peril in which we all stand. If the King become desperate and extend his hand to that other–Pascal, I mean–we are all lost. Though as we told his Holiness, King Henry is most Christian in his faith—'

He broke off there, which was as well, but York's memory somewhat inconveniently supplied 'and most virtuous in the bonds of conjugal chastity', the rest of the quotation. That was how the English bishops had seen fit to describe their prince to their pontiff.

'Will you answer the letter?' York asked after an uncomfortable pause.

The muscles knotted on Gilbert's jaw. 'I must. I have no doubt that what he has said *to* me he has said *about* me. And though, for myself, I had rather suffer in a spirit of Christian resignation, I dare not let such libels go unanswered lest the righteous be persuaded by them into the paths of destruction.' He raised his head to stare challengingly at York. 'I shall tell him that I opposed his election, not because any hopes of my own were thwarted, but because I saw the English church being shamefully deprived of the ancient privilege of choosing her own archbishop. I shall remind him of the indecent haste with which he rushed back to England after Theobald died.' He rose. 'I must write the letter now. Yes, now.'

York seemed a little taken aback but Gilbert thought there was a hint of relief in the speed with which he took his departure. When he had gone Gilbert sat himself down to write the first draft with his own hand.

It did not take long, so swiftly was the quill driven by the vehemence of his feelings. He sat back to read it through. Had he covered every point? He had reviewed the events at Clarendon and at Northampton two years earlier, pointing to the Archbishop's appalling lack of perception in his misjudgement of the King's character and motives. He had commented at length upon the King's exemplary patience throughout, and particularly in the face of such outright insolence as Thomas had displayed in carrying the Cross of Canterbury like a weapon.

No, there was something else. Picking up the quill again, and forgetful for the moment of the exemplary patience, he went on to charge Thomas with cowardice for having fled, leaving his bishops alone to face an enraged King. 'What effrontery then, Father, to invite us to meet death when you showed everyone in the most glaring light that you were terrified of it and seeking to save your skin. It was you who took up arms and held a sword over the hallowed head of the King, and to speak truth, this is the kind of man you are attacking. His dear children, his exceptionally good and noble wife, the many kingdoms subject to him, the riches of the world–all these scarcely dissuade him from spurning all, from stripping himself bare and setting off after our lord Jesus as he carries his cross. And now I may tell you that, in the natural goodness of his heart, he was lately on the point of altering those Constitutions which offended you, and would surely have done so had you remained humble and quiet; but you sent him those terrible letters, savouring neither of the affection of a father nor the modesty of a bishop, and all was destroyed by your threats.'

He smiled to himself when he had finished. The Archbishop might find that difficult to answer.

In that he was right. Thomas never did bother to reply.

In spite of administrative difficulties with so many of his officials *hors de combat* by reason of the fulminations uttered against them, Henry's struggles against the Breton rebels were proving successful. Rafe de Fougères was the last and Henry opined that he would not have to lay siege to his castle for long before he came to his senses. Henry was right. Unlike the Welsh, Rafe played the game of war according to the rules, and the sight of Henry's enormous army told him that he had no hope of holding out. The fact that the Breton barons backed him to the last man had, to his mind, no bearing on his present situation. He was civilised enough to accept a temporary defeat in the certain knowledge that he would be left unharmed to raise another rebellion against the Norman puppet Conan at a more propitious time.

Conan, son of the heiress of Brittany and her first husband, the Earl of Richmond, was bitterly resented throughout the province because he had been intruded into power by Henry FitzEmpress in place of his mother's second husband, Eudo de Porhoët, a Breton lord. Henry's reasons were plain to all. Conan had inherited his father's English earldom and was Henry's vassal.

For years Brittany had simmered under his ineffectual rule until, with his protector and liege fully occupied elsewhere, Rafe de Fougères had risen and rallied the native barons behind Eudo. Their hopes had risen high when news of Henry's illness reached them. Yet here he was, as hale and hearty as if he were under the devil's own protection. As he very probably was, thought Rafe viciously when he was forced to agree that his own daughter should make one of the number of hostages that Henry was demanding as guarantee of his good behaviour.

After the razing of his castle he was dragged to Thouars where Henry forced Eudo himself to do homage to him in the presence of his wife and daughter. The maid was perhaps seventeen at most and beautiful; Rafe could see how the English king's eyes dwelt long on her. So it came as small surprise to hear that she, too, was to go into the tyrant's keeping. For the first time, then, he saw reason to congratulate himself on the lack in his own girl of such maidenly graces.

Certainly Conan, her half-brother, neither would nor could

offer protection to Eudo's lass, he decided a week later in Rennes where Henry was taking formal possession of the duchy. That young man sat limp as a dead fish, and with much the same glazed eye, yea-ing and nay-ing at Henry's command. Yes, he was agreeable that his own infant daughter, Constance, should be betrothed in marriage to Henry's third son, Geoffrey; yes, he recognised Geoffrey as his heir and he now surrendered the whole of Brittany except for the county of Guingamp into Henry's hand to be held in trust until the aforementioned marriage should take place; and no, never in this world would he do or plot aught against his mighty liege and overlord Henry, King of the English, Duke of the Normans. . . .

As the high-sounding titles rolled on, Rafe's wandering eye chanced upon the King of Scots who had an interest here in that his sister was Conan's wife. He might sit on Henry's right hand, thought Rafe, but it was plain he was not enjoying himself. Even a man of small wit might find Henry's dealings in Brittany instructive, especially a man whose own position so closely paralleled that of the hapless Conan. William too held lands in England. Rafe wondered if he were quite so eager to do homage for them now.

October 1166

Henry hesitated with his hand upon the latch. It was still trembling a little with the aftermath of his fury.

He had not intended to come here again but his feet had brought him, regardless. And why not? He was not so simple that he had not known the reason why tonight de Humez, the Seneschal of Normandy and keeper of the hostages, had spoken up for the King of Scots every time Henry had disparaged him. What had he said? That William was virtuous and a man of honour? What he had meant was that Henry was not.

The outrageous assault, ostensibly regarding the tiff which had developed between the Scottish king and himself but more truly, Henry thought, concerning another matter entirely, had finally maddened him. He had ordered de Humez to hold his tongue and stop siding with his enemies; de Humez had fallen grimly silent but at the King's next remark about the unwarranted nature of William's accusations Henry had seen him mutter out of the corner of his mouth to his neighbour. That had been the last straw. He had heard the screaming fury and known it for his own, but he had been as little able to stop it as to hold back a river in full spate. When he was himself again he had found his clothes and his bedcover torn and shredded, the ticking of his mattress ripped apart and the straw scattered in handfuls. His mouth was full of the stuff. De Humez, of course, was gone, and the rest of them only too obviously longing to go too. He had a blinding headache.

He had flung out of the room when the servants came in to set it to rights, and now he found himself here again. Damn de Humez! Damn them all, these old men with their dried-up humours and their outworn codes of what constituted princely honour!

He opened the door and went in to Eudo de Porhoët's daughter.

After Thomas and the Abbot of Pontigny had accompanied the Abbot of Cîteaux to the guest house and seen that he had all he required, they returned to the Abbot's chamber where their interview with the Father-General had taken place. Thomas was prepared to leave the Abbot there and had already bent forward to kiss his ring but the Abbot shook his head and, holding the door wide, invited him to enter again.

Once within, though, he did not seem to know how to begin what he would say but paced about, looking from the crucifix on the wall to the table where the letter the Abbot of Cîteaux had brought still lay, and from there to Thomas who stood by the door with his head bowed and his hands folded in front of him. He coughed several times and finally, stopping in his tracks, motioned Thomas to a stool and said loudly, 'I think it a wretched thing that an Order such as ours, sworn to holy poverty, should be swayed by the loss of worldly possessions.'

Thomas inclined his head dumbly. It was a difficult remark to answer, seeing that the Head of the Order was plainly so swayed. He thought it might have been more to the point if the Abbot had addressed it to him.

'But on my obedience'–the Abbot was muttering to himself–'how can I—? A disgrace to our vows. . . .' He looked at Thomas directly. 'He did say that you must decide for yourself what to do.'

'I cannot see the whole Order injured for my sake. I shall go as soon as I can find somewhere to lay my head.'

The Abbot sat down opposite him. 'Where will you go? To Rome?'

Thomas shook his head slowly from side to side. His mind was only now beginning to function after the first shock of learning that he was to be driven from Pontigny by Henry's threats as he had been driven from England.

'I do not know. I must think.' Rome was a long journey and his purse was practically empty. It would mean appealing once more to Louis for funds.

'Do you believe it possible that your King Henry would truly expel the Cistercian monks from his kingdom and confiscate all their goods? Perhaps if we stood firm—?'

Thomas shook his head. 'My lord, how can you, who saw the swarms of refugees who followed me to escape his wrath, think him incapable? No, I must go.'

'Well,' said the Abbot. 'Well. . . . It is for you to decide. But it shall not be said that you were pressed by us to go.'

After a good deal more in the same vein he allowed Thomas to rise though he kept him a long time in the doorway, doggedly reiterating that for his part Thomas might take as long as he liked to look about for other refuge; it was not until Thomas said that God was his strength and sanctuary and would provide that he removed his restraining hand and let him take his leave. Even then he remained at the door watching him stride away in the October dusk.

Thomas's thoughts were in turmoil. His instant rejection of the Abbot's admittedly half-hearted offer to brave Henry's threats and continue to harbour him had not stemmed from any care for the Order. But he found himself unwilling to consider what it did stem from. It did not matter anyway. He had to go.

Yet when he faced Herbert and the rest with the tidings complete despair momentarily overcame him. 'Let God provide for us now for we have no other help,' he cried.

Herbert had risen to stand in front of him as he sat slumped in his chair but Thomas did not look at him; he had put his hand across his eyes, leaning back with his long legs stretched out and his other arm hanging slackly to the floor. Herbert watched him for a moment while the others watched the two of them. Then he said briskly, 'There is no necessity to repine that I can see. The full authority of the Holy See is behind us and this action of the King's will turn the Pope still further against him. And has not King Louis on a number of occasions promised us sufficient funds to establish ourselves in any city in France?' His head had gone up; he looked almost cheerful.

Thomas took his hand from his face and eyed him. 'I remember. But it seems to me, brother, that you are again yearning for the ostentation of a court and the pleasures of a city which we, who are fettered by the chains of the Gospel, should wish to abandon.' As he spoke his indignation at Herbert's lack of reluctance to leave Pontigny waxed hotter; it ran too near his own desires for comfort. He was searching for a way out of the impasse.

However long they discussed it there appeared to be no way that did not entail applying once more to the King of France.

They all knew that this would further enrage Henry. He would see it as treason; he might even attack Louis because of it. But it was that or surrender, and now that they had caught the tail of the slippery eel success, surrender was impossible.

Herbert volunteered to go to Louis in person at once. 'If the choice is given us,' he said, 'which city will you choose? We should be near the centre of affairs.' But seeing Thomas's sharp shake of the head he went without waiting for an answer.

Thomas gazed into the fire, one log meanly smouldering and that allowed him only because of his bodily infirmity. Sens, he thought. Sens, that lovely city on the Yonne where six great highways met, where there was life and warmth and colour. . . .

November–December 1166

They left the Abbey of Pontigny on a raw November morning of creeping mist, accompanied for the first mile or two by a procession of weeping monks. When they came near the place where the armed escort King Louis had sent awaited them, Thomas called a halt. He had been leading his horse, walking alongside the Abbot; now he turned to him and looked him in the eye, thinking of what he might say to show his gratitude. But the Abbot's glance had gone beyond him to where the glint of pikes and the bright colours of banners showed through the last scanty foliage of the trees. 'You will ride, my lord, with the pomp that befits a prince of the Church.' The Abbot's voice was dry and cool. 'Three hundred men at least wait to escort you. No cardinal could have a more magnificent retinue. And as magnificently, doubtless, you will live in Sens.'

Thomas blinked. 'It was no choice of mine to go. Happily would I have remained a simple monk in holy poverty—'

'Relative poverty, brother, and relative abstinence. We fed you well since your illness; you did not share our poor fare. Nay, I fear that you ate and drank too well. But go back into the world since you must and be sure that we shall always remember you in our prayers.'

'As I you—' began Thomas, but the words of leavetaking dried in his throat when the Abbot did not stop to listen but only gave him his ring to kiss, and then mounted the mule one of the brothers brought forward.

Thomas's little party stood watching the white-cowled figures plod away in an uncertain silence. They walked regimented, two by two, with lowered heads, bare, bony ankles protruding beneath the gowns and sandalled feet slapping in the mud, never deviating to avoid the puddles, as obedient and as apparently mindless as a trail of ants. Not one looked back to sign farewell for all their tears.

The sky had been lightening for some time and as they came round the bend in the road to their escort the first shafts of golden sunlight fell upon them. The sky was delicately blue, the air lit to radiance, and the heaps of fallen leaves showed tawny, russet, amber-gold. Bravely the banners took the sunshine, steel glittered, the horses' quarters shone polished as jet, as new-peeled chestnuts. With a lifting of the heart Thomas spurred forward to join the mighty gathering.

If the leavetaking of the Abbot of Pontigny had been dispiriting, his reception by Archbishop Hugo of Sens and his clergy was not. They welcomed him joyfully and rode with him through the cheering crowds to the Abbey of St Columba just outside the walls. The sight of the sea of delighted faces, roaring approval, heartened Thomas as nothing else could have done. 'Bless us! Bless us!' they shouted, and 'Thomas! Thomas!' the two syllables blending into a staccato drumbeat that quickened his breathing and brought a flush to his cheeks. All the bells of Sens began to peal as they acclaimed him; the sudden dancing carillons brought an unexpected rush of emotion so that for a moment he bent his head; then he raised it again and let the tears flow unashamed. That sent them wild. They showered him with the last fading flowers of autumn; if they had had palms they would have spread them before his feet. Many fainted in the crush and one was trampled, but it was agreed afterwards that Sens would not see such a day for many a year and surely never again such a paragon.

Thomas himself had been at Sens only a day when he saw that life among these Benedictines was to be more comfortable and more rewarding. Their Rule was far less strict than that of the Cistercians, allowing room for the love of beauty and artistic endeavour without which even the soul becomes arid and dry.

The Abbot had told him that during his first days with them he might wander where he would in the monastery. So Thomas set out next morning with Herbert to explore his new home.

They had come into the cloisters, empty now with most of the monks at Terce, and had stood there in silence, listening to the faint, muted chanting. All along the inner wall were the great presses housing the precious manuscripts of the library, opposite them at intervals were the carrels, those little wooden cubicles where the scribes worked at their illuminations. Beyond, through the great arches, the grass showed still green and fresh as summer.

They both jumped as a harsh coughing came from the nearest of the carrels; Herbert, never at a loss and always curious, threw open the door and peered within. Bent over the desk with a tiny brush in his hand was a young monk, thin to the point of emaciation so that his cheekbones stood out sharply under two patches of high colour. When he saw them he sprang up to make obeisance to Thomas and, having kissed his ring, excused himself in case his coughing had disturbed them. He introduced himself as Brother Gilbert and informed them that he had special permission from the Abbot to continue working on his manuscript while the light was good for it was urgently required.

Thomas leaned over, eager to see the book, and caught his breath at the sumptuousness of the work. This must be to the order of a great lord or the King of France himself. Each beautifully painted capital flowed intricately into curves and whorls and the margins of the pages were filled with a pattern of leaves and fruit depicted to the life in shining, brilliant colours. Herbert too stared entranced, exclaiming over birds and beasts with human heads, and then began to laugh, recognising the Abbot's face, large ears, hook nose and all, upon the body of a swan.

'And has he seen his likeness?' he cried when he had recovered his breath, 'or was it in ignorance that he gave you leave to continue?'

The monk smiled ruefully. 'He has not seen that,' he admitted, 'but, see you, I made him very small and the Abbot's sight is not good. It seems to me at times the brush has a will of its own for the likenesses appear despite my will.' He peeped at them uncertainly. 'You will not tell him?'

'Not I,' Herbert assured him, and Thomas smilingly shook his head. He began to examine the pots of colour on the desk and the leaf or two of gold that lay beside them.

The young monk began to cough again and, when it became plain that he would have no more breath to spare for talking, Thomas and Herbert moved away.

Outside, Thomas said slowly, 'I do not like the sound of that cough.'

'He won't live another year.' Herbert began to whistle softly. 'But the book will be finished by then. At least he will leave something to show he once was here.'

'Yes,' said Thomas, 'so he will.' But he could not decide whether it was of any importance if his name was utterly forgot.

A little over a month later Herbert came into Thomas's chamber. Here the bed was long enough so that he might lie at full stretch instead of being forced to choose between sleeping with his knees drawn up or having his feet stick out unsupported from the end as he had at Pontigny, and a coverlet of green say was laid over it. And here a real fire burned; there was even a little pot containing dried herbs on the mantel and the room smelled sweet for Thomas had just strewn a handful on the flames. A press for his gowns flanked the chimney-breast where it might catch the warmth; no longer did he go to change and find the clothes damp and spotted with mould. Painted monograms of Christ, Our Lady and the Apostles decorated the walls, and the window had a pleasant view over the orchard.

Thomas sat beside the fire with a large volume open on his knees. He raised his eyes, smiling, as Herbert entered. 'Would you believe, Herbert, there are even secular works in the Abbot's library?' Then his eyes fell on the package in Herbert's hand. 'A letter?'

'From Nicholas de Monte in Rouen.'

Thomas took it quickly and broke the seals. It was long and it took some time to read. Herbert made to go, then stayed at the sharp movement of Thomas's hand and, pulling up a stool, sat warming his hands at the blaze.

Not lifting his eyes from what he was reading Thomas said, 'The King has arrested the papal courier to whom you gave our letters.'

Herbert's mouth came open. 'Arrested the Pope's letter-carrier?'

Thomas looked at him. 'The courier confessed under torture that the letters were handed to him by you.'

'The King is in Rouen?'

'He is. He has refused even the Empress's demands for the man's release.' Thomas began to walk quickly up and down. 'He has also discovered that that clerk of Geoffrey Ridel's–Master Walter–met with you and he is swearing to punish him for failing to arrest you. Nicholas says that both the Archbishop of Rouen and the Bishop of Lisieux have reproved the King for his actions. Much good that will do!' He bent his eyes to the letter again.

'What other news?' asked Herbert in some anxiety.

'Oh–the Master of the Canterbury hospital is at present in Rouen; he told Nicholas that the Bishop of London has paid all the income belonging to my clerks into the King's treasury.' Herbert opened his mouth indignantly but closed it again when Thomas continued, 'The Prior of Christchurch has imprisoned one of his monks for speaking in my favour.' He worried at his lip. 'Torture and incarceration are the rewards of truth in these evil days.'

Herbert tutted softly under his breath; he was able to accept such things with equanimity seeing that only thus could souls be tried in the heavenly balances.

'Bath is dead,' Thomas announced, 'as is Geoffrey de Mandeville.'

'De Mandeville!' Herbert exclaimed, almost forgetting to cross himself in his surprise. 'How did he die? He was not old.'

But Thomas did not answer and the sudden consternation on his face as his eyes flew over the rest of the letter kept Herbert silent until the last page was turned. He watched in mounting anxiety as Thomas laid the parchments down and rubbed his fingers across his brow. He looked at Herbert at last. 'What was it you said?' he asked.

'How did de Mandeville die?'

'In operations against the Welsh with de Luci. They were attacked while fortifying Basingwerk and suffered heavy losses. De Luci has taken the Cross and proposes to go to Jerusalem.' It did not sound as though his mind was on what he was saying.

'But he is excommunicate!'

Thomas raised his eyes and looked at Herbert for a long moment. 'He is absolved.'

'What—? How—? Has the Pope—?'

Thomas's lips were pinched yet they shook a little. He spoke in a low voice and hurriedly. 'News of a letter which the King has received from John of Oxford in Rome is all over Rouen. Yes, it was true that he actually sent an excommunicate to the Holy Father himself. And he was received graciously by Alexander who granted everything that Henry asked. John was absolved immediately and confirmed as Dean of Salisbury.'

Herbert flushed up to his hair. 'Jesu mercy! Are they all absolved?' he cried.

'The Holy Father has appointed papal legates to settle the King's dispute with me and the understanding was that they would absolve the others when they arrived. But it was allowed that if any were in danger of death in the meantime any member of the clergy might absolve them.' His mouth turned down. 'So Henry has very sensibly sent them all into some kind of danger–to Wales or on a Channel crossing. We may take it, I think, that they are all safely back in the bosom of Mother Church. And I am further forbidden to molest any of them before the arrival of the legates.'

Dismay was written large upon Herbert's face.

'As soon as the names of the legates are announced our friends in Rome will inform us of them.' Thomas smiled thinly. 'I think that when we hear the names we shall know whether Pope Alexander has truly abandoned us. But at least he made John abjure the Customs before he would absolve him.'

'Whatever his reasons, the Pope has served us very ill. Here is principle at stake—' Herbert would tell these papal legates a thing or two they might have missed. He would like to tell the Pope too.

Nor did Thomas rebuke him for the intemperance of his language. Everything Herbert said was exactly true. He had been betrayed when he was on the very point of success. And for what? That the Pope might stand in good odour with Henry FitzEmpress. The armour of meekness and self-discipline that he had cultivated so assiduously at Pontigny sloughed off with an ease that astonished Herbert almost as much as it gratified him. The only person who might not have been surprised at the sight of the Archbishop's white lips and blazing eyes was the Abbot of Pontigny, and he was not there to see.

VII
February 1167

Lent had begun but even the promise of Easter at the end of it brought no balm to Thomas's sore heart. He had spent the past month or two between extravagant bouts of self-pity when he shut himself away for days on end, and composing violently denunciatory letters to his bishops in England. He had even despatched an accusing letter to the Pope informing him, under the thinnest veil of courtesy, that he was as a reed in the eyes of the world. Nor did he regret it though underneath his moods something niggled at him. If it was the loss of the judiciousness for which he was famed, he thought that the bitter satisfaction of speaking his mind more than compensated.

He had heard from the Pope himself since then, though not of course in answer to that letter which must take weeks, if not months, to reach its destination. Alexander's message gave a somewhat different version of the events which had aroused his furious indignation. But it came to the same thing in the end, even when wrapped up in benign phrases. As that, 'Wherefore we ask, command and advise your Excellency to bear with the King patiently, and in the meantime not to decree anything against him or any of his subjects that would hurt or damage him' meant only the blank fact that he was again suspended from his functions as Metropolitan.

As for the legates, there was no mention of their power to judge and sentence, only a carefully-worded announcement that they had been sent to try to make peace. Thomas knew that they were already approaching Provence. Rumour had it that they would venture no further without a safe-conduct through Louis' lands and, in view of the French king's anger with the Pope, might stay there some time. But in the end the evil day would come and he would be thrown to the wolves.

When one of the Abbey servants announced that there were visitors below Thomas merely acknowledged him with an unsmiling nod and was in no mood to go down. But when he entered the guest chamber he saw a small, round, cheerful-looking man who sat there in earnest conversation.

'John Short!' he cried, his face lightening.

John of Salisbury came forward and kissed him warmly. 'See who I have brought you,' he said. 'One whom you had scarce hoped to see again, I think.'

Thomas looked beyond him. The room was dark so that he could not for a moment make out the other's features. He stood there, hesitant, almost as though unsure of his welcome. Then with a shock of pleasure Thomas knew him.

'It is really he, Thomas,' John said. 'William Fitzstephen. He is in France with the King's permission. The foolish fellow had doubts about whether you would wish to see him.'

'You did not? William, there is no one I am happier to see!' His face bore witness to the truth of that. 'But it is so long since I heard from you.' Indeed it was. He had had no more than three letters from Fitzstephen in the two years since their separation.

When they had brought themselves up to date with each other's news, Thomas said, 'You–are not come to stay permanently?'

William shook his head. 'Not because I do not wish it but that I cannot burden you with yet another mouth to feed.

Besides, where I am I can keep you informed of the King's designs; those few I may discover.' He looked at Thomas, seeing with a profound pity the changes in him, the accentuated thinness, the lines of worry graven deep between his brows. 'I had thought you might add two more to your household a little while ago; Worcester and Hereford. They stood out for you so strongly against the King that he told them to go and join you, but with the uncomfortable proviso that if they did they should never come again into England.'

'Hereford?' Thomas was taken by surprise.

'He had a change of heart, though I'm of the opinion that the fear of death had more to do with it than Worcester's arguments. At any rate he's far too ill to travel and looks to get no better in this world. You know that Bath and Lincoln are both dead?'

'I knew only about Bath.'

'He died last summer; Lincoln on the last day of October.'

Thomas nodded with what seemed almost like satisfaction. 'God is making plain his power.' William looked nonplussed; John gave a little cough. 'Yes. God will deal justly even if those who stand in his stead here on earth will not.' He met their eyes. 'You have heard how I am cut down by one who should be my shield and protector?'

They nodded, watching him close.

'Have you heard the names of the men who are to judge me? William of Pavia, purchased by King Henry as a mouthpiece at the papal court, and Otho of Ostia! One treacherous and crafty, the other weak and fickle. Both are avaricious!'

John said mildly, 'Otho is of good repute, I thought–but still, I grant you, a Roman and a cardinal.'

'Yes, honest John, and we know what that means. I am sold and delivered to the followers of Baal by the Pope's own hand. But I shall refuse to all eternity to accept their judgements. The Church goes to her ruin by the crooked paths of riches; she has been prostituted like a whore who is accessible to the lust of any in the streets. Princes fornicate with her at will. Woe to us all!'

The outburst startled the listeners. After a moment Thomas said grimly, 'I have written to William of Pavia. He shall not think that I am under any misapprehensions concerning what they intend me.'

'You have sent it?' John's tone was alarmed.

'Not yet. It is only the rough draft. I will show you.' He rang the little bell that stood on the table and when the servant came told him to send one of the clerks to fetch the papers he had been working on.

John leaned forward while they waited. 'I would have you consider the Pope's position, Thomas. The Emperor is thrusting once more into northern Italy—'

'I know it. His letter to me ended with a plea for alms–not to myself, to be sure, whose purse is leaner than most, but asking me to apply to the Count of Flanders on his behalf.'

'Do you not see that he is not a free agent?'

Thomas's voice was cold. 'I see only that the renowned city which once subdued the whole world is subverted by the craving for human favour. Is the Church's liberty to be exchanged for personal gain?'

Before John could reply the clerk came in with the papers Thomas had sent for. John took them from his hand and went towards the window to get a better light. He did not stand there long. 'You cannot send this,' he said, appalled.

Thomas set his lips together.

'He has not yet done anything to provoke such rudeness. And if he sends it to the Pope the King's case will appear justified. You will be convicted of contumacy by the evidence of your own writing.'

A shadow passed over Thomas's face. He was remembering another letter in which the writer stood condemned out of his own mouth.

'It is excessively full of suspicion and biting sarcasms.

William, tell him.'

William, who had been reading during this exchange, looked up. 'I agree with John. It would be most unseemly to address a cardinal-priest and legate of the Holy See in such terms.'

Thomas sat down. 'You see the anguish I labour under. Now you, my friends, attack me and will doubtless desert me.' His eyes had filled up with tears.

'Attack you? Never!' they both cried at once, and while William ineffectually patted his shoulder John seated himself in front of him and talked, firmly yet kindly, of the great numbers of friends and well-wishers he had, and of how even the Empress herself was said to have cried out upon her son for his behaviour. 'Allow me to address William of Pavia in your name,' he begged, 'and do not lose heart. For of this I am sure–the Holy Father will never see you deposed or unjustly judged.'

William said, 'Do you not remember another time, my lord, when all seemed lost? Yet were we delivered out of the midst of foes by God's hand.' He gazed before him, seeing again the scene in the hall at Northampton when they were threatened by the King's marshals. 'I asked you then to pray so'–he placed his hands together with a meaning look–'when Herbert was urging you to excommunicate our enemies. It seems to me, as it has always seemed, that a display of mildness is more like to disarm rage—'

'If I, William, had done as you and remained in England I should now be dead and the cause lost,' said Thomas sharply. 'You, like many others, persist in believing that this battle is between the King and myself. It is nothing of the sort. It is between Henry and God.'

William reddened and after a moment John stood up. He was feeling sorry for William, who had travelled a long way to see his idol. It was plainly useless to offer further advice to Thomas just now, but he was not too worried. Thomas kicking against the pricks was no new sight but he was too true a Christian to miss the point of William's gentle reminder. After it had worked a while in his mind he would be all the readier to listen to their counsels.

When Thomas had gone he said slowly, 'He must allow me to write that letter for him.'

'I find him changed–much changed,' William muttered. Then, almost inaudibly, 'I had thought him–perfect.'

John saw the pain in his face and looked away. He wondered for an instant whether he should say something but decided against it. Instead he reflected upon the First Commandment and then upon the chief of the seven deadly sins, and not for the first time was led to wonder what dire sin he himself, out of invincible ignorance, regularly committed. But the piercing scrutiny of his own conscience was without result. He, who could see all too clearly the motes in his brothers' eyes, was still unable to discover the beam within his own.

June 1167

The hall of Burgh Castle was quieter now that most of the packing and preparation for the move was completed. Shafts of sunlight lit the damp-stained walls and dusty corners. A fragrance of wood-smoke and cooking drifted through the open windows and mingled with the mouldy smell of the decaying rushes that had been swept up into a great heap at one side. All the hangings had been taken down so that the footsteps of the men who came and went with the last of the great corded bundles rang hollow in the empty vastness.

They did not bother to lower their voices in the presence of the lady who sat in the alcove of the wall under the high window, since every one of them knew that she, who should have been mistress here, was held of no account in any of de Morville's manors but the one she had brought him on their marriage. That was Knaresborough, and they were more careful of her dignity there, but here, on Solway shore in the birth-place of their master, they needed not to bother.

She sat in monumental stillness, guarding a small child in the circle of her arm, a huge woman of a doughy, pallid fairness. One might have thought (as her husband did) that nothing could ever move her as she sat gazing straight before her with eyes of blank slate-blue. But when a different step sounded on the flags the eyes lost their blind look and very slowly, very cautiously, she turned her head.

The hall was empty now except for rubbish; everything had gone below to be loaded on the sumpter mules. Even the garners outside were bare, their contents transferred to the wagons. It was a man carrying a little girl who had entered. Both were black-haired and black-eyed and both were of an extraordinary beauty. But after one look Helwis de Morville returned to her immobility. She was still straining to hear–or to make sure she no longer heard–the far off but all too clear sounds of some creature in an extremity of pain.

Now there was only silence and she could breathe again. It was over. But she feared to stand lest her legs betray her and prove to the man who stood before her that there was indeed a way to undermine the imperturbability that was her only defence against him. Let him think her stolid and insusceptible as an ox. It was safer so, knowing as she did the refined and exquisite cruelty that was, she thought, the only thing that gave him pleasure. She had almost forgotten the girl she once had been, loud, garrulous and light, and too simple to recognise malevolence when she met it. But now she remembered her for some reason and she thought–I can't go on. I can't. I am afraid.

The sense of his words did not penetrate when he spoke; she had to lift her head and stare at him. He was only saying with some impatience, 'Will you sit here all day? Where is your woman? Come below at once.'

She got up then so hastily that she disturbed the little one at her breast and it let out a long, shrill wail. His face moved with disgust; shifting the child to her other arm she drew her gown swiftly across the sagging breast. 'I–I am ready,' she muttered, staring distractedly about her. But he did not mention her forbidden feeding of the child who was now above two years old, though very small.

He said shortly, 'Come then. We are drinking a stirrup cup outside. We shall be away within the hour.'

They were sitting about on the mounting-blocks near the stables, the force of mounted men he had brought with them, drinking ale and cracking jokes, but they sprang up quickly enough when their lord and his lady approached. Standing sipping from the mug somebody placed in her hands she wondered what they were waiting for. But when she saw a gaunt man come with dragging feet towards them she knew.

He stopped a good few yards away and stood with downbent head and arms hanging loosely at his sides; his face was pinched and pale. Hugh de Morville glanced up and then idly away; only the watching woman saw the look of venomous hatred the churl shot him and her face remained expressionless. Finally Sir Hugh desisted from his playful tickling of the little girl he still held and put her by, rising to face the man. 'It is done?'

'As you ordered, my lord.'

'All were there to watch?'

'All. He is dead now. My lord–my lord, may we quench the fire and remove the body from the cauldron?'

The woman moved then, but when Hugh turned to glance at her she was still again. She said, 'Grant him this, husband, I beg.'

'To what end, wife?'

She swallowed. 'That they–may have something to bury.' In her mind's eye she saw what she had been smelling, a pot of stew left too long to boil, rendered down to a brown, amorphous glue but for the white bones.

He stroked the head of the child beside him. 'That cannot be.'

She thought dully, had I not interfered, he might have granted it. He might. His eye would not have fallen on the babe. The old misery took her by the throat as she looked at the child she cradled, at the heavy-lidded, slanted eyes, the too-small nose, the open, drooling mouth.

'They must learn, wife, who is master here. I have been long away but that does not give them leave to touch my harvests.'

She thought, they would have starved else after the last one failed; but she dared not say it.

He turned again to the new reeve. 'Leave him to cook,' he said. 'We shall see then how true your tales of famine are.'

From the passage where she had been hiding Cicely saw Beta come across the hall towards her. She had for a short time escaped Amicia's all-seeing eye because the Lady had left her to deal alone with a pile of sewing while she went to the tower room to ensure that all was well with Lady Maud. Even the madwoman did not frighten her and since Amicia's coming there had been far fewer of the outbursts of shrieking and wild laughter that had been part of the pattern of life in Cicely's early days at the manor house. Lady Maud was quite docile now. That was because she thought she was a little girl again and Amicia her mother, but only Amicia knew that.

Everyone else marvelled at the bravery of unloosing the chain and sitting at the window with the madwoman to feed the birds. No one would even have known of it except that a serving maid had spotted Lady Maud's face peering down and had run screaming lest she be infected by her look. But that in turn had frightened Lady Maud and for the next few days she had grabbed at anything that alighted on the sill. When she finally caught a bird and tore off its wings Amicia had been so angry that she had slapped her; and perhaps that connected in her mind with some early misdemeanour, for after that she would quail at the first hint of Amicia's displeasure.

What she knew of this passed swiftly through Cicely's mind as she waited for her mother, for it was of Amicia she wished to speak to her. Three months in Dorset with that lady had confirmed her original dislike of her. But now she was home again; today was St John's Day and the eve of it was a time of powerful magic.

Beta saw her as she entered the passage, and stopped.

'Did you—?' began the girl.

Beta put her finger to her lips and looked behind her; seeing no one near she took Cicely's arm and walked her along beside her. 'It is done,' she said. 'You need fret on it no more.'

They walked a few steps in silence; Cicely was unsure how to frame the questions she longed to ask. She knew her mother did not like to talk of such secret matters, but she remembered how she had looked when Amicia's words were repeated to her. It had seemed to Cicely that the gentle mask she showed the world had slipped a little and revealed beneath it the blank-eyed face that, crowned with ivy, gazed unmoved on blood and pain and death. Yet Beta had done nothing then, nor mentioned it again until Cicely's womanhood had come upon her. But what she had demanded and taken with her last night proved that that was what she had been waiting for.

She brought it out at last. 'Will–will the Lady die?'

'The Lady?' Beta sounded astonished. 'What has she to do with it?'

'I thought—'

Beta shook her head. Her face was remote and cold again. 'Nay,' she said, 'she shall not be discomfited for me, or you either. It is he who shall be let from his purposes.' She stopped before they reached the kitchen door. 'You will never marry where the baron chooses,' Beta said.

The villeins were folding their beasts in the baron's field for the night and by the gap in the hurdles Herluin the bailiff stood to watch that none slipped craftily by and penned his animals on his own toft, thus depriving his lord's land of the benefit of the dung. He nodded and grunted as each man passed, pretending not to hear the habitual grumbling, but when old Jokkyn who was reeve this year came up, he remarked on the fairness of the evening and they stood together while the rest of the cattle were driven in.

Suddenly a pebble rattled on the path and two dim figures passed on the other side of the hurdles, so closely linked they moved as one. Herluin stiffened and laid a warning hand on Jokkyn's arm. Jokkyn shook him off impatiently.

The young couple were making for the gnarled old elder trees whose arching branches formed an arbour at the corner of the demesne field. The spot had been a trysting place longer than anyone could remember and nothing the baron might say could persuade the villagers that they should be felled. This was because they were sacred to the Elder Mother, most ancient and jealous of the old gods; and here, in this verdant cave, roofed in season by leaves or flowers, she blessed the village unions long before the priest. The pungent scent of elder blossom was bound too closely to the sweet recollections of youth for any man lightly to take his axe to them, and so they remained a refuge for generations yet to come.

Now again the elder was in bloom, the flat, creamy corymbs glimmering ghostly through the dusk. Jokkyn winked and nodded in that direction.

Herluin eyed him haughtily. 'Who was that?'

Jokkyn put on the vacant look that was second nature to a serf. 'Two of the young 'uns going for the Old Gal's blessing.' He cackled suddenly. 'You ain't telling me you've forgot—?'

'It looked to me like Beta's Cicely.'

Jokkyn whistled softly, though whether in surprise or derisive comment Herluin could not be sure. But he was sure the boy had been Weaver's son.

'Was it Cicely?' he said.

Jokkyn pursed his lips. 'Too dark to tell.'

'Have you seen them before?' He nodded towards the trysting place. 'Going down there?'

Jokkyn's voice was injured. 'I don't peep at young lovers.'

Herluin stared at him suspiciously, then looked at the western sky where the last of the afterglow still lingered. 'They'll not be long if they're to be indoors an hour after sunset.'

'It don't take long though, do it?' returned the older man companionably. 'That's a game can be played in a Paternosterwhile. And she's a fine, big girl now–ripe for bedding.'

'It *was* Cicely then!'

Jokkyn tried his vacant look again, with less success. His eyes fell before the bailiff's.

'Very well. We'll wait here for them to come back. And you'll bear me witness.'

Jokkyn was alarmed. 'It's nigh on curfew now,' he objected. 'I'm away home to my supper.'

'Quiet!' hissed Herluin. 'They'll hear if you shout like that.'

'Aye.' Jokkyn lowered his voice not at all. 'I doubt not they've heard us and gone back the other way.' He grabbed at Herluin's arm as the other made to hurry down the lower track. 'Leave be,' he advised. 'Who'll thank you for such news? That lass–who can she marry? Weaver's a freeman, ain't he? She'll do no better.'

'Fool!' shouted Herluin. 'Do you think the baron will let her marry on his manor? Never!'

'Well,' said Jokkyn, content now that the young ones must have heard him and been warned, 'no man of degree will marry with her. She've villein blood.'

'Coin pays for all. She'll be well dowered.'

'Ain't no amount of silver will weigh against her mother's blood,' said Jokkyn with the invincible snobbery of one who accepts his station in life and cannot see why others should not do the same. 'She've done well to get Weaver's lad–if she have got him. Weaver have plenty of coin of his own.'

'Pah!' said Herluin, but he turned and strode towards the manor house. Jokkyn continued to air his views to the darkening sky.

'And he don't do week-work neither. Pays rent for his toft, Weaver do. And if his lad wed with that maid, e'en that may be remitted.' He cast a sardonic eye over the cattle in the baron's field. 'God too always shit on the biggest dung heap,' he observed to them before he moved away.

Manor Court was over and while the baron waited for Robert to return he ran his eye over the last page of Herluin's account of the business done–'dragged him by his hair out of his house, to his damage 4d and to his dishonour 2d' ran the last line.

Robert and Herluin, having shown out all who were not staying to dinner, were whispering together at the end of the hall. If Herluin had something to tell that called for a mediator, it should have been dealt with while his Court was sitting, thought the baron. He rapped sharply with his staff on the chair leg and saw them look towards him; then Robert came hurrying to his side. 'What were you discussing?' he said.

'Oh–just that Leofric pleads time to pay.'

'Hmph! Does he not always?' said the baron. 'Herluin is growing soft if he believes their tales. They do well, those cottars–he and Weaver and Smith. I shall raise their rents.' He pushed at one of the small piles of silver pennies on the board before him. 'Look at that. Little enough revenue I get from fines and amercements now with the King taking the lion's share in his courts.'

Robert inclined his head. 'Aye, it's true the cottars do well. Particularly Weaver.' He paused but the baron was still staring glumly at the money on the table and said nothing. 'He is a hard worker, he and all his family. He deserves reward for such hard labour.'

'The reward he shall reap is a higher rent,' said the baron, 'since by your admission he can afford it.'

'Moreover,' continued Robert as if he had not heard, 'he is a devout man who loves religion—' He turned his eyes suddenly to his father. 'Higher rent?'

'See here, my son,' his father said, 'I know this man you are praising. Yea, it is truth he works hard and, as you tell me, works his children hard. You say he loves religion.' He stretched forth his hand and picked up a shortcross penny, turning it to the obverse side. 'This is the cross he loves. And if he can compass a profit by pulling on his cloth to make ten ells eleven, he will call that good business. Now what is all this about?'

Robert opened his mouth and then closed it again. He knew with what eagerness his father was awaiting the result of his first tentative overtures to Amicia's kin. How could he tell him that the girl for whom he had such grandiose plans was behaving like a village slut? Amicia would be blamed for not keeping her close–and perhaps the whole tale was nothing but the product of loose tongues and evil minds. Best to keep silence and hope it would blow over.

'Oh–nothing,' he said weakly. 'You spoke of raising the rents?'

They began to discuss this and Herluin, sliding quietly back a while later to gather up the money and the parchments, was puzzled; he could not discover in their faces an inkling of what reward he might expect for his faithful care of his lord's interests.

August 1167

The Pope had sent for Cardinal Gratian, his sub-deacon and Notary of the Holy See. While he waited for him he sat fingering an orange stuffed with spices on the desk before him and considered what course of action he should take now in the dispute within the English church. The orange was a safeguard against the plague that was raging in Rome but they had had no cases here in Benevento, neither did Alexander fear any since this was manifestly a visitation upon God's enemies. The victims, dying in their thousands, were those forces of the Emperor's who, a month ago, had stained the very altar of St Peter's with blood. Rainald of Cologne, the schismatic archbishop, was one of them. For he had managed at last to bring his puppet-Pope into the Holy City itself where he had crowned the Empress Beatrice and re-crowned Frederick Emperor of the Holy Roman Empire. And where was the Pope-maker now? Boiling in a tub of brine since that was the only feasible way to get his bones safely back to Germany.

He heard Gratian coming and looked up. 'What news?'

'The Emperor has withdrawn from Rome.'

'*Laus Deo*. Now we shall have a breathing-space to turn our minds to other matters. And principally, I think, to England.'

'Yes, indeed. Even King Henry's Italian connections cannot replace the numbers the Emperor has lost.'

'I think we can afford to be just a little less accommodating towards him.'

Gratian studied the Holy Father. He, who was privy to the letters which warned the opposing sides of intentions so strangely at variance, suspected that Alexander's sympathies had lain all along with Archbishop Thomas. But as Notary he knew better than most what difficulties confronted a pope who must be a politician as well as Christ's Vicar on earth.

'You will not allow the legates final jurisdiction now,' he commented.

'No. We shall write and tell them that their brief is to effect a reconciliation only.' Fiddling with the orange, he knocked it to the floor.

Gratian picked it up. 'I wish I had not sent permission to York to crown the King's son when we had to flee from Rome,'

Alexander said musingly, 'but we were at our lowest ebb and King Henry was insistent. I swear his messengers and envoys wore down the doorsill of our hall.'

'Why should it matter?'

The Pope sighed. 'Canterbury writes to me that it is his prerogative. Though how he knew about it. . . . It may be a cause of further quarrels.' He straightened up in his chair. 'But for now–now we will write to the legates ordering them to use every means in their power to press King Henry to take back the Archbishop into his favour.'

October–November 1167

Henry had just flung down the pen after signing the last of the documents before him when he became aware that the Earl of Essex was at his elbow. This was the new earl, Geoffrey de Mandeville's younger brother William, who had served the Count of Flanders honourably since his father had made their name a stink in the nostrils of decent Englishmen and who was still diffident about returning to his homeland after nearly twenty years. But he filled his place at court with more grace than Geoffrey had ever done, Henry thought, being courteous yet outspoken and entirely lacking in the crawling servility that had characterised his brother. That the difference between the two might have had to do with the masters each had served never crossed Henry's mind. He had taken a fancy to William from the first and admitted him to an intimacy that the rest of the barons thought such short acquaintance scarcely warranted.

'The papal legates are in Caen,' said Essex.

Henry stood up quickly. 'So soon! They've wasted no time crossing Normandy. Well'–he laughed –'they and the Pope as well as myself will be glad to see this business over, I've no doubt. We'll drink a cup of wine to a happy outcome.'

He was in the best of tempers now, cracking jokes and

chaffing Essex. After all, he had waited long for this moment; it had been at the back of his mind this whole year, encouraging him through all the trials he had had to endure–Louis' unprovoked attacks on the Norman border (though he had made him pay dearly for them), another rising in Brittany, rumblings from Aquitaine. And then, only six weeks ago, the death of his mother in the same month that his own little Matilda set off for Germany to become, he hoped, in the fullness of time another Empress of the Germans. He had been surprised at the depth of his grief at their loss; yet the heart-warming conviction that he had the Pope in his pocket had borne him up.

So it was that his welcome of the Cardinals William and Otho lacked nothing in warmth; he had them sit and did them great honour, insisting that they, as princes of the Church, be served with wine before himself. If either of the clerics noticed the irony they covered it well and listened with patience and understanding to the long list of charges their host brought against his Archbishop.

'You may plainly see,' Henry concluded, 'that the real reason for his flight was that debt of forty-four thousand marks which he was determined not to pay me. Or'–he spoke as one moved by a generous impulse –'possibly could not pay, having spent the money on ostentatious living which, as your Eminences realise, is unfitting for an ecclesiastic.'

Cardinal Otho's whimsical, humorous mouth twitched a little at that but the benignity of his glance did not alter as he asked the lord King to enlarge a little further on his accusation that the Archbishop had incited King Louis to make war on him. Henry did so and magnified it to include the Count of Flanders as another recipient of Thomas's evil advice.

Having embellished his case considerably by the end of the afternoon, he went away in a high good humour to await the result of the cardinals' private deliberations, and was surprised to find them seeking another audience before a couple of hours had passed.

'What more is there to say?' he asked Essex, and then, answering himself, 'Some trifle, I suppose, that only a churchman would stickle at. Send them in here.'

It was Otho who came nearest, William of Pavia seeming to hang back. 'Now that we have heard your side of the case, my lord King,' said Otho, 'and before we go to hear the Archbishop's answers to it, we must tell you how far our powers extend; it is not, I fear, as far as you, or even we, were led to believe.' He fumbled within his sleeve and brought out a roll of parchment. 'This message'–he held it out–'was handed to us only two days ago. It clearly defines our jurisdiction.'

Henry put out his hand and Otho advanced a few steps to lay the roll in it. Then he retired to stand beside Cardinal William.

Henry frowned as he took in the Papal Seal. He broke it and flattened the parchment without taking his eyes from the legates. Then he lowered his gaze to it.

When he had finished his breathing was heavy. 'So—' he said. 'It was all a trick to gain time, was it?' He got up so suddenly that the other men jumped. 'No wonder you took nine months to come from Rome! You dallied on the way to see which way the Emperor's cat would jump. And listened to me, all smiles–God damn you! And God damn the Pope, too! You have taken my money—'

Essex saw Otho shake his head; the gesture seemed to enrage Henry further; he began to swear horribly, using those English words such as men hurled at balky horses and at the dogs when they were underfoot. 'Go to Becket then,' he shouted, 'and listen to his twistings and evasions. But this I tell you! You will never move me so you had best take care to move him. Or come not back to me again!' Over Henry's shoulder Essex signalled fiercely at the legates to be gone.

That William of Pavia was obviously only too ready to do

but Otho lingered a moment or two in the comparative safety of the doorway; it was hard to read the expression on his broad, inscrutable face but Essex was sure it was compounded more of interest and amusement than of either fear or horror. He'll have a tale to tell at the Curia, he thought, and a vocabulary unusual in a prince of the Church if he listens much longer.

Then he turned back to Henry. He had flung himself down on the floor where he was drumming with his heels, purple-faced from stuffing rushes into his mouth.

It was on a Sunday almost exactly a month later that the cardinals returned to the King, though this time they found him at Argentan on yet another of his incessant, restless journeys about the province. William of Pavia grumbled sourly about that, too.

'A waste of time, all of it,' he said, 'when one is as immovable as the other. What can Canterbury hope to gain by such intransigence? Refusal to compromise for fear of precedent is the classic folly of weak men.'

'And of martyrs,' Otho remarked urbanely.

Cardinal William ignored that. 'If King Louis had been prepared to listen to my suggestion that Canterbury be transferred to one of his sees— Oh well, we have done our best.'

He had cheered up a little, though, when King Henry rode two leagues out of Argentan to meet them and greeted them with great effusiveness. But he did not much like the interested glances Otho kept shooting at the King; it confirmed his suspicion that his brother cardinal had approached their mission in the wrong spirit entirely and was deriving a great deal of secret enjoyment from proceedings which all right-thinking men would deplore.

He made his report next day in a state of extreme discomfort. 'That we were to have no success with the

Archbishop of Canterbury was plain to me from the beginning,' he announced, 'for there were already whispers going round the conference of a dream he purported to have had the night before–he dreamed that poison in a golden cup was offered him. We were not meant to hear this story, you may be sure, and I merely tell it that you may see that he came unwilling even to consider our arguments. Both he and King Louis denied utterly that he had ever persuaded the French king to make war upon King Henry. When we accepted that, as we were bound to do, they swearing upon oath, we told him that humility and moderation might appease King Henry's anger against him, but to that he only turned away his face.

'We then pointed out to him that his king has loved and honoured the Roman Church and how he is asking no more than the rights and customs his predecessors had enjoyed from the Archbishop's predecessors. But he said'–William swallowed and studiously kept his eyes from Henry's –'that the Pope, in our own presence at Sens, had mercifully absolved him of his previous pledge to obey the Constitutions, and that he would sooner bow his neck to the executioner than consent to them again.' Out of the corner of his eye William saw Henry's sharp movement, and rushed on. 'I asked him in that case if it would not be better for him to resign rather than continue to make such trouble for the Church. And he said—'

Here William lost his voice and began to cough. Otho bent his eyes to the parchment on the table and read from it the Archbishop's answer. 'I will not yield in this cause because that would be setting a pernicious example that would result in the destruction of ecclesiastical liberty and perhaps the ruin of the Christian faith itself. Who would dare raise his voice henceforth? If other pastors similarly gave way, who would rise in opposition and stand as a wall about the House of Israel?'

Most of the bishops dropped their eyes; only Gilbert Foliot and Worcester looked straight back at him, Foliot with his mouth pulled down so that he looked like a jowly, bristling old dog and Worcester with a sudden gleam in his eye as a man has when he hears the charge sounded. But no one said anything.

Having drunk some watered wine, William had recovered himself. But he was not quite sure how he could explain what had followed when he had proposed that the Archbishop should return to his church without any further mention of the customs if the King would allow it. At the time he had thought it most ingenious to argue that, while the world would see that Thomas had won his case, Henry would be allowed the illusion of victory. Now, looking sideways at the King, the fallacy was evident.

It had done no good, anyway, for Thomas had quoted canon law at him: 'He who does not object when he can is assumed to consent' and 'He who openly ceases to protest against misdeeds incurs the suspicion of hidden consent.' He decided there was no point in mentioning it.

'We asked him if he would freely accept our judgement of the dispute,' he said instead, back-tracking a little on events. 'He replied that he would agree to nothing unless the property of his see was restored in full; otherwise he could not afford expensive litigation.'

Henry suddenly banged his hand down on the board before him. 'You failed,' he said.

They did not reply.

'No more to say,' he said. 'You may go.'

Cardinal William stared for a moment in disbelief at such summary treatment, then turned hastily as Henry rose. The King's face was very red, showing how he throttled down his anger.

But when they and their clerks and chaplains went trailing out he followed them as far as the door, three or four of his bishops coming hesitantly after, Foliot and York among them. Cardinal William increased his pace to get abreast of Otho; he did not see why he should feel menaced at the sound of the

King's footsteps behind him, but he did. They passed out together into a crowd of men who had been waiting outside the closed doors; these drew back to make a way for them in a silence that unnerved him further.

He shot a quick glance at the King who stood with one hand on the doorpost, watching them go. But it was the watchers he addressed rather than the legates when he shouted at the top of his voice–'I hope to God I may never lay eyes on a cardinal again!'

Cardinal William nearly tripped over his skirts. 'Take the nearest horse!' he hissed to his chaplain.

Reynold Fitzurse was one of those who witnessed the legates' undignified exit but he saw no more than that for the King went immediately back into the hall again and remained there closeted with the bishops until nightfall. It was not until the evening that he and his cronies learned anything more about what had transpired.

The bishops had come out from the interview looking very sick and shaken and word soon got about that the King was laying all the blame for the fiasco upon them. Reynold heard the talk but contributed nothing to the discussion, mainly because, as always, the rest seemed to be privy to more information than he had. He found it very puzzling, not because there were more threads to the argument than he could ever have imagined (he was used to that), but because it seemed to him that the original actions of the participants had brought it all about. Reynold had the kind of mind that said, 'That man's my enemy; kill him and I have one enemy the less.' He could see, of course, that he might be called to account by the victim's avengers, but then he not only lived by the sword but thought it the only honourable way to live.

He spoke of it to Will de Tracy. 'This business would be all over now had the King executed that traitor archbishop when he had him in England.'

Will fingered his arm where the wound he had got in the

recent war in the Auvergne was just healing. 'The Pope might have had something to say.'

'There's another Pope, isn't there? I thought when the King sent his daughter to the Emperor—'

'Don't speak of that,' said Will with some bitterness. The tax, euphemistically known as an aid, which all the barons had had to pay to the King on that occasion, was still rankling. But he spoke of it himself, just the same. 'He made a good profit on the aid, you know, over and above his expenses. But the marriage didn't mean what you're thinking. Our lord King plays one against the other. He's got a long head, has Harry. That was politics.'

'Politics!' said Reynold in a tone of deepest disgust.

'It's a means to gain your ends without fighting for them. After all, you can't fight everyone at once.' He looked up. 'Here's Hugh coming. He'll know what's going on.'

They had met again, these three who had been Thomas's own knights when he was Chancellor. They had resented him then, an upstart lording it over men of better blood; now they hated him with far more virulence than any of the King's original entourage. That was because they knew him better, they assured themselves.

But Hugh had nothing to add to their knowledge of events; nor did the next day, when messengers were kept busy running between the King and the cardinal-legates, bring any further enlightenment. Apparently tiring of the whole affair, the King went off with his hounds and his hawks on Wednesday while the cardinals held yet another meeting with the bishops. And after that they began making preparations to depart.

Reynold, Will and Hugh were in the group that watched the leave-taking the following morning. The legates stood close to the King, who listened with bowed head to their earnest talk. When the King answered they were amazed at his humble demeanour and the look of entreaty on his face. They were even more surprised to see him mop at cheeks obviously wet.

Cardinal William of Pavia found this circumstance much more to his liking. Moving nearer the King, who was holding his stirrup like a lackey, he scrubbed cautiously at his own eye to induce a sympathetic tear. 'Indeed, indeed,' he said, 'you may be sure that I will intercede with the Pope to rid you of him altogether.' He patted the King upon the shoulder in his most fatherly manner. 'Rest easy,' he said. 'Rest assured. . . .'

The spectacle brought a cough from Otho which sounded remarkably like a derisive snort. And if he could not hide the twinkle in his eye as he raised his hand in a last blessing, it covered his intentions more effectively than Henry's crocodile tears had hidden his.

Riding away, he thought that it grew ever more plain that this monarch wanted nothing less than the Archbishop's head on a charger. Not while I still have a voice, he told himself. Neither shall I ever authorise or consent to his deposition.

Christmas 1167

When the king rose at dawn to find drab fog pressing close around the castle he considered returning to bed. But he decided, in spite of having attended Midnight Mass, to hear the second Mass of Christmas as well, and ordered out his finest garments in honour of the Feast. He rather spoilt the good impression this created by discussing business loudly with some of his officials throughout the ceremony but it did not matter too much to the priest because his constant bouts of coughing effectively deafened him to the chatter of the congregation.

Seeing, when dinner was over, that the fog was not going to lift, Henry decided to fill in time by visiting his children's apartments. He was somewhat put out to find his wife there with them; he had expected her to be at her *toilette*, preparing for the junketings in the hall.

There was a little silence when he entered though they all greeted him with the greatest politeness, the boys kneeling and six-year-old Eleanor performing an endearingly clumsy curtsey before they came forward one by one to kiss his cheek. But when he seated himself beside their mother and gave them leave to continue whatever they were doing, they only glanced warily at one another and sidled away to sit stiffly watching him.

'The babe,' he said, and noticed himself that his voice sounded over-loud and hearty. 'Where is the babe? Not sleeping at this hour?' He meant his latest child whom he had seen for the first time a month ago when Eleanor had brought him from England where he had been born. Now he was just a year old and could already take his first steps.

The Queen rang the little bell on the table and told the nurse to bring the lord John and the lady Johanna. 'We let them play alone together,' she said easily, ignoring the fact that he had not asked after the little girl. 'The others had made them over-excited and both were squalling so that we could not hear ourselves speak.'

The nurse brought in the younger children, Johanna toddling at her side and John in her arms. He was still hiccuping and his fine, dark brows drew together in a look of deep suspicion at sight of a stranger; when Henry took him from her he let out an indignant yell and tried to struggle free. But after a while, talked to and fondled by his mother who nursed the small girl, he consented to sit on Henry's knee with his dark eyes fixed unwaveringly on his father's face.

'How he looks,' Henry said. 'See how he takes me in. Little John,' he continued musingly, jogging his knee, 'what lands shall we give you, eh, little John? Young Henry's to have England and Normandy, Richard's to have his mother's lands, and there's Brittany for Geoffrey. What's left for you?–unless one of the others will give up something.' He looked up suddenly, grinning, and saw the fixed stares of the other boys fall instantly away. 'And I can't see that happening,' he added, 'so we shall have to call you John Lackland, my son.' The moment passed as John made a grab for Henry's beard and everyone laughed.

Things seemed to go better after that; the small girls drew apart to consider and compare their puppet-babies and the boys resumed the complicated game they had been playing with their mother on Henry's arrival. It was not long, though, before the baby's delighted chuckling began to pall and Henry's eyes went more and more often to the golden heads so close to the Queen's. A sense of grievance was beginning to take hold of him. Why were they excluding him? Dandling a baby was no job for a man. He placed John firmly on the floor near the girls and went across to see what they were doing.

He stood behind them, looking over their shoulders. They had a board marked out in squares like a chess board but with counters instead of chessmen, and a die which they shook in a box and threw on the table. 'What game is that?' he asked and then, when no one replied, said sharply, 'You would do better to read a book. You might learn something.'

'It is Christmas,' said Eleanor, 'and a time for good cheer.' She leaned back. 'Let them play, Henry; they read much at other times.'

Henry felt something touch his leg and looked down. John had crept across the floor after him. He bent and picked him up.

'Well,' he said shortly, 'are you not coming to the hall? The festivities will be starting soon.' He turned away to hand the child to the hovering nurse, disentangling himself from his determined clutch with some difficulty. No one answered and, looking back, he caught the exchange of glances and the sullen expressions on the boys' faces. With compressed lips and slow deliberation Richard began to remove the counters from the board.

Angry and hurt, Henry sat on the dais watching the jollity

in the hall. He had looked forward to this occasion for weeks, picturing himself the centre of a merry family group, for this was the first Christmas for years that all his children had been with him. (Except Matilda, of course, who had joined the Emperor's family.) Yet here he sat, as usual, in the midst of a number of elderly lords, Eleanor to one side surrounded by younger men, and the sons who should have been proud to bear him company enjoying themselves down in the body of the hall without a thought for him. One by one they had risen from their seats and sneaked away, even the elder Geoffrey. He could see young Henry, flushed and perspiring with the heat and dancing, pawing at a maid who should have known better than to allow a lad no more than thirteen such liberties.

He stood up suddenly and shouted at him so that even old Cornwall, who was dozing nearby, started out of his drunken stupor. Young Henry did not, or would not, hear and disappeared into the throng. All the lords sitting on the dais began to talk at once, seizing with relief on a suggestion that it was time for the carols to begin.

The King glared across at the Queen, who could scarcely be seen for the host of young gallants around her. So Arundel ordered in the minstrels, a space was cleared, and soon the hall was ringing with the joyous carols.

The King did not join in the singing. He was composing stinging remarks with which to rebuke his wife for the manner in which she had reared their children. Certainly she had, in the devious way of women, pushed him out of their affection. She had spoiled them all, winning their love the easy way, uncaring of the effect on their characters.

He must see to it that she did not do the same with this last child, who was clearly different from the others. The baby John had crawled the length of a room to claw at his father's leg and demand to be taken up into his arms again. None of the others had ever come to him in preference to his mother or his nurse.

Bitterness rose in him. Everything he did was for these boys who did not even trouble to hide their lack of affection for him. And of them all it was upon the eldest, the shining, golden Henry, that he had built his hopes, that prince who was to become by his striving the foremost potentate in Europe—

Had young Henry been aware of what was passing through his father's mind, he would have rejected so preposterous a fantasy immediately. He, like his brothers, had always known that every one of them was no more than a means to the all-important end of feeding and extending the pride and the power of Henry FitzEmpress.

VIII
March 1168

Eleanor the Queen rode with the men in the midst of the muster of nobles and knights who were passing back to the Castle of Lusignan; her excuse for declining to travel with her women was that she preferred the freshness of the wind in her face, though one of the ladies, jolted unmercifully in a litter some way behind, was heard to remark that the freshness of the young men's looks would have been nearer to the mark.

Certainly she was now conversing very courteously with a young knight; what was unusual and what was noted was the length of time that he had been at her side.

The other knights told one another that the only reason the Queen was showing such honour to this William Marshal was because he was the nephew of Earl Patric of Salisbury who, with the Queen, had been left to govern Poitou, but they could not help noticing his easy demeanour and the whiteness of his teeth whenever he smiled; also that he was grave and reflective, listening as closely to the Queen as if she were an elder statesman.

Earl Patric himself was not riding with the Queen because this was dangerous country; he was in the vanguard with the heavily armed men for it was little more than a week since King Henry had marched his army from Normandy and retaken the castle from the de Lusignans. Henry had had to interrupt an important conference with King Louis to do so, and the speed and ferocity with which he had accomplished the task had had as much to do with that as with his chagrin at his wife's failure to control her own duchy. He had wasted no time in returning to Louis, but had appointed Earl Patric to watch over th Queen and his son Richard who, as the heir to Aquitaine, was here with his mother.

Young Richard had been riding just behind the Queen. Now he drew up alongside between her and William Marshal. The Queen turned to him smiling; all saw the softness of her face and they dropped back a little.

Soon the child was chattering to William while the Queen looked idly from side to side as though noting the first cheerful signs of spring. Her eyes roved the scrubby heathland where faint plumes of smoke were visible to one side.

'They are not charcoal burning there?' she said.

William turned from the child–a marvellous boy, he thought, with an interest in the strategy of battle that would put many of his elders to shame–and looked where she pointed.

'Not around here. There are not enough trees.' He frowned, then his face lightened. He wa barely twenty-one and very conscious in his newly-won knighthood that a man must always show himself knowledgeable as well as gentle to women. 'Oh, they are glass makers, without doubt. I had heard it was made somewhere around here.'

'Glass making! How is that done?' She turned the full battery of her melting eyes upon him. He missed the rest of what she said and came back to himself only when she wheeled her mare sidewise.

'My lady,' he cried, 'you must not leave the escort!' But by that time she and Richard both had jumped the ditch and were galloping towards the smudges of smoke in the distance. He remembered then the tales of how headstrong she had been in youth and how fearless and, shouting over his shoulder that a company of archers should be detached to follow, set his own horse after them.

The gelding had much ado to overtake the fleet little mare so that they were almost at the kilns before he came near and, looking back, he saw the group of archers and scattering of knights far behind. 'Madam,' he cried despairingly, 'I pray you, stop! Consider the dangers here.' He saw Richard laugh, and put the whip across the gelding's withers.

The glass makers turned from their tasks to stare at the unexpected visitors, gnarled men, blackened with the smoke of burning bracken. They looked like trolls, he thought, and certainly the product of their trade could vie with any gems trolls might quarry in their underground caves. Out of kilns in the open countryside like these came the shining, jewel-coloured glass that beautified the great churches and cathedrals that were rising all over Europe.

The master glazier recognised his duchess. He led his noble visitors from one place to another, explaining in intolerable detail how the glass was fired; nor could the Queen be detached from the fawning knot of men who pressed near enough almost to touch her. Richard tired of it more quickly and came across to stand with William.

'How do they make pictures with it?' he asked, pushing idly with his toe at the glittering detritus.

One of the men spoke up. 'That's not done here, little lord, but in Poitiers. They cut up the glass with hot irons and join the pieces with strips of lead. But 'tis us makes it all possible. So when you kneel in church and look upon a window that pictures Our Lord or one of the saints, do you think of us.'

Richard turned his head and looked at the man with eyes as expressionless and cold as the blue glass itself. 'We should be going,' he said to William, and went towards the door.

William was momentarily at a loss. Perhaps Richard had been unable to follow the fellow's thick Poitevin accent and had been too embarrassed to admit it, but he did not think so. Seeing the Queen approach he offered his arm, noting how graciously she smiled and inclined her head to these rough fellows. She could teach Richard how to deal with the people who would one day be his.

But she seemed in no hurry to leave. William, in an agony of impatience, did not know how to deal with one at once so wayward and so highly placed. What would his uncle have done, he wondered? Ordered her summarily to horse? And had he done so, would she have obeyed?

Perhaps she saw the worry on his face for she made her adieux at last and permitted him to escort her towards the group of archers and knights who waited with the horses. Richard was already mounted and deep in conversation with the captain; doubtless his talk of military matters held more interest than that of an unlettered churl. All the same, that cold look of Richard's made William uneasy. He believed in the virtues and responsibilities of knighthood and he was very aware that a leader must win the love and respect of his men. King Henry was noted for his openness with the common people.

Not until they were riding away did William address the Queen and even then, as was his habit, he was sparing of words. But he did say it was a pity her Grace had decided so abruptly to leave the safety of numbers in this area and at such a time with so many rebels still at large–and then, weakening a little, added that there was no harm done if they were quick in rejoining the others.

Eleanor listened demurely to the rebuke and, tender to the touching and vulnerable dignity of youth, cast down her eyes. Then they heard the pounding hoofs of hard-driven horses; across the heath a knot of horsemen was coming fast in their direction, waving and shouting.

'Fighting up ahead!' they shouted. 'An ambush!' They reined in, breathless. 'We were sent back to warn the rest and found the Queen gone.' One of them was Henry Fitzgerold, the Chamberlain of her household; he forced by William's horse and laid his hand on Eleanor's bridle. 'Blood of God, my lady, where were you? You gave us a pretty fright.' He blew out his lips and mopped his brow, glaring at William. 'This young man has much to answer for!'

'Nay, nay, you must not blame him.' Eleanor looked quickly at William. 'He would have stopped us if he could. Are my ladies safe?'

'Yes, only the vanguard is involved. It was not a large force that attacked us though the fighting was bloody—' He turned his head to stare. William had kicked his heels into his horse and was away like the wind with half the archers in his wake. 'He'll do no one any good. They'll be gone now, leaving half our good fellows dead.'

Eleanor half rose in the saddle, then sank back again. 'You are sure the fighting is over?'

'Surely.' He still had hold of her bridle, now he glanced sharply about. 'Come, we must rejoin the rest. The sooner we're into the castle the better.'

The Queen dined alone that night in her apartments. It was not a cheerful meal for the thought of Earl Patric's body stiffening along with a dozen or so others in the chapel was uppermost in everyone's mind. The ladies spoke only in whispers and moved about quietly; their mistress's silence was understandable, they thought, seeing it was her own Poitevins who had murdered one of her husband's chief officers. And there were Poitevin servants in the castle now, said to be loyal, but who knew? That night they lay huddled under the covers trembling every time the ancient floorboards creaked in case it was the footstep of an assassin.

Eleanor was not ready for sleep though it was not the sudden ending of Earl Patric's life that kept her wakeful. She was asking herself what more she could have done to remove William Marshal as well as Richard from the danger she had known waited on the road. William had not returned from his wild rush to aid his uncle, neither had his body been found, and that meant he was in the hands of the de Lusignans. Why, she wondered fretfully, had she not warned Earl Patric of the ambush directly she got wind of it? But she knew the answer. She was a Poitevin herself first and foremost, Henry a Norman interloper and Earl Patric his henchman set to watch her. Half her loyalties lay with the de Lusignans in their struggle against foreign interference; they had no quarrel with her, she was sure. But would they revolt against Richard, half Norman as he was, when he became their duke?

And what would Henry do when he heard of this? Ah, Henry. . . . She hoped that he would be too occupied in the north to do anything, as he should be were there any justice. The tale of how he had debauched his hostage, Eudo de Porhoët's daughter, had reached even into Aquitaine so the Bretons themselves could not be unaware of it. It must have been the reason for Eudo's point-blank refusal to aid Henry against the rebellious Poitevins.

Disgust and outraged pride had boiled into fury when she had heard of it. She had raged openly to her ladies in Richard's hearing–something she had never done before–of the shame of this defilement of innocence, of her abomination of her husband's unbridled lusts.

Yes, she had spoken her true feelings, and Richard had not made some excuse and left but listened, quiet and unnoticed by any except herself. So now he knew how it was between his parents and she thought she had done herself no disservice; he was now even more loving and protective than before. She prayed that he would remain so towards all ladies, though there was little evidence of that since he was still at the age when boys prefer the company of men.

She stood up suddenly. 'Send the page downstairs,' she said, 'to discover whether there is yet any word of William Marshal.'

It was Henry Fitzgerold himself who came up to tell her there was no word. 'But they will not harm him,' he said, seeing the Queen's concern and thinking that perhaps she blamed herself for his involvement, 'any more than they would have harmed Salisbury if he had allowed himself to be captured. It was ransom they were after.'

She veiled her eyes. 'I will pay whatever sum they ask. And re-equip him.'

Henry Fitzgerold bowed his head and assured her that never since the world began had any knight a more generous, honourable and gracious lady.

August 1168

This afternoon Cicely went with a few of the maidservants into the woods to gather the bulbs of wild arum; dried and ground up they made a fine, pure starch. It was the best time to dig them now, when the foliage was about to wither. Behind the girls trailed a kitchen lad with trowel and straw bag; he would do the work while they wandered on seeking more or took their ease in the shade of the trees.

Soon the maids found themselves a pleasant spot in a little clearing; some began to talk of the men who were pursuing them and others merely lay in the dappled sunshine, heavy with the heat and sated with the dinner they had just eaten. These were the times they liked best, when they might get out of the house ostensibly to garner the harvest of the countryside but in fact to idle the sweet summer hours away.

Cicely sat with them for a while, putting in a word here and there, but conscious all the time how her presence constrained their cheerful, foolish talk. It was rarely now she had the chance to be with them, and indeed it was not desire for their company that had brought her down here today. At last she tilted one eye up to the sun which was slipping behind the tops of the taller trees and stood up, shaking her skirts to rid them of grass seeds. Carefully offhand, she enquired whether any would go with her to see if the blackberries were ripening.

Those who were not dozing lazily shook their heads. She had known they would refuse, indeed had relied on it, but she still stood a moment as though regretful that none would accompany her. 'Wait for me here then,' she said, 'I'll not be long.' As she moved away, trying not to hurry, she added, 'Do you not go from here or I'll not know where to find you.'

When she had disappeared into the trees one of the girls, a thin, sharp-featured wench, said slyly, 'We'd know where to find her though, eh?' But Cicely did not hear that or the giggles, knowing, half-admiring, that followed.

At about the same time Reynold Fitzurse, Hugh de Morville and Will de Tracy reached the boundary of Fitzurse's lands. They were alone, having left the party they were travelling with at Taunton, and they came on in no great hurry, swapping tales and riddles to while away the miles. Their intention was to break their journey to Devon to visit Reynold's father.

It was not filial duty which had brought Reynold again to Williton but rather a desire to meet the new wife his brother had acquired. The picture he had formed of her was rendering him ever more dissatisfied with Beatrice, and until the sight of her reassured him that he had the superior prize he would know no peace. His father's last letter, informing him that she had happy expectations, had been the spur that had forced him into action; he could not bear the thought that Robert might be granted what he had so long been denied–a child of the better sex. So he had chosen to make his inspection now lest sick jealousy should later prevent it altogether. He had a good excuse for putting in an unexpected appearance for his father had recently been ill; he had had a fall and had been laid up for some weeks. Not that Reynold cared anything about that–indeed he considered it high time a man approaching sixty gave place to his heir.

The three men passed among the trees of a small, outlying wood. Reynold was laughing uproariously, Hugh looked bored; he did not find Will's riddles either as amusing or as difficult to guess as Reynold did. In fact, he was beginning to wish he had not come with them.

'Don't you know any, Hugh?' asked Will.

'I do. But I doubt that either of you could come on the answers.'

'Try us!'

Hugh shrugged. 'As you wish.' He considered a moment. 'I have it. Listen, I'll only say it once. "I'm the world's wonder for I make women happy. I'm a boon to the neighbourhood, a bane to no one, though I may perhaps prick the one who picks me."' He glanced sideways at Reynold who wore a look of deepest concentration. '"I am well set up, stand in a bed, have a roughish root."'

He waved a hand at Will's delighted exclamation. 'Hold. There's more. . . . "Rarely a churl's daughter, more daring than the rest, lays hold of me, rushes my red top, wrenches at my head and lays me in the larder."'

Will was convulsed with delight.

'"She learns soon enough, the curly haired creature who clamps me so, moist is her eye!"'

Reynold struck his thigh. 'Marry! That's good, Hugh! By Cock, that's good!'

'You've said it,' agreed Will. 'But that was easy–easy!' He let out a wild, hooting laugh. '"By Cock", says Reynold! That's good too!'

'Indeed?' said Hugh. 'Tell me the answer then.'

They stared at him with suspicion. He wore a superior smile. 'It's not what you randy whoresons are thinking.'

'Not—? What then? What else?'

'The answerw's–an onion.'

Will closed his mouth and looked eloquently at Reynold.

He began to chuckle softly to himself. 'I must learn that one. That's good, that is. That's clever. Ask us another.'

Hugh suddenly lifted his hand for silence. 'Look there,' he said in a low voice.

All this while they had been ambling, reins loose, through the scattered trees; now they had come to a saucer-like depression, overgrown here and there with thorn and gorse. At the bottom of the dip a boy and girl lay twined together.

They watched, grinning, until Will took Reynold by the elbow. 'Fine fare for serfs while better men go hungry,' he murmured.

Reynold wet his lips and eyed the long, exposed length of the girl's thigh. He swung down from his horse and walked slowly towards the oblivious couple, picking his way with care lest an unwary step betray his presence. He stopped about six feet away from them. 'Unhand that wench, churl,' he said.

They sprang apart as if he had jabbed them with an ox goad. 'Up!' said Reynold going nearer. 'Up, and let me look at you that I'll know you again!'

He saw shock change to fear in the boy's face as he stared past him at the two mounted men. He looked about sixteen and the girl even younger.

Standing over them he said, 'That's a man's job you're about, sonny.' His eyes went to the girl. She was a little beauty, too good for unlicked cubs. Her hands were shaking as she tried to smooth her rumpled skirts. 'Come here, wench,' he said, remembering that long, white thigh.

The boy's face changed and he stepped in front of her. 'Have a care—' he began, but the girl put out her hand to grip his arm and he stopped abruptly. Reynold raised his fist and dealt him a blow on the head that sent him over backwards. 'Come here, wench,' he said again.

The girl's eyes flew to the two watchers and Will gave a shout of laughter as the lad suddenly launched himself at Reynold, yelling, 'Run! Run for the woods!' The girl stared blankly for a split second, then, gathering up her skirts, ran like a hare for the trees. Will put his horse forward to cut her off.

The force of the impact on Reynold's knees had brought him down but as the lad pulled himself erect Hugh wheeled his horse and dismounted directly before him. The point of his short sword just touched the boy's midriff. Sunlight flashed off the blade.

The boy looked down at it, then up at Hugh. He took a backward step past the floundering Reynold. Hugh moved forward so that the sword-point remained in contact. Trembling, the boy drew in his stomach and held his breath, staring transfixed into Hugh's face. He took another careful backward step.

Hugh followed, smiling at him with the utmost tenderness. The boy's mouth opened, his chin trembled, he seemed to be trying to speak. Slowly, gently, Hugh pushed the blade.

The lad made a small noise, his eyes rolled up and he gave a great convulsive jerk. Hugh let his own breath escape in a long sigh and, releasing his grip on the hilt, allowed the body to slump to the ground.

The boy was not quite dead; his eyes wandered and his jaw moved a little. The sword impaling him threw the shadow of a cross on the grass. Hugh stood immobile, looking down at him, then put his hand again to the sword-hilt. Death would come on the rush of blood when he withdrew it. Moved by some impulse he held his hand before him so that the shadow fell on the blind face. 'Time to die, lad,' he said and, with an expert twist, jerked out the sword.

Seeing Hugh was dealing with the cub, Reynold had turned away. His mind was intent on the girl. She had not got far. Will was circling her, closing in, shouting with laughter each time he cut short another frenzied dash in a fresh direction. He was mad with excitement, yelling threats and hunting cries with a fine disregard for the time and place.

He saw Reynold coming and galloped alongside her, leaned

from the saddle and dragged her screaming by the hair for several yards until she lost her footing and fell, leaving a tangle of dark hair twined in his fingers. When he pulled up and swung around, Reynold was bending over her.

Will came up beside them and watched the girl's furious, silent struggling with detached interest. 'Don't worry, sweeting,' he remarked cheerfully, 'you won't miss what you were going to get when we came by. Much better lie still and take it quietly–there, I told you!' as Reynold swore and fetched her a clout to the side of the jaw.

'She's got a lot of fight in her still,' he muttered after a while. Reynold raised a scratched and snarling face. 'Hold her arms down, can't you? Wind her head up in her skirts! I can't do it all alone; she's a very wildcat.'

Will finally consented to kneel upon her chest while Reynold trussed her up, all the while passing derisive comments on men who had difficulty in managing alone. 'Want any help getting your onion out?' he enquired. Reynold ignored it all and singlemindedly exercised his *droit de seigneur*.

A little later Hugh came walking across to them. 'Have you done?'

Reynold nodded at the swaddled, motionless form. 'Do you want her?'

Hugh's dark face was indicative of distaste. 'Not with her head wrapped up. I like to see their faces.' He bent down and began to pull the heavy cloth from her head.

'Where's the boy?'

Hugh's hands stilled. 'Over there. He'll tell no tales.'

Reynold stared. 'You didn't kill him? Christ, what for?' Indignation began to rise in him. 'One of my serfs—'

'One of your father's serfs, I think.'

'There was no call to kill him. What could he have done?' Reynold worried at his thumb nail. 'We'd better shove him out of sight.'

Hugh had finished his unwrapping. 'Her, too. She's dead.

Suffocated.' Moved by a sudden niceness he pulled the skirts over the spread legs. 'What shall we do with them?'

Even Will was silenced. They stared about helplessly.

'God's nails,' said Will at last, 'all for a bit of fun. . . . If the silly little bitch had just kept quiet—'

Hugh looked at the other slope where bracken grew waist high. 'Hide them there,' he said. 'Once the foxes have been at them no one will know what happened. And come on, do; we've wasted enough time.'

Reynold had very little to say on the last mile or two of their journey. He was recalling with some unease that his father's attitude to his serfs differed considerably from that of most lords. And there had been something about that maid. . . . But he could not place the likeness, if likeness it was.

They found his father sitting in the hall in his great chair with his lame leg propped before him on a stool. His face showed no noticeable pleasure at the sight of them but he greeted them cordially enough, asking eagerly for news; little reached them here, he said. So they had to tell all they knew, but it turned out he had heard of most of the important events anyway, all but the death of Leicester, which was evidently a shock to him, and that the Pope had appointed yet another legation to try to heal the rift between King and Archbishop. He brushed that aside and questioned them as to when and how Leicester had died. 'Of old age,' Reynold said, 'a month ago.'

Sir Richard looked at him thoughtfully. 'He was not much older than I. I mind well the first time I met him—' He told them a long and rambling story of how it had come about in the days when Stephen was king and brother fought brother. Reynold was not interested and looked about him, wondering when Robert's wife would put in an appearance.

'De Luci is sole Justiciar then,' said Sir Richard at last. 'He will not go to Jerusalem now. Well'–he eased himself to a more comfortable position–'tell me how the fighting goes in

France.'

When he had heard that, and they had much to say for they had been there on knight service a few months earlier, he looked again at Reynold rather narrowly and said, 'You will be glad to hear your lady mother is much improved, both in health and spirit.'

Reynold was taken aback. It was not exactly true to say he never thought of his mother, for he prayed for her regularly, but she had long since been relegated to the list of Holy Souls whom he recommended to God's mercy. He stuttered out some sort of reply and found himself agreeing to go up and visit her when Amicia should come–'for it is she, I am bound to say, who has worked this miracle,' the baron concluded. It was a minute or two before he realised Amicia was Robert's wife.

She came soon after, and Robert with her. He looked much the same–more assured perhaps, as would any man who discovered himself overnight transformed from a landless knight into a lord of many acres. The woman was short and squat, and round as a barrel; had he not known of her condition he never would have guessed it. He realised with relief he would not have taken her at any price. Still, she had good teeth and no obvious deformities so no doubt Robert found her an improvement on his first wife.

She ran her eyes over him in a very bold, open way as they climbed the tower stair. 'How did you get those scratches on your face?' she enquired. The tone, not gentle and commiserating but insistent on explanation, reminded him unpleasantly of Beatrice. He put his hand to his cheek. 'A branch of thorn,' he said, 'coming through a wood. I did it yesterday.'

'It looks fresher than that.' She opened the door. 'Do not be surprised if she does not recognise you. Speak to her as you would to a child.'

The tower room was clean and comfortable, the shutters set wide to the warm, summer evening. His mother sat on a stool, gazing out. He saw that the hair under the veil was now quite white. A rush of feeling disturbed him. It was as though she had been long dead and had risen again.

'Mother?' he said. 'Mother, it's Reynold.'

She looked about as if seeking the person he was addressing, a faint, puzzled frown creasing her brow. He came nearer and knelt before her. 'Bless me, mother.'

Her eyes went to Amicia for guidance, then she looked back at him. 'It is Reynold,' he repeated.

She lifted her hand and slowly, hesitantly, touched his cheek. 'Reynold?' she said vaguely. He seized the hand, covering it with kisses, then began to cry over it. But he let it go without protest when she pulled away from him.

After a minute he rose up rather sheepishly and brushed his knees. He said to Amicia, 'She does not know me.'

'No. But you see she is happy and well cared for. That must be a great comfort to you.' He thought she was eyeing him with more kindness than she had before. 'I think–I think we might let her come below to dine with us tonight. It may do her good–she may know you in those surroundings.'

He was about to shake his head when he saw she was not even looking to him for consent or denial. It confirmed his half-formed opinion of her as a masterful woman. No, certainly nothing to envy here!

At the door to the hall they were met by a serving-woman who engaged the mistress in anxious colloquy; Reynold heard her muttered exclamation, 'Drat the girl!' and, perceiving the signals of some small domestic crisis, passed hastily on.

The servants were setting up the trestles and boards for dinner with all their usual heavy-handed clumsiness and a pleasant smell wafted on the air. Will and Hugh were still talking with the baron but he looked distrait; his eyes wandered down the hall as if he sought someone who had not come. That person was manifestly not his wife for when Reynold, watching him closely, told him that Amicia was bringing Lady Maud below to dine with them, he merely shrugged without interest. That showed Reynold it was not new for those other than the master to make decisions; he dwelt in silence upon so curious a circumstance until his mother came, leaning on Amicia's arm.

He had an idea, though, that she knew his father when they seated her beside him, and he saw her eyes go from the baron's face to his own once or twice while they ate. Dusk had come down by the time the meal was over and a couple of young lads brought tapers to light the candles on the board; in the spreading golden glow she looked younger, more like the mother of his youth, especially when she leaned back and, signing herself, placed a morsel of the bread on which the meats had been served on her tongue as if she houselled herself; he could recall her doing that from his earliest years. So he smiled gently at her and she smiled back, nodding graciously to him as to one with whom she might have some small acquaintance.

At that moment there came a noise from outside the open door: the sound of men's voices muttering and another raised above them, loud with anger or distress. The baron's head came up. 'Who's there?' he said sharply, and to Robert, 'Go and see.'

Amicia half rose too, staring. A woman came in and a group of men following, bearing something between them on a hurdle. Robert stopped dead when he saw who had entered.

She came on until she stood before the high table, a woman obviously of the people, her pleasant, plump face empty and fixed in shock. She looked only at the baron. From grey lips she jerked out, 'Go look, Fitzurse, at what they bring you.'

In that instant everyone there but Lady Maud knew what the men bore.

Reynold sat rigid, hand still outstretched to the goblet in front of him and his mouth half-open; when someone nearby let out a harsh and startled cry he jumped and overturned the cup. Wine ran out like blood over the white, scrubbed board.

The woman was Beta, she who in the old days had been the baron's leman.

At her utterance the baron had come to his feet with a violence that almost overturned his chair, too full of dread to know he stood upon the leg he had thought never to use again. He strode down the hall to the group of silent men and their burden. Beta followed and, after a moment of stunned inaction, Robert too.

The cry that had caused Reynold to spill his wine had come from Lady Maud. She had sprung up in the same instant, her face contorted not with fear but with rage and recognition. The sight of Beta had broken down barriers and let in knowledge; now for her the years rolled back to the days when she was mistress here and this woman–and her brat. . . . She stood quite still, glaring down the hall after them.

Amicia saw the sudden change in her, the lucidity, reason even, in her face. She gaped, amazed, as this stranger turned on her and imperiously demanded to know what had happened. 'Cicely,' she whispered. 'It must be Cicely.' Abruptly she hurried to her husband's side.

Sir Richard had uncovered the hurdle.

Jokkyn the serf was one of those who had borne it hither; his square, brick-red face was swollen with crying. 'Men have been at her,' he choked out.

Slowly the baron raised his head. 'Men. . . .' Stiffly he turned and stared at the three visitors at his table. 'Strangers here. . . . ' He lifted his arm, pointing at Reynold. 'You! By Almighty God—' His rising voice died to a gurgle, he turned the colour of tallow and, still with arm outstretched, swayed and toppled like a falling tree. Beta did not even look his way. Her eyes were fixed upon the hurdle's load as if they would never again see anything else.

Robert looked blindly from the dead girl to the fallen man, then gazed wildly at the three guests who sat stiff and wary, guilt plain on their faces. But it was Reynold he cried out to. 'Blood of God! This is our father's child! She is our sister. What have you done?'

Through the appalled silence Lady Maud began to titter. 'Ah, Robert, Robert,' she said, not loud but very clear. 'How should he know that? Did not your father deny her and pass her off as Miller's child? Reynold–poor Reynold–believed him.' She relinquished the grip she had taken on Reynnld's arm and straightened herself. The intensity of hatred on her face was shocking, and worse the exultant triumph in her voice as she screamed, 'On his own bead be it, liar and perjurer as he has proved himself to be! Truly God hath repaid him—'

'Hush!' wailed Amicia and burst shrilly into tears. 'Hush, for Jesu's love! They are both dead. Is not that enough?'

Lady Maud stared at her blankly. 'Dead? He–is he—? No. . . .'

'Yes,' said Robert.

Hugh and Will had snatched their daggers from the board and backed slowly from the table; they pushed Reynold along between themselves and the wall as they edged towards the door. He went like a sleepwalker; they, like the trained warriors they were, back to back, right hands on sword hilts. No one moved to stop them. The eyes of all were on the stricken face of the old woman as she hobbled slowly from the dais to where Robert and Amicia knelt by the baron.

Neither did any notice Beta go. She went outside and up the stair to the tower room, but she passed its door and continued up the last narrow spiral to the battlemented walk. There, leaning between the crenellations, she turned her face up to the uncaring sky.

From below came the drumming thunder of hoofbeats on the bridge as the knights raced away but she did not hear them or the shouts of the villagers who had gathered in the courtyard. The last thing she ever knew was the great soundless explosion of light as her skull cracked like an eggshell on the paving sixty feet below.

If Robert thought that God would not be mocked he never allowed it to surface in his mind, but that, whether he acknowledged it or not, was why he had sat by unmoving while his brother made his escape, and it was for the same reason that he did not report the deaths to the sheriff for a full week afterwards. But he wasted no thought at all on Beta, having no fellow-feeling with those who spit upon the countenance of God. She was shovelled hastily into a pit of quicklime at the crossroads and dismissed from prayers and memory alike.

Robert was left in full, if temporary, possession until the heir should come forward and accept his punishment according to the law. He had still not done so two months later when Lady Maud, never having spoken another word, died quietly in her sleep. Five weeks after that Amicia gave birth to a son.

Reynold returned to his wife at Barham half-way through Advent, having spent the intervening three months skulking with Will on that isolated manor of his where the three knights had taken refuge after their flight from Williton. Hugh left for the north after a week or so, though whether he went because retribution was more unlikely there, as Will believed, or as a result of the devastating quarrel that had blown up between himself and Reynold, the latter was unsure. Reynold was certain of one thing only: he hated Hugh and must have done so for a long time without knowing it.

It was what Hugh had said that made him realise it. For Reynold was suffering most unfamiliar pangs of remorse–not for the sakes of those untimely dead, but rather because of what might happen to him in consequence. It was not worldly penalties he feared; few sins were gross enough to raise from him more than a mildly jeering comment, but there was one written in letters of scarlet, a final tabu, and it was the knowledge that he, though all unwitting, was guilty of such an enormity that lay like a ton weight upon him.

Thoroughly unnerved, he had little to say for days after they fled. The other two left him alone at first, riding off with the reeve about the small, mean place and trouncing the latter soundly for the neglect that was everywhere apparent. They did that only to relieve their anger at being cooped up on a lonely, desolate moor, knowing full well that a handful of villeins could scratch no more than a bare living from the poor soil. Then a spell of rainy weather deprived them even of that occupation. There was nothing to do but dice and gamble and try without success to draw Reynold into conversation.

They were all sitting thus in the tumbledown hall one day with a dish of soft, red apples between them and the summer rain leaking through the roof in half a dozen places when Will burst out irritably, 'Mass, will the rain never stop! We shall be afloat before long.'

'The angels weep for our sins perhaps,' remarked Hugh lightly and cast a glance at the morose Reynold.

'For a man who's not a monk you dwell overmuch on sin,' Will said sharply. 'It would appear it's the sin, not the deed, that's your pleasure.'

Hugh ignored him, looking still at Reynold. 'A pretty jest,' he murmured. 'Your own sister—'

'Shut your mouth!' said Reynold violently.

Hugh's nostrils widened a little. 'Incest. . . .' he said softly. 'You have outdone us all.'

Reynold was on his feet and standing over Hugh before Will was aware he had moved. 'Christ's Blood! Could I know that? God knows I never saw her since she was a babe. And that she should be his get–that whoremaster–that pimping sod that locked away my mother. Christ!'

'Reynold,' entreated Will. He had never cared how Reynold spoke of his father while he was alive, but he felt a certain superstitious discomfort in hearing the dead described in such terms. Neither of the others took any notice.

Hugh had stood up and put his hand on Reynold's arm and, as though the touch had triggered something in him, Reynold shouted, 'You! You call me incestuous! Aye–and envy me that sin. What manner of man are you, de Morville?' His face was contorted, his hand on his dagger hilt.

Hugh spoke swiftly, softly, hurrying out the words so that Will did not catch it all; he thought in sudden wonder that the other man was suddenly afraid. 'Do you not see what a mighty vengeance you have taken?' he was whispering. 'His name you have dishonoured and thereby caused his death. How many times have you sworn that he should pay for every affront to your mother? Was all that empty talk? I'll not believe it. You had planned this; it smacks of your ingenuity.'

Careful, Hugh, thought Will, tensely watching.

'I did not know her,' Reynold muttered, 'and if I had, I thought her Miller's child.'

'Yet is your mother free of him.'

Enunciating every word clearly and distinctly Reynold said, 'Keep your filthy tongue off my mother's name.'

Hugh looked as though someone had flicked him in the face.

The silence stretched dangerously. No one speaks to de Morville like that, Will thought in unbelief. He was mightily relieved when Hugh strode out and left them.

The next day he was gone. Reynold and Will stayed on, but as winter began to close in Will became restive and began saying that they must get away before the roads became impassable; Reynold knew the real reason was that he had tired of the reeve's daughter but since worry about his inheritance was now looming larger than the fate of his soul, he agreed that the time had come to return to their normal courses and take their punishment. However high the fine–and it was likely to be high–he could pay it out of the revenues that would come to him from his father.

It did not take Beatrice long to get most of the story out of him. She did not know of the existence of the baron's youngest child and he saw no need to tell her of the sin into which he had been tricked by fate. He would not have told her anything beyond the fact of his father's death had she not almost immediately given him proof that the King's justice now stretched its tentacles into every corner of the land.

He treated her to a garbled tale in which his two companions had played the major parts, and after one disgusted look at him she had thrown the tail of hair Ilaria had been braiding over her shoulder and got into bed. 'I suppose you know what this means,' she said. 'You have put paid to any advancement you might have had. You will be lucky if the King does not let you from his counsels altogether.'

Reynold's mouth opened. It was something he had not thought of. 'The King won't hear of it,' he said. 'He is in France. Why should he concern himself with so small a matter? By the time I join him again for my knight service it will all be forgotten.' But he spoke with more confidence than he felt. He was remembering how King Henry would sit at the end of a hard day's campaigning going over the official documents a courier had brought, and how he would slap down his hand and shout whenever a familiar name caught his eye.

He wished that Hugh had had that bloody girl as well. (He was able now to forget that she was anything other than he had supposed her to be.) Then he and Will could have got together and laid all the blame on him. They had not meant to damage her while he–he had murdered that boy in cold blood for his own perverted pleasure.

Gervase of Cornhill, the sheriff, called again within the week. Closeted alone with him, Reynold came a little nearer to the truth.

Gervase rubbed his chin. He had no more information than what was contained in the document empowering him to apprehend Fitzurse for suspected rape and murder. This did not sound so black to him as he had first thought. And Fitzurse was no mere squire but a lord of the soil and one of his peers.

'A mountain made out of a molehill,' he grumbled as he stood up. 'These new justices go about the country snooping into matters that are none of their business. But I shall have to serve a writ on you to appear. No need to worry, though–it will take a year or so.'

He bade Reynold goodbye but turned back at the door. 'One thing,' he said. 'You'll not be able to step into your inheritance till this is over. A strange coincidence that Sir Richard should have died at the same time–unfortunate. Were I in your shoes, I'd lie low for a bit–keep away from the King.'

IX
January 1169

King Henry leaned back in his chair and allowed a faint breath of satisfaction to escape him. More good had come of this conference than he had dared hope. He had ceded very little and he had gained both a truce and a worthwhile treaty.

He was glad enough of the truce. He had spent the whole of the previous year campaigning, first against his own rebellious vassals of Poitou and Brittany and then against his overlord, Louis, who had been treacherously aiding them. And he was sick of it. For every French town he had burnt Louis had retaliated on one of his until it had begun to seem that warfare might drag on forever with no decisive result. Apparently Louis had come to the same conclusion, for Henry's overtures towards peace had been seized on with alacrity.

Here in Montmirail, on the Feast of the Epiphany, they had thrashed out the terms. Henry was to hold Normandy as before, paying fealty to Louis and his son Philip; young Henry was to have the hereditary Seneschalcy of France and to hold Brittany, Maine and Anjou directly of Louis. (Henry had not liked the words *sine medio* but, certain of his influence over his son, had allowed them to pass undisputed.) Richard was to hold Poitou and Guienne, also *sine medio*, and was to marry Louis' daughter Alais, and Geoffrey was to hold Brittany of young Henry as mediate between himself and Louis. Louis had also agreed to hand over to him certain Bretons and Poitevins who had taken shelter in his domains. Yes, he was well pleased with the day's work. He lifted his cup to Louis in salutation.

Louis nodded to him blandly. He had remarked the English king's complacency and, now that the meeting was breaking up, decided it was time to spring his little surprise. He said softly, 'Since we are to be allied once more by the hope of mutual grandchildren, cousin, may I beg a favour of your courtesy?'

Henry shot him a look of sudden suspicion and tried to hedge. 'If it be within my power, cousin.'

'Who has more power than the King of the English? If France had half such power, should I be badgered as I am by the Pope? Here at my court are two more papal envoys, and it is their commission and their dearest wish that you will consent to a meeting with Archbishop Thomas. Believe me, cousin, they will give me no rest unless I can persuade you.'

Henry frowned, less at Louis' suggestion than at the reminder of one over whom, it seemed, he had no power at all; but he badly wanted the treaty which he now saw hanging in the balance. And if Louis wanted it as much as he did, it might be that he and the papal envoys would knock some sense into Thomas's head. At any rate, nothing would be lost by making the attempt. He remembered, with some thankfulness, the letter he had received last summer from the Pope, promising to suppress Thomas's legatine authority and his censures until peace should be made between them. That had been the only thing that had stopped him from accepting the offer of an alliance from the Emperor last September.

'I am, as I have always been, prepared to make my peace with the Archbishop,' he said. 'As you well know, I am not the prime mover in the quarrel. I shall be happy to meet him if you can arrange it.' He looked consideringly at Louis. 'Who are the papal envoys?'

Louis named them amiably as Simon and Engelbert, both priors of unimportant monasteries, and Bernard de Corilo, a monk of Grammont. 'It may be that the Pope feels that simple monks may succeed where cardinals have failed.'

'Please God it may be so.' Henry rose. 'With that hope, cousin, on this holy day on which three kings offered gifts to the King of Kings, I commend myself, my sons and my lands to your keeping.' He made a rather lower reverence than was necessary to a brother monarch. Outdo that in pious cant if you can, he thought. But Louis made no attempt to do so; he merely doffed his hat and watched him go. Neither Henry nor anyone else saw the faint, close-lipped smile that lifted the corners of his mouth for a second, and of all those who knew him only Eleanor might have guessed the reason.

Next day when young Henry and Richard knelt and placed their hands between his, promising to be his men, Louis guarded his eyes carefully, keeping them on the downbent, red-gold heads lest Henry read the triumph in them. *His* men, not Henry's. A mouse may outwit a lion given time, he thought, especially a greedy lion who has no intention of sharing with his cubs.

For he had not missed the look on Henry's face at the words *sine medio*, and he knew that Henry would never allow his sons autonomy in their lands while he lived. But he, Louis, was now these boys' overlord and to him they might legally appeal for help in gaining their rights. Not for years, maybe, for young Henry was scarce fourteen and Richard only eleven, but the day would come. . . . Oh yes, it would come. . . .

And he would be Richard's father-in-law, as well as young Henry's, when he married Alais. That bridal was costing him no marriage portion either. He wondered if the old fox realised how he had been paid back for his trickery in wedding Margaret and young Henry so prematurely, and thereby gaining the Vexin years before time. He hoped he did.

The ceremony of homage was nearing its end and he turned his thoughts to the meeting between Henry and the Archbishop, so soon to take place. His feelings about it were ambivalent. For so long he had been sure that Henry desired not reconciliation but revenge, yet something in his demeanour yesterday had put a doubt into his mind. Could it be that some of his old fondness for the Archbishop still remained?–enough to make him genuinely wish for peace between them? On the one hand, their quarrel was injurious to the Church but it had given him the best opportunity he had ever had to discompose Henry FitzEmpress and settle his accounts with him; he would be loth indeed to lose that advantage and have Henry regain a friend.

All the same, Archbishop Thomas was costing him a great deal of money. Besides, for Thomas's own sake. . . . But even that could not prevent him from dwelling pleasurably on the second letter from the Pope that was to be delivered to the King of the English if the meeting brought no good result.

Henry's sons, flushed with delight and self-importance, kissed the French king's hand again and made their adieux. They were not to remain for the rest of the business.

Louis permitted himself a smile at Henry. There was movement and bustle by the great door at the other end of the hall; he saw Henry's head go up like a pointer's. But it was the Pope's envoys alone who were entering; the Archbishop and his friends and advisers were still in the outer chamber.

By the time all the formalities of introduction were done Henry was obviously becoming impatient. Even the usual Papal letter, proffered by the Prior of Mont Dieu, was handed on at once to Richard de Luci who scanned it swiftly. He turned to King Henry, pointing to the date. 'May of last year,' he murmured. 'Nearly eight months on the road.'

'What does he say?'

'No more than we might expect. He hopes to hear of peace between you—'

Henry was not listening. His eyes were fixed on the outer door and the throng that was pushing in. Among them, two heads close together, one fair, the other dark and greying, overtopped the rest. Herbert of Bosham was whispering feverishly in the Archbishop's ear.

Thomas, wearied by the conflicting advice showered on him by the various members of his entourage, hardly heard him. He stared down the hall for his first sight of Henry in four years. His long sight was still excellent and he saw him clearly, leaning a little forward, hands on wide-spread knees. But Thomas was not near enough to make out the King's expression beyond the fact that he neither scowled nor smiled.

He heard the last of Herbert's whispered counsel. 'Walk warily, my lord. I say to you from conscience that if in this mutual concession you omit the words "saving the honour of God" as you once in England omitted "saving my order" when the question of the royal customs was involved, your sorrow will be renewed. You will, of course, recall the words of the Psalmist, "I was dumb with silence; I held my peace even from good and my sorrow was stirred."'

Thomas looked at him almost blankly, then he glanced at the faces around him, all mouthing last-minute advice; he shook his head sharply as at the buzzing of tiresome gnats and increased his pace so that they fell a step or two behind. Almost running the last few steps, he closed his eyes and threw himself at Henry's feet.

In the relief that swept over him he recognised that he had run to Henry as to a sanctuary from the miseries he had endured in his exile. He was bone-tired–sick of the contention with his king, with his bishops and the Pope, weary of countering his followers' homesickness and his own longings for security. Everyone was tired of the dispute; but nothing had really changed. If he did as the papal envoys desired and submitted to the King's will, it would all have been for nothing. So Herbert, irritating Herbert, who based all his advice on Holy Writ, was right.

He felt his cheeks wet as Henry gently took him by the shoulders to raise him. Each gazed into the other's face. Henry's hands tightened on him, his mouth moved as though he would have liked to smile.

The emotional moment was quickly over and Thomas launched into his formal speech. It was directed as much at King Louis and the Pope as at Henry. He begged Henry to be merciful to the Church in England, blaming his own sinfulness for all the trouble that had come upon it. He did not look at Henry as he spoke but at a point midway between him and Louis so that, after a period of trying to catch his eye, Henry dropped his own and seemed to consider the point of his shoe, his expression withdrawn and noncommittal. Louis shaded his eyes with his hand, apparently from the occasional gleam of wintry sunshine which struck through the high windows; it enabled him to look from Henry to the Archbishop unobserved.

So that when Thomas specified several offences the King of the English had committed against the Church in his land, he saw the sudden compression of Henry's lips and, removing the obstructing hand, bent a cold stare on the Archbishop. Thomas saw it, hesitated, and let himself look directly at Henry.

'On the whole matter in dispute between us, my lord King,' he said, 'and in the presence of the lord King of the French and the princes, lay and ecclesiastical, who witness this, I throw myself on your mercy and pleasure'–with the yearning to be done with it all the words came from his heart, and as easily the phrase that followed, without a breath between–'saving the honour of God.'

It had come without conscious volition as though something–or someone–had drawn the words from him. Nor did he feel regret; it had not been Thomas of London who spoke. In the face of all those varying expressions of rage, horror and bitter disappointment around him his control returned. He heard Henry's loud, grating voice raised in fierce denunciation, and the words vanity, ingratitude, and pride, without a tremor. Royal generosity was quoted, the high-flown ambitions of underlings, the secret desires to unseat his liege lord and reign in his place.

All Henry's long-cherished resentments had boiled up, momentarily overcoming reason. He was remembering how the citizens of Northampton had begged for this commoner's touch; fuming, he screamed, 'Can you deny that you took oaths of allegiance from my subjects when you were Chancellor in order to disinherit me?' Purple with fury, he rounded upon Louis. 'It was for that reason that he outdid me in magnificence and acted so liberally in your lands!'

Completely taken aback, both by the event and by the preposterousness of Henry's allegations, Louis raised his eyes and hands to heaven.

'My lord!' exclaimed Thomas almost as fiercely. 'My lord, ever since I left your service you have reproached me for my actions as Chancellor! It is jealous anger that leads you to rebuke me for what should earn gratitude. Everyone here knows what I did for you, the loyalty with which I served you. It would be improper for me to remind you–especially here–of what advantages I gained for you. The world knows the truth of it!'

Tears stood in Henry's eyes; he breathed as though he had been running hard. Turning again to Louis, he cried, 'He dares to taunt us both, this man who foolishly and vainly deserted his church, fleeing away by night in secret although no one drove him out of the kingdom! Now he claims his cause is that of the Church and that he suffers for justice's sake! He has deceived many eminent men by his casuistry.' He paused to draw several deep, shuddering breaths. 'I have always been willing, and still am, to allow him to rule over his church with as much freedom as any of his predecessors. But take note of this, cousin; whenever he disapproves of something he says it is contrary to God's honour and so will always best me. Let me propose this to him that none may say I am a despiser of God's honour–let him behave to me as the most holy of his predecessors did towards the least of mine, and I will be content!'

Louis gazed at Henry for a long moment, noting the shaking lips and the trembling hand with which he rubbed his tear-stained cheeks. From the body of the hall came angry cries. 'Is not that sufficient?' 'The King of the English has humbled himself enough!' And from the back a jeering yell, 'Who will rule in England if he goes home?'

Louis' face had hardened. 'My lord Archbishop,' he enquired coldly, 'do you wish to be more than a saint?'

With a sinking heart Thomas answered that he was ready to return to his see under those terms but that he could not admit new customs to the Church. 'It is true that there have been archbishops greater and holier that I,' he added quietly, 'but every one of them had to deal with abuses against the Church. And if they had been entirely successful I would not now be facing this ordeal.'

He saw Louis swing impatiently towards Henry and then his view of them was blocked by the angrily expostulating men who swarmed round him, the Pope's envoys foremost among them. He shut his lips tight, not answering the bitter reproaches that were flung at him from all sides until his old friend, John Belmeis, now Bishop of Poitiers, took him by the elbow and hissed at him that such obstinacy could lead to the destruction of the Church.

Thomas allowed his eyes to rest upon the hand that grasped his arm. 'Have a care, brother,' he said coldly, 'that it is not yourselves who destroy the Church. God willing, I shall never do so.' John removed his hand as if it had been stung.

Above the urgings from the papal envoys to change his mind he could still hear Henry's angry, upraised tones insisting that the Archbishop must swear, precisely and absolutely, to keep the customs. He had been right, then; nothing was changed except that he and Henry were four years older, more set in their determination. How would it end? Henry must have been hoping that his antagonist would weaken. Now they both knew the other had not done so. Evidently his advisers were realising the same thing for they were falling silent and withdrawing a little so that he and Herbert stood alone in the centre of a ring. He could see Henry again now, rising and preparing to depart. And he saw the papal envoys hurrying away to join him.

The little group around him saw them too and followed them with eyes that returned to rest accusingly on him. He ignored the worried murmurs they were exchanging concerning Louis' protection. And when both he and Herbert tried to rally them they seemed singularly unresponsive, drawing closer together and keeping them at a distance.

On the way back to Sens the two of them rode solitary in the midst of the procession. Disappointment had stilled the most garrulous tongue; it was an unwontedly silent cavalcade; consequently, when one of his knights, Henry of Houghton, began having trouble with his mount, his irritated commands to the animal were clearly audible. 'Get on,' he ordered. 'Whoa, there! Gee up–saving, of course, God's honour, Holy Church and your order.'

Henry was still talking to the Pope's envoys 'I did *not* expel the lord of Canterbury from my realm,' he exclaimed with some heat, 'but–I offer this out of reverence for the lord Pope–if he will do what he ought and obey me in those matters in which his predecessors obeyed mine, he may go back to England and have peace there! I cannot say more.'

They eyed him dubiously. 'Will you then write an open letter to the lord Pope?' asked the Prior of Mont Dieu. 'Sealed with your seal, that we may give him some definite information as to your intentions towards the lord Archbishop.'

Henry looked at him sideways. This prior looked a simple enough fellow but was probably as slippery as all ecclesiastics. 'That is unnecessary. And you must remember that by the time he might receive it, circumstances may have changed. The letter you brought me was three-quarters of a year on the road.'

He saw them glance at one another. 'We have another letter for you,' said the Prior of Val St Pierre. He was a very thin man with a long, corded neck in which his Adam's apple bobbed convulsively as he spoke. 'We were to deliver it only if these talks failed.' He searched about inside his robe and finally located a thin and dirty roll of parchment.

Henry broke the seal and cut the cords that tied it. When he had finished reading he raised his eyes to them. They were watching him closely.

He slapped his hand down on it, his mouth twitching a little. 'He thinks to frighten me by threats?' he said softly. 'I do not fear them. Nor do I fear they will be carried out. You have seen the Archbishop–seen his behaviour towards me, his liege lord. And I tell you this. Nowhere else in all the world does the Church enjoy such freedom as in England. Nowhere else are the clergy treated with such honour.'

The monk Bernard spoke for the first time. 'That is as it should be, my lord King.'

'You think so? They are thieves and robbers for the most part, filthy and savage'–Henry's voice was rising– sacrilegious, seducers of virgins, incendiaries, murderers!'

Bernard blinked. Henry retrieved his slipping control and tapped the letter again. 'I shall send a messenger to the Pope with my answer to this.'

'And you will allow the Archbishop to return in peace to his own see?'

'I have told you that he can never enter my land until he has promised to obey what others obey.'

The Prior of Val St Pierre's throat began to work again. 'Surely we have heard him promise that?'

'He must take the oath without saving clauses.'

'My lord King, the Holy Father has placed great hopes on this meeting. You have read his letter—'

Henry's fingers began to tap on the table. 'I am prepared to summon the English bishops and ask their advice.'

There was an audible breath of relief. 'How soon may they arrive?'

'I am not in a position to set a definite date.'

'But surely you may set a date far enough ahead that they may—'

Henry rose. 'I cannot set a date. I suggest that you turn your attentions and persuasions on the Archbishop. Clerical quarrels are not the only concern of kings. If you have come to mediate, go and mediate. You are wasting my time!'

February 1169

When the Queen's sons were shown into her bower she sent away her ladies that they might talk freely. Henry was allowed the floor first and launched at once into a graphic account of the great feast at which he had served as Seneschal of France.

'King Louis conversed most graciously with me while I served him, mother,' he announced importantly, 'for I am one of his chief vassals now. He told me how happy he will be when my father cedes Anjou and Maine to me, that I may take my rightful place in his counsels. Also he asked very kindly after my wife, his daughter, and wished to know when we shall be bedded.'

Eleanor lowered her lids. She did not doubt that Louis would be happy at such uncharacteristic behaviour on the older Henry's part. Young Henry did not notice her lack of response; he continued to pour out opinions, impressions and hopes for the future in a state of high excitement. 'When may I see Margaret, my wife?' he enquired eagerly. 'Has she grown? I hope she is not so lean as when last I saw her.'

Eleanor gestured towards the corner. 'See how thoughtful a mother you have. Did you think I would not guess what was closest to your heart?'

A girl who had been sitting quiet as a mouse with some embroidery in her lap came shyly forward. She had long black hair, very smooth and straight, and a narrow elfin face. Her nose was too large for prettiness but when the rest of her face filled out a little she would make an attractive woman. She stood with her hands demurely folded as became a maid but the rather full dark eyes were devouring Henry.

Eleanor smiled faintly. That those two young things were well satisfied with each other was clear. She prayed that Richard might be equally pleased with Alais, and Geoffrey with Constance, Conan's daughter.

For herself, these new arrangements meant the addition of two more small girls to her family; the household was, in her opinion, already overburdened with females. However, it was a method of increase infinitely preferable to childbearing. She was glad to be done with that.

Life was a risk from the cradle to the tomb, of course, but she had long considered it to be unfairly loaded against women. She had been lucky; of the ten children, two to Louis and eight to Henry, that she had borne, only one had died in childhood–but there were many women who reared only two or three out of ten or more, or died worn out before their thirtieth birthday. It did not incline one to think highly of God's arrangements for the multiplication of mankind.

She thought of Margaret's narrow hips with sudden doubt and, looking her way, saw Henry's golden head bent down to hers as he held forth upon the court they would set up in Angers. She said warningly, 'Do not place overmuch reliance on your father's allowing you a free hand in your provinces as yet.'

Henry's eyes opened wide at her. 'What do you mean? I am full fourteen. Why, at my age my father had led troops in battle.'

'Only with older, wiser heads to make the dispositions.' She saw his colour rise and wished she had not spoken in front of Margaret. Both of them looked resentful. She turned back to Richard who all this time had been telling Geoffrey about last summer's event in Aquitaine. He was describing the ceremony at Limoges where he had contracted a symbolic marriage with St Valerie, patron saint of the province.

Henry too listened now, his expression growing ever more peevish. Finally he said sharply, 'I cannot see why Richard was carried about your duchy thus. My father has never done as much for me although I am the elder. Why should I be kept hidden in England while others, lesser, younger, travel far and wide?'

'That's not strange, seeing you are heir to England,' Richard said. 'And you were not hid; you had your own household.'

'A household, not a court! Tutors and masters and grey-beards to watch me! I was made to study while you were gadding abroad having gold rings pushed on your finger by bishops. Only I, who am nearly grown, am unknown in my own lands!'

'Come, come,' said Eleanor soothingly, 'it is unmannerly to raise your voice in the presence of ladies. You shall have your court as soon as you are crowned, I am sure.'

'And who will crown me while my father will not allow the Archbishop of Canterbury into England?' Henry stared at her with his lip pushed out. 'Even King Louis is against him now.'

'There is always York.' She paused a second. 'Has Louis turned against the Archbishop?'

'Oh–I know not.' He flung round petulantly. 'So some were saying. I did not see him; they took good care of that.'

'I saw him,' announced Geoffrey.

'Why did you not tell me? How did he look?'

'Tall–very thin.'

'I know that, you simpleton. I don't want to know what he looks like but how he is!'

'How can I know? I would not have known who he was but that the serving-men were going to him for his blessing.'

No, thought Eleanor, Geoffrey would not remember. Half his lifetime is forever to a boy of ten, and it is longer than that since Henry and Becket were inseparable.

'I was sorry to hear the quarrel was not mended,' she interposed easily. 'You were not present at their meeting, I suppose?'

They shook their heads. Young Henry still looked ruffled and Margaret close to tears.

'It was not our father's fault that it was not,' said Richard.

Young Henry rounded on him. 'What do you know about it? You don't know him, any more than Geoffrey does.' He was bristling at Richard again, ready to defend his foster-father against all comers.

Eleanor sighed inwardly. What was it about Becket that he could arouse such steadfastly diverse emotions in all who knew him?

'You are upsetting Margaret with your squabbling,' she said coldly. 'Are you unable to converse civilly together?'

After that reproof they mended their manners somewhat but she thought it well to steer clear of the subject uppermost in her mind. So they talked of lighter matters, including the younger children and their half-brother, the other Geoffrey, who had been laid low with an ague that had gone to his chest and left him with a racking cough. It seemed that reminded Henry of something.

'Shall our other little brother join your family too, mother?' he asked her. 'William, I mean, who lives at Woodstock.'

For Eleanor, the linking of that name and place meant the firstborn son who had gone too soon into the dark. 'Woodstock?' she said from a great distance, trying to suppress the painful memory.

But she realised what he must mean even as the word passed her lips. She made herself smile. 'No. My family will be large enough, do you not think?'

The quality of the silence told her that the two eldest boys, at least, recognised young Henry's blunder. She leaned forward, facing him. 'It does not matter,' she said gently. 'It is not something I am–unused to.'

He raised a crimson face. 'You should have me beaten,' he blurted.

Her glance went beyond him. 'Why should you pay for what is not your fault?'

Margaret had cast down her eyes, her mouth prim. She looked more than usually like Louis. She mumbled something about getting her sewing and went over to the corner.

'Is the child's mother with him at Woodstock?' asked Eleanor quickly.

He fumbled and coloured even more deeply. 'I think so–I am not sure–people talk of it so openly I had thought you knew.'

'I know now,' she said, 'but I am not one of those who blame the messenger for the evil of the tidings. Have you heard her name?'

He hesitated.

'Is it the de Clifford girl?'

He answered only with a nod. She gave an angry laugh. 'Then it is not such news to me. And now no more. Go fetch your little bride from the corner where she is hiding. And Henry—' He turned back to look at her. 'Do not ever treat her thus,' she said. 'Keep a decent reticence at least.'

She dismissed them all soon after and heard the boys go leaping and whooping down the stair, all embarrassments forgotten. She had not learned much that she wanted to know. As for what she had learned, she supposed she would have to get used to it. It was not as though she any longer cared.

But Woodstock, she told herself fiercely, Woodstock, a royal palace! Her angry thoughts jostled, unco-ordinated, but after a little her face grew gentler; she was remembering another palace in a different world. Oh to be in Poitou, where arcaded walls gave upon sunlit gardens, where there was poetry and song, and fragrance lingered on the evening air. . . .

March–April 1169

As Thomas heard it Henry soon found an object on which to vent his frustration. He spent six weeks in preparations for war and early in March took his army back into Poitou against the Counts of Angoulême and La Marche. No news of his doings there had filtered through as yet.

His own worries were more immediate. Without the continuing financial aid of King Louis he and his companions would soon find themselves in desperate straits and no provisions had been received from him since they had returned from Montmirail. Much as it galled Thomas, only the charity of John Belmeis of Poitiers and William of Sens had kept them afloat. It was beginning to seem that he must dismiss most of his clerks and retire with Herbert (who resolutely refused to be dismissed) into Burgundy.

He had been discussing the situation with a few of his intimates when a messenger from the French court arrived, requesting his presence there. The spark of hope that rose in Thomas was plainly not shared by the rest of them, for the man was scarcely out of the door before Hugh of Nunant announced gloomily that this was the end; the French meant to drive them out of the kingdom. Murmurs of glum agreement came from the others.

Thomas had shaken his head. 'You are no prophet, nor a prophet's son,' he commented briefly.

Even now, entering the French king's presence chamber, he felt no real trepidation. Louis had risen, his expression mournful but somehow appealing. He gazed at Thomas, then came towards him with extended hands and, falling on his knees, clutched at the heavy folds of the long *cappa*. Surprised and embarrassed, Thomas remembered how this king had once similarly abased himself before Bernard of Clairvaux.

Louis was weeping. 'Forgive me, my lord Archbishop. You were right from the beginning. I should have believed you and supported you at Montmirail.' It was difficult to hear the words, muffled by the cloth and choked with sobs. Absurdly, Thomas felt his legs begin to tremble and stiffened them instinctively.

Louis raised a wet face and pulled himself erect but he still clung to the Archbishop like a remorseful child. 'In my presence he made peace with Poitou and Brittany and has now perfidiously broken his word. He cannot be trusted. He has broken the pact.' Louis wiped his nose with the back of his hand. 'I beseech you to forgive me. If I had only followed your example of prudence, foresight and discretion—'

'Say no more, my lord, I pray you. But if it is my place to forgive you I do so freely.'

'Your attitude is that of a true Christian. I can scarcely bear to tell you what King Henry has done.' Nevertheless, he proceeded to do so, detailing how the King of the English had despoiled the lands of many of the nobles, had seized the possessions of others, and had thrown the lords into prison where he was keeping them in chains. 'Never again shall I desert you,' he ended. 'King Henry is henceforth my enemy for he is an enemy of truth and fair dealing, and, as you yourself have pointed out, an enemy of the Church.'

Louis seemed to expect some reply to that but he received none. He continued after a pause, 'Sit at my right hand. You are welcome to stay in my kingdom as long as you wish; I shall support you as before. If the Pope were only still in my lands everything would be as clear to him as to me.' He stopped again, then added with a determined air, 'I shall write to the Holy Father myself.'

Riding back to Sens Thomas considered their conversation. He was aware that Louis would like him to excommunicate Henry, for he had linked his name with those members of the English clergy who were Thomas's avowed enemies, and he was of course aware that the suspension that had kept the Archbishop's hands tied this last year was automatically lifted at the beginning of Lent.

But what were Louis' motives? Sudden irritation rose in him. Was he becoming over-suspicious? With letters and messages from the Pope taking months to reach him, he was thrown entirely on his own resources. If Alexander had stood by him and had given him a position at the papal court in the beginning instead of effectively banishing him from the scenes of action, these states of uncertainty would never have arisen. Alexander's vacillations were the cause of half his troubles. . . .

Well, he could only do as he thought best. He listed the names of those he had decided to excommunicate. But Henry's was not among them.

On that same day in Benevento the Pope, with many pauses for thought, dictated a letter to Archbishop Thomas of Canterbury. He stated that he had refused the demands of King Henry's ambassadors, and he enjoined moderation and conciliation. Then he sat so long remembering the man and wondering, in view of the news from Montmirail, whether moderation was any longer in him that the clerk raised his eyes and gave a gentle cough.

The Pope jumped a little and then ordered the Archbishop not to sentence King Henry's person, realm or officers until the newly-appointed nuncios, Gratian and Vivian, had fulfilled their mission. 'Any sentence already pronounced,' he continued softly, 'but no–strike that out. He could not–have done so.' He sat drumming his fingers on the table while the clerk waited. 'But then again. . . . Aye, set it down. Any sentence already pronounced must be suspended until that same time.'

He too felt a sudden sharp exasperation. Who but Christ Himself could make peace between two such unyielding men?

April–May 1169

In the guest chamber of Clairvaux Abbey on Palm Sunday the windows were still unshuttered though Compline was over. A peach tree across the court, laden with pink blossom, stood limned against the wall in exquisite clarity, every flower and unfurling leaf as sharp and clear as a painting in a Book of Hours.

John of Salisbury did not see it as he listened to the men behind him discussing the ceremony they had witnessed that day: the second excommunication of Gilbert Foliot, Bishop of London. It was little more than a month since the Archbishop had loosed the thunderbolt at nine others who had offended him, the Bishop of Salisbury and the Earl of Norfolk among them, and today he had announced too his intention of visiting the same punishment on half a dozen more on Ascension Day.

John turned round quickly when he heard someone enter and, seeing it was Herbert of Bosham, joined the group by the fire.

'The letters are written,' he told them with evident relish, 'certifying to the clergy of London the Archbishop's acts and intentions. And those to Salisbury and London themselves informing them that the sentences involve interdicts on their sees.'

There was a hushed silence as all those present took in the implications; then Hugh of Nunant, always prone to pessimism, observed that it would surprise him if any of the letters reached their destinations, what with the close watch the King was keeping on aliens who entered England and the dire punishments he was threatening against any who dared carry messages from the Archbishop of Canterbury.

But Herbert merely tapped his finger on his nose and grinned and, in case they did not catch his drift, nodded meaningly towards the door. Lombard of Piacenza, who had grown very deaf, pulled at Alexander Llewellyn's sleeve. 'What is it? Is someone without?'

'No, no,' said Alexander impatiently. 'He means the Archbishop has a messenger he trusts to get the letters through.'

John got up and went out of the door.

Thomas was kneeling at the Prie-dieu when John entered but he signed to him to remain and soon rose to his feet. They spoke for a time of general topics but soon came round to the King, and Thomas had bitter words to use of his obduracy. John's look was wry. 'He has no premium on obstinacy, Thomas.'

'He is so certain he is always right there is no moving him. But he was always thus–when he fears he is losing an argument he flies into a rage and will not try to see another point of view—'

'Do you? Nay—' John raised his hand. 'Hear me out, at least. I hold no brief for him–you, of all men, should know my mind on that matter. Yet I should not be a true friend if I did not speak frankly, and this I must tell you. Your own accusations against the King betray you. All men see their own faults mirrored in others.'

Thomas spoke stiffly. 'You think me in the wrong?'

John sighed. 'I believe you are in the right but you seem to forget our adversary is our sovereign lord. Be not stiff-necked with him–gentleness will serve our cause better than truculence. You think him opinionated and wilful but he thinks you arbitrary and perverse. Where there is no goodwill there can be no reconciling of differences.'

'You do not know him as I do.'

'I saw his face when he greeted you at Montmirail.'

Thomas's eyes fell away. 'It may be true,' he said very slowly, 'that he has still some feeling for me. But do you not see that will make no difference? Can you not see that with him love is always subordinated to power?' He shook his head. 'I have to win. It has been given me to show him he too has a king. If I did not love *him*—' He swallowed. 'Even you do not understand.'

'I see only a battle of wills.'

'I know. That is all the world would see.'

'And to win it you will risk thousands of innocent souls.'

'Innocent souls are never at risk.'

John closed his eyes.

'If I pleased men,' said Thomas, 'I should not be the servant of Christ.'

The rain that had threatened all morning began to fall in torrents before the small ship was well out of harbour so that William Bouhert and Berengar the Frenchman were forced to seek shelter in the foetid cockpit which was the only cabin space. But at least the downpour flattened the turbulent waves and lessened the rolling and pitching which had already caused William Bouhert's high colour to wane.

It would have taken a great deal more than that, though, to make him repent of their hazardous undertaking. He had exiled himself willingly with the Archbishop but that, to his passionate devotion, had seemed nothing; he had longed for some sterner way to prove himself. Now at last his chance had come; he had been chosen to accompany and, if necessary, protect the messenger who carried on his person the precious packet of letters which would announce to the Archbishop's enemies their banishment from Christ's fold. The importance of the mission lay in the fact that the sentences possessed no legal validity until they had been served on the offenders, and with King Henry as determined to keep them out of his realm as they were to get in the risks were great indeed. That made it all the better, and an offering worthy of the master he revered.

He explained all this to the Frenchman several times, and as often asked him if he had the packet safe; Berengar, expressing deepest understanding, had patted his breast on each occasion but his eyes, after a while, had grown a trifle glassy. When he said he thought he would go up on deck, William nodded.

On deck Berengar, who had never felt seasick in his life, sighed faintly. He had little faith in the value of William's high sentiments should it come to torture in one of King Henry's gaols. So he went to find the captain, a Breton whom he had used before; they understood each other well because neither would have thought of tempting fate for anything but money.

It was early evening when the passengers and their horses were put off to splash through the shallow water to a lonely pebbled beach near Sandwich. To the west the sky was a pale, clear green with one star burning in it like a white lamp. All was silent.

They too were silent, riding down the stony track towards Eastry. They would lie there that night in safety, for the prior was a secret friend of the Archbishop's and asked no awkward questions of men who appeared from nowhere. Tomorrow they would make for London and, all going well, would deliver the documents in Paul's on Ascension Day. Under his cloak Berengar crossed his fingers. He was as Christian as the next man but it did no harm to invoke other powers as extra insurance against disaster.

It was evening again when they came over London Bridge and their eyes flew about, noting the heavy load it carried; they had to wait some time before they could edge into the stream of wagons and pack horses that was crossing. Already, only five or six years after erection, it was patent that its builders had not foreseen the volume of traffic it would draw. Still, it was the pride of London and it bestrode the Thames arrogantly. It was all of elm, cunningly jointed and pinned;

the rails, breast high, were as thick through as a man, and the planks beneath the horses' hoofs as thick, yet still they creaked at the great weight upon them.

To their right the White Tower loomed, not white at all now but as delicately pink in the sunset as the puffs of cloud overhead. William Bouhert did not look that way; his eyes were fixed on the growing spire of Paul's ahead; they had got on with the building since last he had seen it. Thursday, he thought, Thursday at this time, we shall either have passed back over this bridge or be lying in a dungeon. He clenched his hands upon the reins and glanced quickly at Berengar, but he was looking about with the same faintly derogatory air as William had seen on the faces of Englishmen in Sens or Soissons.

Many men came to drink at the small and very dirty hostelry where they slept that night, rough fellows some but others whose manner and bearing bespoke the journeyman or even the master. Little but a nod or a knowing look passed between them in the taproom; but when Thursday came at last and they pushed up to Paul's great door William recognised many in the crowd around them. After they had thrust and elbowed their way to the front rank nearest the altar those same faces surrounded them. One, a huge, red-bearded fellow, stood hard by; when William looked his way, his eyelid drooped infinitesimally.

As the High Mass began they were pressed close against the altar-rail amongst those who held purses or small leather bags; these waited to present offerings to be laid upon the altar. It was not Gilbert Foliot himself who officiated today but a priest of the diocese named Vitalis, one who was noted for the speed with which he could rattle through the rite. So it was not long before he descended the chancel steps and moved along the line, gathering up the tributes; he was doing that at a good clip too.

William held his breath and fixed his eyes upon the great,

painted crucifix over the altar; he tried to pray but found he had forgotten every prayer he knew. Out of the corner of his eye he saw the priest's hand come out to snatch the package Berengar held out, and he knelt stiff as the image he had been watching as the Frenchman put out his other hand to hold the priest motionless while he called loudly to epistoller and gospeller to witness his command in the name of the Holy Father that one copy of the letters he was presenting be given to the Bishop and one to the Dean. Then, turning to the congregation, Berengar cried in the tones of a herald–'Know ye all that Gilbert, Bishop of London, is excommunicated by Archbishop Thomas of Canterbury, Legate of the Holy See!'

In the moment of silence that followed William swung up his cloak to cover Berengar, they slid under the arm of Redbeard and ducked swiftly through a press of men who might have had neither sight nor feeling for all the notice that was taken of their movements. By the time they came among strangers everyone else was shoving this way and that, craning and stretching to see what had happened; they too turned to stare in the direction they had come and pulled at arms to enquire what voice it was that had cried the sentence.

At the altar all was confusion. A low groan rustled down the nave as it became apparent that the clergy were leaving with their business only half completed. In an instant the first excited witnesses were pouring out from Paul's doors to spread the word all over London. Soon Cheapside and Thames Street were full of running figures, all eager to be first with the sensational news.

Gilbert Foliot passed under the gate arch of Westminster Abbey very early for his meeting with the barons of the Exchequer and the clergy of London. There had been an untimely frost that morning; the new leaves hung like blackened rags charred by fire; it reminded him hideously of another, more eternal, fire which surely awaited the unprofitable servant.

Wido Rufus, the Abbot, greeted him effusively but Gilbert was not pleased to see behind him the tall figure of Richard of Ilchester. He had hoped to see Wido alone first; Richard was too much a king's man to be allowed to overhear his own most inward doubts expressed. Yet Richard too looked pale and ill-at-ease, his wall eye wandering even more uncontrollably than usual, and Gilbert began to suspect that Wido's long-windedness was a cover for inner dismay. He saw that they were looking to him to hearten them against this fresh blow; doubtless they thought he had called the meeting for that reason.

If they but knew the agonies of uncertainty he was suffering! Whatever might be said of that monster across the Channel, he was still their metropolitan with the power to bind and loose, to deny them the sacraments, to cut them off from salvation. The sweat rose on Gilbert's brow as he thought of the anathema cried upon his name, the snuffing out of the candle-flame that symbolised his soul.

He had been furious at first at the injustice of it, had declared that he would travel to Rome himself to appeal to the Pope, but in the black, sleepless spaces of the night fear had set a cold creeping in his bowels. He was old, he might fall sick unto death. . . . He, who had always held as fervently to the letter as to the spirit of the Church's law, could not now make himself believe it meant nothing. Neither, he saw, could these others. They were as frightened as he was.

But it was unjust. What had he done but obey his prince? Could he have refused to act as receiver for the incomes of those clerks of the Archbishop who had fled to him? Everything he had done was at the King's express orders. Gilbert's mind did not go quite so far as to censure King Henry but he considered the fact that he was still in good spiritual odour while those who worked his will were excommunicate.

The letter he had received from Henry speaking of the

wrongs done by 'that traitor Thomas, mine enemy'–a phrase which once he would have given much to hear–had merely swelled his resentments. Easy enough for Henry to say that he would pay for Gilbert's journey to Rome, easier still to give him a choice of remaining in England or joining the court in Normandy as he should deem most expedient for his own interests. . . . Gilbert saw the offers as Henry's means of salving his conscience. Was the cost of a journey the price of his immortal soul?

He could not eat any of the breakfast the Abbot offered. But he managed to pull himself together sufficiently to hatch some elaborate arguments to justify their disobeying the Archbishop.

He laid them before his clergy an hour or two later in as confident a manner as he could attain to. 'The canons clearly provide,' he announced grimly, 'that no one shall be condemned unsummoned and that no bishop can excommunicate a man unless his guilt be proved. Since, then, his lordship has acted unjustly, we trust in God that his sword shall smite nothing but air. We anticipated this blow by appealing to the Pope and an appeal made at the beginning of Lent must nullify a sentence passed on Palm Sunday—' He talked on and on, knowing that as he could not deceive himself, he could not deceive them.

No one spoke. The silence, and the way their eyes avoided his, told him all he needed to know. Before he had said half he had planned to, he stopped abruptly. Seeing his bad colour Richard of Ilchester hurried to him.

Gilbert found himself sitting with his head between his knees. As the dizziness cleared he heard someone say far off, 'What is going to happen then?' and another voice reply, 'God knows!'

He knew then he would go to Rome.

August 1169

War had troubled Aquitaine all summer; the southern lords had something to avenge this time, apart from ancient feuds with their Norman overlords. Last year one of their number, Robert de Silly, had surrendered honourably to superior forces and submitted to King Henry; despite this, he had been refused the kiss of peace, loaded with chains and cast into a dungeon. There he had been starved to death.

The rebellious barons might be united in a common cause but they could not sink their differences sufficiently to formulate an overall plan of campaign. King Henry marched his well-trained army from one rock-girt stronghold to the next and they fell like wheat before the sickle; by June Poitou lay quiet and a month later Gascony was subdued. At the end of July, certain he had taught them a lesson they would not soon forget, Henry turned north for home.

He did not hurry for he knew what awaited him in Normandy. Two more papal legates, lawyers this time. They had made better time from Rome than had the cardinals two years previously, being, he supposed, less puffed up with their own importance. Well, they could wait upon his pleasure. He did not even want to think about the subject they came to discuss.

Early in the year he had proposed to the Holy See that Becket (even he now used that derogatory pseudonym) be transferred from Canterbury, and he had offered to pay all the Pope's debts if Alexander would grant him permission to fill all the vacancies in the English church. He had begged Louis to expel the Archbishop from his domains. None of it had availed him anything. So he had pushed it all out of his mind and gone off to Aquitaine to execute summary justice. There news of the fresh excommunications had reached him.

Gilbert Foliot had accepted his offer and set out for Rome but he had got no further than Milan when the Pope sent him word that he had empowered the Archbishop of Rouen to absolve him provided he swear to obey papal instructions on the matter in dispute. Henry had read the bishop's abject terror between the lines of his letters and he knew very well that Gilbert would jump at the chance of absolution on any terms. And, once accepted, he would obey them, including the one to mend the quarrel. So what was left to do?

Always, when he got as far as this, he flew into a rage, refusing to think further about a conflict it seemed he could not win. It was why he lingered so long in Anjou on the way home to see work begun on a long series of embankments along the Loire to prevent the river from flooding the fields every spring.

So it was the third week in August before he arrived in Domfront, dusty, tired, but looking about with that sharp, narrow-eyed look that made men run hither and yon, pretending to a quite unnecessary busyness. Young Henry was there to greet him in the midst of a score or so of lads his own age, members of his household and the older sons of the greatest houses of England and Normandy.

He ran his eye over them. Not a one to touch young Henry, either for looks or bearing. That was how it should be; one should be able to pick out a king instantly. And his boy was a king indeed. He swelled with paternal pride.

Leaping from his horse he hastened to kiss him, to stand beside him with one hand on his shoulder. Not yet fifteen, the lad was as tall as he. 'Are the papal envoys here?' he asked in a low voice, under cover of the noise and excitement of arrival.

'No,' said young Henry, 'they wait for you to send for them, no doubt.' He gave his father a quick glance. 'They know better, I suppose, than to approach me.'

The King laughed. 'That's as well. Men like that are masters of statecraft. They'd run rings around a boy. I only thought they might be here because they'd guess I'd come where you were. But I'm glad they're not that we may have some time together before all that begins.' He turned to go in.

'Think of me arguing with lawyers while you are out enjoying yourself hunting.'

Young Henry looked stiff. 'Shall I not be present at the talks?'

'You? No, lad; you go off and pleasure yourself.'

Young Henry followed. 'Why not? How shall I learn statecraft if I am not to hear?'

His father kept on walking. 'Time enough for that.' He was at pains to keep his voice easy but he wondered what the tutors had been up to that a boy should bandy words with his father so.

Young Henry persisted. 'I sat with you at Clarendon.'

The King stopped and faced his son. 'Yea, so you did.' He thought of his tears for the Archbishop on that occasion. 'Perhaps it would have been better if you had not been there.' Gripping the boy's arm, he said, 'Enjoy your boyhood while you may; it's too soon over. I had none.'

He saw the sulky look and slapped him on the back. 'How are you off for money? I warrant you've run through all I left you. There's armour we captured in the baggage, and swords, some of them jewelled, very fine. You take your pick. You don't want to worry your head about anything else yet.'

Money, thought young Henry, and loot. I am to be paid off like a child who wants something he cannot have. He will never let me rule, or even learn to. Nor will he permit me to sit in the councils, as our mother did Richard in Poitou, and hear the talk of men.

He turned his back upon his father without another word and went to rejoin his friends. He would take them down when the baggage was unloaded and share out the plunder from Poitou. That was something Richard should not get.

September 1169

Gratian the lawyer said coldly, 'I can see no point in

remaining here any longer.'

Vivian, the other papal legate, did not answer. He was a brown, bulky man with a square jaw and considerable determination; he was not yet prepared to wash his hands entirely of Henry FitzEmpress.

Gratian, he thought, lacked staying power; the negotiations' sudden collapse just as success had appeared within their grasp had discouraged him. But things had looked as black before–blacker even, with King Henry threatening to join the schismatics and later shouting at them to do as they pleased, he didn't care an egg for them or their excommunications. Yet under all the bluster Vivian had sensed that he was unsure of himself. He was therefore ready to hang on a little longer.

The two legates had been following King Henry about between Domfront, Bayeux and Bures for more than a fortnight now. Henry had begun with menacing demands for the absolution of his men and had been pulled up short by Gratian's haughty retort, 'Do not threaten us, my lord. We come from a court that has been wont to give the law to emperors.' As one stormy interview followed another, they had managed to hammer out some sort of settlement.

Gratian had consented to absolve those of the King's men who were present on an oath of unconditional obedience to their commands, and Vivian had agreed to travel to England to absolve the rest. In return, Henry had conceded the Archbishop's demands for the restitution of Canterbury's property and promised him safe entry into England. And then the King, out of sheer pettiness, so Gratian believed, had yesterday insisted on the inclusion of the words 'saving the honour of the kingdom'. The Archbishop's representatives had countered with the demand that 'and the Church' be added. Neither side would budge an inch.

'I see no point in continuing,' Gratian repeated. 'It is clear, to me at least, that King Henry does not want peace with the

Archbishop. If he were sincere, he would never have sent that last order to England.' He searched about among the parchments on the board before him for the copy they had secretly acquired. 'Look at it again.'

Vivian gave a slight shake of the head. 'I remember. The last throw of a desperate man.'

' "Anyone found with letters of the Pope or the Archbishop shall be instantly taken and executed as a traitor," ' read Gratian inexorably. ' "No one shall be permitted to leave the country without licence; anyone, from bishop to layman, observing the interdict shall be banished with all his kin and have his goods confiscated—" Does that sound like a man who has peace in mind? And'–his voice rose with indignation–'Peter's Pence is not to be sent to Rome but collected for the King.'

Vivian, still keeping his detachment, saw that Gratian had gone over entirely to the Archbishop's side. 'He is trying to cover himself against all eventualities,' he said.

'I shall return to Rome and inform his Holiness that this king is completely untrustworthy.'

'I understand. But you will not object if I remain and try once more?'

Gratian stood up. 'You will be wasting your time.'

'Well, perhaps. But I feel I must make one last effort.' He did not say what was in his mind: that this might be easier with his inflexible brother-legate gone.

Apparent goodwill, he sensed, would confuse King Henry, might even disarm him. Then, as a friend, he could point out the dire consequences of a refusal to compromise; he must know that his people would not quickly forgive a king who brought interdict upon them. His subtle brain leapt ahead, laying plans; he was not aware of Gratian any longer.

Gratian, seeing it, looked at him hard. He knew of Vivian's reputation for venality. But the Pope knew of it too so it would not matter. His own was the voice that would be listened to.

Certainly he did not believe that Vivian could out-manœuvre King Henry in a battle of wits.

November 1169

Archdeacon Vivian had succeeded in his work so well that King Henry was on pilgrimage to the shrine of St Denis in the great new abbey church built by Abbot Suger in Paris. At the golden altar he offered a sumptuous pall and eighty gold coins of Byzantium; King Louis was deeply impressed at the evidence of such a change of heart. He laid on a splendid reception when the King of the English arrived on Montmartre–the site of St Denis's martyrdom–where he was to meet the Archbishop and make his peace with him at last.

Henry had given way on every point. He would abandon the customs and would permit his clergy freedom to appeal to Rome over his head. He would even cede all the property that the Archbishop claimed belonged to Canterbury, though some of it had passed through several hands in the last five years. In return he asked only the omission of all saving clauses. And the Archbishop had agreed. All that remained was for both to sign the documents setting forth the conditions.

It was unfortunate that the Archbishop was later in arriving than the King but Henry waited with every appearance of good humour.

When he arrived the afternoon was well advanced. Vivian immediately presented King Henry with the petition upon whose wording he had worked so hard.

Henry laid his finger on the last line. 'That should read that the Archbishop shall have his church and his possessions as his predecessors in the archiepiscopate had them,' he said.

Vivian gently shook his head. 'Nay, my lord King. You agreed to restore all the churches and prebends which fell vacant after the Archbishop left the country that he may deal with them as his own.'

Henry looked sharply at Vivian, but said no more. Thomas bit his lip. He did not look at Henry and Henry did not look at him.

This apparently was Henry's last attempt at evasion. He publicly accepted the rest of the conditions without further argument.

'We come now,' announced Vivian, 'to the question of the seizure of movable goods—'

'Thirty thousand marks seems to the Archbishop an equitable sum,' said Rotrou of Rouen.

Henry looked at Thomas then, and quickly away again. His mouth twisted a little.

'So necessary and desired a peace should not be impeded over a matter of money,' put in King Louis anxiously. 'Is it in your mind a fair sum, cousin?'

Henry's eyebrows went up. 'It is too high, of course. But I will pay whatever sum is determined between the Archbishop's advisers and my own.'

Vivian almost rubbed his hands. The long struggle was over. 'While they consult together then—' He caught King Louis' eye; they had previously agreed to avert any prolonged confrontation between the two principals.

Louis rose and went across to Henry. It was already growing dark and he was more than ready to concur with Vivian's unspoken signal. After bowing to the assembled company they departed arm-in-arm, deep in what appeared to be amicable conversation.

Vivian was actually rubbing his hands as he came over to Thomas and his advisers, the Bishops of Rouen and of Séez. 'All has gone most satisfactorily, do you not agree, my lords?'

Thomas's nod was guarded. He was not sure how deeply committed Vivian was to Henry. 'There is still the matter of what guarantees the King will give that he intends to keep his promises. Not that I have so far any real reason to distrust him'–he carefully kept his voice noncommital–'but I know many of his vassals hate me and will do all they can to violate the terms of the peace, especially those who now hold property that belongs rightfully to Canterbury. However, I have been in touch with the Holy Father on this question. He tells me I must be satisfied with the kiss of peace from him.'

Vivian, still delighted with his success, foresaw no difficulty there. It was, after all, the only thing a priest could ask, oaths being forbidden to him. 'I see no reason why you should not have it immediately,' he said. 'I will go to King Henry myself as soon as your representatives have agreed with his upon the proper sum that should be paid in restitution.'

'Thirty thousand marks,' said Thomas firmly.

'Yes. . . . Very well.' He went over to where the officials were still arguing.

But it was more than an hour before he came bustling back and unctuously informed them that he would now carry the Archbishop's request to the King. While he was gone–and it was a long time–the Archbishop and the two bishops sat talking quietly together. None of them could quite believe that it was all over, or that if it was how different life would be.

When Vivian came upon King Louis, King Henry was no longer in his company. He was already preparing to leave, Louis said, for the quarters that had been assigned to him at Mantes, more than thirty miles away. Together they hastened to catch him before he departed.

Suavely Henry listened to the request and as suavely answered that nothing would please him more than to kiss the Archbishop; he no longer bore him the least ill-will but he had once sworn in anger that he would never grant him the *pax*, whatever happened. This was too solemn an oath to break.

Vivian and King Louis walked back to the Chapel of the Martyrdom in silence, the fate of Robert de Silly in both their minds.

Thomas showed no surprise; his suspicions were now confirmed. He knew Henry's conception of feudal honour too well to miss the implications. 'You may tell him I shall never make peace without it,' he said with finality, and turned away.

Riding down the hill with his men to their lodgings at the Temple, he noticed the dejected slump of Hugh of Nunant's shoulders. 'I'm sorry, Hugh,' he said softly as he came abreast. 'I long to go home as much as you do.'

Hugh raised a tear-stained face. 'The peace of the Church has been discussed today in the Chapel of the Martyrdom,' he said in a tone harsh with accusation. 'I am beginning to believe that only through your martyrdom will it ever be attained.'

Thomas swung round as if he had been stung. 'Would to God she might be delivered at such a price,' he retorted. 'If I thought my blood could save her—' He heard his own voice shake and clamped his lips hard together.

A number of the company heard the exchange and even those out of earshot caught the open rancour of the tone. Thomas kept his chin high. He was sharply wounded but, worse, he was also angry.

That some people agreed with Hugh became apparent after the night office. Thomas came out of the chapel to find a small crowd waiting for him. No one seemed to wish to be first to speak but finally one of the clerks stepped forward and informed him haltingly that they could approve his cause no longer. The King had yielded every point and was ready to restore everything he had seized; there was no reason now why they should stay in exile while the Archbishop held out for so personal a matter as the *pax*.

Thomas listened with grave attention. Anger had died in him; a heavy ache in his chest remained. Almost indifferently he told them that without the kiss the peace meant nothing, but that if it was their wish he would go back to England, there to suffer whatever the Lord might decree.

That took them by surprise. There was silence and he turned to go. 'My lord,' called the clerk who was spokesman.

Thomas looked back at him. Tears were streaming down his face. He made a gesture but Thomas could not bring himself to respond. He turned on his heel and left them.

X
June-July 1170

Sunlight streaming in through the coloured windows of the church of the Abbey of Westminster struck sparkles from the jewels studding the trefoils of the crown poised above the young King's head. Archbishop Roger of York held it high a moment in the expectant hush, then brought it slowly down to rest upon young Henry's brow. At that moment the sun went behind a cloud, the shining tableau dimmed and the candle-flames upon the altar became visible once more. The close-packed crowd of witnesses saw the new crown dull to brass and the boy's bright hair to dingy brown; ever ready to see omens on such occasions, they shifted restively as the bannered trumpets spilled showers of silver notes across the lofty nave. For Canterbury, not York, should have been crowning the heir to the kingdom.

But the trumpets sang their triumph to Roger for himself as much as for young Henry. This was the supreme moment of his career for which he had worked and waited. He, despite all censures and prohibitions, was officiating at this most important coronation as Primate of England with the Bishops of London, Salisbury, Durham and Rochester acting as his assistants. It was he who would afterwards address the congregation on this hopeful and joyous event while the old

King listened from his chair of state in the forefront, and (he hoped) took due note of the loyalty and obedience of the one Archbishop he had in England.

Henry noted it. He had forgotten, along with much else, that he had ever disliked Roger of York. But then, the man of thirty-seven, obsessed to the point of mania with the need to prove his ascendancy, was not the same person as the neophyte ruler who, fifteen years before, had had such a fine conceit of his own omnipotence.

Even seven short months ago he had never imagined that his denial of the kiss of peace to Archbishop Thomas would raise such a storm of protest all over Europe. That in itself had annoyed him; when the Pope wrote personally to him, absolving him of his vow not to give it, perversity deepened into a mulish obstinacy. He would not be pushed. Thomas should have the kiss when he was ready to grant it and not an hour before.

The Pope had threatened his continental lands with interdict. That was more frightening, for they could not so easily be sealed off from the letters of anathema as could England. But Henry had still maintained an intractable silence. Pope Alexander knew when to press an advantage and when to hold fire. He confirmed temporary absolution of the men Thomas had excommunicated and sat back to await events.

Henry sailed for England in February. He was determined to follow the Emperor's example of the previous year and crown his heir, and if the furtive and distrustful Becket would not return to fulfil his duties, the honour should be given to Roger of York; Henry had been careful to preserve the letter of permission the Pope had imprudently granted two years earlier when papal fortunes were at their lowest ebb.

A violent storm blew up on the crossing; one of the ships was lost and the rest of the fleet limped battered into different ports along the coast. It seemed that even the elements were conspiring to thwart the King; he arrived in a black rage that the state of affairs he found in England did nothing to dispel. For it appeared he had been seriously deceived by his officers; so far from the new laws he had promulgated bringing any improvement, the sheriffs had seized their chance in his long absence to indulge in a variety of malpractices to their own profit and to the hardship of those he had sought to help. Furious, he dismissed most of them out of hand and replaced them with men of lesser blood who were directly under his control.

But at least the arrangements for the coronation had gone smoothly with the King himself in England to see that his orders were carried out to the letter. Then, the very day before the ceremony was to take place, a letter was delivered from the Holy Father, flatly prohibiting Roger's invasion of the Archbishop's privilege.

York insisted that it had been conveyed direct from Becket by a nun, but fortunately the whole affair was shrouded in such secrecy that it was not difficult to suppress it altogether. Whispers there might be but few had certain knowledge. Beside himself with rage, Henry burnt the missive personally.

There were no more setbacks. On this fourteenth day of June Henry watched his fondest dream realised as young Henry was crowned and anointed King of the English. Now the kingdom was safe; if he should die, his beloved eldest son was set securely in his place.

His heir, shining in cloth of silver, the crown upon his head, steadily descended the chancel steps. Henry smiled upon him tenderly as he approached. But young Henry passed him by without a look and the great earls of the land moved forward to take their places in the procession, blocking off his view.

It's his day, Henry told himself, and he's overcome with the solemnity of the oaths he's sworn before God's altar–the same vows he himself had taken, to guard the Church and preserve the customs of the kingdom. Did he imagine it or had the boy hesitated on that?–remembering perhaps the day at Clarendon when the foster-father he had so dearly loved and who should have been officiating had uncompromisingly refused to accept them?

That was not the only qualm Henry felt that day. To honour his son, he himself served him as a page at the great feast that followed, carving for him and handing him the bowl to wash his fingers between each course. Walking away with the scented water he overheard the Archbishop of York's obsequious comment that no prince in the world could have enjoyed such distinguished service.

Young Henry's clear voice rang out in answer above the general hubbub. 'Why should you be astonished, my lord? Should not my father do so? He, the son of a duke, is lower in rank than I who am descended from a line of kings.'

Henry managed to swallow his doubts about his son and, leaving some of his most trusted advisers to watch him, took ship again for Normandy a few weeks later. It was being whispered that the Pope, encouraged by the Emperor's overtures to him now that his anti-Pope had died, had authorised the letters of interdict to be delivered. That must be stopped. But now that he had shown the world he was not to be trifled with and had got what he wanted, Henry was ready to appear to submit.

He was quite cheerful as he rode from Barfleur towards Falaise where Queen Eleanor and the Lady Margaret, young Henry's wife, awaited him, debating with himself how best to explain away the breaking of his half-promise that he would send for both of them in time for the coronation. The approach of a group of horsemen interrupted his thoughts.

He recognised his cousin, Roger, Bishop of Worcester, with a crowd of clerks in his train. They should have been at the coronation–he had marked their absence–but Roger had always been a partisan of the Archbishop and had doubtless stayed away as a mark of disapproval. Henry began to shout at him when he was hardly within hailing distance.

'Where have you been, you traitor? I ordered you to be present at my son's coronation and named the day. You refused to come, proving you have no love for me or desire for my son's advancement. The truth is you favour my enemy and hate me!'

Roger waved his hand wearily before his face as though to brush away the irate words.

'Don't do that at me! I can unmake you!' Henry yelled. 'You won't look so nonchalant when I strip you of the revenues of your bishopric. You're not fit to be a bishop.'

By this time they were face to face and their retinues drew back to leave a space round them. Roger sat his horse calmly as the King heaped threats and abuse upon him. 'You are no son of the good Earl Robert, my uncle, who had us both taught our first lessons in manners and letters together,' he proclaimed loudly enough for all to hear. 'What have you got to say for yourself?' He was sweating heavily for the day was very warm and indignation had made him hotter.

Roger looked him straight in the eye. 'I had every intention of attending the happy ceremony,' he answered coolly, 'but while I waited to embark at Dieppe a letter forbidding me to cross was delivered to me. Nor am I sorry now that I was prevented for I would not have wished to be present once I knew who was officiating. It was wrong and contrary to God's will because the man who crowned your son presumed too far. Had I been there I would not have allowed it.'

Henry was momentarily silenced by this bold attack.

'As for your remark that I am no son of my father,' Roger continued implacably, 'you yourself never gave any fitting return to the house of the uncle who brought you up with due honour and who fought King Stephen for sixteen years for your sake. One of my younger brothers you kept in a state so poor that for very poverty he relinquished his knighthood and bound himself in perpetual servitude to the Hospitallers of Jerusalem. That is the way you reward your friends and their dependants.'

The allusion to the Archbishop was plain. Henry grew even redder but let the impudent comments pass. 'What letter?' he demanded. 'I sent no letter. Are you saying it came from the Queen or the Constable of Normandy? The Queen is in the castle at this moment and if the Constable's not, he soon will be. I shall get to the bottom of it.'

'I am not saying it came from the Queen. Out of fear of you she might suppress the truth and then you would be still angrier with me; or if she confessed it you might rage madly against her, and I would rather lose a limb than that that noble lady should suffer one harsh word.'

Henry breathed deeply. Noble lady, indeed. He was well aware that Roger's remarks, like his own, had been aimed as much at the listeners as at their apparent target. He also knew that his cousin was not afraid of him and he had an uncomfortable suspicion that Roger had long ago come to see his public displays of rage as the tactical manœuvres they were. Nonetheless, he must feel himself in a strong position to be so openly defiant.

The offended muttering of his own men was growing louder. Several of them began to shout rudely at the bishop. Henry turned on them. 'Do you think, you miserable dogs, that if my kinsman and I say what we like to each other it gives you leave to dishonour a bishop? 'Come,' he said curtly to Roger, 'return to Falaise with us. We will speak there alone.'

That evening after supper Henry listened quietly to the clerical reproaches concerning his confiscation of Peter's Pence and then calmly began to discuss the best methods of gaining the Archbishop's forgiveness. The writing on the wall was plain enough, after all. And his attitude had been coloured by the Queen's admission that she and the Constable had sent the letter because they were convinced that once

Roger of Worcester learned that Becket was not to perform his lawful office he would contrive to disrupt the proceedings. So it had all been a misunderstanding. But it was another piece of news entirely that had made his immediate surrender vital.

'Louis,' Eleanor had said, 'is already raiding in the Vexin. He is bitterly affronted that Margaret was not crowned with young Henry and is swearing he will seize back her marriage portion. Why, in God's name, did you not send for us as you promised?'

Thinking of all the harassments he had had to contend with in England, he had answered her sharply and a pretty quarrel had blown up between them over his omission. 'Were you not so mulish,' she had thrown at him as a Parthian shot, 'you could have had Becket in England by now. He could have fulfilled his duty and crowned our son–and after that'–she had laughed–'he would have been in your power.'

Then, perhaps sensing something in his silence, she had stopped, her face altering. 'Oh,' she said, 'I see–I see. . . . You really mean to forgive him. You fool. You will be the laughing-stock of the world. All this–for what?'

If he had stayed he would have hit her. He walked out.

But when his anger cooled, he was ready to face the truth. He did want Thomas back–and even more if she did not. Thomas would be the ideal mentor for that wilful youth he had made his equal in England. Surely gratitude would persuade him to that, at least?

Henry's old dream of a chancellor-archbishop was a long time a-dying. But he did not mention it to Roger.

Left alone, Eleanor recognised that Becket had but to make the smallest gesture and all would be forgiven. There had never been any way that she could touch Henry, either by love or hate; always he turned and twisted like an eel and wriggled off the hook. Becket would return and all would be as it had been before. She had lost the only weapon that might cut

Henry deep.

Except–except that there were many who saw Becket's return as irretrievable ruin. They would not sit idly by and watch him triumph; they would spin their webs of intrigue and stir up discord if they could. For one moment she wondered vaguely about the man himself. Did he love Henry as Henry so evidently still loved him? It did not matter. He was not real to her, only a means to an end. And the end was not yet. . . .

Hot suns and cool, night-time rains had combined to bring the Traitor's Meadow outside Fréteval to its lushest summer green; the last buttercups and milkmaids straggled up through the long grass where it was not bruised and flattened by the trampling of horses. Under the heavily-leafed trees round its borders were deep pools of shade; most of the Norman court waited here but the King sat his horse alone in the centre in the full sun.

It was with mixed feelings that he saw Thomas and the Archbishop of Sens approaching, followed by many French bishops and nobles, though he recognised with relief that Louis had acceded to his request and stayed away. It would be easier to trim his sails without that fishy eye on him. They had made up their differences in the last two days, but with evident reservations on Louis' part and only at the cost of Henry's solemn promise to send Margaret at once to England to be crowned.

Determined not to be blamed if anything should go amiss this time, Henry swept off his cap the moment he saw the Archbishops' arrival; now he spurred forward and greeted them with the utmost politeness. The onlookers watched silently, not stirring a muscle until the Archbishop of Sens rode back to the French entourage. Then they relaxed; he was wearing a broad smile.

Thomas was struck instantly by the change in Henry's

demeanour. Gone were the sidelong, veiled glances; the King met him eye to eye and asked after his health as if the assurance that Thomas was well truly mattered to him. It was not long before confidence in his good intentions had risen high enough for Thomas to broach the subject that constantly preoccupied him. 'Have you truly repented, my dear lord?' he queried softly. 'Can you now accept that all my care was for your eternal soul?'

Henry dropped his eyes then, but in the manner of one who is abashed rather than in any attempt to hide resentment, Thomas thought. Nor did he raise them when Thomas himself excused him by saying that he knew how he had been misled by evil counsellors.

Watching closely, Thomas judged that he might speak his mind. 'It was very wrong in you, nonetheless, to allow York to crown the heir to England. The Holy Father forbade it and we have reason to believe that York received the interdiction. But he has always been led astray by blind ambition and hatred of myself.'

Henry made a faint, protesting noise. 'Who crowned King William who conquered England? And what of King Henry, my grandfather? Neither of them were crowned by an Archbishop of Canterbury.'

Thomas was not to be confused by historical precedents. In his eagerness to refute them he did not notice that the King had not answered his pointed allusion to the Pope's prohibition. He replied that they were special cases, for Stigand, in William's time, had been no true archbishop but a schismatic, and Anselm had been in exile when the King's grandfather was crowned. Perhaps he saw the flaw in his own argument there for he hesitated and then added that, though obliged to make this protest, he had no wish to diminish the young King but rather to ensure that in future years no man should say he was crowned and anointed unlawfully.

Seizing eagerly on this promising opening, Henry answered

warmly. 'If you are concerned for my son, you have every right for you became his second father when I gave him to you to nurture, and I know how well he loves you. I will tell you this–he cannot endure the sight of your enemies. Yea, and I know he will avenge you if an opportunity offers.' He had been speaking almost at random, trying to lay the groundwork for the realisation of his desires, and the last sentence had sprung unbidden to his lips; it was not a thing he had consciously apprehended before but he recognised its truth as he voiced the words.

Solemnly, not taking his eyes from Thomas's, he went on, 'I do not doubt that the church of Canterbury is among the noblest in the West, nor would I deprive her of her rights. Rather, with you to advise me, I will take measures to restore to her all her ancient dignities. As for those who have betrayed both you and me, I will answer them as the merits of traitors deserve.'

He thought he had put the implication rather well–not so forcefully as to sound like blackmail, yet clearly enough not to be missed–but he was amazed at the effect of his carefully-chosen words. Thomas sprang from his horse and knelt before him.

Henry himself was out of the saddle in the next instant and holding the Archbishop's stirrup for him to remount. The easy tears of an emotional man stood in his eyes; his voice broke as he whispered, 'Need we go on? Come, Tom, let us renew our old affection; let each of us show good to the other and forget former animosities.' He stopped and swallowed. 'But, I beseech you, show me honour in the sight of those who watch us.'

Thomas kissed his hand. His own throat was too full for speech. But the clause that meant so much to Henry had escaped him entirely; only the King's last words sang like a paean in his mind. Now his sorrows were over; now he could go home.

Henry's delight was as evident as his own. All the barriers between them had broken; both talked at once, each of them overwhelmed by the sudden miraculous tractability of the other and eager to open his heart. It was a considerable time before they moved towards their followers who, seeing the way the wind blew, had gradually merged and mingled.

Herbert had edged close to Archbishop Rotrou of Rouen. He, though of the King's party, was trusted by the Archbishop's men, being incorruptible and (more to the point) courageous enough to have taken issue with Henry on a number of occasions over his treatment of those who sided with Thomas. Hard-headed, commonsensical, he was known as a man able to see both sides of an argument. Even Herbert respected him, so he was ready to listen to his comments on this unexpectedly happy turn of events.

Henry stopped, facing the expectant crowd, and put out his right hand towards his companion. 'Behold,' he said, 'my friend and subject, Archbishop Thomas. I have this to say to all of you in his hearing. If I, when I find him prepared to every good, should not myself be good to him, then were I the worst of men and should prove the evil things said of me to be true. Nor do I believe that any advice is more honourable and useful than that I study to surpass this man in kindness and charity.'

There was a moment's silence, then a great cheer went up. Herbert whispered in Rotrou's ear. Men were swarming forward, eager for the Archbishop's blessing now that such an action was acceptable to the King. Rotrou went with them and came to Henry's side. 'My lord,' he said softly, 'it would be most apt and fitting were you and Archbishop Thomas now to exchange the kiss of peace in the sight of all.'

Henry's eyes flickered towards him and back to the press that engulfed Thomas. 'Later,' he said, 'later— In my own land, my lord Archbishop, I will kiss him gladly—on his lips, his hands, his feet. But to do so now would accord ill with my honour, seeming to be the price of settlement.'

He did not know whether Thomas had overheard. But he was sure Herbert of Bosham had, just as he was sure he had put the suggestion into Rotrou's mind. He shot him a glance of cold dislike. Let him stew a little longer.

But though Thomas gave no sign, his ear, finely attuned to every inflection of the King, had picked up the exchange. It unsettled him, seeming to make nonsense of the King's former warmth. And, fearing a more public rebuff, he did not mention the matter.

He and Henry continued to talk familiarly together over the next two days but there was a constraint in Thomas and wariness was growing. Why should Henry refuse the kiss if he had meant what he had said? So when Henry asked him to accompany him to Normandy to show that reconciliation was complete, he declined, saying that as a guest of King Louis he could not honourably leave without first paying his respects to him.

The King nodded grudgingly. He rose soon after, telling Thomas to send him one of his clerks in a week or two; he would give him letters to his son and the Justiciar and the clerk could cross to England and take possession of Canterbury's property. And after asking for and receiving Thomas's blessing he took his departure without making any further arrangements to meet him again.

Puzzled and ill-at-ease at this inconclusive ending to their conference, Thomas tried to reassure himself by recalling how disorderly and chaotic were Henry's usual methods of business. Still the doubt remained. A hundred times his excellent memory dredged up word for word what had passed between them in the Traitor's Meadow. He could not be mistaken, Henry had promised to punish his evil counsellors. And had looked on him with love. Yet, once more, what he longed for seemed to be slipping away. It could not be— O God, it could not be that Henry was so far gone in wrongdoing that—

No, he would not even think it. For if it should be true, nothing would be left but to die—

August 1170

Henry half-wakened very early in the morning when it was still quite dark; he tried to move and could not, and for one appalling moment thought that he had died and the glimmering candles he could faintly see were the lights about his bier. He gasped; the glorious feeling of air rushing into his lungs delivered him from terror.

Someone beside the bed bent over him; he felt a hand upon his forehead, then he was lifted and a cup was at his lips. A voice said, 'Drink, my lord. The fever has left you.'

Heavy on the man's arm, he tried. Three sips were enough. Falling back, he lay feeble as an hour-old calf. But he had cheated death.

A week ago he had been suddenly struck down; sweating and shivering he had tried to carry on until, in the middle of a tirade against some sin of omission by an underling, he had crashed headlong to the floor and lain as one dead. For days after he had raved in delirium and had come to himself to hear the tinkling of a bell as the priest approached with the pyx. A deadly lassitude was upon him.

So he had resigned himself to death and somehow whispered his last instructions: that his lands be divided between his sons as he had arranged by treaty with King Louis, and that John be brought up and provided for by his eldest brother. For himself, he would rest among the Good Men of Grandmont, most penitential of orders. They had tried to argue with that as unbefitting to his royal dignity but he had ignored them. Dignity and pride had been nothing to him then.

But now that he knew he would live and the dread of Judgement had receded again into that small corner of his mind where all things spiritual were relegated, he was as much at ease as any man who rests after labour. He lay content in the great bed while servants moved softly about the chamber ministering to his needs, and bishops and acolytes rustled in to kneel and give thanks for his recovery.

It was a grey, close day with a threat of rain. Swarms of people were moving about the bailey and the inner wards; as always when a king's demise was imminent, the vultures had gathered, ready to seize on anything of value before the new king's officials should arrive. Forestalled this time, they hung about watching fresh arrivals. Among them came the Queen.

She was taken immediately to the sickroom, ceremony for once laid by. Propped up on bolsters, Henry saw her enter, saw the way her eyes flew to his face and dwelt there; he recognised disappointment with a sudden, blinding shock.

She had come to look upon his corpse. Answering her grave enquiries only in monosyllables, his mind chewed on the monstrous fact; finally he shut his eyes to silence her and heard her move away to whisper with the physicians. Hot tears formed under his closed eyelids.

After a while he wiped his nose surreptitiously on the sheet. He was not going to give way to self-pity, even at his weakest. He had never wept for Tom; why should he do so because a woman he had never loved had shown she cared nothing for him either? The tears he had shed a few days since when he thought he was dying did not count; in those circumstances he had naturally felt remorse for his long refusal to give Tom the kiss of peace. After all, he had thought then it was too late.

But God in His mercy had spared him. If Tom came to see him, he decided, he would greet him with the kiss. He had always intended to grant it in the end—once Tom had suffered enough. Warm in the warm bed, he began to drowse again, seeing in his mind the Tom of long ago whom he had loved and trusted as no man before or since. Surely when they had kissed he would prove his gratitude by accepting a secular post in government. . . ? They would go forward in amity and peace together, he and his ablest servant. . . .

Each night the Queen dined with him in his bedchamber, and he came gradually to look forward to her coming; at least the clear mind and sharp wit were unchanged. Her grasp of outside affairs was as quick as ever, and as long as he did not meet her eyes too often he could manage, if not to forget the unwelcome revelation, at least to cover it over.

She spoke of course of the Archbishop, but only in a roundabout way and with no harshness, as if she too remembered the time when they were as close as brothers. He asked her once if she thought it well that he should again become young Henry's tutor and adviser.

'I cannot think it,' she said and, when pressed for her reasons, shook her head. 'Why do you ask me? Well, if you will have it, he will not do it, nor can I see that it would do good to our son.'

He ignored the latter part of her remark. 'Why should he not?'

'Henry is too old to serve an archbishop as page; he has had his own household for years. And you will not persuade Becket to neglect his archiepiscopal duties for any reason.' She smiled. 'Why should he? He has gained all he wants, has he not?'

Henry was silent, staring at her. 'What else could I have done?' he suddenly burst out. 'It seems this Pope will live for ever. And with even the Emperor now treating with him—'

'I do not say you had any other choice. But you must face facts, Henry, however unpalatable.' She rose, tall, stately, handsomer still than many women half her age. 'Becket has won and you have lost,' said she.

It was a few days after that, while Henry was still confined to his bed, that John of Salisbury and Herbert of Bosham came from the Archbishop. Henry refused to see them; he disliked them both but that was not the reason. Every day thereafter word came that they waited on his pleasure; finally he said grudgingly that they might be brought before him, but only for a short interview; he still had not recovered strength.

He found them all complaints. News had come from England from those of the Archbishop's lieutenants who had returned home that their revenues had been collected already and had vanished into the sheriffs' coffers, houses were stripped and bare and barns demolished. The King's officers had left them nothing, all valuables had been carted off, woods cut down and livestock removed. And the Canterbury manors were still firmly in the hands of the Archbishop's enemies.

Henry listened sourly. They crouched humbly on two stools that Herbert had brought forward; that had annoyed him–he would have liked to keep them kneeling.

'If you will give us letters, my lord King, ordering that Saltwood Castle and Rochester Castle be restored to Canterbury, we may proceed at once to England. Without that authority'–John glanced at Herbert–'the Archbishop fears to return.'

Henry moved his head sorrowfully from side to side. 'Why does he not trust me? I have so agreed and ordered.'

'Then the orders have not been obeyed,' declared Herbert roundly.

Henry let his eyes slide towards him. He was a saucy knave, this one. 'You see how sick I am. When I have my strength again, I will see to it.'

John persisted. 'If we may have letters, sealed with your seal—'

Henry sighed. 'Business is beyond me for the moment. In a little while, when I am well, it shall be done.' He closed his eyes.

They did not rise to go but whispered together. At last John said, 'We beg, my lord, that you will send word to the young King that Saltwood Castle, at least, be taken out of the hands of the de Brocs. For it commands the coast and without it we have no security.'

'Saltwood we must have,' said Herbert.

Henry leaned up on his elbow and stared at them. 'Must have?' he said. 'It seems to me you must have too much.' He fixed John with his eyes. 'I shall by no means hand over the castles to you until I first see you acting differently towards me than you have acted in the past.' He waved his hand at them. 'You may go. I will discuss this with none but the Archbishop himself.'

Outside the Archbishop's men looked eloquently at each other. 'We cannot proceed to England without some safeguard,' John said, then moved on, away from the doorkeeper who was listening avidly, and lowered his voice. 'The Archbishop was quite clear on that point. We shall have to go back to him at Sens.'

Thomas was on the point of leaving to make his farewells to King Louis when they returned. He accepted their reports of the King's evasions in silence. An interval spent in writing to friends all over Europe to announce the reconciliation had helped to obliterate his inward doubts. Now they returned.

'He was ill, you say?' he asked after a moment.

'He was abed,' said Herbert succinctly.

'He did not–ask that I go thither?'

'He did not. He lay there peeping under his eyelids at us. He was not so sick as he pretended.'

John put his hand on Thomas's arm. 'We feel you should not sail for England without the kiss. It alone will serve as a visible sign that the King means to honour his promises. Unless it is reported to his henchmen in England—'

'Well. . . .' Thomas's old, cheerful smile, too rare now, was on his lips. 'I shall not go without seeing him again first. I will hear what King Louis thinks about it. Fare you well, my good friends.'

They raised their hands to him as his procession began to

move forward. The sun caught the great silver cross carried at the head in a sudden blaze of light, the banners of saints in bliss swung lazily on their poles; only the blink of steel was lacking, otherwise one might have thought a proud and puissant noble was in transit.

John knew it was King Louis' bounty paid for all of this. How would Thomas manage in England unless the King made reparation for the stolen rents?

October 1170

Thomas was waiting with the Archbishop of Sens in the chapel of Amboise Castle. He had followed the King here from Tours in the hope of extracting the longed-for kiss by guile if he could not get it in any other way. For, kneeling beside him at Mass, Henry would be obliged to transmit to him the *pax*, the holy kiss indicating brotherhood in the faith.

The King had at last granted the letters ordering his son to see to it that all Canterbury's possessions were restored. Yet still the thing hung fire. The young King's advisers, among them the hated Geoffrey Ridel, had temporised, saying that it would take time to inform the present holders of these commands and even longer for the evacuation of Saltwood and other castles to take place. The Archbishop's envoys who had carried the orders into England had eventually contrived to see young Henry alone but he had professed himself helpless to aid them. And they reported deep misgivings on the whole situation; few people, apart from the common herd, had wished to be seen associating with them.

It was this that Thomas and the King had discussed at Tours, but Henry had not offered the kiss and Thomas had not asked for it. It was becoming an obsession with both of them, a silent battle of wills.

Nigel de Sacville, the King's chaplain who was to sing the Mass, had seen the two Archbishops enter the chapel; now, instead of hurrying to vest himself, he loitered near the door as the King approached. He had something else on his mind apart from his office.

'Faith!' exclaimed Henry, seeing him there. 'Are you not ready yet? Come, man, shift yourself.'

'My lord King.' Nigel came close. 'I waited to warn you. The Archbishop is within with his Grace of Sens.'

Henry scowled and peered round the door, then turned back with a smothered oath. He eyed Nigel suspiciously. 'What is it to you?'

'Nothing to me, lord,' Nigel disclaimed hastily. He hoped the King would not call to mind that prebend of the Archbishop's he held. 'It–it merely occurred to me that if your Grace still feels bound by your vow never to grant him the kiss of peace, there is yet a way that you may keep it while hearing Mass in his company.'

'Oh?' Henry's eyes seemed to be boring through to the back of Nigel's head. 'What way?'

'The *pax* is omitted from a Requiem Mass.'

'Ah. . . . Good fellow! See to it then.' He looked back at the knights and barons behind him. 'Here's a man has my interests at heart. Well, let's get in and get it over.'

Kneeling at Henry's side, Thomas saw the colour of the priest's cope with a curious sense of fatality. So slight a mischance, a requiem where none had been expected, yet it showed him clearly that all his struggling to avoid the destiny he had foreseen so long ago was vain. For years something had been forcing his unwilling steps in a direction he did not want to go; now, in this trifling event he saw at last there was no escape.

He thought of his own half-jesting words to the King of France when they had made their farewells. 'I am going into England to play for heads.' 'So it seems to me,' Louis had said gravely. 'Hear me, my lord Archbishop–never put your faith in King Henry unless he gives you the kiss. Remember Robert de Silly.' And then, quite suddenly, he had stretched out his hand and cried, 'Stay here! As long as King Louis lives you will never lack the food, the wine, the riches of Gaul!'

Touched and taken by surprise, Thomas recognised for perhaps the first time that Louis liked him as a man; but he could only murmur formally, 'God's will be done,' as he had bent to kiss his hand. In the doorway he had turned for one last look and had said, almost without volition, 'I am going into England to die.'

So he had known it then deep in his heart; now his mind knew too. That was the only difference.

Henry took the Gospel book from the priest, kissed it, and passed it on to him to kiss. And in a last desperate attempt he put his hand on Henry's and, speaking strongly, said, 'Lord, I have come into your lands; for the sake of the place, the time, and our agreement, give me the kiss of peace.'

Henry kept his eyes firmly to the front. 'You shall have it as much as you wish when we are in England.'

That was all. Neither of them ever mentioned it again. But outside the chapel Henry turned once more to Thomas. 'As you are here, will you act as my counsellor at my meeting with Theobald of Blois?'

Thomas nodded silently. He could not refuse without making matters worse between them. Yet as they rode along Henry began again to recapitulate all the old, wearisome reproaches, reminding the Archbishop of all he had received at his hands. Thomas refused to be drawn, answering only as he had before that Henry had forgotten how well he had served him. And, oddly enough, Henry nodded as if satisfied.

Matters went well at the meeting with the Count of Blois; Thomas's adroitness in argument succeeded in gaining Henry everything he wanted and he turned a friendly eye on the Archbishop when it was over. 'You are wasted on anything but statecraft, Tom,' he said.

Thomas smiled feebly.

'When we are back in England'–Henry crossed his legs and leaned back comfortably–'when we are there again, I shall need you more than ever. God only knows what has been happening there these years I have been away.' He began to talk of the new sheriffs he had appointed; it was almost like old times, Thomas thought, except that they were now two different people.

After a while Henry seemed to notice he was not getting the replies he expected; he raised his eyebrows once or twice at Thomas's laconic rejoinders and then fell silent and studied him. When he spoke again, though, his voice was friendlier than ever. 'Tom—?' He leaned forward, wonderfully gracious and familiar. 'Will you not accept the Seal from me again? I ask it both out of my need and that you may prove to me that you truly have my interests at heart.'

Thomas, torn, did not know how to reply. He could not accept but neither did he want to stir up the quarrel again. Silence lengthened between them.

'If you will,' Henry said softly, 'I will give you everything.' He gazed at the Archbishop eagerly, earnestly, willing him to accede to the thing he wanted above all else. This was the only way he could turn defeat into victory, and for what he would gain he would count the rest well lost.

But for Thomas it was as though Satan himself sat there before him and spoke in a voice of brass. 'All these things will I give thee, if thou wilt fall down and worship me.' He brushed a hand across his eyes and the image faded. It was only Henry sitting in front of him, outlined against a wall-hanging that swayed slightly in a draught.

'Do not refuse me,' he was saying in an almost wheedling tone. 'Consider it, I beg you.' His eyes probed Thomas's. 'You will think on it?'

When Thomas still said nothing he got up and, going over to the fire, stared fixedly into the flames. After a minute he said crisply, 'It will be best if you proceed at once to Rouen. I will meet you there and settle your debts, then we will travel together to England.' Coming back, he clapped Thomas on the shoulder. 'We both have many arrangements to make. Have you listed everything you will need?' He continued to talk for some time of those necessities, more to dissipate the atmosphere that still hung in the room than for any other reason, Thomas thought. 'Go in peace,' he finished. 'I will follow you and see you in Rouen or in England as soon as I can.'

'In England?'

'In Rouen or in England,' said Henry with some impatience. 'Whichever is convenient to me.' He turned away.

Thomas looked at his back uncertainly. How to voice his fear of entering England unprotected? 'My lord,' he said hesitantly, 'something tells me that I shall see you no more in this life.'

Henry whirled round. 'Do you take me for a traitor?'

Thomas's hand came up in an instinctive gesture. '*Absit a te, domine!*'

'Such a thing is far from me indeed,' snapped Henry. Indignation strangled further utterance.

He sat burning with resentment when Thomas had gone. This from the man he had given way to on every point! His ingratitude was boundless. Well, let him go to England alone. That might show him which side of his bread the honey was on.

November 1170

'The King is not here, then?' said the Archbishop.

The Constable of Rouen Castle stretched out his hands to the fire and answered for the third time that the King had left a letter of explanation, which letter the clerk was even now bringing. He begged the Archbishop and the reverend gentlemen with him to remove their cloaks.

In a moment the clerk hurried in. Thomas held out his hand for the letter. While he was reading it he heard someone else come in; and, after he had taken in the contents, it was no surprise to see John of Oxford standing there. John came forward to kiss his ring; seeing Herbert stiffen, Thomas made the faintest sideways motion of the head at him.

'How things change,' he remarked coolly to the top of John's head. 'The Archbishop of Canterbury ought to be providing you with safe conduct to England–a little safer than you can provide for him.'

It appeared, though, that irony was lost upon John. He was affability itself to the whole party, greeting each one by name and title; if he felt any discomfort at all in facing the man who had contested his right to the Deanship of Salisbury, who had denounced him, excommunicated him and charged him with heresy, it was not apparent. He gave orders for their comfort and saw them to their quarters in person; finally bowing out on a wave of effusiveness that left even Herbert speechless.

'What—?' said Herbert explosively when he had gone. 'What was in the letter? Why is the King not here?'

'He says that friends of his in France have informed him that Louis is preparing to attack his vassals in the Auvergne. And, as you heard, that swearer is to escort us to England.' (That was how they all referred to John of Oxford since the Diet of Wurzburg.)

They looked at each other, sharing the same thought. 'What are you going to do about the papal letters now?' asked Herbert. He meant the letters Thomas had received from Pope Alexander suspending the Archbishop of York and placing London and Salisbury once more under the ban for crowning the King's son in direct defiance of his orders. Disobedience towards the Archbishop was one thing, a challenge to papal authority quite another. They had come from Rome with extraordinary speed in answer to Thomas's plea for some weapon against his enemies in England. But the

Holy Father had had understanding enough to authorise Thomas to use them at his own discretion.

Thomas seated himself without answering. He had hoped never to have need of them. But already Henry was breaking faith. . . .

'I do not know,' he said. 'If we carry them with us and we are searched on entering England—' He seemed to meditate a moment. 'I think I must consult with the Archbishop of Rouen.'

Rotrou, having heard of their arrival, came to the castle late that same day. He was ushered in to them by John of Oxford himself. When the latter had taken himself off–'Keep the door for me, Herbert,' Thomas said drily–Herbert went out with a meaning nod, and Rotrou's chaplain with him; both Archbishops knew then that they might talk freely.

But they did not say anything at all at first, only sat there side by side on the bed, gazing at the glowing red of the charcoal in a brazier in the middle of the room.

'He is not coming,' Thomas said briefly.

Rotrou shook his head but it was agreement he meant to convey.

'Nor has he sent me money. Herbert asked John of Oxford.' (He would not call him Dean of Salisbury.) 'He said there was no silver here to spare and that the King must have forgotten. How am I to pay my debts? My creditors have followed me and are waiting in the town. Honest tradesmen, most of them. I cannot see them defrauded.'

'I have money.' Rotrou's shame was evident.

'My debts amount to at least three hundred pounds.'

'You shall have that sum tomorrow.'

Thomas's mouth set. 'I think it a foul shame that a king as rich as Henry should be so remiss. I have lived on Louis' charity for years while he has pocketed my revenues; surely at this point he could overcome his avarice sufficiently to reimburse me enough to pay what I owe. . . ? But I thank your

Grace for your beneficence and accept with gratitude. I shall, of course, see that you are repaid as soon as I am settled in England again.'

Rotrou's large, slate-coloured eyes opened to their fullest extent. 'You intend to go? After this?'

'What else can I do? If I do not, King Henry will say that it is I who am breaking faith. Besides, I am in his castle, surrounded by his men, and he has left orders that–that John of Oxford is to escort me there.'

'Are you not afraid of what may await you?'

'Afraid?' Thomas smiled twistedly. 'Yes, if I let myself think on it. So I do not.'

Rotrou leaned forward. His rather fat, soft-looking face seemed to grow firmer. 'I will come with you.'

'No. I thank you again. But no.' Abruptly he told Rotrou about the Pope's letters. 'So you see the danger?'

Rotrou sucked in his lip but offered no advice. He said instead, 'Then I will come to Wissant with you. Yes, indeed I shall. You cannot prevent me.' He laughed but there was not much humour in it. 'Am I not one of your creditors now?'

They were in Wissant a week later, and there they sat, waiting for a wind that would carry the ships over the narrow sea to Dover. It seemed it might be a long wait, for thick, white fog had blanketed the little port the last three days.

One day about sunset one of the men came in and announced that the weather was turning with the tide; he had felt a stir in the air down by the harbour and the seabirds were on the wing. Sure enough, that night they saw the stars, fugitive between clouds, and by morning the fog had cleared. But what wind there was blew out of the north-west; no hope yet of making landfall on an English shore.

Herbert of Bosham and the Archbishops of Canterbury and Rouen were down at the quayside the next afternoon; weary of being pent so long within doors they had come out for a breath of air. Several small ships lay at anchor with furled sails, most of them deserted but one with a stir and scurry on its deck as men shouted and passed crates and bundles from hand to hand. They watched with quickened interest. It was discharging cargo.

Above the voices of the sailors another, closer at hand, was calling urgently. Thomas turned, half recognising the man approaching, yet unable for the moment to place him. 'My lord Archbishop,' he said breathlessly. He stopped, appraising Thomas's companions, then bowed to Rotrou. 'Your grace–and Master Herbert.'

'It's–Milo, is it not?' said Thomas. He recalled him now that he heard his voice, having heard it often enough when he was Chancellor and this man in the service of the Count of Boulogne. 'What are you doing here?'

He nodded towards the ship they had been watching. 'I'm pilot on the *Grâce à Dieu*. We're out of Dover, my lord.' He drew nearer, looking about warily. 'Step with me in here.' He led them into a kind of open warehouse which stank strongly of fish.

'I heard you were here as soon as we landed–the town's full of it–but I never hoped to meet you thus. My lord, you should not go to England. Everyone there knows the King's men will have your life if they can. It's common talk.' Thomas lifted his hand but Milo rushed on. 'You'll get no help from the bishops. I was told by one of the Bishop of London's own men that they know you carry letters of excommunication against them and they're bound and determined to stop you by some means.'

Thomas looked at his companions, his face tightening. 'Do you know what they mean to do?'

Milo shook his head. 'Appeal to the King, some say. But others think worse. I do know three are in Canterbury–London, York and Salisbury. And it's said they've seen Ranulf de Broc.'

'Those three!' exclaimed Herbert. Thomas put out his hand

swiftly to silence him. 'I thank you for this warning,' he said to Milo. 'Is there anything else?'

'Dover is full of armed men waiting for you. Still—' He smiled faintly. 'They might get a surprise. I reckon half the men of Kent will be there as well and a billhook may bring down a mounted man. They'll not come empty-handed in your defence against men with swords.'

Something clinked in Rotrou's hand as he held it out to the pilot. Milo did not move his head but his eyes slid that way, then up to rest scornfully a second on Rotrou's face. He looked back at Thomas. 'Give me your blessing, my lord.' He knelt down on the dirty floor to receive it. Rotrou blessed him too, in some confusion, but he did not seem to think quite so much of that, standing up again before it was half over.

Walking back to the horses they chewed on what they had just heard. 'It's worse that I feared,' said Thomas. 'I had thought we might be searched but now they know what they are looking for. John of Oxford will not try to stop them. And if the townsfolk attempt it there will be bloodshed.'

Rotrou did not reply for a moment. He was deep in thought. Patently, the common folk were behind the Archbishop to a man. He said slowly, 'If the de Brocs are expecting you in Dover, could you not land elsewhere? A word to the captain or the helmsman, perhaps?'

Thomas brightened. 'Indeed. If we land at Sandwich—' He gazed thoughtfully ahead, then seemed to come to some decision. 'I shall send the papal letters ahead to be delivered into the hands of those in Canterbury. I have no other weapon and, even supposing the King's intentions are honourable, I do not believe he can control his henchmen from a distance. . . . If the censures have already been delivered before I enter England, it may appear they do not emanate from me.'

'How will you send them?'

'I will send messengers immediately to Milo. He will get them over on the first ship.'

But Herbert, as usual, had the last word. Evidently his thoughts had been running on a different track, for as soon as they were mounted he delivered himself of a long homily, backed by many biblical references, on the felicity of martyrdom. They heard him out in silence. When he wound up his oration they were within sight of their lodgings.

Rotrou allowed a faint sigh to escape him. Being of a pragmatical turn of mind he found it difficult to make any connection between martyrdom and political assassination. Martyrdom was to be cut down by heathen Dane or Muscovite, to be forced to choose between Christ and a Roman Emperor. . . .

The Archbishop's face was white and drawn. He spoke curtly as he dismounted. 'Your word is true but hard. Who can fulfil it?'

Yet when Rotrou begged him again that evening not to go he would not consider it. He has reached the end of his tether, Rotrou thought. And he saw how a long-time prisoner might be driven to venture through a sudden yielding door and take his chance upon a trap. That was how it was with him. England was his free air, his home; to England he would go, whatever the outcome. Nothing was left but to pray.

XI
December 1170

A high sea was running as the ship carrying the exiles home drew nearer England; what with that and a following wind they were making good speed. Already the chalk cliffs showed up, white against the grey of sea and sky. The Archbishop eyed them apprehensively but breathed more easily as they slipped by on the port bow, proof that they were truly heading for Sandwich.

He had been surprised at John of Oxford's ready acceptance of his change of plan. John stood beside him now, his eyes narrowed against the blown spume, the over-large head sunk between raised shoulders as he gripped the rail and peered towards the land. 'England . . . ,' he said. 'After how many years?' He was doing his best to be friendly but the expansiveness grated still on Thomas. John had not left his side for a moment during the voyage and had kept up a flow of empty pleasantries the whole time. 'There will be friends to greet you, I doubt not,' he said, showing all his teeth.

'And officials,' said Thomas gently.

'Officials? Oh well, word runs ahead. But now that all is well between you and the King you will be welcomed with honour.'

Thomas addressed the handful of his friends who stood near.

'Let the Primatial Cross of Canterbury now be set up in the bows that all who wait to greet us may see under what sign we come.'

'Indeed, yea, indeed!' cried John for all the world as if his permission had been asked. In the end it was he who saw to the ordering of it and, when the great shining silver symbol towered proudly erect, took his place beneath it by the Archbishop as of right. So they beached at Sandwich, a procession ready to disembark, with the sailors crowding curiously along the rails to get a good view.

They heard the noise of cheering before they took in the size of the enormous host packed solid on the shore and splashing into the water to grab the lines the crew cast towards them–poor fisher-folk for the most part, but with a scattering of burghers amongst them. It was the keen eyes of Herbert that spotted the group of armed men pushing through; he gripped Thomas's shoulder warningly and nodded towards them. By the time the gangplank was in position they were waiting at the bottom.

John of Oxford had seen them too but apparently the apprehension on his face was not for himself for he stepped stoutly in front of Thomas. 'Greetings to Gervase, lord Sheriff of Kent, and to Sir Ranulf de Broc,' he called loudly. 'We who are aboard this ship come into England at the lord King's express command.'

Ranulf inclined his head. 'And greetings to you, my lord Dean of Salisbury. You may pass as you will but behind you stands one with whom the sheriff and I would speak.'

A little movement ran over the suddenly hushed crowd. John came a few steps down the gangplank. 'I am to tell you in the name of the King that if any harm the Archbishop or his men he shall be adjudged guilty of treason. For the King has made his peace with them.'

'Harm? We intend them no harm. Our only intention is to search this ship lest this Archbishop'– he enunciated the word as another might a term of vilest opprobrium–'bring in anything—' That was as far as he got.

A low, growling murmur rose as the crowd swayed suddenly nearer. Further off, voices were raised in anger. The sheriff ranged up beside Ranulf and whispered urgently to him.

Thomas put John of Oxford gently by–he saw now that he had misjudged both his intentions and the King's–and took the first step on the gangplank to disembark. As one the great host swarmed forward, engulfing the King's officers. There were smiles and tears of joy, acclamations and caps flung aloft, and a voice crying over and over, 'Blessed is the father of orphans, the judge of widows; blessed is he that cometh in the name of the Lord!' Pushed to one side, the sheriff was yelling, 'You have come back, bringing fire and the sword. You want to take away the young King's crown!'

Thomas took the last step and stood on English soil. Silently he put his hands palm-to-palm on his breast, bowing his head. Across the heads of the people who had fallen on their knees before him he replied to Gervase. 'You are wrong. I have not come to undo the young King's coronation. I would give him four more kingdoms if I could.'

'Liar!' Ranulf de Broc came back. 'We know you have excommunicated the Archbishop of York and other bishops for doing the King's will. Unless you change your ways it will be the worse for you!'

Thomas glared at him. 'I have punished those who defied God by usurping the right to crown him. How can it bring fire and sword to punish the sins of bishops?'

'Hush! Hush!' implored John of Oxford from behind. 'Do not answer them.' He went unheard.

'You will get nowhere by threatening me,' Thomas continued coldly. 'I have come to risk my neck for truth and justice.'

By now the applauding cries quite drowned any further comments Ranulf or the sheriff might make. But as the

Archbishop was carried forward by the excited crowd he cried loudly in their general direction that he had the King's permission to punish the bishops and that if they had any more to say they might seek him at Canterbury.

Hugh of Nunant, almost lost in the crowd, caught and clung to Herbert's elbow. 'I never thought to find myself in agreement with John of Oxford,' he panted, 'but unless the Archbishop will learn to bridle his tongue we shall all be in the utmost danger.'

'They are going,' Herbert said. He peered down at Hugh. 'Will you curb truth?'

'No,' puffed Hugh, 'but there is a time when the snaffle is useful.'

'Say you so?' enquired Herbert with heavy irony.

But it was lost on Hugh who did not hear. He was promising himself, though, that he would have a private talk with John of Salisbury at the first opportunity; he was perhaps the only one who could persuade the Archbishop to something resembling meekness under threat.

Ranulf de Broc and Gervase the sheriff received reports of the Archbishop's triumphal progress back to Canterbury at intervals during the course of the following day. They found it hard to credit that a ten-mile journey could take so long. But it was close on sunset before the procession arrived at its destination by reason of the huge crowds that blocked the roads.

Half the inhabitants of Kent, it seemed, had turned out to welcome their father in God; the rejoicing multitude flung down bracken and branches, even the clothes from their backs, to make a carpet for the feet of the returning exiles. The cavalcade was held up at every vill by parish priests and their flocks who met it with hymns and *Te Deums* and accompanied it miles along the way. And Canterbury greeted its Archbishop with trumpets, choirs and a joyful pealing of the cathedral bells.

'One would think he was another Christ entering Jerusalem,' Ranulf commented sourly when they sat together after supper.

Gervase, toying with his wine-cup, did not answer. He did not like that comparison at all, considering it close to blasphemy; besides, it aroused thoughts he would rather not admit to consciousness. It was manifestly impossible that such an overbearing, sharp-tongued, vengeful fellow could stand for eternal truths. No, he was in the game for what he could get out of it–riches, power and prestige–like all the rest.

Could they have known the Sheriff of Kent's thoughts, the majority of the English barons would have agreed with him. Certainly they wanted the Archbishop back no more than he, loosing his thunderbolts as he pleased, and more especially if he were to be ranged alongside the King. For they were far from happy about Henry either.

They had supported him against the Church on the Constitutions of Clarendon–for freedom's sake, they would have said; meaning, as do all men who mouth that catchword, freedom for themselves and their own class. Yet far from showing gratitude, the first thing the King had done was to deprive them of many of their prerogatives by interfering with the old laws of feudal homage, wardships and reliefs. They had all lost money when pleas that had always been heard in the baronial courts were transferred to his own. And, not content with that, he had continued to tax them unmercifully to pay for his wars, his bribes to the Curia, even his daughter's marriage.

Until the last few months they had merely groaned and muttered under his exactions. But the news that he was reconciled with the man he had so often named traitor had come like a thunderclap. It was true that most of them had been afraid of interdict but they had trusted him, wily as he was, to find a way out short of surrendering to Pope and

Archbishop. Now they felt betrayed. Many of them, short on logic, were certain that the Archbishop was returning to wreak vengeance upon them for taking the King's part. Others, remembering how as Chancellor he had helped the young monarch crush those of their number who resisted royal authority, saw the old combination of him and Henry as more than they would be able to bear.

Ranulf was not one of those who had feared interdict, or excommunication either. No dread of hellfire or twinge of conscience had ever disturbed him. His concern was with things material, and notably with Saltwood Castle which he had come to think his own. He was determined to hold it against all comers, whatever Archbishop, Pope, or even King Henry might say. So he, like Gervase and many others, had thrown in his lot with the clique who were whispering to the young King that now he was crowned he should be allowed to rule in England.

'By now,' Gervase remarked with apparent inconsequence, 'Becket has had time to eat plenty of bread.'

Ranulf's nostrils widened. He understood the comment only too well since it referred to his frequently-shouted threat that the Archbishop should not live long enough to eat a whole loaf of bread in England. 'Well,' he said, 'what could we do? It's plain enough the news of a reconciliation was true or it would not have been the Dean of Salisbury acting as escort.'

Gervase eyed him slyly. 'And so–you will do nothing?'

Ranulf crashed his fist down on the board between them. 'Nay, by God, I will do something! Tomorrow we shall go to Canterbury and demand that he absolve the bishops. You do not tell me the King agreed to that. I'll not believe it!'

'He said he had the King's leave.'

'Some twist of words. But if he had— Listen. There is always the young King—'

They put their heads close and began to whisper together.

In the choir of Canterbury Cathedral at that same time Thomas was receiving the monks of Christchurch one by one and giving them the kiss of peace; he had prepared the way by sending John of Salisbury ahead to absolve and reconcile those who had communicated with the excommunicates during his absence.

The great church was gorgeously adorned with rich hangings and tapestries in his honour; tears had filled his eyes when he saw it and had overflowed entirely when he seated himself again, after six years, on the Throne of Augustine. Most of the monks, too, wept for joy, clinging to his hands, each loth to pass on and make way for the next. Even Herbert blinked a little and turned away his eyes from the light that blazed in Thomas's.

Later, in the chapter-house, he preached to them, taking his text from Hebrews: 'Here we have no abiding city but we seek one to come.' There was a long silence after he had finished; he stood with a face remote and rapt, looking over their heads, and it seemed none cared to call him back from where he gazed. One after another murmured soft goodnights and left until only he and Herbert remained.

It took a lot to overwhelm Herbert and even more to reduce him to silence. All at once he thought of something he could add. 'Now, lord,' he declaimed, 'it is no matter when you depart hence for in you this day the Bride of Christ has won the victory. Christ conquers, Christ reigns, Christ rules!'

A pity, he felt, that he had not said it before the others left. But he was very pleased with his own definitive ending to the splendid day.

The small town of Canterbury was still humming like an overturned hive the next day and the stir penetrated as far as the guest chamber of St Augustine's monastery. The Bishops of London and Salisbury who were temporarily in residence took note of it.

Gilbert Foliot sat fidgeting with the tarnished silver crucifix that hung from a thong around his neck. 'Will they never come?' he exclaimed. 'They have had thrice the time they need to do their business.' He was speaking of the bishops' chaplains who had accompanied the King's officers on their errand to the newly-returned Archbishop.

'It is surely a good sign that they are taking so long,' said Jocelin of Salisbury. 'Had he refused point-blank to listen they had returned before this.' But his long, grey, sheep-like face did not express the same hopeful sentiments.

'And where is Roger?' demanded Foliot. 'Even he cannot be still abed.' He got up to pace impatiently about, taking no notice of Salisbury's nervous murmur that he understood the Archbishop of York was feeling unwell. A lot of his annoyance was due to Roger de Pont l'Évêque's absence. He could get no comfort from Salisbury, who was a miserable, hand-wringing sort of man; York, for all his faults, had the capacity to bolster his own lost confidence. 'Go you and fetch him,' he ordered peremptorily. Salisbury got up in haste to do his bidding.

He scratched on the door of York's bedchamber and, after waiting a second or two, opened it softly. Roger was bending over a pretty, fair-haired boy who sat on the edge of the bed; the child, who looked about ten years old, giggled and squirmed like a girl. Salisbury saw that he was one of Roger's *castrati*, the choir of singing boys he carried about with him everywhere. He sprang nimbly aside when he saw the door open.

Roger turned, quite unabashed. 'Have they returned?' he enquired.

'No,' said Salisbury. 'It is that–that London is asking for you.' He stood hesitating on the threshold in some discomfort as the boy slipped past. 'I trust–I trust you are recovered,' he twittered.

Roger calmly buckled a jewelled belt about his girth. 'I am always improved by the sweet voice of one of those lads hymning the praises of the Lord,' he pronounced unctuously. 'My headache is quite gone, I thank you.'

Passing along to the guest chamber he shot a narrow look at Salisbury, wondering if he would repeat what he had seen–or might have seen. His brother in God's cheek was somewhat less pallid than usual, that was all. On the whole, he did not think so. Salisbury was in no position to criticise others when everyone knew the young man he passed off as his nephew was really his son.

When they came in to Gilbert they found the Abbot with him. Clarembald was a man of immense bulk; his jowls shook as he held forth upon the monstrous act of injustice that had been done his guests. They stood waiting politely till he finished running through the reasons why he did not scruple to ignore this new ban.

A bell began to ring somewhere within the monastery; Clarembald cut himself short, saying he must go but he would see them later at Collations. So they sat down–York in the seat the Abbot had vacated since it was the better one–and prepared to chew over once again all the old grievances they cherished against their metropolitan.

They had barely begun when there was a sharp knocking on the door. All their heads came up at once as three men entered, London's and Salisbury's chaplains first; York's seemed to hang back a little.

'Well?' said York.

The Bishop of London's chaplain addressed him. 'My lord, the Archbishop has at last consented to restore you to the communion of the Church on condition that you swear in his presence to obey all future commands of the Pope. We strove long for it for he refused at first, saying that it was the Holy Father who had passed judgement and an inferior could not undo the verdict of a superior—'

'And me?' cried Salisbury. 'What of me?'

'You too, my lord. But'–he carefully kept his eyes from

Roger de Pont l'Évêque–'my lord of York he would not speak of, insisting that he had no authority over his peer.'

Roger raised his hand. 'Did you insist on the use of the phrase "saving the honour of the kingdom" in the oath that they must take?'

The Bishop of London's chaplain quailed visibly but continued addressing his master. 'When first we were taken into his presence the sheriff and Sir Ranulf were speaking hotly against him, saying that what he had done infringed the custom of the realm and injured the King, but that if he would absolve all three of you immediately you would come to him and make submission. And though he replied calmly, my lord, it was evident he was angry by reason of that clause which they also demanded. He refused as I have told you and would say no more while the sheriff's men were menacing him.' He stopped and swallowed. 'It was we, my lord, who begged them to desist and allow us to try, and finally we moved him as I have said.'

'You did well,' said Gilbert. 'I shall go to him at once.' Relief was evident in the sudden relaxation of his clenched hands.

York drew a deep, angry breath. Was he to be left alone, the only one unshriven? 'If you do that, how may you expect the King ever to trust you again?' he burst out fiercely. 'Have you heard that he has suspended the Constitutions?–for I have not! No, if either of you break his laws you will never enjoy his friendship again. Rather will he call you what you are, faint-hearted deserters and evil traitors! He will drive you both out of his realm as the law provides, and confiscate all your goods. Tell me–where will you go, homeless wanderers, stripped of everything and shamefully put down?'

Salisbury gazed in anguish from him to the stricken Gilbert.

Roger moderated his tone. 'Come now,' he said, attempting to rally them, 'I am not penniless, you know. I have eight thousand shining golden bezants in my treasury, God be praised, and I will willingly spend it all to reduce the wilfulness and obstinacy of this archbishop, and to put down his pride and presumption. I beg you, my brothers, do not let him weaken your determination. Ignore his threats; let us instead go together to see the old King who has so splendidly sustained us all along against this enemy.'

He could see that they were torn. 'I will send a warning to the young King,' he said, 'that Becket intends to depose him.' His face was suddenly vicious but fortunately the others, taken up with their inward struggles, did not see. He infused his voice with pleading. 'Shall we not stand together as we have always done?'

Gilbert rubbed his hand across his face and nodded wearily. 'I will bear the cross that has been laid on me a while longer. As you have said, our duty is to the King and to the young King. In threatening us he threatens them.'

The Queen bent her head and played with the rings on her fingers. Her Chamberlain sat and watched her. They had been discussing the latest move of the Archbishop, news of which had just reached them.

She pulled off a small, pearl ring and weighed and dandled it on her palm. 'You have a safe messenger?' she asked. Henry Fitzgerold nodded. She held out the ring to him. 'Send this to the young King in England with a message from his mother. He is not to see or speak with the Archbishop. Tell him–tell him that his father's advisers are waiting only for that to stir up more dissension between them.' She smiled at the Chamberlain. 'I will not have my son drawn into this coil if I can help it. But best not to put it in writing.'

Christmas Day 1170

The packed congregation in Canterbury Cathedral hung on the Archbishop's discourse as he enlarged upon the wonderful humility of the Lord who had submitted to being wrapped in swaddling clothes and laid in a manger, and many a one felt that the words were addressed to him alone, so gentle and intimate was the tone. Even when he turned to the morals of the people, urging them to shun sin and honour the Church, few closed their eyes to allow the familiar exhortations to flow past unheeded.

Not always, he told them, were the priests of God vouchsafed the reverence due to them; he himself had had to endure the contemptuous spite of those who feared man more than God. It was more than possible that he would not be with them much longer. Protesting cries began to rise as he continued that the church of Canterbury had already one martyred archbishop, St Alphege, and might soon have another.

Thomas paused there, looking down from the pulpit at his people. Arms were stretched out to him imploringly as scores of voices expressed their desolation. He hardened his heart; he would not allow even their grief to deflect him from the step he was about to take. His face was pale, his eyes dark-circled; the last three harrowing weeks had left their mark on him. He knew now it had been a mistake to come to England but to admit it would be to face defeat and that he could not do. So he must use the only weapon at his command.

That the country was seething with intrigue and unrest he had seen for himself when he made a progress through his diocese a week after his return. Before he set out he had sent three fine destriers as a gift to the young King with a request for an audience, because even then he had been afraid that the reason for the bishops' excommunication was being presented to his foster-son in a distorted light. For he had had no word from him–no welcome from the boy he had loved and who, he knew, loved him.

The progress itself had been a mingling of triumph and disaster. London had welcomed its long-lost son with as great jubilation as Canterbury but, in the midst of it, outside the church of St Mary in Southwark, a woman well-known in the city as a seeress had screamed at him repeatedly, 'Archbishop, beware the blade! Beware the blade!' The words had rung in his head all night. And the next morning the Earl of Arundel had arrived with a message: the young King would not see him; he was to return to his place in Canterbury, stay there, and keep the peace.

Only one old friend was in London, Reginald of Cornwall, and he sick abed of a tertian fever. Thomas sent a monk, disguised as a physician, to ask his intervention, but the man was recognised and the sick earl had packed him hastily off with a warning to the Archbishop that his life was in danger. Thomas saw that if even Earl Reginald dared not openly stand with him the situation was indeed serious. Everything depended upon Henry's early coming. He took with him a bodyguard of knights on his return journey to Canterbury.

But Henry did not come and the last weeks of Advent slid by. Thomas's birthday came and went. He was fifty-two years old. Now not a day passed without tidings of some new depredation committed by Ranulf de Broc who evidently still considered himself administrator of Canterbury's estates. He confiscated a shipload of wine sent by the King; he hunted constantly in the Archbishop's woods with the Archbishop's own hounds, and on Christmas Eve word came that his brother Robert had docked the tail of a Canterbury sumpter horse. That act, so trivial-seeming, was the spark to start a conflagration. To any feudal overlord it was a calculated insult, a symbolic emasculation. Thomas saw it thus.

Remembering, his voice changed when he declared that peace could be granted only to men of good will. Since his return evil men had been doing their utmost to destroy his peace, and yesterday the culminating outrage had been perpetrated by Satan's minions, the de Brocs. Coldly, implacably, before the awed and silent congregation, he consigned each of the de Broc brothers to perpetual anathema and, for good measure, the false incumbents of Harrow and Throwley too. As he threw down the candles, he proclaimed a curse upon all who came between himself and the King.

After his frugal evening meal the Archbishop had complained of a headache and retired early to bed, leaving his small circle of intimates to talk with the guests who had come to spend the Christmas Feast with him. They were not many and they were all religious, but the sight of even a few new faces had cheered the returned exiles considerably. William Fitzstephen was one of them; the rest were strangers, amongst them Thomas's long-time admirers and correspondents, Edward Grim from Cambridge and Henry of Auxerre who had travelled from Burgundy.

They sat now talking somewhat constrainedly, none of them wishing to be first to mention what was uppermost in all their minds. When Herbert, who had gone out with the Archbishop, came back they turned their eyes on him eagerly but he only gave voice to his worries for Thomas's health at great length; after a while William Fitzstephen, feeling Herbert had audience enough in the others, began to whisper to John of Salisbury. His talk too was of Thomas, but of his safety rather then his wellbeing.

'Ranulf de Broc,' he said, 'has been thirsting for the Archbishop's blood ever since he came home. Will not these fresh censures give him the chance he has been waiting for?'

Robert of Merton, Thomas's confessor, who had overheard, leaned their way. 'Excommunication will not trouble the de Brocs,' he assured them. 'Robert de Broc is an apostate Cistercian–when he was threatened before he laughed aloud and declared he had always lived as an excommunicate.'

'I think you are missing the point,' said William anxiously. 'There are still those vicars who refused to hand over their churches to Canterbury's bailiff. They will not laugh.'

Herbert had fallen silent; everyone was listening. 'Are you

saying that the Archbishop should not have done what he did?' he demanded.

Edward Grim, the Englishman, suddenly cleared his throat. He was a big, brawny man who looked more like a man-at-arms than a monk, and his words did not belie his appearance. 'I see the Archbishop as a man who will not be swayed from the Christian path by human considerations. He fights God's fight and he is a warrior before all else. When he was Chancellor, was he not ever in the forefront of his troops? Who can enumerate the numbers of persons he did to death in those days, the numbers he deprived of all their possessions in a right cause? He destroyed cities and towns, put manors and farms to the torch, and showed no mercy to the King's enemies. Nor will he now show mercy to the enemies of God.'

Herbert nodded complacently at this evidence of a kindred spirit.

William Fitzstephen had felt himself at a disadvantage with those who had shared the exile but his sensibility did not extend to this stranger. 'Blessed are the meek,' he pronounced firmly.

Edward Grim was equally firm. 'The Archbishop is God's champion.'

'Does God need champions?' It was John of Salisbury, suspiciously innocent, who posed the question.

There was a little pause before Edward said, 'What would God have of us then? Why are we here at all if not to work His will? If we sit by with folded hands the wicked will flourish unchecked.'

'Aye, that they will,' cried Alexander Llewellyn, 'and the godly be cruelly oppressed. Have we not seen it?'

'I think we none of us have trust enough in God,' returned John quietly. 'Should we not rather fear to impose our human will on His unknowable designs?'

'It cannot be God's will that the de Brocs murder our Archbishop,' said Robert of Merton faintly. 'Surely. . . ?'

'Murder can never be God's will, only man's. But it is only through meekness that men of violence may be disarmed.'

John saw several of the listeners shake their heads in gloomy disagreement. Herbert said, 'You will never persuade me that Christians should not fight for truth.' He had the old, familiar glint in his eye.

John forbore to argue with him. Some men, it was plain, were born to fight. A number of others of the company took up the challenge, however, and were treated to a long dissertation on the law and the Prophets by Herbert. The Old Testament suits him best, thought John, suits most men best until they reck the consequences. It's easy to talk of standing firm and holding fast to truth, but doing it's another matter when the world raises its mailed fist against you.

The thoughts had come from some subterranean level he had not known existed in him–thoughts at complete variance with everything he had ever preached. Am I craven then? he asked himself. Is that why I lean always to the soft answer that turns away wrath? Was it cowardice made Thomas flee and new-found courage brought him back to face whatever might befall? In short, did Thomas of London discern the will of God more clearly than John of Salisbury?

Herbert was not having all his own way in the argument that was raging. Hugh of Nunant cried out that the Lord had miraculously restored to the High Priest's servant the ear that St Peter had cut off, thereby showing that he had mercy on God's enemies; and Lombard of Piacenza recited solemnly, '*Multifarie olim Deus loquens patribus in Prophetis novissime diebus istis locutus est nobis in Filio.*'

Herbert announced that he had never supposed that the Prophets spoke more truly than the Son but that, '*Christus factus est pro nobis obediens usque ad mortem, mortem autem crucis.*'

John closed his eyes. Was that how Herbert and Alexander, and presumably this Edward Grim, saw Thomas?–obedient even unto death.

He prayed long and earnestly that night before he slept but God did not see fit to lighten his darkness. He had to wait four more days for that.

Reynold Fitzurse and Will de Tracy had been hanging about at Bures for a week when the Archbishop of York and two other bishops arrived to see the King in the middle of December; but even they, with the court but not of it, did not have to wait long to hear the reason for their coming. Henry howled his fury at the news they brought loud enough for all to hear. Only York had appeared before the King in person, being merely suspended from office; the other two, who turned out to be London and Salisbury, lodged themselves some distance off lest the dread taint of their excommunication contaminate him.

Reynold and Will had a fellow-feeling with them. They themselves were neither excommunicate nor exiled, yet both felt they might as well have been. Everyone knew that they were *persona non grata* with the King, and everyone knew why.

Each of them had been run to earth on his own manor by the sheriff of the county when he had finally returned home after that miserable incident at Williton; each had skulked there for months, quaking in his shoes at what might happen when the time came to fulfil his knight-service and he must face the King. Reynold had managed to quell his anxieties by resolving upon a frank and soldierly regret, tempered by manly camaraderie—did not everyone know that no woman was safe from the King himself? But Beatrice had not left him long in that fool's paradise. Indeed, she informed him so often that his one hope of regaining the King's favour lay in the performance of some deed that would quite overshadow his former misconduct, and harped so bitterly upon the ruin he had brought on them, that he had threatened to break her arm if she mentioned it again.

Nonetheless, he had gone to France ready and eager for

feats of derring-do only to find that he was dismissed both from scenes of conflict and the King's presence, and set to tasks more fitted for a squire than a noble knight. It was no accident, for the same treatment had been accorded Will; they had returned home deflated and gloomy, and ready to blame anyone but themselves for their misfortunes. Their tour of duty the next year had followed the same pattern, and at the end of it news of the rapprochement between the King and the Archbishop had broken. At home their cases still had not come up for hearing; the dismissal of so many of the sheriffs had had far-reaching consequences.

Unable to face the prospect of their wives' nagging tongues, they had remained in France and fetched up at Bures for the Christmas Court. There, large as life, hobnobbing with various officers, they had seen Hugh de Morville. They gave him the barest acknowledgement, and the King, who knew every one of his men by sight if not by name, ignored all three of them.

They were all there, though, on one of the lowest tables at the great Christmas Feast; disregarded or not, they were King's men. From his place beside Will, Reynold could see Hugh seated with his own kinsman le Bret further up the board. On the dais the Archbishop of York had the place of honour at the King's right hand.

The atmosphere was far from festive for it was plain the King was in a dangerous mood. Reynold and Will kept their heads low over their trenchers. This was no time to be noticed.

Roger of York had started the evening by magnifying Thomas's small bodyguard and the cheering crowds who had followed him into a band of armed men and a disorderly mob who were making a circuit of the countryside to the terror of the populace; now he was expatiating on the risk of the young King's deposition. He watched the King carefully as he spoke.

Henry's face was working. He had come to the Christmas festivities in an ill humour, having been forced to conclude a humiliating truce with Louis when he had found an army of vastly superior numbers drawn up and waiting for him in the Auvergne. And now this. . . .

'If all who crowned my son or were present at his coronation are to be excommunicated, I am not like to escape either,' he said abruptly. He turned directly to Roger. 'What am I to do?'

Roger shook his head. 'That is not for me to say, my lord King.' His eye slid to the silently listening magnates along the high table. 'You should seek counsel of these goodly barons and knights.'

But they only began to murmur and argue among themselves, not a one putting forward any constructive suggestion. Henry's lowering gaze roamed over them. He was not unaware of the disaffection in the rank and file of their class; now he read something more than mere indecision in the manifest unwillingness of his closest advisers to commit themselves. They cared nothing for him, any of them; he must do it all—guard against the Scots and Welsh on his borders, circumvent Louis, juggle with Pope and cardinals, and somehow find his way through this new web of intrigue that Thomas was weaving in England.

Roger muttered something. 'What?' he said. 'What? Speak up.'

Roger's whisper was hurried. 'I am telling you, my lord, that while Thomas lives you will have no peace, nor quiet days, nor a tranquil kingdom.'

Henry's precarious hold on his patience snapped. His lips drew back from his teeth, the breath hissed through them. 'Fools and dastards have I nominated in my realm,' he bellowed. 'Disloyal cowards, not one of whom will avenge me on this lowborn clerk!' He screamed on and on until his howling died away in strangled curses, the notorious fury running its usual course through hair-tearing to tears.

Everyone in the hall had caught the first words but, having heard similar outbursts a hundred times before, few gave them much consideration. Reynold, more concerned with his personal affairs than the larger issues that perturbed the King, had been peering through the fingers of his sheltering hand at Hugh throughout; thus it was, with the attention of all other men diverted, he alone saw the conspiratorial muttering between him and le Bret before both rose and slipped away.

He jogged Will with his elbow. 'Where are they going?'

Will stared at the empty space on the bench with suddenly dawning comprehension. 'By God—' he said. 'By God's Wounds, they're taking him at his word this time!' He gripped Reynold fiercely by the arm. 'Come on! Jesu, if we can get there first—'

'What?' said Reynold. 'What? Where—?'

'England,' said Will tersely, 'to arrest Becket–what else? Le Bret has been praying for such a chance for years and it's Hugh's road back to the King's good graces. Why not ours?' He hustled Reynold before him through the door. One quick look back assured him that the departures were noted by no one. 'To horse, my friend! If they think we're going to be cut out of this one, they're wrong. We'll make for Saltwood and the de Brocs, and I'll wager you a pound of silver we'll find them there!' He was laughing, lit with excitement and eagerness after the long months of inaction.

Pounding along beside him in the darkness, Reynold warmed himself with remembering the feel of the sword-grip in his hand and the deadly joy when the keen blade whistled down upon a hated enemy. But it was not the Archbishop he saw cowering beneath it.

St Stephen's Day 1170

When John came to his chamber just before Compline to look up a text he had been arguing over with the Abbot, William Fitzstephen was waiting there for him. 'What is it, William?' he asked.

'He is sending Herbert and Alexander to King Louis, and Gilbert Glanville to the Pope.'

John did not need to ask who 'he' was. His heart jumped a little but he put on a judicial air. 'To King Louis? Why not to King Henry?'

'To tell him–so says Herbert–what they have seen of this peace of King Henry's which is no peace but a turbulence.' He sat on the bed and put his hands between his knees, pressing them close. 'Herbert himself told me. He said he pleaded that someone else might be sent, but that our lord Archbishop replied that he must go because the King holds him in greater suspicion than others where the cause of the Church is concerned.'

John stood watching him. Not more than I, he thought, surely not more than I? But he said only, 'When do they go?'

'Tomorrow.'

The faintest sense of relief washed over John. Without that truculent pair to urge Thomas to further excesses the pot might come off the boil. God send it might be so. He became aware that William was still speaking.

'Herbert wept bitterly, saying it is hard that he should be sent away, nevermore to see our lord in the flesh, and harder still that he should be cheated of the fruit of his consummation—'

Something rigid in John's stance stopped him. After a minute John said tonelessly, 'Nevermore to see him in the flesh?'

'He said they were the Archbishop's own words.'

There was another silence. William said tentatively, 'You think as I do?'

'I think,' said John, 'I think he is sending away those two to save their lives.'

'Then–what of us?'

'The rest of us?' Surprisingly John laughed. It was not a pleasant sound. 'He knows we shall do nothing. We have sworn by turning the other cheek too often.'

Holy Innocents' Day 1170

Reynold and Will arrived at Saltwood Castle this day to find de Morville and le Bret already there. But if their greeting of the newcomers was less than welcoming, Ranulf de Broc made up for it. He led them to the head of the table where, early as it was, a noisy drinking session was in progress. 'Two more!' he shouted. 'Two more to join our gallant band! Any more on the way? No? It matters not. I've half a hundred trusty fellows of my own will follow me through the gates of hell if I give the word. We'll lay that damned Archbishop by the heels tomorrow, never fear!'

He was drunk. His sword lay unsheathed beside him on the board and every now and then he would grab it up and make jabs and hewing motions to the immediate danger of any in close proximity. More than half his exuberance was due to the news de Morville had brought–that the old King's patience with that upstart who wanted his castle had run out–for it meant that he need no longer involve himself with the faction who surrounded the young King and who, strangely, had evinced extreme reluctance to admit him to their ranks. But the others did not know that.

He looked round, his small, watery eyes squinting through the haze of smoke that filled the hall. 'It's Canterbury for us long before dawn tomorrow, lads–Clarembald will let us lay up in St Augustine's. No more coming, you say? No matter, no matter. We'll be close on four score and if we can't hold those burghers down—'

Hugh de Morville spoke. 'Are you thinking he'll come quietly, de Broc? He's a doughty swordsman as I remember.'

Ranulf's swag belly swayed from side to side with his laughter. 'Have you forgotten he's a churchman now?'

'So's Hugh of Horsea.'

Ranulf focused on the unfrocked clerk who sat nearby. 'Will you take edged steel in hand, Mauclerk?' he demanded. 'It seems de Morville here has little stomach for it.'

De Morville allowed his eyes to rest for a second on the silver chalice that Ranulf was using as a drinking cup. 'All I am saying is that it will not be as easy as standing off a few sailors and peasants to plunder the Archbishop's baggage. Did you not see him at Northampton? He was ready to brain any that stood in his path with his own archiepiscopal cross.'

'I shall take him,' said Reynold through his teeth, 'trussed like a capon to the King.'

De Morville looked at him and smiled. 'Ah–Reynold. . . . Ever in the vanguard where there's danger. But are you not his man?'

Ranulf's little eyes swivelled round to Reynold. 'I'm a King's man,' snarled Reynold. 'Make no mistake on that, de Morville!'

Le Bret pulled at de Morville's sleeve. 'What are you at?' he muttered.

There was a great deal of noise in the hall, for Ranulf had begun acquainting the new arrivals with particulars of the ambush they had laid for the Archbishop's men when they had stolen half his goods, and the air was ringing with lurid oaths and laughter. So none but le Bret heard Hugh's answer. 'Let the great ox take the lead if that's his wish. There's a debt I owe him for which it may be requital.'

Seeing his shaking shoulders, le Bret stared. It was the first time he had ever seen Hugh de Morville express amusement by other than a superior smile; neither could he see anything even faintly humorous in the situation.

Glowering across at Hugh, Reynold had just recalled that he also was the Archbishop's man. He shouted something to that effect but in the hubbub no one heard and he was left to fester inwardly until bedtime.

Thomas said Matins at midnight in his own chamber. John of Salisbury and William Fitzstephen took turns with the responses, promptly but mechanically. Each was busy with his own thoughts. A number of strangers had put in an appearance at dinner this day, availing themselves of the hospitality of the Archbishop's board. They had caused no trouble and indeed had had little to say beyond the common courtesies of the table, but their unaccountable presence and their close, hard looks at the company had brought about a noticeable loss of appetite among the monks. The memory of this was in their minds.

When they had finished Thomas rose up and went to the window, laying back the shutter. It was black night outside, very still, with a tang of frost and a million glittering stars. He stood there, looking out over the leafless orchard and, without turning, said, 'Can I reach Sandwich by daybreak?'

'Easily,' said William, 'easily. . . .' John said nothing. They waited, hardly breathing, and in the silence heard him sigh, and the rustle of his clothing as he squared his shoulders. His voice came to them thin and attenuated from the outer air: 'God's will be done. Thomas will wait on His ordering in his own church.'

Tuesday 29 December 1170

The frost which had whitened all at midnight had gone before dawn with the wind that had arisen. It was blowing gustily when Thomas wakened; he heard it throw sudden sharp spatters of rain against the shutters. He got up and lit a candle, and sat again on the bed and gazed at the small flame which trembled and swayed sinuously in the draught. For a moment his mind was as blank as a new-scrubbed board.

Then came memory and with it a great weight of fear pressing down on him. Sinking on his knees at the bedside he forced all his will into the narrow channel of acceptance, closing out the urge to foresee, to plan, to evade. To live each minute as it came was the only way, even an entreaty for deliverance the first, thin edge of disobedience. He had stopped praying for Henry's return nearly a week ago.

An hour or so later, when he was dressing, there came a sharp knocking on the door; it was a servant with a message that a group of citizens waited below with tidings of importance for the Archbishop. Thomas went down to them.

Three burghers stood there, twisting their caps in their hands. One of them stepped forward. 'My lord,' he said, 'the streets are full of armed men. We came to warn you that you must lock your gates. Mailed and armed with broadswords, my lord—' He was ashen-faced and trembling.

Holding out his hands for them to kiss, Thomas said sombrely, 'Let them do as they will; I am ready for the end. I know that I shall die a death of violence but'–his voice became suddenly fierce–'they shall not kill me outside my church.' He withdrew his hands from them and raised them aloft in blessing. 'It is you who must bar your doors. Keep off the streets–and may God be with us all.'

He heard Mass and visited all the altars in a kind of blank suspension of feeling; only when he saw Robert of Merton waiting on a faldstool with his stole about his shoulders to signify that he was ready to hear the Archbishop's confession did his mind seem to take up its usual activity. He went and knelt a little behind and to one side of him and murmured that, Father, he had sinned, but then the strange oblivion to outside events descended again. He could hardly remember why he was kneeling there. Of course, to confess his sins–for the last time. So long a catalogue of offences and so oft repeated; God surely knew it all by now and recognised how he repented it. . . .

When he spoke at last, it was not Robert he addressed. 'Lord,' he said, 'Thou knowest that I expect death hourly in Thy service. If I have done aught I should not, believing it to be Thy will, forgive me my culpable blindness. And if I have not done what Thou wouldst, I ask Thy pardon. Above all, grant me strength to die for Thee as Thou didst die for me.'

Robert of Merton was crying; Thomas had to touch him gently because, in the pity and excitement that moved him, he had forgotten to pronounce the absolution, let alone a penance. Thomas, though, did not forget; he underwent the discipline thrice during the morning.

He had not ordered the gates locked but no outsiders came to share his dinner; cathedral, monastery and palace lay peaceful and quiet within the sheltering walls. The winter's day was nearly over but, oddly, it was growing lighter as the heavy clouds drew back to reveal a sunset red as blood; the lurid glow painted the faces near him like a leaping fire. He found that he could eat no more but sat on until the rest had eaten the pheasant and drunk the good wine; it was, after all, a feast, and it was well they should not face empty-bellied what was to come. So he smiled and chatted and pretended to drink from an empty cup.

The wine had raised their spirits; after he had led his intimates to his own chamber they were conversing more animatedly than they had done for weeks. That was why they did not hear the gruff, unfamiliar tones in the hall, and the voice of William Fitznigel the seneschal answering them. But Thomas heard them. It seemed an age until the seneschal peered round the door.

'My lord, four knights from the King's court are asking for audience.'

'Make them welcome. Let them come in,' said Thomas from his place on the bed. He was cold as ice now that what he dreaded had come, but he signed calmly to Robert of Merton to continue what he had been saying before the interruption.

Robert tried but his wits had left him; he could not recall the point he had been trying to make. John of Salisbury prompted him. 'The will of God may be seen—'

The four knights entered and seated themselves in a row on the floor while Robert stumbled and hesitated. Thomas saw they were unarmed and fixed his eyes firmly on the speaker. That only made his confessor's agitation worse. 'By invisible signs,' he at last got out, 'may His will be known–by the eye of faith–and His very present help in trouble—'

'Aye, may He help you–you will need it,' said the largest of the strangers with a harsh bark that passed for laughter. He had a coarse, heavy face, darkened by weather to the colour of wood, and neck and shoulders like a bull. Thomas looked at him. It was Fitzurse, who had been one of his own knights until the exile.

Reynold stared implacably back at him. He had come here determined to take the lead, no matter that it had been not his but de Morville's plan to reconnoitre the ground before attempting to take the Archbishop. Not by such a transparent stratagem would he be deprived of any credit for the coup, even though that old fool Ranulf de Broc had been taken in by it. He had acquiesced immediately, agreeing to surround the palace while the spies were within. 'That way we may be sure none other gets in to help him,' he had said, 'and you may let us know how many knights he has about him there.' Reynold had had no intention of letting de Morville and le Bret make the arrest alone. 'Will and I go too,' he had announced, and finally Ranulf had allowed that four was not too many and he had got his way. He had decided then to make it clear he was in charge of operations. Unfortunately he had given little thought as to just how he was to do it. Speaking first, he felt, had helped.

'Greetings, my lords,' the Archbishop said gently, gazing from one to the next. 'Welcome to you all–Fitzurse, de Morville, de Tracy and—?' His glance at the last member of the party was interrogative.

Reynold settled on the tack he would take. 'Our names need matter nothing to you. We are here in the King's name on the

King's business. He has spoken his mind to us and we shall utter it to you. Will you hear it in the presence of these men or alone?'

'That is for you to say,' said the Archbishop in the same mild tone.

'Alone,' snapped Fitzurse.

The dozen or so monks and scholars rose and began to file out, but something in their anguished looks at him and the meaning glances he intercepted between Fitzurse and de Tracy made Thomas suddenly wary. 'No,' he said abruptly, 'I have changed my mind. I can see no need for secrecy.'

William Fitzstephen, John of Salisbury and Robert of Merton hurried back, followed by Henry of Auxerre and Edward Grim. They grouped themselves about him. 'Now I will hear your message,' said Thomas. 'Tell me the King's mind.'

'It is the King's command that you come with us to Winchester to pay honour to the young King, for the old King knows how you have been plotting to deprive him of his crown and raising the countryside to insurrection—'

'As God is my witness,' said Thomas wearily, 'I am not trying to deprive him of his crown. I have tried to see him and have been refused—' He looked at them sharply; these were the same accusations that had been levelled at him by de Broc. He was suddenly certain they had not come from the King at all.

'Will you absolve the bishops, lift the suspensions, and submit to judgement?' interrupted Fitzurse harshly.

'I have already offered to absolve them. It is they who refuse to pledge that they will accept the judgement of the Church. In any case, the King himself gave me permission to punish them—'

'Do you hear that?' Reynold's voice fairly cracked with rage. 'Do you hear that, men? This fellow is accusing the King of selling his trusted servants to him for the sake of peace!'

Thomas's jaw set. 'I cannot loose those the Pope has bound.'

'It was at your instigation that he bound them!' shouted de Tracy. 'If you will not undo it, it will be the worse for you!'

Anger was swelling in Thomas at the malignant injustice of these assertions, and the stupidity and obtuseness of those who made them. 'You, Fitzurse, as one of the King's chief barons, must know I am reconciled with the King,' he snapped. 'You were there at Fréteval!'

'I was not!'

'You were. I saw you there.'

'I was not there,' bellowed Reynold, roused to greater rage at the reminder of his banishment from the King's counsels.

Drawn by the commotion, numbers of monks and servants had come and clustered round the open door, the bolder ones among them pushing in to listen. John pulled at Thomas's elbow. 'Why do you not speak privily with them? All this will lead to is a senseless affray.' He motioned to the entry where the more stalwart serving men were ranging themselves, stiff and bristling like dogs about to fight.

'Cease your threats and let your wrangling be stilled,' Thomas ordered the knights coldly. 'I trust in the King of Heaven who suffered on the cross for His own. It befits King Henry not to command me through you; I have endured insults enough from his men.'

'We trust in the King of the English,' sneered Broken Nose. Le Bret–that was his name, Thomas suddenly remembered.

He put by John's restraining hand. 'No one who disobeys the orders of the Roman See shall have mercy from me,' he said and, glaring at Fitzurse and de Tracy, added, 'Moreover, you know what there is between you and me, and I am appalled that you should threaten in his own house an archbishop to whom you have sworn fealty!'

He heard someone laugh and guessed it was de Morville, lurking in the shadows. 'And you,' he added through clenched teeth. 'And you, de Morville. You are my men, all three of you. King Henry would not have sent you to me with such words.'

De Morville stepped out then into the light. 'You speak in peril of your head,' he said.

'Ah. . . ,' said Thomas, lightly but dangerously. 'Have you come to kill me then?' He took a step closer to the knights.

Hugh laughed again and held out his empty hands.

Thomas turned away. 'I have committed my cause to the judge of all; I am not moved by your threats, and if your swords are ready, so is my soul for martyrdom.' He swung back suddenly. 'If all the swords in England hung over me, you could not turn me from God's justice and obedience to the Pope!'

'Let's go,' said Reynold. He preferred to return later with reinforcements than to lose the initiative to Hugh. 'It's no use to bandy further words. He refuses the King's commands but he'll soon see we have other means in our power.' He faced the throng that now filled the room, his big voice booming out. 'We tell you in the name of the King that if you are loyal to him you must utterly abandon this traitor! And see you guard him well for us until we return.'

Thomas was after them in four long strides as they thrust through to the door. 'I shall not run away,' he blazed. 'Here–here you shall find me! Once I was a timid priest, and fled— No more!'

He stood, gripping the door post, glaring at their retreating backs as they clattered down the stairs, and saw them meet the seneschal coming up, his account rolls in his hand. He must have been shut away, poring over his lists, knowing nothing of what was going on above.

They seized him as they passed; he shrieked wildly, 'My lord, my lord, do you see what they are doing?' and the rolls went bouncing away down the steps as they dragged him along with them. Thomas clenched his hands. 'I see,' said he. 'They are the force and the power of darkness.'

John had come up behind him; he immediately recognised the paraphrasing of the Lord's words to those who came to arrest him after the kiss of Judas. He was shocked at the implication that William Fitznigel had turned his coat. He spoke coldly. 'It is a very strange thing, Thomas, that you will never take advice but always say and do what seems good to you alone. What need for a great and good man like yourself to follow those evil fellows to the very door? They were deliberately trying to provoke you to anger that they might ensnare you in your own words.'

Thomas bent his head; he was shaking so that he could hardly stand. He said grimly, 'We must all die, nor should we be diverted from righteousness by fear of death. I am more ready to undergo death than they are to inflict it.'

'The rest of us are sinners and not yet ready to die,' returned John sharply. 'I see no one here prepared for death but you.'

Thomas sucked in his lower lip but made no direct answer, only as he moved away muttered again that phrase that was beginning to exasperate John beyond all bearing. John did not follow him. What could you say to a man who was utterly convinced that his own blind, implacable, remorseless will was God's?

The knights had plunged down the stairs and through the hall, yelling 'To arms! To arms!' which was the signal that it was safe to enter. It was pitch dark outside and unseasonably mild; black, rain-heavy clouds obscured the smallest gleam of light from the sky, even the shapes of the trees could not be discerned against it. Only the answering cries of 'Réaux! Réaux!' told them that Ranulf's men were into the great court.

In the murk Reynold cannoned into a serving-lad and forced him to help him don his hauberk in the porch. He could hear others near him doing the same, curses and the clang of steel on stone came to him muffled through the helmet, and then a louder crash as the portal slammed shut and the bar thumped home behind it. The lad's fumbling fingers had just fastened the last strap. Reynold kicked him aside.

'Will, Will!' he shouted. 'They've barred us out.'

Men were already hammering on the door with the hilts of their swords; the din was tremendous. Someone brought a torch; by its fitful light Reynold saw Hugh de Morville close by. He was mailed but not yet helmeted. In the smoky, orange glare he looked like an infernal angel.

'Will!' Reynold yelled. 'Where are you, Will?'

Robert de Broc appeared beside him. 'Will's here,' he said, 'and le Bret and de Morville.' He nodded at the door. 'They'll never break that down.' The heavy oak was not even dinting. 'I know another way. Come on.'

They panted heavily along behind him, round the palace to the orchard at the back. The younger de Broc knew the layout well, having quartered himself here for a time during the Archbishop's exile. They came to a flight of wooden stairs. 'There,' he said, 'that leads up to the solar and so into the chamber where you saw him.' Evidence of the quality of his stewardship was in the dilapidation; the stair was broken and splintered and hanging askew. But the door at the top was also locked.

It was raining now, splats of thunder-rain big as pennies. From the bottom of the steps de Broc called that there were carpenters' tools here where the damage was being mended–would an axe be any use? They used it to smash through a shuttered window and a partition, and found themselves again in the great hall instead of where Robert had promised. A swarm of terrified servants ran screaming at their entrance; Will and le Bret herded them along and unbarred the outer door. They had to cut down several fellows to do so. Ranulf's men poured in, yelling like fiends and brandishing their weapons. Then they all started to force their way through to the Archbishop's apartments.

The ringing crash of axes and the rending of wood was clearly heard by the frightened men in Thomas's chamber; now when the great roar of triumph as Ranulf's men gained entry came swelling up, they stared wildly at one another. Most of them ran from the room; in the warren of interconnecting apartments there were many ways to go, many places to hide. No more than a dozen stayed with Thomas; only those five who had listened with him to the first words of the knights, and a handful of the more courageous monks. One of them, an old man who had remained from sheer inability to run, had fallen on his knees, crying piercingly on God and the Virgin for aid in their extremity.

'Not so loud, good brother,' said Thomas as one gently reproving a scared child. 'Neither our Blessed Lord nor our Blessed Lady suffer from the human infirmity of deafness. They will hear if you pray silently.' No flicker of fear showed on his face.

'We cannot stay here,' cried another of the monks. 'We must go to the church; we shall be safe from them there.'

'You may go if you will,' said Thomas. 'Monks were always cowards. I shall stay here.' None of their pleadings and expostulations could move him. 'I told those miscreants they would find me here,' he repeated, 'and here I stay.' And he seated himself determinedly on the bed.

'For God's sake,' John exclaimed. 'Are you mad?' He grabbed Thomas by the arm, Henry of Auxerre took the other, and an undignified tussle commenced. Somewhere far off a bell began to ring. 'It is time for Vespers,' cried John desperately. 'It is your manifest duty to attend.'

Thomas shook off the hands that were dragging him to the door. 'If I go, I go in the proper manner,' he said, 'with my cross carried before me.' The monks ran ahead towards the little-used passage that led to the cloisters. Henry of Auxerre snatched up the cross and Thomas's friends hustled him along behind it. But once more he thrust them off, refusing to be hurried, and settled himself to the slow, deliberate pace befitting an archbishop in the performance of his religious duties.

The first monk to reach it was trying to force the normally locked door at the end of the passage; it flew open so suddenly that he was precipitated through to land upon his knees and cry his thanks to God for a miracle. The Cellarer, who had unlocked it on the other side, called on them, 'Hurry, hurry!' and another unceremonious struggle began to push the unwilling Archbishop more swiftly along the north side of the cloisters. They could all hear the shouts and war cries from the south where the maddened aggressors were trying to break in.

The sweating, terrified men finally pulled the Archbishop bodily into the north transept of the cathedral. The monks, warned by some boys from the town, had broken off their Office; they came swarming to the door at this further interruption just as the knights burst through, bellowing curses, into the cloisters. Quickly, one of the monks clapped shut the door and barred it.

Outside in the rain-spattered darkness a large group from Thomas's household was cowering; a terrible screaming went up as the door closed.

'Open it!' Thomas shouted. 'Open the door! I command you on your obedience. The church shall not be made into a fortress. Let anyone enter who wishes.' When they stood frozen he pushed past, lifted the heavy bar, and pulled in those who had been left outside. They raced past him like mad things, intent only on finding a hiding place. When the last one was inside and Thomas turned, only Robert of Merton, William Fitzstephen and the visiting monk Edward Grim were still at his side.

It was more than an hour after sunset on one of the shortest days of winter and the only lights in the vast cathedral, apart from the ruby eyes of the sanctuary lamps and the votive candles, were in the choir where Vespers had been in progress.

His three faithful followers urged Thomas towards them. This time he went; he would sit upon his throne and face his fate.

All around were rustlings, quick, uneasy breathing, and the muffled, sputum-choked coughs of winter, for the church was full of townsfolk who had thought to find refuge there from danger. The four ecclesiastics had reached the south-west corner of the transept when the armed men stampeded through the open door. One of them shouted, 'Where is Thomas Becket, traitor to the King and the realm?'

Thomas stood quite still. That was an insult he would not answer. Then came the harsh, unmistakable voice of Fitzurse. 'Where is the Archbishop?'

At that he stepped forward. 'Here,' he said. 'No traitor but a priest of God.' Stopping by the pillar between the Chapel of St Benedict and the Lady Chapel he demanded, 'What do you want of me?'

They came rushing forward, able to make out his dark figure by the wavering gleam of the votive lights. A great crowd of de Broc's knights was behind the four who had set themselves to take him; among them, though well back, Hugh Mauclerk of Horsea. 'Absolve those you have excommunicated,' he bawled, 'and restore to communion those you have suspended!'

'There has been no satisfaction; I will not absolve them under threat.'

'Then you shall die!' 'Kill the obstinate fool; he deserves it!' the shouts went up.

'I embrace death,' Thomas whispered, 'and I commend my soul to Blessed Mary and the saints of this church.' Only Edward Grim heard him; the other two had slipped behind the pillar out of sight. The Archbishop's voice grew louder. 'God forbid I should flee your swords but by the authority of God I forbid you to touch my men.'

'Come with us; you are our prisoner,' ordered Reynold brusquely, pushing through and seizing his cloak. Thomas twisted furiously sideways, wrenching the cloth from his hand. Reynold grabbed at him again, and with le Bret and Mauclerk on the other side almost succeeded in lifting him off his feet. 'Here, Will!' Reynold shouted. It was in his mind to haul the Archbishop forcibly across Will's back, he being the shortest of them, and thus have him carried ignominiously away as a hunter a dead doe. But Will misunderstood and came within reach of the wildly-struggling Archbishop's hands.

Fury lent Thomas strength. He grasped Will by the hauberk and threw him against Mauclerk. Both of them crashed to the stone floor. Edward Grim grappled with le Bret. Thomas faced Reynold with blazing eyes. 'Take your hands off me, Fitzurse, you pimp! You owe me fealty. How dare you use violence in this place?' Yet his own hand itched for a sword. He sensed someone on his other side and whirled to face the threat. It was de Morville and he was wearing his odious smile. Thomas felt his flesh creep. God, how he hated the man. He had always been there at the worst moments of his life, disdaining him. Now he laughed aloud. In a light, almost conversational, tone he said, 'You are inviting death, Archbishop.'

Beside himself with rage alike at the deadly insult and at Hugh's appearance, Reynold drew his sword. It described a great arc over Hugh's and the Archbishop's heads. 'I owe you no fealty against my fealty to the King!' he yelled. Thomas felt the wind of the sword in his hair. 'I commend myself and my church to God and Blessed Mary, to St Denis and St Alphege,' he recited as quickly as he could get the words out.

Hugh de Morville sprang backwards but his smile died only momentarily. When he turned back to where the braver of the townsmen were creeping from their hiding places, confronting them with drawn sword, he was again showing all his perfect teeth. It stopped them dead.

Weighted with mail as he was, Will de Tracy had managed to struggle erect, leaving Mauclerk groaning on the pavement. His blood was boiling at his humiliating overthrow by a mere cleric. He swung up his great two-handed broadsword and brought it down in a mighty stroke just as le Bret fought free of Edward Grim and sent him staggering against the Archbishop.

Edward saw the blow coming and threw up his arm instinctively against it. The blade sheared half through his forearm, glanced off the bone and sliced across the crown of Thomas's head. Blood poured in a torrent over his face.

'Strike! Strike!' de Tracy yelled at the others. 'Will you let this bastard live?' He fetched his own sword down again on the bleeding head.

Still the Archbishop remained upright. 'Into Thy hands, O Lord,' he jerked out. Reynold struck again. Thomas staggered and fell to his hands and knees.

A great screaming and crying sounded in the church but Thomas did not hear it; he heard nothing but a low, soft roaring in his skull. Slowly he slid down into the sticky blood and it was warm and pleasant under his cheek. Darkness descended on him, spilling down like fold upon fold of black velvet.

Lying against the pillar, so close that his head almost touched the Archbishop's outflung hand, Edward Grim heard his last whisper. 'For the name of Jesus–and the defence of the Church–I–embrace—' Death, Edward's slipping thoughts furnished. Death. When his consciousness began to ebb, he imagined he was dying too.

Richard le Bret, his face contorted, raised his sword over the moribund Archbishop. He dealt such a stroke that the blade clove clean through the frontal bone to the paving beneath and snapped in two. Mauclerk stepped forward, inserted his sword-point in the terrible wound and churned it as a goodwife stirs her pottage. Brains and blood splashed out over the floor. 'Let's go, men,' he shouted exultantly. 'This fellow isn't going to trouble anyone again.'

Thomas's long battle was irretrievably lost, sublimely won.

An unfamiliar sweetness assailed the nostrils of Edward Grim as he swam back to consciousness. His eyelids fluttered and he looked across a field of flowers, red and white. Roses, he thought confusedly, roses and lilies, and the sea is near, I hear it surging.

But in the next split second he knew the sound for what it was, no voice of ocean but the soughing lamentation of a great mass of people; and, the darkness clearing from his mind, he saw clearly the horrid sight before him.

The Archbishop's mutilated corpse lay not a yard away. All round it men and women were dipping shreds torn from their clothing into the pool of blood and brains that had spread over the pavement. They trod about in the slippery mess, gathering their precious relics, and all the time they groaned and wept and called upon God to witness that another martyr had joined the heavenly throng.

Now the monks were coming back–too late, too late, his mind screamed at them–pulling at the townsfolk with ungentle hands, crying out on them to go and leave the Archbishop's body to his own.

Edward Grim looked up into the drawn, stricken faces of William Fitzstephen and Robert of Merton, and tried to speak. His stomach was strong but he had never been in battle. He vomited over their feet.

The knights rushed out of the cathedral into a night of storm and driving rain, following in the wake of Ranulf's retainers who hurried to join the men-at-arms already looting the palace. It was like the sack of an enemy town. They had loaded the Archbishop's horses with everything that was conveyable; vestments, plate and books were scattered on the ground and trodden underfoot. Reynold, Will and le Bret stared speechlessly at one another. Hugh was nowhere to be seen.

They found him upstairs gazing down into the Archbishop's

smashed and broken treasure chest, empty but for a few silver coins that had rolled into the corners. He looked into their pallid faces. 'Alas!' he said in a tone of gentlest commiseration. 'It seems there are not thirty pieces left for you.' Lifting his head he listened as the unseasonable thunder rumbled and pealed overhead. 'But I doubt not you will get your just reward.' With a complete change of manner he turned abruptly on his heel. 'I am for Knaresborough,' he announced briskly. 'If you take my advice you will ride with me.'

They followed him like frightened children.

January 1171

New Year's Day supper was over and King Henry just retired to his private chamber when a messenger was hurried through the hall by the seneschal. Few noted him as he went by; there was nothing out of the way in the sight of an exhausted courier arriving at court at any hour.

But a minute or two later their heads came up as one. All through the long silence, deadly and unaccountable, that followed, the echoes of that one wild, lost, despairing cry rang in their minds.

When the news was brought to Queen Eleanor she was seated with a couple of ladies by the window of an alcove in the thickness of the wall. The messenger was tired and mud-spattered, showing he had ridden hard and carried tidings of weight. He had not come from the King but was one of her own people.

The ladies looked apprehensively from him to the Queen and rose hurriedly enough to drop the silks they had been winding, but they went only out of earshot, not out of sight, and waited there that they might gauge the measure of the news from the Queen's expression.

They did not learn much from it, for Eleanor heard the

message with a composed face, then slowly rose and turned her back on all of them, staring out of the window. The court outside was empty of people; only a scattering of little, dun-coloured birds hopped and pecked on grass that was still patched here and there with melting snow. Over them a few gulls, driven inland by wintry weather, appeared hovering; the smaller birds rose in a sudden rush and flew away.

She spoke as if to them. 'How has the King taken this news?'

'He is mad with grief, madam, so they say. He has shut himself away and will speak to no one.'

After a minute, when she said no more, the messenger bowed and went away.

Eleanor raised her eyes to the sky. Black cloud on grey raced tumultuously before the wind, parting occasionally to show tumbled heaps of cumulus like snow mountains in the highest air; through fugitive gaps small patches of blue were now and then discernible. Even as she watched one grew and grew, ever more radiant and glorious; she saw it in her fancy as the floor of Heaven. .

She closed her eyes and leaned suddenly on the stone mullion. When she opened them again the shining, azure lake had been swallowed up, and she was glad; it was as though the driving storm-clouds obscured something in her mind she did not want resolved.

She gave herself a small, sharp, angry shake. If ever a man brought death upon himself by sheer wilful obstinacy and pride, Becket had. And however it appeared to the rest of the world, she knew Henry's hopes had been set at naught; he was crushed, defeated, tumbled down. That was all she cared about.

He was disgraced, and by an action the lad who was the apple of his eye would never forgive. Excommunication and all it brought in its train would be his portion. Fierce exultation rose in her. Who would blame her if she withdrew herself from him and retired into her own duchy? Never before would she have dared such a feudal dereliction, but now. . . . She gazed at the snow-caked, frost-bitten grass below but saw nothing of winter's tokens. Her world shone bright with sunshine.

In Argentan Castle Henry roused again from stupor. He had eaten nothing and drunk only water for three days but even starvation could not silence the newly-awakened voice of conscience. He beat his clenched fists on his temples but it did no good. He was finally face to face with what he had become and there was no escape.

Somewhere along the much-travelled road between England and Normandy he had mislaid the boy who had dreamed of justice and incorruptible power. He had thought well of himself, that boy; but the man who began again to weep with dry, tearing sobs was all too well aware of why he had never achieved it.

He had used his easily-aroused rages with the same deliberate intent as his Norse ancestors had done, to terrify his opponents into submission. And it had grown to be a habit in the grain, the censor at the threshold of his mind atrophied from lack of use. He had exploited to the full his ability to make men tremble; aye, enjoyed it, gloried in it, using it to feed the pride that always whispered that he was greater, cleverer, craftier than all of them.

All except Tom. . . . He, in his inmost soul, had never trembled, never been deceived. It was Thomas's refusal to fear him that had driven him past the point of no return, to excesses he had never meant to commit, to savage threats he had never meant to implement. And, once too often, he had opened the floodgates to a tidal wave of fury against a petty irritation, not pausing to consider who might come to shipwreck–for he had never taken seriously those wildly improbable tales coming out of England. But Tom had died and he–he too might go under. There was no one who would believe his innocence of evil intent; he would stand condemned in the eyes of the world.

But it was not fear of the Church's judgement that tortured Henry; he had no liking for Pope or clergy, and scant respect either. It was bitter grief for the one man he had truly loved that bent him double as a man huddles over a mortal wound. Sharper than any devil's pitchfork was the terrible remorse. He saw Thomas dying on the altar steps in a welter of blood and tried, unavailing, to close his mind to the picture of his hands (those long, white hands) piteously upraised to ward off the bright, flashing steel. Or had he submitted meekly, easily, to cruel death, believing it to be the expressed will of the King? Could he have believed that?

Remembering how he had sent him, alone and helpless, into England, and the crafty stratagem by which he had avoided giving the kiss of peace which might have safeguarded him, he knew that to be only too likely. He had acted the part he had written for himself too well; how could Thomas–how could anyone–have known how gladly he would have forgiven him? All he had wanted was Thomas's compliance.

But he could never break that iron will that put God first, that believed shadows were more important than realities. Thomas had been a fool not to have seen that he could have done anything, had anything, for the pretence that Henry came first. His pride, after all, was greater than mine, Henry thought bitterly; he would never pretend, while my pretences deceived everyone, including myself, the greater part of the time. But not now, not now. He wept aloud.

His imagination began to work again on the scene in the cathedral and he sprang to his feet to pace up and down as though he could outrun the images in his head. When he had gone two or three times round the little chamber he stopped and rested his head against the tapestry on the wall and let the tears run down.

Suddenly he ground his teeth together. Who had done it? He could not remember the names. But they should suffer. He would have their blood-stained hands off–and the eyes that had watched Tom die without a tear should never look upon a smiling sky again. He would see to that. . . . The familiar rage was welling like a bubble in his guts. When it burst. . . .

Like a lightning stroke words spoke in his mind: '—forgive them for they know not what they do.' Who had said it? Thomas? He stood still, feeling his hands begin to shake. So nearly had he let the devil in again to destroy him.

He forced himself to be rational. He could not punish the assassins as he longed to do. Men would say he was sacrificing his tools that they might not bear evidence against him. Try as he might he could get no further than that in thought for the future. He could think of nothing but blood and death and irremediable loss.

Some words of the messenger's came back to him, hurried, uneasy, of a vision one of the monks had had within hours of the murder; some nonsense of the body rising from the bier 'dazzling white and red, comely of face and beautiful to look upon'. And the monk whispering, 'Are you not dead, lord?' and Thomas replying, 'I was dead but am risen again.'

Surely close to blasphemy, that. Yet something pricked disquietingly at Henry as it had evidently done at the messenger. He shook his shoulders and shivered, telling himself that dead men do not rise, or at least, not in these latter days. Had they ever? And he stared again at the finality of death, that door that closes too fast behind each departing soul for any glimpse of what may lie beyond.

That brought back all the pain.

Towards evening a dreadful doubt assailed him. Beside it the certainty of excommunication was nothing. Had he ever truly loved anything but his own will? Even Hikenai?–or had he merely enjoyed the feelings she aroused in him? He loved his children, yes, but they were *his*. Was that why?

His mind groped helplessly with the concept of selfless love.

It seemed impossible. All outward manifestations of the emotion are ultimately selfish, he told himself; even self-abnegation warms with conscious virtue those who practise it.

But doubt remained. He could be as wrong in this as in so much else. Light-headed with hunger, he began to drowse and dream; and suddenly jerked wide awake. Perhaps the answer lay at Woodstock.

Historical Postscript

Despite the legends, the four knights suffered nothing worse than excommunication for their crime; the very principle Thomas fought for saved them. Only the Church could punish the murder of an archbishop in his own cathedral. They lay low in Knaresborough Castle (in Archbishop Roger of York's see) for a considerable time but were eventually received back at court. The evidence of what became of them thereafter is inconclusive and contradictory but one record states that William de Tracy gave a manor to Christchurch Monastery, Canterbury, in penance for his part in the murder, another that Hugh de Morville died in the reign of King John about the year 1202. There is, however, a possibility that this was a different Hugh de Morville.

Two charters of Reynold Fitzurse are extant. By one of these he confirmed to the church of St Andrew at Stoke Courcy, called therein 'Sutinstocke', a grant of two-thirds of the sheaves of Williton. One of the witnesses was his brother Robert. By the other he granted to Robert Fitzurse a moiety of Williton and of the house there, the other moiety having been granted by him to the Knights Templars in alms for his soul. Among the witnesses to it were Hugh de Morville and Richard le Bret. He never had a son; Maud remained his only child and heiress. She married a certain Robert de Courtenay.

Ecclesiastical opinion in Europe did not doubt that the murder was at King Henry's instigation. The Archbishop of Sens immediately imposed interdict on all Henry's continental lands and Pope Alexander, who had given orders that no Englishmen were to be admitted to his presence, confirmed it. Only heavy bribes to the Curia and abject promises to submit to whatever penance the Pope ordained saved England from a like fate and Henry from excommunication. Alexander announced that he would send legates 'to observe the King's humility' before he would consider absolving him of complicity. Roger of York and Gilbert Foliot remained in suspension for more than a year.

Duke Conan died in February 1171 and Henry took a large army into Brittany to secure the province for his son Geoffrey. With this successfully accomplished he launched the invasion of Ireland which has bedevilled us ever since. He had two purposes; to put the sea between himself and the approaching papal legates and to mend his reputation by the fiction that he had taken the Cross in order to bring back the Celtic Church into the Roman fold. Queen Eleanor retired into Poitou while he was away, leaving Richard de Luci in charge of England and young Henry. The only public comment the young King made upon the murder of his foster-father was, 'Alas! Yet I thank Thee, God, that I knew nothing and that none of my men had any hand in it.' Whether it did, in some small part, motivate his subsequent rebellion against his father we shall never know but Henry's prophetic words to Thomas at Fréteval lead one to believe that he must have thought so. The remark is well authenticated because Thomas himself quoted it in a letter to the Pope almost immediately after the reconciliation.

After the murder and the scenes of wild excitement in the cathedral that followed on the discovery of Thomas's hair shirt (in the twelfth century sure evidence of saintliness), Robert de

Broc sent word to the monks that if they did not bury the body immediately he would drag it out and throw it in a cesspool. The monks promptly buried their martyr in the crypt and there he lay between the altars of St Augustine and St John the Baptist for half a century until the splendid shrine built for him was completed. He was canonised by popular acclaim from the time of his death; many miracles were worked by his infinitely diluted blood. Officially numbered on the roll of martyred saints little more than two years later, his feast was celebrated yearly on the day on which his life ended.

Gilbert Foliot founded the Hospital of St Thomas at Southwark in his honour, Richard de Luci the Abbey of Lesnes. Pilgrims came to the place of martyrdom for more than 350 years until another King Henry, as greedy, as self-willed, but immeasurably more dangerous, tore down the glorious shrine, stole the gem-encrusted plates of gold that covered it, and treated the venerated remains with the same contempt a long-dead de Broc had once threatened. All that remains is a flight of stone steps worn hollow by the knees of the faithful.

Bibliography

Appleby, John T.: *Henry II*, G. Bell and Sons 1962

Bagley, J. J.: *Life in Mediaeval England*, Batsford 1960

Barber, Richard: *Henry Plantagenet*, Barrie and Rockliff 1964

Barlow, Frank: *Feudal Kingdom of England*, Longman 1955

Barrow, G. W. S.: *Feudal Britain*, Arnold 1956

Brooke, Christopher: *From Alfred to Henry III*, Nelson 1961

Brooke, Christopher: *Twelfth Century Renaissance*, Thames and Hudson 1969

Coulton, C. G.: *Social Life in Britain: Conquest to Reformation*, Cambridge University Press 1918, revised edition 1956

Duggan, Alfred: *Thomas Becket of Canterbury*, Faber 1967

Eades, George E.: *Historic London*, Queen Anne Press 1966

English Historical Documents, Volume II, (ed. David C. Douglas and George W. Greenaway), Eyre & Spottiswoode 1968

Eyton, R. W.: *Court, Household and Itinerary of Henry II*, Taylor 1878

Hay, Denis: *The Mediaeval Centuries*, Methuen 1953

Hughes, Pennethorne: *Witchcraft*, Longman 1952

Hutton, William Holden: *Thomas Becket*, Cambridge University Press 1926

Kelly, Amy: *Eleanor of Aquitaine and the Four Kings*, Cassell 1952

Knowles, David: *Episcopal Colleagues of Thomas Becket*, Cambridge University Press 1951

Knowles, David: *Thomas Becket*, Cambridge University Press 1970

Lyte, Sir Henry C. Maxwell: *Fitzurse, Somerset Archaeological and Natural History Society Proceedings*, 1922. Vol. LXVIII, pp. 93–104

Murray, Margaret: *Witch Cult in Western Europe* Oxford University Press 1963

Murray, Margaret: *God of the Witches*, Oxford University Press 1933

Quennell, Marjorie and C. H. B.: *History of Everyday Things in England: 1066–1499*, Batsford 4th ed. 1957

Stenton, Doris Mary: *English Society in the Early Middle Ages*, Pelican History of England, III, 1951

Stuart, D. M.: *London through the Ages*, Methuen 1956

Warren, W. L.: *Henry II*, Eyre Methuen 1973

Webb, Clement C.: *John of Salisbury*, Methuen 1932

Winston, Richard: *Becket*, Constable 1967

Fic
Butler, M.